Readers are raving about

CUT & RUN

Cut & Run

"Ty and Zane were so heartbreakingly beautiful and so realistic that these two will go down as two of the most fascinating characters written in this genre."
—*Literary Nymphs*

"A touching erotic romance as well as an intriguing murder mystery."
—*Romance Junkies*

Sticks & Stones

"I was slightly infatuated with Ty and Zane after reading *Cut & Run*, but I fell in love with them in *Sticks & Stones*."
—*Joyfully Reviewed*

"Filled with moments both brutal and tender, *Sticks & Stones* is a fast, compelling read, and I can't wait for the next chapter in Ty and Zane's saga."
—*Night Owl Reviews*

Fish & Chips

"This is the third book in the series and each one just keeps getting better."
—*The Romance Studio*

"This is one of my favorite series in the whole wide world…"
—*Dark Divas Reviews*

Divide & Conquer

"Between the passion that exists between the main characters and the suspense that the authors have skillfully woven throughout the story, readers will be more than satisfied with this new addition to an outstanding series."
—*Literary Nymphs*

"*Divide & Conquer* is a triumph. It will make you cry, it's fun, it will lift you up, and ultimately give you the best reason to continue reading books."
—*Reviews by Jessewave*

http://www.dreamspinnerpress.com

THE CUT & RUN SERIES

Cut & Run
Sticks & Stones
Fish & Chips
Divide & Conquer
Armed & Dangerous

BY ABIGAIL ROUX

According to Hoyle
The Archer
My Brother's Keeper
A Tale from de Rode
Unrequited

BY MADELEINE URBAN AND ABIGAIL ROUX

Caught Running
Love Ahead
Warrior's Cross

ARMED & DANGEROUS

ABIGAIL ROUX

Dreamspinner Press

Published by
Dreamspinner Press
382 NE 191st Street #88329
Miami, FL 33179-3899, USA
http://www.dreamspinnerpress.com/

This is a work of fiction. Names, characters, places, and incidents either are the product of the author's imagination or are used fictitiously, and any resemblance to actual persons, living or dead, business establishments, events, or locales is entirely coincidental.

Armed & Dangerous
Copyright © 2012 by Abigail Roux

Cover Design by Mara McKennen

All rights reserved. No part of this book may be reproduced or transmitted in any form or by any means, electronic or mechanical, including photocopying, recording, or by any information storage and retrieval system without the written permission of the Publisher, except where permitted by law. To request permission and all other inquiries, contact Dreamspinner Press, 382 NE 191st Street #88329, Miami, FL 33179-3899, USA
http://www.dreamspinnerpress.com/

ISBN: 978-1-61372-512-2

Printed in the United States of America
First Edition
May 2012

eBook edition available
eBook ISBN: 978-1-61372-513-9

To those who stay the course.

Flying solo, especially with this book, was a difficult endeavor. I could not have done it without the unwavering support of everyone reading this. And without the unseemly likes of Jaclyn "the Canadian" Kean, Amanda "the Flash" McDonough, Stacey "That's What She Said" Sheiko, Nik "Glitterpants" Simmons, Jennifer "Smurfette" Taylor, and Ely "the Baking Panda" Verdesoto, this book would not be what it is. They are the best friends I could ever ask for.

~Chapter 1~

THE scratch of the Montblanc pen whispered in the quiet, well-appointed office. Thick stone walls and double-paned bulletproof glass worked to dampen the traffic noise of downtown Washington, DC, and sumptuous carpet and soundproofing in the walls kept his office a haven of solitude amidst one of the busiest cities in the world.

Richard Burns, executive assistant director of the Criminal Investigative Division of the Federal Bureau of Investigation, flipped through page after page, initialing and signing. The Bureau may have moved into the digital age, but paperwork still made the gears turn. With a sniff, he closed the folder and tossed it into his outbox for his assistant to pick up. At least he didn't have to write out his full title every time.

He was reaching to replace the fountain pen in its box when the buzzer on his phone interrupted him.

"Sir?"

"Yes, Nancy?"

"Security just called, sir. You have a visitor," his assistant's tinny voice announced over the speaker.

"Who is it? I don't have any appointments until two."

"The ID provided is for a Mr. Randall Jonas. Central Intelligence Agency."

Burns looked at the phone in surprise. "Send him through," he said as he stood and began straightening his tie and suit jacket.

It took five minutes, give or take, and the buzzer went off again. "Sir, the escort is here with Mr. Jonas."

Burns walked around his desk to greet his old friend when he came through the door. Randall Jonas had been one of three men in Burns' original Marine Corps squadron who had returned from Vietnam. Earl Grady was the other. They were like his brothers, and Burns would never turn down a surprise visit from one of them. But when the door opened and Jonas was shown into his office, Burns knew immediately that something was wrong.

"You look like hell," he said before he could think of a more appropriate way to say it.

Jonas nodded. "With good reason."

Jonas didn't look at all like the sharp CIA section chief Burns saw for an occasional drink at an upscale DC bar. Jonas looked worn, mussed around the edges, wild around the eyes. He was a large man with a lantern jaw, trending toward heavy in recent years, with gunmetal gray hair and eyes that were a washed out brown. He was usually full of good humor and charm, more a mischievous gnome than a spook. Right now, though, he looked like a bear being chased through the woods by bigfoot.

Burns offered him a hand to shake and then gestured toward the leather sofa in the corner of his office. "Forgive me for skipping over the pleasantries, but it seems like you might want me to. What's happened?"

Jonas dragged a hand through his hair. "I really stepped in something nasty, Dick. I was about five minutes from being detained at Langley," he said as he thumped onto the couch and pulled at the knot of his tie.

"You what?" Burns sat down across from Jonas.

"I came across something I was never meant to see. Long story short, someone within the Company has been using government assets to pull personal jobs for profit, and then offing the assets when they got wise. They turned the CIA into a hit service."

"What?"

"There was some paperwork that made me suspicious, so I started snooping around. And when I followed the trail, that son of a bitch led right back to me."

Burns blinked at him. "What?"

"Richard, focus for me here. Someone's setting me up to take the fall for ordering private hits. I found out before they got everything in place. So I picked up and ran." Jonas waved a hand, dismissing any further detail of his escape from Langley.

Burns nodded, frowning hard. Abuse of power happened in the alphabet agencies just like anywhere else. Only it usually ended with death and destruction instead of bankruptcy, bailouts, or moving a factory to China.

"Someone within the CIA is eating their own. And you're the fall guy. I gather following the trail in reverse can't prove your innocence."

"No, they're just notes from one lackey to another, issuing orders," Jonas said, leaning forward, bracing his elbows on his knees. "It's bad, Dick. I'm being framed for misuse of resources, running operations on my own authority, unsanctioned elimination of personnel, and if it really goes bad, treason. I'd definitely be put in jail for the rest of my natural life. That's if whoever is responsible doesn't just come after me as well. Assets are being cleaned. People are losing their lives."

"Jesus, Randy."

"I need some help, and you're the only one I trust right now."

Burns realized he was staring, and he nodded curtly. He knew this man, had known him for the better part of forty years, and he knew if Jonas said it, it was the truth. Even if he was a damn spook. "What do you need?"

"I need a contact brought in."

"A contact?"

"From what details I was able to pull together before I ran, there's just one guy still alive who has the information needed to point to the bastard in charge of all this. They tried to clean him a year ago, but he got away." Jonas shook his head. "They've been eliminating agents, Dick. Agent and handler teams going down or disappearing—for a couple of years now. Slowly, almost randomly, and I can't say I would have caught on without coming across that file and getting suspicious."

Jonas nodded as he sat up and then leaned back, looking truly miserable. "I've worked my ass off for the Company, Dick. I'm not going to let it go down this way. There's a cell inside, one that's not sanctioned and not supervised. I'm not sure how high it goes, other than too high if they're gunning for me."

"Do you have the stats on this contact? The one with the information?"

"Sort of. He went dark over a year ago. I've been in touch with his former handler."

"Okay. We'll get him pegged down and then I'll send an agent after him. We'll bring this to someone we can trust."

"You can't dispatch FBI resources, Dick. They'll be monitoring everything."

Burns raised an eyebrow at the paranoia, but that was a spook for you.

"Look, Richard, I don't know much about your operations, other than the CIA uses you and whatever assets you've cultivated over here for certain jobs. I know you've got the means to do this off the board."

Burns pursed his lips and scratched at his nose, trying to hide the discomfort. "I might know someone. I'll mobilize him. And until we can get this mystery asset of yours in, you'll stay here. Even the CIA isn't going to storm FBI headquarters to get to you. Who's the contact?"

"He's a foreign national named Julian Cross. Records say he'd been taken out, but then he popped back up on the radar and rumor was he was still alive. When I talked to Blake Nichols, his former handler, he confirmed Cross is alive. For now. But he can't get Cross to come in." Jonas tapped his fingers on the arm of the couch, visibly agitated. "I have an address, and I can only hope this guy has the information I need. He's the only one who could have it. All the others are dead."

"Julian Cross," Burns muttered as he scratched at his chin. "Why does that name sound familiar?"

Jonas shrugged.

Burns stood and went to his desk, waking his computer to type in a search. It returned nothing. But he knew the name. He tapped in a code and then searched again. This time the computer searched through a cache of hidden files, and it popped up with one file.

Burns snorted when he scanned the information contained in the file. Paris. Of course. He looked at Jonas. "Give me all the information you have. I'm putting my best man on it," he said as he pulled a cell phone out of a locked drawer.

"If Cross doesn't know who was giving those kill orders, no one does. But I have a feeling he put everything together and he thinks it was the CIA trying to kill him. That's why he went off the grid. He won't be easy to bring in," Jonas said as he walked over to the desk, pulling a folded piece of paper out of his pocket. "This is it. Name, contacts, addresses. And your man should know Cross is a high-level federal asset and wet works operative—considered armed and extremely dangerous. He's... very capable"

Burns nodded as he dialed, and he couldn't help but smile. "They'll get along famously."

*I'm sorry. Walls are closing in and I need to go.
Love you.*

ZANE sat straight up in the bed, soaked in sweat, ears ringing as his lover's name echoed off the walls. He had been dreaming, his mind taking him back to Ty's living room and the dance they had shared. Ty's name was still on his lips. He could still smell him and feel his arms around him as they swayed together. But that had been over a week ago.

It seemed he could still hear the music.

Zane shuddered and leaned over to grab up his cell phone. He swiped the screen to answer the call, interrupting the ringtone. "Ga-Garrett."

"Zane."

The smooth voice struck Zane hard enough that he fell back onto one elbow, struggling to swallow the butterflies. He was too caught up in the dream. He wasn't sure he was awake at all.

"Ty?" he said after too long a pause. It sounded plaintive. He rubbed his hand over his face.

"You sound horrible. Are you okay?"

Zane shook his head, and his gaze fell on the shaft of moonlight that painted the wall across the room. He tried to focus his eyes on it. It was just enough to provide a soft blue glow in the room. He wiped a hand across his forehead. It came away damp. "I… where the fuck have you been?"

"Calm down and I'll tell you."

Zane growled. He leaned over and groped for the almost empty bottle of water on the nightstand. It was tepid, but he took a few swallows anyway. "Calm down, my ass. Where are you?"

"Well," Ty said, the word drawn out. Zane recognized the tone of voice Ty used when he was trying to figure out how to explain something that didn't happen to normal people. "I've been told I'm in Tennessee. Or Kentucky. It wasn't really clear. That's not why I called."

"Are you in one piece?" Zane asked. He curled his free hand into the sheet.

"So far. But listen, Zane, I don't have much time. I got a call from Burns."

Zane shivered and shifted back to lean against the headboard. That meant Ty wasn't coming home any time soon, Zane was sure of it. When he spoke, his voice was dark and just barely controlled. "I'm listening."

Ty was silent for a moment. "I miss you," he said. He sounded wrecked, which didn't help Zane feel any better. "But I have to go dark. He didn't give me a choice this time."

It was on the tip of Zane's tongue to demand an explanation, but the regret in Ty's voice stopped him. With anyone else, this conversation would have been ludicrous. Zane rubbed at his eyes. He'd only gone to bed a couple of hours ago, and far earlier in the evening than normal. Ty wouldn't have expected to wake him.

"You scared the hell out of me, Ty."

"I know," Ty said, and though he sounded sympathetic, he didn't necessarily sound contrite. "But I had to go. I don't...."

Zane had known Ty wasn't himself after their two weeks of hell. Zane had known, and he'd hoped to have the chance to help once they'd both caught their breath. But Ty's midnight exit had upset that plan. Frustration and anger swamped Zane again, drowning his brief feeling of relief. "Do you know what I thought when I woke up without you?"

"Hopefully that you couldn't wait to see me again? I left you a note," Ty said, voice hopeful.

"Yeah, and you know what? It didn't help!" Zane said, giving up on trying to be understanding. "That's not something you want to find when you wake up to what's supposed to be the first day of the rest of your life!"

"The what, now?"

Zane groaned, turned sideways, and flopped down onto his side. He pulled a pillow over his head and then talked anyway. His words came out muffled and stilted. "Beaumont. Tyler. Grady."

"Wait, whoa, full names? What the hell, Garrett?"

"I told you I loved you, and the next day you were gone."

Ty was silent, but Zane could hear him breathing. When he finally spoke, his voice was low and hoarse. "I'm sorry. I didn't think of that."

"Did you think at all?"

"Zane."

"Asshole!"

"I love you, Zane. I do, and you know it. And when I get home, we're going to sit down and talk this out. I promise."

"I told you I loved you."

"And I appreciated that."

Zane pulled the pillow away and rolled onto his back to stare up through the dark at the ceiling. "I told you twice."

"Zane."

"What the hell does Burns want now? You're supposed to be on wellness leave."

Ty didn't answer for a long time, long enough that Zane checked the display on his phone to make sure the call was still connected. Then he heard Ty huff. "God, I love it when you're cranky like this. Promise to still be pissed when I get home, okay?"

"I don't think that's going to be a problem."

Ty laughed affectionately, and Zane's body responded to the sound despite the anger still washing over him. Zane grunted. There was no denying that his exasperating lover would be able to charm his way out of this. Damn him. But Zane was by far too angry to let it go so easily. "Are you saying you knew I loved you before I said it?"

"Come on, Zane. I'm a trained profiler. You really think I can't tell when someone's head over heels in love? You were just crunching the numbers."

"The first time I told you—"

"You were scared shitless."

Zane was silent. He wanted to deny it, but Ty was right. The day Ty had danced with him in his living room, he'd told Ty he loved him before he'd even realized the words were slipping out.

"You were terrified as soon as it came out, weren't you?" Ty asked.

"Yes."

"If I hadn't given you an out, what would you have done?"

Zane closed his eyes.

"You would have freaked out. And you were already freaking out anyway. Do you know how much it hurt to dismiss that? But you weren't ready. And I needed you to say it for you. Not for me."

Zane sniffed, feeling somewhat mollified. "Jesus, Ty. You know me too well."

"Tell me about it."

"Head over heels, huh?" Zane's lips twitched into a very reluctant smile, and he rubbed at them, then dragged his fingers through the dark beard he'd let grow in during the past weeks as he'd been blind. He was still angry, but he tamped it down for the moment, just relieved to hear Ty's voice. "What else do you know about me?"

Ty hummed. "I know you're sleeping in my bed right now."

Zane glanced around Ty's bedroom and sighed. Dammit. "I'm still upset," he muttered, not admitting anything. "I understand you were strung out, but goddamn, Ty. You could've said something, you could have talked to me about it instead of just—"

"I have no excuse. Sometimes I'm a selfish asshole."

Dregs of the scare still sloshed through Zane, enough that he didn't want to let it go, but he knew it wouldn't solve anything to harp at Ty over the phone. He sighed instead. "What did Burns want?" he asked in a more even tone, knowing it was a question he wouldn't have asked a week ago.

"I'm sorry, Zane," Ty said, refusing to answer.

Zane's jaw clenched. For good or for bad, Zane knew the drill. "You were ordered to go dark?"

"Yes."

"Meaning immediate deployment off the grid, no contact with noncombatants, no trail to trace, no idea when you'll be back."

"I had to call you."

Zane swallowed hard as that sank in. With this call, Ty was breaking protocol and disobeying a direct order, something Zane knew Ty didn't take lightly. All sorts of responses crowded on his tongue before a wry observation won out. "I hope there's not a trace on your phone, or we're seriously busted."

"Quite frankly, Zane, I don't care if we are," Ty said with conviction. "Not anymore."

"Grady," Zane said, throat aching. "Do what you have to and then get your ass home."

"I'm sorry, Zane. I'll make this up to you."

"There better be groveling involved," Zane muttered.

"Sleep well."

The call disconnected. Zane was left with silence and a sudden overwhelming sense of helplessness and worry. Ty was out there working a job alone, and Zane didn't know any more now than he had a day ago. He swallowed hard and let the hand holding the phone fall to the side. After several minutes of focusing on trying to sort the upset from the lingering anger and not having much luck, he climbed out of the bed, yanked the sweaty sheets off the mattress, and headed down to the basement to put them in the washer.

He needed a shower and some iced tea—preferably from Long Island, but that wasn't a good idea, so instant mix would do. He just hoped he could find enough work to keep him distracted until Ty returned and he could kick his ass.

RANDALL JONAS sat on Dick Burns' couch with his head in his hands. There was a cot in the corner with pillows and folded blankets where he'd been sleeping, and there were whispers going around the office about why Burns wasn't taking meetings.

When the cell phone in his pocket rang, Jonas nearly jumped out of his skin. Burns bit his lip to keep from smiling. His old friend had been out of the game too long for this cloak and dagger stuff.

Burns glanced over at him from where he sat at his desk. The phone was a burn phone, the number only known to two people: Burns and Blake Nichols, Julian Cross' former handler.

Jonas turned the speaker on with an obvious sense of relief. "Nichols," he said in a grave voice

"Hello, sir."

"Tell me."

"I was able to get in touch with Julian Cross, sir. He understands the situation."

"Thank Christ."

"But he wants no part in it."

"Excuse me?"

"He told me that he's out and intends to stay out, sir. He wants no part in any of it. He said if anyone is sent to pick him up, they'll return in a body bag. Since you know where he is, he's packing up right now and preparing to move."

Jonas closed his eyes. Burns slid his palm across his mouth.

"Cross is my friend, sir," Nichols' voice said on the speaker. "I don't want him hurt. But I also know that if this doesn't end he's going to be a target for the rest of his life."

"What are you getting at?"

"I want assurances that after this is over, Julian will be left alone."

"Assurances?"

"Your word will do."

Jonas met Burns' eyes across the office. "I'll go to bat for him."

"I suppose that will have to do. He won't be easy to detain, but I may have a way."

"What do you propose?"

"I can arrange for his boyfriend to be at home at a certain time. If he calls Julian, Julian will come and could possibly be detained. But it has to be today."

"That can be done."

"Julian won't go gently."

"We're aware of that fact."

"Even so. If I were you, sir, I'd sure as hell send more than one guy."

THE heavy thuds of wrapped fists hitting a punching bag echoed off the concrete block walls, as did the soft grunts of effort coming from the man abusing it. The FBI Baltimore field office gym was almost empty in the very early morning. That just meant Special Agent Zane Garrett didn't have to deal with people watching him beat the stuffing out of a bag.

Again.

He focused on his target, using hands, feet, arms, legs, whatever combination worked as he let his body attack and his mind empty. Then, after one vicious kick, the stationary bag swung backward and a deep oomph and a hard thump interrupted Zane's concentration.

"Garrett, what's good, man?" Special Agent Fred Perrimore muttered wryly from where he sprawled on his ass on the mat behind the punching bag he'd been holding in place.

Zane lowered his fists and wiped the trailing sweat from his forehead with the back of his forearm. "Sorry, Freddy. I figured you were paying attention."

"I was!" the stout, muscled black man said from the floor.

Zane offered him a grin and a hand. He helped the man to his feet.

"Need to talk about the prickly thing that crawled up your ass and died?" Perrimore asked, rubbing his hip with one hand.

"What do you mean?" Zane asked as he walked to the nearby bench and picked up his towel.

"You've been pissed for days, Garrett. You'd think your fifteen minutes of fame would make you friendlier, but no."

"Don't talk about publicity with me." Zane had not enjoyed the continued media attention after his touchdown run with a bomb at Green Mount Cemetery last week. His snowflake of a partner had been granted a reprieve, three days off work to deal with the mental fallout. But not Zane, no, because he had used up all his comp time being blind and helpless.

"I'm just glad Grady hasn't been here. You two would be taking each other apart in the ring," Perrimore said with a nod to the boxing ring in the middle of the gym. He sprayed his face with his water bottle. "How the hell does he have so much damn leave time, anyway? Is he on psych eval again?"

Zane shrugged. He'd been a little on edge ever since he woke up and found a good-bye letter in bed next to him instead of his lover. Zane didn't even know if Ty's little mental health trip had helped him. That phone call had been two days ago, and no Ty in sight.

"He needed some time after the building fell in on us," Zane murmured.

"Hell, Zane, I don't doubt that. I'd be shocked if he were here. In fact, I'm shocked that you've been here." Perrimore crossed his arms and focused his disapproval on Zane. "You were blind for a week. And being in that building when it came down on you and Grady? You should have taken time too. The docs would have signed off on the leave, no question."

Zane edged up one shoulder as he punched halfheartedly at the bag, watching it waver. "I had plenty of time to sit and think when I couldn't see. I need to be doing something, even if it is just paperwork. Mac's not letting me go out, anyway."

"Yeah," Perrimore said with a firm nod. "Because you're mean. He can't risk the PR nightmare if you were on the streets."

Zane didn't think his behavior had been that bad. "You're exaggerating."

"You told Clancy to take her pom-poms and go home."

Zane wrinkled his nose. "She was going on about how great What's-His-Name from Financial Crimes is."

"Yeah, well, you probably ought to apologize."

"I'm not apologizing when she's dating the guy." Zane's phone, sitting on the bench with his towel, began to chime. He turned to pick it up.

"They hooked up? Michelle and What's-His-Name?"

"Yeah. Keeping it quiet, though, so keep your mouth shut," Zane said as he looked at his phone's display. It was a Washington, DC number, one he didn't know.

"Why is she dating a guy from Financial Crimes?" Perrimore asked. He sounded exasperated.

Zane shrugged and hit the button to answer the call. "Special Agent Zane Garrett."

"Garrett, Burns here," the caller said. He didn't offer his title, even though it was an impressive one. He didn't even offer a hello. "I need you on a plane in less than two hours."

Zane figured he must have looked surprised, because Perrimore frowned and pointed at the phone, mouthing, "Who is it?"

Zane shook his head. "A plane to where?"

"Chicago, but I don't have time to explain further. There will be information in your locker," Burns said, sounding harried and impatient.

Zane glanced at the clock high on the wall. It was almost five in the morning. Normally a call at this time would have caught Zane still in bed. "Guess it's a good thing I'm at the office."

"Should I tap someone else for this, Agent Garrett?" Burns asked, his customary composure somewhat lacking. "Because I've got less than fifteen minutes to find my man a backup, and I recall that you used to be less talkative."

Zane frowned. There was something weird about this. "No, sir. I can leave immediately."

"You do that, then. Take a lesson from your partner, Zane. Every minute you spend being a smartass is one minute on the other side that you're not there for someone who's counting on you." He ended the call without waiting for Zane's response.

Zane pulled the phone from his ear and looked at it as if it might lunge and snap his head off. "What the hell?" Whatever had happened had Burns more riled than Zane had ever heard him. Zane looked at Perrimore. "I gotta go." He grabbed his towel and took off at a run for the locker room.

"Hey, what's going on? Garrett!" Perrimore called after him.

Zane didn't stop to answer. He could be showered and dressed and in his truck in ten minutes. BWI wasn't far away.

~Chapter 2~

IT HAD been a whirlwind few hours. A single card of information—airline and flight time out of Baltimore; a time and place in Chicago—had been waiting on the top shelf of Zane's locker, along with a ticket for a nonstop to O'Hare.

Zane had, upon occasion, worked with less information. And he knew enough about how Burns worked not to even be bothered with his methods.

He'd made it to BWI with barely enough time to change into the suit he'd had in the truck. He'd taken the time during the past two days to repack the small duffel bag he kept in the truck for when he needed a change of clothes and more than a couple of spare magazines for his Glock. He'd been able to check the duffel, along with his arsenal.

That he was in a hurry to serve as backup for another agent, he understood. Why it all translated into Burns being so tense, he had no idea. It was more than a little unnerving, actually, because it brought back memories of clandestine assignments he'd thought he'd buried. It made him wonder what Ty could possibly be doing for Burns that Burns needed to call Zane in on a job. This wasn't the first time Zane had worked for the assistant director at the order of a single phone call. It was just the first time he'd done it since he was sober.

Zane tried to clear his mind as he waited for the plane to land and taxi to the gate. After the all clear, he pulled on his wool coat and headed up the skyway with a purpose. His plane was on time, not too surprising for an early morning flight, and his contact was supposed to meet him at the security point where the gate let out of the concourse proper, near baggage claim.

At quarter to seven, O'Hare was bustling, and it helped Zane shrug off the last of the lingering unease from the flight. He had to walk at least half a mile through the sprawling terminals, maneuvering through throngs of people as he tried to get out, but he made it to the security point in under fifteen minutes. Right on time. Now he just had to find his contact.

He got stuck behind a group of college kids, some kind of sports team, as he came through the terminal exit. He stopped to try to look around and over them, searching for anything that might give him a clue as to whom he'd be meeting.

Suit and tie, he would guess that much.

Several people fit the bill as he surveyed the milling crowd. A man in an expensive suit with no luggage other than a briefcase was reading a newspaper. A woman in a sharp pantsuit and her hair in a tight bun stood near the entrance to a café, checking her watch. Zane gave her a second glance before his gaze coasted past a well-built man leaning over into a cold drinks case, wearing an expensive trench coat and a T-shirt and jeans. The T-shirt and trench combo didn't get rocked often.

Zane smiled when it made him think of Ty. The pang of hurt that had lodged in his chest a couple of days ago twinged, and he rubbed at it, ignoring the frazzle of irritation that followed. Ty would wear something like that. He would probably get to Chicago, think *Damn, it's cold*, and then go right out and buy a high-dollar trench to wear with jeans and a T-shirt because he'd be able to wear it at work when he got home, and who cared what he looked like in the meantime? Zane chuckled despite the frustration and lingering sense of loss. It would make sense to Ty, anyway.

He tipped his head to one side to try to see what the T-shirt said. The man straightened and brought into view the face of one Special Agent B. Tyler Grady.

Zane did a literal double take, hardly able to believe who he was seeing.

Ty.

Ty looked up and met Zane's eyes across the crowded terminal, and shock registered on his handsome face. He was wearing a pair of jeans Zane had intimate knowledge of and a T-shirt he had never seen before. It was pink and vintage-looking with an orange half circle on it. There were two cartoon characters in front of the circle, an alligator and a crocodile, one saying, "See you later," and the other replying, "After while." He hadn't shaved in a day or two and looked a touch harried, but he also looked healthier than he had the last time Zane had seen him, less worn and more at peace with the world. As Zane drew near, he could see that Ty's hazel eyes were the same as he remembered: alight with life and humor.

"Zane! What are you doing here?"

Zane was torn between a nearly overwhelming urge to pull Ty into his arms and the driving need to shake him silly. Zane curled his hands into fists, all too aware of the people all around them. "Burns sent me."

Ty turned his chin. "You're my backup?" he asked, a smile forming as he spoke. His eyes sparkled, and the smile lines around them appeared before he took an impulsive step forward and hugged Zane tight. Then he kissed him, heedless of the crowds milling through the terminal.

Zane clutched at Ty's arms in surprise, but the warmth of Ty's lips melted the shock away within seconds, and Zane squeezed his eyes shut as everything else faded.

It seemed like forever before Ty broke the kiss and took Zane's face between his hands to look at him. "I thought it'd be days before I got to see you."

Zane turned his head just enough to press his lips to Ty's palm before he frowned. The swell of absolute relief and ridiculous happiness didn't stand a chance against the stored-up anger and frustration. He pulled back and took Ty by his shoulders, shaking him just like he'd wanted to. "What were you thinking?"

Ty laughed and grabbed him. "Stop! Okay!"

"I should shake you until your teeth rattle," Zane said as he let Ty go.

Ty nodded as his smile fell away. His hands dropped from Zane's face, his fingers dragging against Zane's skin.

Zane had almost a week of frustration built up, and he wasn't about to let it go that easily, even if Ty did look like a kicked puppy because Zane sort of wanted to kill him. When he spoke again, he was surprised that it came out in a growl. "Where the hell have you been?"

Ty shrugged, looking away at the thinning crowd. "Here and there. In theory, Tennessee was involved. Or Kentucky. I'm still not sure." He looked back at Zane. "Which one has the bluegrass and which one has blue grass?"

Zane barely resisted the impulse to shake him again. It wouldn't help, but it might help him feel better. "I'm not asking where Burns *told* you you were."

Ty nodded, refusing to comment on that.

Zane shook his head and then glanced up at the ceiling before meeting his lover's gaze again. "You just left," Zane said, and he made no effort to hide his upset.

Ty glanced around the terminal, then looked back at Zane and flopped his hands. "I had to. I don't know how to explain it; it's just sometimes it feels like… like the world is shrinking around me. Like if I don't get out and away that it'll catch me and crush me. And I know that sounds stupid, but it's a real feeling and I panic. I woke up that morning and I just had to go." He reached up and put his palm against Zane's cheek again. It was like he couldn't help himself. "I tried to wake you, I really did. I even shook you!"

"You shook me."

"Well… I poked you."

"Ty!"

"I know! You were sleeping so soundly and…. You looked happy and safe so I let you sleep."

"I was," Zane said, too loud, and Ty glanced around. Zane stopped and gritted his teeth before continuing, his voice lowered again, "I was. And then I woke up."

Ty met his eyes with difficulty. Even with the fear Zane could see, Ty was more rested and pulled together than he had been five days ago, when he'd resembled a train going off the rails. He looked so much more like himself. Zane recognized just how stressed Ty must have been before taking off, and he could see that wherever Ty had been, it had helped.

"When I left that morning I intended to be back that night. Or at least the next morning. I swear, Zane, if I'd known I'd be gone this long I would have tried to stick it out." Ty waited a few breaths and then added, "I'm sorry."

It didn't help Zane feel any better about the situation, especially when Ty's sincere remorse highlighted how he was acting like a stereotypical jilted lover. Jealous, demanding, cranky. Zane grimaced. It just wasn't fair that he had been the one left behind and yet he still looked like the asshole. "There's no way I'm going to come out of this looking good."

Ty grabbed his arm as Zane turned away, stepping in front of him to face him. "What do you care if you come out of it looking good? The only person seeing you is me, and I know what I did was shitty. What do you care if we fight in front of a bunch of strangers who'll never see us again? I know you're angry, Zane. Show it. Just get it out so it doesn't sit inside you and blow up later."

Zane looked into his eyes and saw the near desperation there, and suddenly he could see the core of what had been bothering Ty. Neither of them had ever felt comfortable showing what they were feeling. For the first time, Zane could see just how badly Ty needed that. But Zane was too close to losing his temper as he stood there and looked into Ty's eyes. "What do you want me to say?" The words came out graveled and curt.

Ty put both hands out, palms up. "I don't know, bitch at me? Tell me it's okay? Say *something*. I'm damn near groveling, here, Zane."

"You scared me, Ty. Scared me," Zane snapped back, loud enough that people started glancing at them.

"I know," Ty said, still calm. "I'm sorry I scared you. I'm sorry I bolted without saying anything to you. I'm sorry I left when you needed me. If I could go back, I'd do it differently. But I'm not sorry for going. You and I both know I needed it. And somewhere in there, you know I needed to do it alone."

"I wouldn't have stopped you," Zane said in a more controlled tone.

"I know, Zane."

"Then why the hell didn't you wake me?"

"I was afraid… I was afraid if I woke you and looked into your eyes I wouldn't be able to go. And I had to go, Zane, I had to."

Zane sighed. The anger was melting away, even after almost a week of percolating. Zane wanted to resent Ty for being so easy to forgive. He had expected to be hit with Ty's charm, not this disarming sincerity. Even though fear and worry remained, they were blunted by the desperately happy part of him that just wanted Ty with him, no matter what. And he was glad to see Ty looking healthy again.

Ty nodded. "You're understandably pissed."

"You're damn right I am."

"Why don't we go get your bags, take a cab ride to my hotel, and you can take it out on me there?"

"Take it out on you. As opposed to what, the world?" Zane asked as he turned and started to walk through the breezeway.

Zane heard his partner sigh, but Ty kept his mouth shut as they walked.

Zane suspected he was overreacting, and he tried to swallow the anger. This wasn't how he'd wanted to see Ty again. He was not supposed to be angry and hurt and Ty all understanding and apologetic, making him feel like a caveman for being upset.

After checking the directory sign outside baggage claim, Zane found the baggage conveyor for his flight and stood waiting for his black leather duffel to scroll past. Ty stood at his side, silent and close. Zane could feel him. He took a steadying breath and turned to look at Ty.

He was watching Zane, eyebrows raised.

Zane sniffed in annoyance. "Still upset," he muttered, the words almost lost under the shuffling sound of people moving around them. But he sighed and relaxed a little; just being able to see Ty and feel the bundle of energy that was his partner allowed that.

Ty gave him another serene, amused smile. He glanced over his shoulder, and then he stepped forward and took Zane's elbow. Before

Zane could do anything but draw a breath, Ty kissed him again, right there in the middle of baggage claim.

Zane grabbed his elbows, holding him still so he could deepen the kiss. To hell with whoever was watching. Ty felt so good in his arms, and he smelled like sandalwood, of all things. Zane didn't care why Ty was suddenly so comfortable with the PDAs. He was going to take advantage while he could.

"Does it make you feel better to know I missed the hell out of you?" Ty whispered, lips moving against Zane's. "And I hope you're still just a little angry when we get to my hotel room."

Zane let out a shuddering breath. "It'll be more than just a little."

Ty hummed, the sound deep and anticipatory. It was almost a purr. "Promise?"

Zane gripped Ty's upper arms tight. "Absolutely."

Ty smiled rakishly, damn him, and took a step back, looking Zane up and down before nodding at the conveyor belt. "There went your bag."

Zane glanced around and had to dart after his duffel. When he pulled it off the belt and looked back at Ty in exasperation, Ty was still smiling.

"Come on. I'll show you the hotel Dick ponied up for," Ty said as he turned to head for the exits.

"You really have a hotel? But when do we move?"

"I don't know."

Zane slung the small bag over his shoulder and loped after Ty. "Why was Burns in such a hurry to get me here this morning if the meet isn't set?"

"Probably because he knew I was here alone with nothing to do but something stupid. I've been stalking this guy for two days now," Ty said as he dug around in his pockets, fussing with the heavy trench coat he wore. "Took me a full day just to get a whiff of him. Burns needed to give you time to get under. It'll be this evening, so we'll have time to buy you some new clothes, give you time to scruff yourself up. Maybe give me time to scruff you up."

"What do you mean scruff me up?"

"I mean screw you through a wall," Ty said, waving his hand up and down at Zane.

Zane laughed in surprise. That idea sounded pretty damn good.

"And you look like a Fed. We're not supposed to look like government on this one, so we'll need to find you some new clothes."

"If you say so. All I know is I'm backup. And a lot happier to be here than I was thirty minutes ago."

Ty's hand snaked around Zane's waist and pulled him closer as they walked. "Burns didn't give me anything but the city and 'hurry' and that he'd call me to give me an address later. Then I sat here cooling my heels for two days because he decided I needed backup. I didn't even get a chance to run down this dude, who apparently is pretty good at not being found."

"Who is he?"

"I don't know. Do you really want to talk about a case we'll be handling in less than twelve hours, or do you want to go see my kickass hotel room and discuss your feelings instead?"

"Are you seriously asking me that question right now?" Zane said as he moved his duffel to his other shoulder so it didn't hang between them.

"Is that a no, then?"

Zane reached to dig his fingers into Ty's ribs, smiling when Ty twisted to get away. "You might get there without being mauled in the back of a taxi, but I'm making no promises."

"Fair enough. So how was your week, anyway?" Ty asked, passing through the glass doors and out into Chicago's frigid March morning. He began to search his pockets again, not looking where he was going.

Zane stopped their forward progress toward the curb after Ty almost ran down a couple of nuns dragging neon paisley rolling cases. "What are you looking for?"

"I got you something," Ty said as he lifted one side of his trench coat and peered under it. "This damn thing has so many hidey holes I can't remember which one I put it in."

Zane couldn't help but laugh again. "You got me something?"

Ty looked up, his eyes wide and sincere as he nodded. God, he was handsome. Zane had to shake the urge to kiss him again, and he let the warmth in his chest spread through him as he met Ty's eyes. Ty, as always, remained outwardly oblivious to the effect he often had on Zane.

"I've been here an hour or so. Walked through the gift shop." He flopped his hands and gave up the search. "It'll fall out eventually," he muttered as he smoothed his hands down the front of his coat. He'd definitely bought it for the exact reason Zane had thought.

"You didn't need to bring anything home but yourself," Zane said, sighing as he took Ty's arm and got him moving again, following the ground transportation signs toward the taxi queue. It was the same Ty Grady he knew and loved. Really loved. And wasn't that still an odd thought?

"I didn't know when I'd get home after this," Ty said with a wave of his hand. "I couldn't call you. I was pretty sure you were going to be frothing at the mouth by now, so I had to have a plan B in case a sincere apology and groveling didn't work."

"I wasn't frothing at the mouth."

Ty cleared his throat and glanced at Zane with a knowing look.

Zane shoved his hands in the pockets of his long overcoat and tried to ignore him, but he could just feel Ty watching and waiting. "Okay, so I was a little put out." He shrugged as he glanced over at his partner.

Ty nodded as they came up on the cab in the front of the line waiting for passengers. He opened the door and they both climbed into the back of the car, and Zane stashed the duffel between his feet. Ty said something to the cabbie Zane couldn't make out over the traffic noise, and the car was moving a few moments later.

"I am sorry I left like that," Ty said as soon as they were sitting next to each other, a careful two feet of empty seat between them.

The structures whizzing by outside cast weird shadows into the cab, but Zane knew the features of Ty's face without having to see them, and a short glimpse in the sunlight showed him that Ty was watching him, eyes intent.

"I'm sorry you felt you had to."

Ty gave an elegant shrug and smiled. "Shit happens," he said as he looked away.

"Usually because you're full of it," Zane muttered, leaning back in the seat to take the first easy breath he'd been able to draw in days. He glanced at Ty and felt more of the pressure in his chest ease away.

Ty rested his head against the seat and turned to look at Zane. "Nice suit."

Zane looked down at himself. It was a deep black suit with sharp lines and tiny charcoal pinstripes, bought to replace the suit ruined last week at Lydia Reeves' funeral and picked up from the tailor's just yesterday. The jacket had been cut a little fuller to allow for his gun holster, and the sleeves a little longer to cover his knives. "Burns caught me in the gym. This was what I had for work, since I didn't have time to run home."

Ty was still watching him, his head lowered, his lips twitching as he fought a smile. "No, Zane," he said in a low voice, an entirely different tone to the words. "I meant *nice suit*."

Zane's mouth went dry as the honey-smooth tone of Ty's seductive voice seeped into him. A slash of light caught in Ty's eyes, and they glittered green with flecks of gold, focused on him. Zane felt his cheeks flush. "Well. I… uh."

Ty didn't respond. He continued to watch Zane as the city passed by the cab's windows. Zane raised an eyebrow, and Ty smirked. Zane knew that look. He knew it very well, and the cab could not get to the hotel fast enough.

TY LED Zane through the lobby of the hotel Dick had put them up in, bypassing the front desk in favor of the elevators. Technically, they had two rooms for the day. They wouldn't need both.

Ty had to admit that he was nervous. He'd been nervous ever since the morning Richard Burns had called him and he'd realized he wouldn't be able to get back to Zane before Zane completely flipped out. As soon as the elevator doors closed, Ty glanced at Zane and breathed in deeply to calm himself.

Zane turned to lean against the side wall, facing Ty, watching him. His dark eyes didn't stray, not that Ty had anywhere to hide.

"You mad?" Ty asked, lips twitching as he fought a smile.

Zane's eyes narrowed, and the calm façade melted into something that looked a little more dangerous. A thrill ran through Ty's body, and he could not suppress the shiver.

"You want to talk?"

"Is there more to say?" Zane asked. His voice carried a cautious undertone. "I'm angry, you're sorry."

"Honestly?" Ty said, losing the teasing note. "I think we have shit tons of things to talk about."

Zane frowned, looking pained. But he nodded in agreement.

The elevator lurched as they reached their floor. Ty waited for the doors to open before he stepped closer and took Zane's hand in his.

Zane laced his fingers with Ty's, and the frown faded, replaced by an unusual vulnerability. "This isn't going to keep me angry."

"Yeah, that's not exactly my plan," Ty whispered as he led Zane down the hallway. They passed a few people on their way to their door, but he never let go of Zane's hand. He didn't let go of it as he fished his key out of one of his many pockets and unlocked the door, and once they were inside, he didn't let go of it after he let Zane drop his bag. Instead, he pulled Zane closer to kiss him.

Zane's free hand dug under Ty's trench coat to slide around his waist, pulling Ty to him as their lips met.

Ty's eyes fell shut and all the tension drained out of him as he wrapped around his lover. Zane was so warm, and his familiar scent seeped into Ty, pushing away all the worries he'd been harboring. He reached out and slid his hand along Zane's waist, pulling at his shirt. "I love you, Zane."

Zane sighed, leaning to place a soft kiss at Ty's temple. "I know."

Ty turned his head to instigate another kiss, delving into it with more heat. "I've been looking forward to this for days."

Zane clutched him close, heat and anticipation building between them, and Ty heard a soft groan escape Zane as the kiss continued. The sound went straight through Ty, and his hands began tugging at Zane's dress shirt, undoing buttons, pulling at his belt as they shuffled further into the room. Ty was forced to take a step back to keep his balance. He found himself against the side of the wet bar, and he just had to laugh and lean against the edge of the counter. Zane shoved Ty's coat off his shoulders and pulled at his T-shirt.

"Been too long," Zane said before claiming another kiss.

Ty nodded, not able to say anything in reply. He pushed onto his toes and sat on the marble counter so he could slide his knees against Zane's hips and pull him closer. Zane wedged in, obviously determined to have skin on skin contact sooner rather than later.

Ty began to laugh again, pushing off Zane's shirt and dragging his hands against his shoulders. He leaned in to get another kiss, but just as their lips touched, Ty opened his mouth to say one last thing before he forgot and let it slide too long. Zane spoke first.

"Ty," Zane said between kisses, his hands firm on Ty's body. "Be mine, just for now. There's time."

Ty reached for Zane's face, meeting his eyes. "I was always yours," he said with difficulty.

Zane pressed his fingertips to Ty's lips. "Why?"

Ty shook his head, searching for the answer. His chest tightened and breathing became difficult, but he landed on the words he needed. He met Zane's dark eyes and realized he was feeling light-headed as he answered. "Because… you make me the kind of person I've always wished I was."

Zane was silent, his gaze tracing over Ty's face. Ty held his breath until Zane spoke. "I've always wanted you just like you are. As much as you infuriate me, you're who I want."

Ty couldn't put his finger on what those words felt like. It was somewhere between relief and elation. He didn't have any more he could say, so he just leaned forward and kissed Zane again, hooking his feet behind Zane's thighs so he couldn't get away.

With a groan, Zane started pulling at Ty's T-shirt to get it over his head.

"Don't hurt it! It's new," Ty said with a grin as he lifted his arms for Zane to pull the shirt off. It hit the floor, and Zane's hands splayed over Ty's chest and ribs while he latched on to Ty's neck. Ty moaned and let his head fall back, cursing when he banged it against the mirrored cabinet above the wet bar.

Zane sank to his knees, tugging Ty off the counter, mouth still on Ty's body, his beard leaving a trail of prickles. His hands slid into Ty's jeans, and he pulled them down as he moved.

"Zane," Ty said, breathless as he looked down at Zane on his knees. He put his hand on Zane's head and pulled at his overgrown curly hair.

Zane dragged his tongue down the dark trail of hair along Ty's abdomen before he tipped his head back to look up at Ty.

"Is this a bad time to tell you that I hate that beard?" Ty asked.

"You'll deal with it," Zane said, that spark returning to his almost-black eyes.

Ty laughed, his hand tightening in Zane's hair. Zane retaliated by dragging his cheek down Ty's hip. Ty tugged at his hair harder. "Come back up here."

Zane stood in one fluid motion, reaching out to cup one hand over the back of Ty's neck as he pulled him into a voracious kiss.

Something inside Ty flipped over, and he dug his fingers into Zane with a grateful moan. Something about Zane's touch felt different. There was more confidence in him, something more firm than just the muscles of his back that Ty was digging his fingers into. Something more certain.

Zane pulled him closer and squeezed him tight, then reached down to slide his hands under Ty's ass and lift him with a grunt. Ty wrapped around him so he wouldn't fall, and Zane swung around and took the three steps to the bed before tossing Ty down to the mattress.

Ty was still bouncing when Zane crawled over him to kiss him again. He remembered the first time they'd ever tried this: Zane had picked him up like that, in the bathroom of that damn Holiday Inn in New York City. If Ty told Zane that he enjoyed it, he'd be getting tossed around all the time. He'd probably end up with a broken arm or something. Or Zane would ruin his back.

He let Zane take over, letting his lover's touch brush away all the stress and worry of the last few months, letting himself forget everything he'd been holding onto, letting Zane wipe the slate clean for him. He tangled his hands in Zane's hair and kissed him like it was their first time.

When their mouths parted, both of them gasping for breath, Zane set his forehead against Ty's and slid his hand through Ty's mussed hair. His body was heavy against Ty's, his heart racing, warmth and anticipation flowing between them.

"This feels different," Ty said, breathless.

"Yes." Zane shifted down to one elbow, laying all of his weight on Ty and pressing closer, nosing against Ty's chin and cheek.

Ty spread his legs wider, letting Zane settle between them. It had taken a few months, but he'd finally gotten comfortable with just how much he enjoyed having Zane top him. He'd taught himself quite a lot on that cruise ship job over Christmas.

He reached up to slide his fingers into Zane's hair, meeting Zane's eyes and lifting his hips, making Zane's breath catch.

"Ty," Zane drew out, a shudder coursing through him and into Ty. "You make me crazy wanting you."

"That's the way I like you," Ty said as he dragged his fingers up Zane's back. "Come on, we have time."

Zane shifted and ground down against Ty's thigh. "Good. I intend to make you as crazy as I am," he said against Ty's ear before pushing himself up and to his knees. "And I believe you invited me to work off a little aggravation."

"Less talky, Zane," Ty said with a smirk he knew would get Zane even more riled.

Zane gave him that narrow-eyed glare again and scooted back and off the bed. "Get those jeans off now if you want them to be wearable later," he said as he stripped off the rest of his clothes.

Ty did so without ever letting his gaze leave Zane, watching his lover disrobe with a shiver of anticipation. Then he spread himself out flat and stretched his arms above his head. He met Zane's eyes, laying his body out to offer up control. If Zane deserved anything from him, it was enough trust to give him that.

Zane growled low in his throat and again crawled up Ty's body, rubbing his chest and cock against all the skin he could as he worked his way up, leading with his tongue… and that damn beard. Ty dismissed that obscenity to fuss about later, pushing his body up against Zane's, forcing his hands to remain above his head instead of touching Zane like he so wanted to do.

"How do you want me to touch you?" Zane asked in a voice that rasped against Ty's skin.

"I just want you."

Zane rubbed against him more insistently as they kissed, hard and long and wet. His hands squeezed and petted until one followed the lines of Ty's muscled arm to close over his crossed wrists, holding them fast. "I thought you weren't kinky."

"I'm not kinky."

Zane hummed. "Want me to hold you down while I fuck you senseless? Is that why you've got your hands up like this?"

"Yeah." Ty could barely get the word out as he stared up into Zane's eyes.

"I can certainly oblige," Zane said, voice raspy and dark. He pushed down on Ty's wrists as he ground their hips together.

Ty whimpered at the tone of Zane's voice and the promise in it. "I should do this for you more often," he said in a tortured voice.

"Do what?"

"Give you everything I have."

Their eyes met in the breathless silence. Ty could feel Zane's heart beating fast against his chest. Zane finally kissed him in a violent rush and then pushed up and away from him.

"Stay there and spread your knees. I want to see you."

As Zane left the bed and disappeared into the bathroom, Ty did as he was ordered, placing his feet flat on the mattress and letting his knees fall to the sides. Zane had certainly gotten comfortable with his inner Alpha. Before Ty could form another thought, Zane was back, on the bed, between Ty's legs and licking his way up the inside of Ty's thigh to his cock.

Ty sighed, an almost inaudible release of air. The look in Zane's eyes was something Ty had never seen. It was intense and heated, possessive, filled with emotion that made Ty's chest hurt all over again, like the first time he'd ever looked into that fire in Zane's eyes and known that there would be no one else in the world for him.

Zane worked his way back up Ty's body before saying, "I love you, Ty."

Ty didn't have time to respond before Zane was kissing him, his lips and tongue demanding on Ty's, his body pressing down, insinuating himself between Ty's open legs.

One hand gripped both Ty's wrists as Zane rested his elbow against the bed near Ty's head. The other hand groped its way down Ty's body, a languorous, intimate exploration of the space between them. Ty closed his eyes as warmth and pressure spread through him. He felt Zane's long fingers, slick with cool lubricant, slide under his balls to rub.

"Fuck yes." Ty's back arched and his fingers stretched for anything to grab onto as Zane held him tight. He hooked one leg over Zane's hip and moaned into the kiss. He could feel Zane's cock, hard and demanding against him, and every inch of Zane's body was tense where he touched Ty.

"Zane," Ty whispered shakily.

"It's been too long since I got to do this," Zane said, his voice rasping and harsh. The head of his cock pushed against Ty, and Ty pulled his leg up higher to help the entry.

"All you have to do is ask," Ty said, unable to catch his breath over the rapid butterfly beating of his heart.

Zane nodded even as he turned his head and deepened the kiss. Ty lost himself in the sensations, submerging in the familiar scent of his lover and the absolute joy of being touched and taken like this. Then the head of Zane's cock pushed into him with a slow rocking of Zane's hips that forced him into Ty, little by little.

"Jesus, Zane." Ty pulled at his hands as the pain seared through him, desperate to be able to drag his fingers down Zane's back, but

Zane held fast. His other hand came to rest on Ty's thigh, fingers digging in, pulling at Ty's leg as he worked himself in with infinite care.

Ty pulled his knees up higher as the pain ebbed into something dull and throbbing, letting Zane spread him wider and push deeper into him. He absolutely loved the feeling of Zane's hips, warm against the inside of his thighs and pressing against him. Loved the sensation of the shaft of Zane's cock sliding against tight muscles, of being pushed into as he was held down.

Grunting as he stretched out over Ty's body, Zane flexed his hips until he was as deep inside Ty as he could get. A soft moan escaped him, and after kissing Ty again, he began to move, a slow rocking motion that built into a real rhythm. The first true thrust wrung an involuntary gasp out of Ty, and he pushed his hips into each one that followed. It spurred Zane on, his movements sliding Ty's shoulders against the expensive sheets, the bulk of Zane's weight on that one hand forcing Ty's wrists to sink into the mattress.

Ty couldn't describe how it felt to be pinned beneath Zane and taken in such an intimate, forceful way. Sex with Zane in any form was always enjoyable, but this was something different, something more than he'd ever given anyone.

He wrapped his legs around Zane's hips, his back curling as he met Zane's thrusts. A desperate stutter of a moan passed his lips, and he jerked his head to the side as Zane shoved into him. Zane's free hand came up to grip Ty's hair, pulling his face back so he had to look up. It was an odd feeling, looking into the eyes of the man who moved inside him. It wasn't uncomfortable, though. Far from it.

Zane flexed his hips as he bit at Ty's lip. "Kiss me," he said, voice hoarse and demanding.

Ty nearly whimpered. His hands moved to reach for his lover, but Zane's restraint on his wrists stopped them. Ty gasped instead and rolled his hips again, then pushed back with his shoulders to lift himself just enough to press his lips to Zane's.

Zane crushed their mouths together, the passion flaring out of control as he sank deep. Ty's ears were filled with the thuds of their bodies meeting, the barely there gasps that wrung out of him, Zane's grunts of effort and pleasure against his neck. He curled to combat the brutal pounding, a cry escaping as his fingers splayed. Zane leaned even more of his weight forward on Ty's hands, thrusting in and then grinding close before pulling back, only to push in again.

Ty writhed and let out a shameless whimper, then moved again to hook his ankles behind Zane's lower back for lack of any other way to hold on to him. Zane moaned as the angle of his entry changed, and the soft sound ratcheted up the heat inside Ty, pleasure curling in his groin. Zane hissed before shifting to start in on him harder, his hips ramming against Ty's ass. As it went on and on, Ty cried out, and the hoarse sounds weren't quite words.

He twisted as Zane pounded into him, unable to do anything but open himself up to the vulnerability of pleasure. Breathing hard, Zane started to slow, changing the hard thrusts to long, smooth slides. He lowered himself to lie against Ty, reaching up with his other hand to pull Ty's wrists down. Zane kissed him, slow and sure. Ty moaned and spread his captive hands, letting Zane's fingers thread into his, feeling helpless in Zane's grasp but loving that he could trust Zane with that feeling. Not once did it cross his mind to panic or try to escape the grip of Zane's fingers. At that moment, he was totally Zane's.

"I love to see you like this," Zane whispered against Ty's ear, causing a shudder to travel through Ty's body. "So fucking perfect."

Zane must have felt Ty's reaction, because he gasped and snapped his hips hard and then moved back up on his knees. He let go of one of Ty's hands, then reached down to slide his free hand against Ty's hip, holding on to him. Ty arched into his touch, reaching out to drag his fingers over Zane's shoulder and down his chest. Short, tortured breaths escaped his parted lips. He couldn't force himself to open his eyes as Zane started to move inside him again.

"Ty," Zane said as he released Ty's other wrist and moved his hand to splay his palm across Ty's chest. "Look at me. Open your eyes, baby."

Ty whimpered with the words, almost a pained gasp as he forced his eyes open.

Zane swallowed hard as he drew a shaky breath. "Are you feeling this too?" he asked, breathless as he rolled his hips against Ty.

Ty met his eyes for a brief moment before the pleasure and the proximity caused his eyes to fall shut once more and his body to jerk as he reached for Zane's neck and pulled him close. Zane's fingers tightened in his hair, holding him there.

"Yes," Ty answered, surprised at how desperate the honest answer sounded. He moaned, licking his lips as he tried to process through the haze, and then pressed his mouth to Zane's ear. The flare of heat had Ty's blood pumping so hard that at first he couldn't be sure the words were coming out. He couldn't hear a thing but his own heartbeat. "I'll always be yours, baby."

Zane shuddered against him, managing a dozen more thrusts before tensing hard. He shouted as he came, and his hips stuttered with each abbreviated thrust as he moaned Ty's name. Through his climax, Zane continued rolling his hips, providing the friction Ty needed, and it was enough to push Ty over the edge. They held tight to each other as they shared their pleasure, letting the world spin out of control for a few short moments together.

~CHAPTER 3~

ZANE stood on the bathroom threshold, looking out into the shadowed hotel room at the man he'd left sprawled across the bed in a mess of sheets and sweat. The light shining from behind Zane lit Ty's face, highlighting long lashes that lay against flushed cheeks and lips Zane could tell were swollen.

He smirked as he turned the small box over and back in his hand. He'd discovered it in his duffel bag, tangled up in a clean undershirt from the drawer where he'd kept the box hidden.

It was like Fate had intervened and tossed it into his bag while he wasn't looking.

Zane wanted to be angry at Ty, he truly did. But dammit, he just couldn't hold onto it. He was in love with a man who was flighty and spontaneous and headstrong all wrapped into one gorgeous, fun, frustrating package. Ty was a walking emotional hazard, and Zane had known that from the start. Zane huffed and leaned against the doorframe, wanting to burn into his memory the vision of Ty lying there after being thoroughly fucked.

Ty stretched, and the tangle of sheets muffled his low hum. He didn't look back at Zane, but he turned his head. "You're lurking."

"Admiring," Zane said as he took his time looking Ty up and down.

"Well. Go ahead, then."

Zane allowed himself a small smile. "I expected to be angry at you for longer," he said as he moved to the bed and settled on his side next to Ty.

Ty stretched again, his muscles tensing, body flexing like a large cat sunning. He smiled at Zane, eyes sparkling. "But then?"

Despite the fact that he had just about fucked Ty into oblivion not fifteen minutes before, a stroke of heat ripped through Zane as he watched the play of Ty's muscles, and he rolled his eyes in resignation. "Too happy to see you."

Ty reached out to slide the tips of his fingers down Zane's cheek. He scooted himself closer until he could press his nose to Zane's, and he draped his leg over Zane's hip. "I did miss you. And I *am* sorry."

Zane nodded as he slid his hand down Ty's hip and pulled him close. He knew he needed to let the anger go; it wouldn't change what Ty had done. "Did it hurt so much?"

Ty's expression softened into sadness, but it passed so quickly that Zane could have imagined it. "Sometimes I… I just need a break. Up here," he said, tapping his forehead. "I have to go somewhere on my own to let life hit me. If I don't, too much piles up and… I end up not really able to deal. I just have to get away sometimes."

Zane didn't understand; he wasn't sure he could without having seen the things Ty had seen or living the things Ty had lived. He supposed that when he had to take something apart and analyze it from all sides, it was his way of coping with an issue that would otherwise be too big to deal with. Ty's way of coping was to walk into an open space, either figuratively or physically, and let the problem hit him with its full force. It was one of the ways he and Ty were wired so differently.

Ty sighed and rolled to his back again. "Running for a few days is better than the alternative."

"Meltdown."

"Yes. It's happened before, and it's not pretty. Taking off gives me time to think, gives me clarity."

Zane totally believed that. He couldn't imagine living inside Ty's head was easy. He laid his cheek against Ty's chest, listening to the steady heartbeat as he tried to convince himself not to brood about it. His hand clenched on the small box he still held.

Ty's arm snaked around him, pulling him close and tight. Zane shifted and moved his head to Ty's shoulder.

"Zane?"

Zane realized he'd been staring at the headboard without really seeing anything, and he blinked back into focus to look up at Ty by resting his chin on Ty's chest. Ty's fingers curled around a lock of Zane's hair to play with it.

"Next time… next time I need to go, will you go with me?"

Whatever remnants of anger still lingering had no chance against a request like that. Zane would have sworn that he felt what remained of that hard knot he'd carried in his chest for the past several days melt away. "Yeah," he said, reaching to trail his fingers over Ty's cheek.

Ty gripped his hand and smiled, looking relieved. "Even if it involves the wilderness?"

Zane couldn't help but laugh. "Even if it involves the wilderness."

Ty hugged him tight and let out the breath he'd been holding in a rush. "I love you. I will always be yours, Zane—no matter where I am or where you are. I promise you that," he said, the words as serious as Zane had ever heard Ty utter.

Zane felt flushed all over, light-headed, and more than a little off-kilter. What Ty promised… it was more than Zane had ever expected to want from anyone ever again. But he did want that from Ty, desperately. He drew breath to speak, but it caught, and he had to try again before he could get anything out. "You—you grovel pretty damn well."

"I do everything well."

"Ha!"

"See, that was one thing I thought a lot about while I was gone," Ty said as he rolled Zane to his back and gave him a quick kiss.

"Groveling?"

"No"

"Being awesome?"

"No, Zane, shut up and let me talk."

Zane bit his lip to keep from smiling. He looked up into Ty's hazel eyes and found himself getting lost in them as Ty spoke.

"See… there's no reason you shouldn't know exactly how I feel about you. Or how I feel about bagels or loafers or the color blue."

"Bagels?"

"Yes. There's nothing we need to hide from each other. And I know it'll be hard for both of us, and we might need to share some things gradually, but I think we should give it a try."

Zane settled, his arms curving around Ty's waist, his gaze still riveted to Ty. "I think that sounds pretty damn good," he said, knowing it would help keep insecurity—and jealousy—at bay. He slid his hand over Ty's hip and up his side. "How do you feel about bagels?"

"Zane."

Zane smirked and ran his hand down Ty's arm.

"But that means you have to do the same for me," Ty continued. "No more hiding from me."

"I don't hide."

"Yes, you do."

Zane looked up into his eyes, wondering how he'd found a man who knew him so well inside and out. "You know, once I make my mind up about something…."

"I know."

Zane nodded. "I love you." Then he lifted his head enough to press a kiss to Ty's lips.

"I know," Ty said with a smirk as he pulled Zane closer. "And what the hell do you have that's poking me?"

The hand still clutching the box was pressed against the small of Ty's back, and Zane shifted enough to pull his arm free, propping himself up on that elbow as Ty lay back and watched him. "You know how I spent all that time… crunching the numbers?" he asked as an odd calm swept over him.

"I was aware, yes. Why?"

Zane smiled and then placed the little wrapped box on Ty's belly. He'd been envisioning this moment for months. In every permutation of his imaginings, they'd been wearing more clothing.

Ty had to duck his chin to see what it was, and he was looking at Zane oddly when he reached for the box. "What's this?"

"I bought it for you while we were on the cruise ship."

"And all I got you was this stupid T-shirt," Ty said as he lifted the tape at one end of the box.

"Don't fuss." Zane poked him in the ribs. Ty grunted and jerked away, reminding Zane that he was probably still sore from his collision with a very large fireman at home plate a couple of weeks back.

Ty glanced at him and opened the box like it might be rigged to explode. He set the lid aside and opened the case.

Set off against gray velvet and still gleaming after all those months was an elegant, polished white gold slide pendant hung on a length of tightly wound black cord. The slide was about the size and shape of a nickel, and the inset boasted a two-tone compass rose. Each of the eight points terminated in a tiny diamond chip set into the round seal.

Ty stared at it, speechless as he took in the intricate, uneven detailing of the hand-tooled piece. The imperfections reflected that it was one of a kind. Just like Ty.

"Zane," Ty finally managed to say. He sat up, not seeming to notice that he'd disturbed Zane's lounging, and looked down at Zane, agape.

Zane waited, feeling a slight trepidation niggling at him as he tried to decide what the reaction meant.

"This cost you a fortune," Ty said, aghast, as he lifted the necklace off the pad.

Zane edged up one shoulder in a tiny shrug. He hadn't even looked at the price tag. He'd seen it and known he had to get it. And seeing the amazement on Ty's face just now was worth every cent.

Ty just looked at him, his hazel eyes boring clear into Zane's soul. Sometimes Zane found himself wondering what Ty saw when he looked into him like that.

"Thank you, Zane."

"You're welcome," Zane said, swallowing hard as he sat up. "Want to see how it looks?" Because he did. Desperately. He'd visualized it uncounted times now.

Ty gave him a crooked grin and handed him the necklace. He sat so Zane could hook it around his neck. Zane unwound the leather cord and unfastened the clasp before moving it to settle it around Ty's throat. It took a few seconds to get the clasp closed—Ty's gaze on him was too distracting for Zane to get his fingers to work—and finally Zane pulled the pendant down so the necklace hung as it was supposed to.

Ty was still watching him. Zane touched the compass rose as it fell below the hollow of Ty's throat.

"Looks great," Zane said, starting to feel a little self-conscious under Ty's unwavering gaze.

"Why a compass?" Ty asked. He hadn't taken his eyes off Zane's yet.

Zane smiled and ran his thumb across the pendant. "Because you gave me direction when I was lost. You showed me the way." He looked up to meet Ty's eyes. "You're like my very own compass."

"Zane."

"I know, I know. I'm a sap."

"Maybe. But you're my sap," Ty said fondly. He reached for Zane and leaned in to kiss him.

Zane laughed against Ty's lips. "This from the man who asked me to slow dance in his living room. I think you've still got me beat."

"You loved it."

"Yeah." Zane touched the compass rose again. "I hope you'll wear it sometimes," he said, reaching to trail his fingers along the leather cord.

Ty reached up and gripped Zane's hand, meeting his eyes. Zane gazed at him; he couldn't get over how handsome he was.

"Thank you, baby."

Zane allowed himself a moment to soak in that smile and those sparkling eyes before pulling Ty into another consuming kiss. He didn't want to brood about the future or be embarrassed about the past anymore. He was taking a page out of Ty's book and concentrating on the now. And right now, the only thing he wanted was Ty.

He laughed as Ty wrapped his arms around him and pushed him back to the bed, then climbed on top of him to straddle him and hold him down. Zane gripped his hips, more than eager to see if Ty would ride him wearing nothing but that necklace.

"Now," Ty said with a grim note in his voice. "About this beard you've got going."

AFTER being convinced that the beard and mustache only lent to the image that they weren't Feds, Ty insisted that the best place to find Zane something else to wear for the job was the Magnificent Mile. Later that afternoon, they exited the cab away from the stores in order to stroll, because they had the time and why the hell not?

Ty's exodus had done him good, more than he'd expected when he'd gotten up that morning last week in a panic and bolted. He no longer felt heavy, no longer felt burdened by the past or the future, no longer felt the impending doom of walls closing in on his mind. It had been a good move on his part regardless of the backlash. A mental health break.

And to top off his improved mood, he and Zane were together in a city halfway across the country from anyone who knew them. Ty could feel the weight of the compass rose around his neck, and it was one burden he was happy to bear. He gave in to the impulse and reached out to slide his gloved fingers into Zane's bare hand. Zane's chin snapped around, and Ty could see his eyes widened in surprise, but Zane didn't pull away. Instead, he curled their hands together and gave a gentle squeeze. Ty's feeling of elation was borderline ridiculous.

Ty brushed his shoulder against Zane's as they walked along Michigan Avenue. "I figure we're tourists for a few hours. We can do whatever we feel like."

Zane smiled and his shoulders relaxed. "That sounds great."

"First thing is to find you some new threads. We can eat a late lunch, do the tourist thing while we have the chance."

"How long do we have?"

Ty shrugged. "We move when Dick calls."

They walked along the bustling avenue, passing high-end stores that included Disney, Apple, Cartier, Crate & Barrel, and Saks Fifth Avenue. After a quick meal, they went into several stores, Ty picking out clothing he claimed appropriate for the job and Zane shooting it all down as being made for a teenage hipster.

Ty was on the verge of getting frustrated when he found a pair of jeans he liked, forced Zane to try them on, and paid for them before Zane could argue or even take them off. He threw in a vintage burgundy Henley that cost a solid hundred dollars, a brown leather and suede jacket that would have bought him new tires if he had his Bronco back, and a pair of boots he thought he might end up stealing. He and Zane could share shoes and shirts as long as the shirts weren't tailored. Zane's height was the only thing that precluded them from sharing pants as well. It was a shame, because Zane's casual wardrobe could use a little help.

Ty eyed the finished product with a very real desire to get Zane back to the hotel and take it all off again.

Hands on his hips, he pushed at the back of his upper teeth with his tongue as he looked Zane over. "I don't think I've ever been gayer than I am right now."

Zane boggled at him, and Ty couldn't help but laugh. Zane shook his head and looked down at the clothes, then up at Ty with narrowed eyes. He tipped his head to one side and pulled up the collar on the jacket, ran his hand through his hair to ruffle it, and reached out to pluck Ty's aviators off his collar and slide them on. He ran his tongue over his lower lip and raised an impertinent eyebrow toward Ty.

"Oh God. Okay," Ty muttered, rolling his eyes and turning to leave. "Now you're just embarrassing yourself." He smirked and glanced back, though, because Zane made embarrassing look pretty damn good.

Zane grinned as he followed, carrying his suit over his shoulder in a bag. "I used to dress like this a lot in Miami, you know."

Ty hummed as he pictured all the many forms he'd seen Zane's style take in the past. His Miami attire had probably involved mesh shirts, snakeskin pants, and Thai silk. Aside from his partner knowing what walking shorts were, he seemed to be competent about dressing himself at home. Ty had to bite his lip to keep from laughing. He reached out to take Zane's hand again, angling them toward Navy Pier and the waterfront.

"If you like these jeans that much, maybe I should get some new clothes for at home. Been a while since I've bought anything but suits for work," Zane said, assuming an idle tone, though Ty knew full well it was meant to needle him.

"Agreed," Ty said, adding a nod to emphasize that, yeah, Zane needed an all new wardrobe, preferably one that showed off his incredible shoulders and back, because Ty had to admit, that was his favorite part of Zane. He glanced sideways at Zane and smirked. "We're going to Navy Pier now. There's something you should see."

"Should I be worried?"

"Always."

They walked several blocks south, then cut east past Pritzker Military Library to make for the lake. From the circle where cabs were coming and going, picking up and dropping off, they could look down the length of the ordered chaos that was Chicago's Navy Pier. The Ferris wheel and other rides, the yachts and touring boats moored at the docks, the seemingly endless array of shops and restaurants, extending as far as the eye could see from where he and Zane stood together.

"What is Navy Pier?" Zane asked as he followed Ty through a red metal arch bearing those words.

"It's... I don't know. It's got a Ferris wheel," Ty said with a careless shrug. "It's like the Field Museum and Wrigley Field. You have to go do it if you go to Chicago."

"Everything I know about Chicago I learned from *The Blues Brothers*," Zane said, distracted as they walked past small booths and ticket stands.

"Jesus, Zane," Ty muttered. "So I came here last night very briefly because I needed a drink. You need to see this." He gave Zane's hand a tug, leading him inside the shopping area and wending through the mass of people, shops, and mobile vendors. When he stopped, they were standing in front of Garrett Popcorn Shop. Ty waved a hand at it with pride, as if it were somehow his doing.

Zane pulled off the aviators and laughed. "That's great," he said as he looked in the window.

Ty put his hand on the small of Zane's back and ushered him in, pointing to the far wall where the shop had several T-shirts hanging. The white one in the middle, the same one Ty had bought yesterday and stowed in his bag, had yellow-orange cheddar cheese and golden-brown caramel handprints on the chest and the slogan "Love Can Be Messy" above the word Garrett and the shop's logo. It had been too perfect for Ty to pass up.

Zane's lips pressed together into a thin line, and when he glanced at Ty, Ty could see the amusement in Zane's eyes. It made them shine, the dark brown warm and inviting. Ty's chest tightened as he looked at his lover. Why the hell couldn't every day be like this?

"That's pretty good. I ought to get one," Zane said, plucking at the sleeve.

Ty stepped up behind him, letting his hand linger on Zane's back, soaking up the feeling of being with him again. "You can borrow mine," he murmured, smiling.

Zane turned his head, letting his nose brush Ty's cheek.

Ty closed his eyes and allowed himself to enjoy the moment. "Come on," he said after a few seconds of content silence. "Let's go see the sights for a few hours. Pretend it's real."

Zane's brow wrinkled. "Pretend what's real?"

Ty slid his hand down Zane's arm and linked their fingers again. "That I can hold your hand without worrying about being recognized," he said with a smile. He tugged at Zane's hand, wanting to get out of the shops and back onto the pier to see the water and the view.

Zane's smile reappeared and he nodded. "Anytime you want."

Ty gave him a melancholy smile, squeezing his hand. It was a shame they didn't get to go out and hold hands like this at home. A crying shame. But they couldn't risk being recognized and outed at work. As soon as they both retired, though, Ty intended to hold Zane's hand everywhere they went.

"WHAT are you going to tell them?" Randall Jonas asked as Burns dialed the number for his man in Chicago.

"As little as possible," Burns answered. He was silent as he waited for an answer, and when he spoke he was using some sort of code that Jonas didn't begin trying to decipher. "Your father says hello," Burns told his agent. It must have been some sort of activator.

Jonas watched him as he exchanged a few more seemingly mundane pleasantries; then he broke the code and just outright said the information he'd intended to pass on. "Consider your mark armed and extremely dangerous. He's a federal informant who's gone off the grid, and we need him here, in my office."

Jonas frowned, confused by Burns' methods. But then, Burns had never had regular methods to begin with.

"I don't care how you do it, just get him here. In one piece. Don't 'yes, sir' me, you little shit, just don't get dead." He hung up and looked at Jonas with a worried frown.

"Can your men really bring in Cross without any backup?" Jonas asked.

Burns pursed his lips. "Yes. I'd put these two against any of your spooks, any day of the week."

Jonas raised an eyebrow, and he couldn't help but smile at his old friend's confidence. "Them's fightin' words."

"Bring it, old man."

~Chapter 4~

"We should be getting close," Zane said as the cab cut through the architectural jungle of downtown.

"How do you want to play it? Go in soft or heavy? Good cop, bad cop? Shoot first and ask questions later?" Ty asked with a hint of sarcastic amusement.

Zane shrugged. "Are you expecting trouble?" Out of long habit, he slid his hand into his new jacket to check his weapon.

"From this guy? Almost certainly," Ty said. "Dick talked about him like he was Batman."

"How so?"

"Long list of connections to the CIA, organized crime, a laundry list of arms dealers and mercs, foreign and domestic."

"Why does Burns want him? And why us?"

Ty was silent for a moment. "I've learned not to ask those questions," he said as he looked at Zane with a smile to mitigate the harshness of the words.

Zane nodded. He looked at Ty with warmth he probably shouldn't have been feeling while officially on the job. Ty seemed closer than he had been just a moment ago, close enough for Zane to smell him, the unusual musk of sandalwood that was so unlike Ty and the more familiar combination of Tide, gun oil, leather, and sweat that turned him on like crazy. But Zane felt a pang of yearning for a whiff of Old Spice.

"I'm also expecting him to not actually be at this address. If he was this easy to find, he wouldn't be Batman," Ty said, drawing Zane out of his reverie.

"If he's there, it would be novel for it to go so smoothly," Zane said as the cab came to a stop in front of an old building converted into condos.

Ty checked his gun and got out as Zane paid the driver, who didn't even blink at the weapons and nodded when Zane told him to wait. Ty clucked his tongue, trying his best not to smile as Zane joined him on the curb. Ty had been told not long ago that he shouldn't enjoy the almost-getting-killed part of his job as much as he did. Zane didn't know who had said it, but ever since, Ty had been making a concerted effort to hide his unholy glee during melees. It was still pretty clear to Zane, though.

He surveyed the light traffic passing by on the side street. It was evening, and there weren't many people out and about. Hopefully that would work in their favor.

"Ready?" he asked Ty.

Ty glanced up and down the street, then nodded and stepped up to the double glass doors of the building. They would have to be buzzed in, which never helped the element of surprise. Ty stared at the panel for a moment, obviously contemplating how to go about it. He glanced back at Zane and shrugged one shoulder, then pushed the number they'd been given.

After a short pause, the small speaker clicked. "Hello?"

"Hey, Jimmy!" Ty practically shouted, startling Zane. Ty's words slurred as he leaned toward the speaker. "Dude. You should not have left early tonight."

There was a short pause. "I think you have the wrong apartment."

"Come on, man, don't be like that! I swear I didn't know you were into her! I left my good pants on your couch. If I go in to work hungover in my boxers again, they'll can me for sure. Four strikes and you're out, brother!" Ty bit his lip to keep from laughing as he turned his head away from the speaker box.

Zane grinned and shook his head, covering his mouth and reminding himself that they were trained federal agents. Professionals. In theory.

"You've got the wrong apartment. There's no Jimmy here."

"Oh," Ty drew out. "Shit, man, I'm sorry! Didn't mean to go buzzing you so early in the morning." The last glance at his watch had told Zane it was nearing six in the evening. "But hey, do you know Jimmy, man? Could you grab my pants for me?"

There was a longer pause, long enough that Zane thought the man on the other end of the speaker had abandoned the conversation. But then the box clicked again.

"There's no Jimmy here. Buzz somebody else." The words ended with some ring of finality.

Ty clucked his tongue again and shrugged at Zane. "Worth a try," he told his partner with a smirk. He reached out and hit another button. A moment later a woman answered. "Delivery."

"I didn't order anything," she said brusquely, and that was that. Four more tries later—one no answer, two immediate denials, and a bizarre conversation with a stoner about the phases of the moon during which Ty had way too much to offer, in Zane's opinion—Ty huffed in frustration.

"How many more are you going to try?" Zane asked. They didn't really have the time to call the Chicago field office and ask for a warrant. Not to mention that would go over really well with Burns, who obviously wanted them to keep this as low as it could go. Was this the kind of thing that Ty was always doing for Burns?

Ty glanced at him stubbornly and pushed a button at random. Zane rolled his eyes. As soon as there was an answer, he stepped closer to the speaker and said, "Federal agents, ma'am."

"Nice try, asshole," the woman said smugly; then the speaker box clicked off.

Ty growled dangerously. "I hate this town," he muttered as he took his gun out from under his coat.

Zane straightened in mild alarm. "What are you doing?"

Ty yanked a glove off one hand and wrapped it around the butt of his gun, then turned smoothly and rammed the handle into the glass door. The mottled glass cracked and shattered, but there was mesh wire embedded inside that kept it from falling in. Ty used the muzzle of his gun to clear out the window, ripping through the wire, raining pieces all over the sidewalk and Ty's feet. He reached through the iron bars and pushed the handle, opening the door and holding it for Zane with a gallant wave of his hand.

"Why, thank you, sir," Zane drawled as he walked through the mess, already thinking of ways to make sure Ty would be the one writing up the report for this trip.

"Assholes," Ty muttered as he looked up at the floor display above the elevators. He stopped in front of the fire alarm and looked at it for just a moment too long for Zane's comfort. Zane cleared his throat pointedly.

Ty looked at him almost guiltily and then followed him toward the stairwell. Zane didn't know if there were any sort of alarm on the door, but they needed to move a little more quickly regardless.

The condo they had targeted was on the second floor, not nearly a long enough hike up the steps to pacify Ty's annoyance. Zane pushed past him and started checking doors until they found the number they'd been provided. He glanced at his partner, knocked on the door, and listened to what sounded like a rush of feet that immediately retreated. Zane frowned and reached out to rap on the door again, but someone approached from the other side and stopped. Zane figured the man was looking out the peephole, so he held up his badge. Behind him, Ty did the same. "Federal agents."

A bolt slid and the door opened just a bit, blocked by the chain, and a slim, wholly average-looking man peered out.

"Cameron Jacobs? I'm Special Agent Zane Garrett, and this is Special Agent Ty Grady. We're looking for Julian Cross."

CAMERON stared through the four-inch gap as he studied the two tall, capable-looking men holding out badges that looked pretty official. They could be federal agents. Or not. With Julian's past business, there was no telling who might come looking for him. It was the "or not" that was scaring Cameron right now, and his hand gripped the doorjamb so tightly that it hurt. "I don't know who that is."

"Perhaps you know him better as Julian Bailey?" the man called Special Agent Grady said drily. "Or Sir? Maybe even Boss?"

Cameron frowned as he shook his head. Surely federal agents would be nicer than this. He looked them up and down. And better dressed. "I'm sorry, but you have the wrong...." He frowned harder as he remembered the last time he had said those words, maybe fifteen minutes ago. "Was that you on the speaker?" he asked in outrage.

The man who had introduced them smiled slowly. To Cameron, it was like a dangerous animal showing its teeth. He frowned, looking over the man's windblown, curly hair, piercing eyes, and a crooked nose that had probably been broken at least twice. The smile was probably meant to put him at ease.

Special Agent Grady flipped over the badge he'd been holding and pulled aside his leather jacket to slide it into an inner pocket. The move revealed a fairly large weapon in a holster under his arm. Whether he did it on purpose didn't really matter; his point was made.

"Would you mind opening the door so we can have a word, Mr. Jacobs?" Special Agent Garrett asked in a businesslike tone. "Or you can just point us toward Cross and we'll be out of your hair."

"I do mind," Cameron objected, his back straightening as he pulled his hand back to slam the door shut.

Grady's hand shot out in a flash, stopping the door from closing. He stepped closer and lowered his head, as if he might be about to share a secret. Everything about him screamed military to Cameron, from his gruff tone to his quick reflexes to his impressive athletic build.

"Do you have any idea how much trouble it is to fix a chain that's been ripped off a doorjamb?" Special Agent Grady asked calmly. "Or how much it hurts my shoulder to put it through a solid oak door? This is oak, right? It's very nice."

Cameron pushed hard against the door, and it made no difference at all. He glanced at Special Agent Garrett, who was taller, darker, and not offering any sympathy. This was not looking good. Not at all. So

Cameron nodded jerkily and reached to unhook the chain, aware that Julian would read him the riot act for this.

Of course, Julian would yell at him for opening the door in the first place. But only a little bit.

Chain undone, Cameron took several steps back and gathered himself to reach for his phone and Julian's speed dial emergency number as he watched his four calf-high white Westies charge the strangers entering the apartment.

Special Agent Grady moved in slowly, his body turned almost sideways as his eyes scanned the room. His hand was on his weapon.

Cameron had seen Julian enter rooms in a similar fashion, and it set off even more warning bells. The man looked down at the four dogs and balked, side-stepping and gesturing for his partner to come in.

It was Cameron's chance. Cameron reached into his pocket for his cell phone and fumbled with it, trying to be inconspicuous about it. He hoped that he managed to hit the key combination for the prewritten text he needed to send.

Special Agent Garrett shut the door gently, and the strangers moved steadily into Cameron's condo. The more he watched the agents, the more they reminded him of Julian. They were on guard but confident. "I don't know who you're looking for. There's no one else here."

"We know," Grady told him. He smiled and nodded to the pocket Cameron still had his hand stuffed into. "He'll be here soon, though. Take a load off, kid. It won't be so bad." He stretched out broad muscles and rolled his neck, the movement shifting his coat, revealing a specialty T-shirt. Grady turned to look down at the yipping dogs in distaste, and then he looked up at his partner.

Special Agent Garrett tipped his head to one side before focusing on Cameron. From twelve feet away, his eyes appeared to be flat black, and Cameron felt like he was pinned in place.

"How do you know Mr. Cross, Mr. Jacobs?" he asked. His voice was calmer than Special Agent Grady's, more polite, if still a bit cool.

Cameron pressed his lips together in a bid for silence. At least this was one of the possible scenarios Julian had outlined for him when they had set up the alert system. Despite Cameron's protests, his dangerous lover had insisted he'd rather come here to protect him and eliminate the problem than stay away in dubious safety.

Movement caught his eye, and Cameron glanced up to see one of Julian's large orange cats sinuously padding around the screen that sectioned off the bedroom. It was Smith, followed closely by Wesson.

The two very big cats stopped midstride upon seeing the strangers, and Cameron could have sworn he heard one of them growl.

"Now see, that's what I'm talking about," the churlish agent said as he pointed at the cats. "Those are guard dogs, Zane. Pound for pound the most effective killing machine in the world."

"So you say, Meow Mix," Garrett answered. He sounded like he was humoring his partner. Zane Garrett, Cameron remembered from the door. And Ty Grady, he reminded himself. Garrett and Grady. It sounded like some obnoxious men's clothing store. Zane pointed at Ty. "You keep your hands off the wildlife."

"Shove it, Garrett," Ty said with a huff. He moved around the couch and knelt several feet away from Smith and Wesson. He reached out his hand. "What are they, Maine Coons?" he asked Cameron with what seemed like genuine interest.

Cameron watched as the man put himself well within range of a serious tangle with pain. He swallowed and glanced at the digital clock next to the television. It had been three minutes. "Yeah," he said quietly.

"Ty, I said keep your damn hands to yourself," Zane snapped. "We don't have time for a field trip to the hospital if that cat decides it wants a taste of you."

Ty blithely ignored his partner's admonition, still holding out one hand and talking to Smith and Wesson in a low voice, a smile on his face. He turned and glanced over his shoulder at Zane. "If the big one didn't eat me, I think I can deal with two little ones."

Smith and Wesson sat side by side, watching him in the way only a cat could watch an inferior being. Cameron figured he looked like he was watching Ty like the man was an idiot. He also wondered what cat the man could possibly have tangled with that was bigger than Smith or Wesson.

Zane gave an aggrieved sigh and walked a little further into the room, though Cameron noticed he kept both the front door and him in sight. "We're not going to bite, Mr. Jacobs," Zane said, trying to placate him, Cameron could tell. Zane's lips twitched. "No more than the cats, anyway."

"The last stranger who messed with them ended up with stitches from temple to lip," Cameron mentioned to Ty.

Ty merely made a clicking sound with his tongue, not moving as he continued to hold his hand out to the cats. Wesson began to move slowly, slinking toward him. "Come on, handsome," Ty crooned to the cat. Smith lowered his head, his tail twitching as he watched, but Wesson continued to move toward him. He sat and graciously allowed the man to rub one finger under his chin.

Cameron's jaw dropped. Those stupid cats wouldn't even let him touch them, and he'd been living with Julian for over a year now. He swallowed his feeling of dread. If this guy got hold of Wesson and hurt him, Julian would maim him, and that would be a mess. A moment later, Ty had gathered the big cat into his arms and was standing again, holding him over his shoulder, rubbing his ear gently. He turned to grin at his partner. "Like playing the bagpipes," he joked about the large feline.

Cameron could hear Wesson purring from where he stood across the room.

Zane shook his head, clearly exasperated. "Make yourself at home, Ty. Want to check the fridge, see if there's any beer?"

Ty snorted loudly at him and shook his head. He bent and set the cat down carefully, giving his ear a last twirl with one long finger before standing back up and brushing at the cat hair on his shoulder, then looking at his watch. Wesson wound his large body around the agent's ankles, still purring to the point he was almost vibrating. Cameron had never seen anyone besides Julian handle either cat like that.

Ty bent to pick the cat up again, turning him upside down and holding him like a baby in his arms as he rubbed him under the chin.

Cameron's jaw dropped.

"Come on, Zane, don't be scared of a little pussy," Ty told his partner with a sly grin. Zane circled one finger in the air, dismissing the... insult?

Cameron's brows lifted about as far as they could go. "You two are supposed to be FBI agents?" he asked in disbelief.

"And your guy is late," Ty commented as he nodded. He watched out the balcony doors for a long moment before he set the cat down and calmly reached into his coat to pull his weapon. He glanced at Zane with narrowed eyes and then nodded toward the door as he checked the gun in the same manner Cameron had seen Julian check his, with utter calm and competence. Zane pulled a gun out from under his jacket, handling it capably.

"Mr. Jacobs, will he come in firing, or will he be concerned for your safety?" Ty asked, without a hint of real worry that Cameron could detect. It seemed like both men were accustomed to the idea of imminent peril.

But they didn't know Julian. He was a whole different level of danger.

"Don't worry about me," Cameron murmured. He shook his head and crouched, calling for the dogs. He gathered them and put them into their playpen in the far corner of the room. His gaze settled on Smith and Wesson. While the two cats tolerated him because Julian kicked them out of bed if they didn't, they didn't like him that much. Cameron wasn't too sure he could get them back into the bedroom without damage to himself. So they'd just have to take care of themselves.

Ty and Zane moved together in the middle of the living room as if drawn by magnets, putting their backs to each other, standing maybe four feet apart. Zane faced the door while Ty faced the balcony, synchronized like they'd been doing this a long time. The dogs began yipping plaintively, and Smith and Wesson both sat down in the opening to the bedroom, ready to enjoy the show.

Cameron cocked his head, listening. He could hear nothing over the complaining of the dogs.

The door burst open suddenly, kicked hard from the hallway, splintering the doorjamb. Julian's gun was drawn already, trained on the two so-called federal agents. Zane was already facing him, gun up and pointed. Ty didn't turn to face Julian. He kept his gun trained on the silent balcony.

Julian moved into the room, hulking and livid. He pointed his gun at Zane, and the two men stood there aiming at each other, silent as they sized each other up. Cameron was struck by the strong resemblance between them.

"Julian Cross?" Zane finally asked evenly.

Julian answered by pulling back the hammer on his gun.

Cameron saw the trigger move. It was just a tap away from a bullet now. He swallowed hard and forced himself to keep his eyes open. But Zane didn't even blink.

"We're here on orders from Richard Burns, assistant director of the Criminal Investigations Branch of the Federal Bureau of Investigation, to call on your status as a registered federal informant," Zane rattled off efficiently, neither his weapon nor his voice wavering.

Cameron's eyes widened in surprise as he saw Julian's gun waver ever so slightly.

"And we would appreciate it if you'd put that gun down," Ty added without turning around. "And tell your buddy I don't appreciate the feeling of his crosshairs on my forehead."

Julian's eyes darted between them and Cameron. "Are you okay?" he asked Cameron.

"Yes," Cameron said, resisting the urge to run over to his lover. He was using Julian Bailey's American accent, and Cameron remembered that Julian had told him that was a warning sign, that it meant he didn't know or didn't trust the people they were with. "They didn't touch me."

Julian's black eyes moved back to pin the man in front of him. "Put your weapon down. Then we can talk."

"I'm telling you right now, Cross, tell your buddy on the roof next door to stand down," Ty interrupted in a gruff voice.

"Put down your weapon and we'll discuss it," Julian repeated slowly.

"Don't think I won't shoot your Irish ass just 'cause I'm a Fed," Ty growled. "We don't need you to be walking."

Zane's gun was still trained on Julian. As far as Cameron could tell, he hadn't even twitched as Ty talked.

Even though Ty wasn't even looking at Julian, the threat still made Cameron shiver. Somehow they knew Julian wasn't American. Cameron had to swallow hard on a fresh wave of fear.

And Cameron didn't know how Ty knew someone else was out there at all. Cameron knew that it was Preston, Julian's ever-present, forever silent driver and cohort, which meant that if Ty even twitched he'd be on the floor, and Zane wouldn't be but a second behind. Cameron really didn't want corpses of federal agents in their apartment.

"Julian, please."

Julian waited another breathless moment before lowering his weapon. He eased the hammer down and then held it up sideways as proof that he'd done so. He slid it carefully back into its hiding spot.

"My man on the roof stays trained on your partner while you show me a badge," he bargained.

He held up his hand in a signal to Preston. Cameron looked between Julian and Zane as Zane moved the hand bracing his gun and slid it into his jacket. He pulled out a leather wallet and tossed it to Julian.

Julian caught it deftly with one hand, then flipped it over to look at the identification within. He stared at it for a moment before looking up at Zane.

He made a "quit" motion with his hand toward the balcony. "You can tell Richard Burns to stick it," he finally said as he handed the wallet back.

Zane snorted as he pocketed the wallet and lowered his weapon somewhat. "If you know Burns, you know that won't help."

Julian's eyes darted between the two men. "Get out," he ordered.

"Also won't help," Zane said, sliding his gun under his jacket. "We're here to escort you to DC. If we don't get you there, someone else will, and much less comfortably, I assure you."

Julian's shoulders tightened. He lowered his head and shook it. "I told them before. I will not be involved. I'm sorry you've wasted your time." He glanced at Cameron, his expression softening. "Perhaps you should see the sights before you go home, make the trip worthwhile," he told the two agents. His voice was polite, but he couldn't fool Cameron. He was angry and tense.

Though Zane was the one talking now, Cameron paid more attention to Ty. He still had his gun out and in hand and was staring devotedly out the balcony doors.

"No misunderstanding, Mr. Cross," Zane said, his voice genial enough under such odd circumstances that it pulled Cameron's attention away from Ty. "This isn't a request."

Cameron stiffened when Zane's eyes turned to focus on him speculatively, and Cameron bit down on his tongue to keep from blurting out what was sure to be a stupid question.

"Then so be it," Julian finally answered stubbornly. "Anyone else looking for me will follow the bread crumbs you've left behind you, no doubt. The longer you're here, the more you become my problem."

"Okay," Ty said impatiently as he stuffed his gun into his holster and moved around the couch, approaching Cameron. "Mr. Cross, I understand you won't be accompanying us to Washington willingly, is that correct?" he asked brusquely, continuing before Julian could answer. He moved toward Cameron as he extracted a pair of handcuffs. "Cameron Jacobs, you are under arrest for harboring a federal fugitive."

"What?" Cameron yelped, putting his hands behind his back and backing away. "Harboring a fugitive? Julian, what is this?"

"Stay calm, love," Julian requested, though the undertone in his voice told Cameron he was having trouble following his own advice.

Whoever these two men were, they knew physically threatening Julian would have no effect on him, and physically threatening Cameron would just piss him off. Arresting Cameron, however....

Ty gripped Cameron's elbow and pulled at him, turning him around with alarming strength as he clasped one cuff on his wrist.

Cameron looked up at Julian, hoping he knew what he was doing.

"You're bluffing," Julian said as he looked at Zane. "You have no grounds to arrest him, and you can't force me to Washington."

"Actually, yes, we do, and yes, we can," Zane replied. "It would be a shame to find an unregistered firearm in Mr. Jacobs' possession, especially if he threatened a federal agent with it."

Cameron gasped. "That's awful and you know it!"

"Yeah, you're breaking my heart." Ty's hand tightened on Cameron's shoulder as he secured the handcuffs, and his voice was low and gruff in Cameron's ear. "You have a good evening now, Mr. Cross," he said in a louder voice, pushing Cameron in front of him toward the door.

Cameron tried to dig in his heels, but he was no match for Ty. Both the FBI agents were closer to Julian's size than his, and since the top of his head did well to reach Julian's nose, it wasn't much problem for Ty to push him around. But Cameron was determined to stay calm, like Julian had told him, though it wasn't looking good as Ty propelled him forward. At least he was almost certain these guys wouldn't kill him.

"I'm sure you have ways to find us," Zane told Julian as he walked toward the door, somehow managing to look casual but keep facing Julian the whole time. He was still holding his gun. "If you decide to change your mind."

Julian sidestepped, stopping their progress. He didn't budge as Ty moved Cameron toward the door. Ty's fingers dug into Cameron's shoulder to stop him.

"Zane, I think Mr. Cross is a little more attached to Mr. Jacobs than we realized," Ty said casually to his partner.

"Well, leave it to intel to miss important little details like that," Zane muttered. He offered Julian an insincere smile. "Your choice, Mr. Cross. In a manner of speaking."

"Either get out of the way or have your man on the roof shoot us," Ty told Julian, sounding as if he hadn't a care in the world.

Julian narrowed his eyes. He glanced to the side, looking at Zane as he held up his hand and slowly reached into his coat with the other.

He extracted his cell phone carefully and slid it open. He looked back at Ty as he pressed a button and put the phone to his ear. "Preston," he said slowly, "shoot the stupid one."

"Julian!" Cameron snapped, annoyance flaring. Julian was supposed to be helping them!

Julian shrugged. "What do you mean, which one?" he said to Preston, whose voice could barely be heard on the phone.

"Let me guess; Preston drives the clown car?" Ty asked, unimpressed.

"Preston, don't you dare!" Cameron yelled at Julian's phone. "How is this going to help?" He looked around at the three men, and Cameron realized what a mess this was. There was nothing here but a lot of testosterone. He hoped. "Are you going to keep threatening each other, or is something going to happen besides someone dying on our floor?"

Zane raised an eyebrow. "He's got a temper," he observed as Cameron pulled at Ty's immovable hands.

Julian closed the phone in his hand in disgust and glared at the two agents. "You realize you put both our lives in danger with this stunt."

"We can live with that," Ty said. "Now do you want to do this nicely, have time to pack your Uzi in your underwear, or do we get to cuff you and drag you out?"

Julian's jaw tightened. "I won't go without Cameron."

"This isn't a vacation, Cross," Zane said.

"He's exposed now, thanks to you. I go with you willingly on the condition I keep him by my side."

Ty was already unlocking the handcuffs on Cameron's wrists. "Tell the clown on the roof to protect him," he told Julian. "Not our job."

Cameron darted straight for Julian once Ty let him loose, moving to stand behind his imposing lover. "Is this something important? This informant stuff?"

"Not to me," Julian said as he slid one hand into Cameron's, squeezing his fingers. He hadn't taken his eyes off Ty, who was holding up the handcuffs and smirking.

"You look like the type who enjoys these," the agent drawled.

Julian sighed in a rare show of exasperation. "Are you two really the crack team they sent after me? This is almost insulting."

"What you see isn't always what you get," Zane said. He glanced at Ty for a long moment, and Ty sniffed, looking somewhat disappointed that he didn't get to use his handcuffs. Zane looked at his watch. "Fine. Jacobs goes with. We've got two hours to make our flight to DC."

Cameron pressed against the back of Julian's arm. "Julian, I can stay here with Preston and Blake," he said, naming the two men who often worked with Julian on his clandestine "jobs," his driver and his boss. Cameron still wasn't exactly sure what Julian did, but he knew for certain he didn't want details. He slept better at night without them.

Julian turned his head, looking back at Cameron while still keeping an eye on the two men. "Preston and Blake will be busy. Go pack a bag. Quickly. Please," he was careful to tack on.

"What about the animals?" Ty asked. "Who the hell needs this many dogs anyway?"

"What's wrong with being a pet owner?" Cameron asked.

"Yeah, you pronounced 'hoarder' wrong."

Glancing around, Cameron kept his mouth shut and looked to Julian for direction. Julian was looking at the agent with the equivalent of a glare for his stoic lover.

"Preston will take care of them," Julian answered, jaw tight.

Cameron swallowed hard, and after one last look at Ty, he hurried over to the bedroom to pack for both himself and Julian. Zane followed behind him, intending to watch what he packed. Cameron glanced at the man uneasily. He had only an inkling of what was going on, but he did know they were in deep trouble this time.

Ty turned and watched Cameron disappear into the bedroom. He looked back at Zane and shook his head. It wasn't a great idea to take the boyfriend along. Two prisoners would be harder to handle than one, but it could prove a useful way to control Julian Cross if he got unruly. Zane took a few steps toward the dividing screens of the bedroom and stood where he could watch Cameron's movements and see what he was packing in his bags.

Ty ran a finger along his eyebrow and turned to stroll into the center of the room again, looking out the balcony doors at the roof of the building across the street. He'd seen the dying light glint off a piece of glass on the roof as he'd been petting the cat and recognized it for what it was. How the sniper had gotten up there so quickly was the real question. It didn't matter, but it bothered Ty.

Ty smiled crookedly and gave the man on the roof, Preston, a cheeky little wave.

He heard Zane snort. He stayed across the room, keeping between Julian and the door and keeping Cameron within his line of sight. Not that it looked like either man was going to run.

"You do realize that you're going to be held in a federal cell or safe house for the length of this thing," Zane said to Julian. "You really want him stuck there with you?"

"I sleep better knowing he's not in harm's way," Julian said. He looked at Ty. "He will shoot you, you know."

"You told him to shoot the stupid one," Ty said as he pointed at Zane.

"Yeah," Zane said. "The one standing out in the open in front of the window, waving at the sniper."

"The one that knows where the sniper is to wave at him. If he was going to shoot me, he would have." Ty looked at Julian. "Does that kid have any idea what you're about to drag him into?"

Julian was silent, glaring at Ty for a moment before looking away and sighing.

"That's a no," Zane said. "Does he know what business you've been working in?"

"That is none of your concern. You and I both know I'll never set foot in a cell or a courtroom if I make it to DC. We know what this is. He doesn't need to."

Ty looked at Zane, trying to conceal the question in his expression. Apparently Cameron Jacobs wasn't the only one being kept out of the loop.

But Julian was perceptive, and he caught Ty's look. He laughed and shook his head. "No one told you. They just sent you here like good little errand boys."

Zane leveled a look at Ty that would have crushed a lesser man, but Ty was immune. He also had no clue why Zane wanted to be such a hardass in front of this guy. The Batman types were the most fun to annoy.

"We're supposed to escort you to DC, Mr. Cross," Zane said. "Anything beyond that is need-to-know."

"Someone must really have it in for you two."

Ty rolled his eyes. He half suspected the man was just trying to screw with them, but he knew Richard Burns well enough to think he probably had kept something from them. Ty was used to it. That was just the way Burns operated. Ty trusted him implicitly. He didn't ask questions.

"Look, O'Doul, I have the patience of a bouncy ball right now, so how about shutting your mouth and getting your friend in there to hurry the hell up?"

"Ty," Zane said in that quiet, calm-down voice that Ty hated.

"Zane," he responded in the same tone. He turned to Julian. "Get him out here. I don't care if he's packed."

"Cameron?" Julian called without taking his eyes off Ty. "The irritating one is getting more irritating."

"His name is Ty," Cameron called back from behind the screen.

Ty saw the big man give the entry to the bedroom a curious glance, as if wondering why he should care what their names were. Ty snorted at them both in annoyance. He glanced at Zane, raising one eyebrow and tilting his head toward Julian. They would have to restrain him before leaving. There was no way they could trust him. Ty was all for using Cameron to keep him under control, but they were damn sure tying Cross up and making sure he couldn't do any damage either way.

"He's got five seconds," Ty said as he looked at Zane for one more moment.

"Cameron," Julian called. "Unless you want the irritating one to help you pack, I suggest you hurry."

"He always do the heavy lifting for you, Cross?" Ty asked the man in a low, amused voice.

"Yes, he does. Cooks and cleans too. Makes me feel more like a man," Julian said without a hint of sarcasm. "Wanker."

"At least you'll have someone to argue with," Cameron said as he emerged with two bags, one on each shoulder, one of which Julian took as soon as Cameron stopped beside him.

"I would prefer to shoot him, not argue with him," Julian mumbled. He adjusted one of the straps and looked up at Ty and Zane, raising his chin. "I suppose you'll be wanting to confiscate my weapon?"

Ty glanced at Zane and smirked. "He's got the stiff upper lip going now," he said as he pulled his gun.

"That would be the British," Julian said.

"Same thing," Ty said, knowing it would upset an Irishman. He pointed his gun at Julian's feet. "Guns on the couch. Mr. Jacobs, if you would please join my partner over here," he said with a tilt of his head at Zane, mimicking Julian's proper speech, "he'll be kind enough to handcuff you again and frog-march you downstairs."

"Do you work at being this rude?" Cameron asked. Ty could hear Zane choking on what might have been a laugh.

"I said please."

Zane was tamping down a smile as he took Cameron in hand and cuffed him. "Now, Mr. Cross," Zane said, "I'm betting that you're going to be quite willing to cooperate as long as we treat Mr. Jacobs well."

"Is not treating me well a possibility?" Cameron asked, his voice wavering as he kept his eyes on Julian.

Julian shook his head as he looked at Cameron. He extracted the weapons hidden on his person and put them on the couch as he'd been told, continuing to keep his eyes on Cameron. They seemed to be communicating. Ty recognized the way one lover could speak to another without words. He cleared his throat and moved toward Julian with care.

The man put his hands up behind his head, but something about him still made Ty wary. He could almost smell the capabilities of the man. He very carefully moved his hand up one of Julian's arms and down the other, then slid the handcuffs onto one wrist and clicked them into place.

"Those are some impressive cats," he said as he holstered his gun and used both hands to secure Julian's behind his back. "How long have you had them?"

"As long as they can remember," Julian answered without looking away from Cameron.

Ty looked over the man's shoulder at Zane and rolled his eyes. He snapped the other cuff down hard, then patted him down. He found a long sliver of metal embedded in each sleeve, just at the cuffs, but no other weaponry.

Julian sighed in annoyance as Ty removed the lock pick pieces.

"Poor hired killer, took away his toys," Ty said in mocking sympathy. "We're good," he said to Zane, patting Julian on the back.

"Don't worry, Mr. Jacobs," Zane said. "You'll be in DC in about seven hours, and dealing with us will be but a happy memory."

"Thank God for small favors," Julian murmured. He turned. "That second bag is quite heavy. Do mind your back, Agent Grady," he said with utmost sincerity, then smirked and began moving toward Zane and the door. Cameron shifted away from Zane as Julian approached, but he didn't try to move any further.

"If we want to make the plane, we need to go now," Zane said.

Ty thought seriously about leaving the bags on the floor, but even he wasn't that much of a bastard. He bent and hefted both bags with a muttered curse. He nodded, turning one last time to salute the man he knew was probably still on the opposite roof, watching them through a scope.

"Let's get this show on the road," he grunted as he headed for the door. "Mr. Jacobs, you're going to need to stop cowering. Garrett won't hurt you. Much."

"Actually, in my experience, it's the tall, dark, and silent types who are the most dangerous," Cameron said as he preceded Zane out the door.

"Oh Christ, he's one of those, isn't he?" Ty muttered.

"You have no idea," Julian said in return.

PRESTON watched through the scope of his Parker Hale Model 85 as the two agents led Julian and Cameron out of the apartment and shut the door behind them. He raised his head to look down at the street and the cab waiting.

One thing was certain after seeing the face of the man waving to him in his scope: he couldn't just take them out from up here. He didn't know why, but the man looked familiar. He didn't wait for them to emerge on the street, instead packing up and moving as he pulled out his cell phone. He dialed the only number he really could in this situation.

"Hello, sir," he said as soon as Blake Nichols answered.

"I know you call Julian 'sir' to annoy him, but do you really have to do it to me too?" Blake asked, amused.

"I apologize, sir, but we have a problem."

"What kind of problem?" Blake asked, tone changing.

"Two federal agents have just taken Mr. Cross into custody."

"What?"

"I said, two federal agents—"

"I heard you, Preston!"

"Of course, sir," Preston said as he trotted down the steps of the building he'd been using as his sniper's nest.

"What agency?"

"I can't be certain. They had FBI badges, but one of them—"

"Were they CIA?"

"Possibly, sir. I couldn't tell."

"That was fucking fast. Stay on them, Preston, but do not move on them, understood? I'll get back to you."

"Yes, sir."

Preston flipped the phone closed and picked up the pace, hurrying to the ground level so he'd have a chance to catch up with that cab.

~Chapter 5~

TSA used the screened-off area for security searches to pass through airline crews, law enforcement, and VIPs. It was quicker than going through as a regular passenger but still a lot of scrutiny, especially when it came to checking prisoners.

Ty and Zane had debated over whether to go through the law enforcement line since they were supposed to be operating dark, but the risk of taking Julian Cross through the searches without being restrained was too high, and trying to explain that he was handcuffed because he wasn't coming willingly without identifying themselves as FBI would get awkward.

So there they stood at Midway airport as one uniformed man each patted Cameron and Zane down. Ty rocked from side to side, checking the time on his cell phone every few seconds. Zane knew he didn't want to miss the plane, but he figured Ty also wanted to get rid of Julian as soon as possible. Zane didn't blame him; he felt much the same. Julian Cross was dangerous. Even standing sedately in front of them, his hands cuffed, Cameron's jacket thrown over them to hide the restraints from the general public, he made Zane uneasy. Obviously Ty felt the same way. And there was an added element in that Julian seemed to especially dislike Ty and vice versa. The animosity between the two was solid in the air, and Zane couldn't figure out why, other than Ty sometimes had that effect on people.

The TSA officials reported them done and waved Zane and Cameron over to the side. Zane holstered his gun when the guard spoke up. "Next," he said, gesturing for Julian to step forward onto the screening mat. The other screener waved Ty forward.

They stood side by side, Ty annoyed with the whole process and Julian calm and serene as the TSA agent took Cameron's coat from him to reveal his handcuffs.

Ty had his arms up, hands held out to the sides as he was given a cursory pat down. Julian looked sideways at him, then at the TSA agent. After another moment he calmly said, "He has a bomb."

Zane whirled in place so he could see Julian just as the agent said, "Excuse me?"

Ty's head snapped up, and he looked at Julian murderously as Julian repeated, "He has a bomb."

Ty would have lunged and throttled him right then and there, but the TSA agent who'd been searching him wrapped his arms around Ty's shoulders to restrain him.

"Cross," Zane said in warning, "they've already checked our ID." Attempting damage control, he took a couple of slow steps to put himself between Ty and Julian. Cameron hovered on the other side of the mat, looking mortified.

"Their IDs are fake," Julian told the TSA agents with supreme confidence. He was even using his Irish accent as he spoke. He looked at Ty with what appeared to be heartfelt sincerity. "I can't let you kill innocent people."

"Shut up!" Ty growled at him. He pointed a finger in Julian's face. "If I get a cavity search because of you, I will kick your ass!"

"Grady, enough," Zane said, pointing at him before he turned to Julian. "You're not helping yourself, Cross." He pulled out his wallet with the utmost care and held out his ID and a confirmation card with the appropriate security numbers, hoping to head off a mess.

Julian actually smirked and winked at him. Zane resisted the urge to roll his eyes and maintained his calm, professional mask as a worried-looking TSA agent took his cards and made a beeline for the phone on the desk. Zane could practically hear Ty vibrating with outrage behind him.

Several minutes later, two very large security agents returned with the first and flanked Ty. "You're going to have to come with us, sir."

Ty growled and pointed at Julian, looking at Zane as they dragged him away. "I hate him."

Zane quashed a sigh and nodded. It wouldn't help to rail against the very excitable TSA, and he turned to nod at Julian. "Go ahead and search him. Thoroughly," Zane told the agents. Worst case, he could leave Ty and Cameron and take Julian to DC himself, though he'd get no end of shit about it from Ty afterward.

Julian was still smiling as he held his handcuffed hands up to be searched.

"WHAT if they'd just locked us all up? What would that have accomplished?" Cameron asked Julian as they walked alongside Zane, following in Ty's wake. He was talking on his cell phone as he stalked toward the airline desk.

"It would have delayed the inevitable," Julian told him with a negligent shrug. He was smirking, something he only did when he was feeling particularly evil.

Ahead of them, Ty stopped in his tracks as he spoke on the phone. "What do you mean, rent a car?"

Julian began to laugh.

The delay at Midway had caused them to miss the last flight to DC for the night. When they'd missed that one, whoever was giving Ty and Zane orders had told them to haul it to O'Hare to catch the midnight flight, which they had tried to do, but they'd hit the ever-present Chicagoland construction, and it had taken them a full three hours to get up to O'Hare. By then the last flight was gone, and they were grounded until morning. Which was exactly what Julian had wanted.

Cameron wasn't sure what surprised him more, the ten-minute-long nearly incoherent rant that had come out of Ty's mouth as they'd sat in traffic in a minivan taxi with no shocks, or the extent to which Julian seemed to be enjoying himself.

"Antagonizing him probably isn't the best idea," he said as they stopped as well. Ty didn't seem to have a lot of patience to work with, and Cameron knew that Julian could try the patience of a saint if he felt so inclined.

"I've had worse," Julian murmured.

Ty snapped the phone closed and turned to Zane. "He told us to rent a fucking car. He doesn't want us to hang around until morning. He wants Batman and Robin here on the move and away from the TSA."

"Sounds like he wants us to scramble," Zane said, just loud enough for Cameron to discern.

"Exactly, but I'm not sure why. We're not on anyone's radar. Unless he's not telling us that either."

Julian hummed but didn't comment. Cameron watched as Zane just looked at Ty, and after a long moment, Ty sniffed, shoved his phone in his pocket, and turned on his heel to head toward the rental cars. Zane turned back to him and Julian. "Ready for a ride, gentlemen?"

"A ride? In a car? With the three of you?" Cameron asked, horrified. "To Washington, DC?" He would have sworn he saw a twinkle of humor in Zane's eyes before the man looked away.

Ty stomped back up to them and grabbed Julian by the elbow. "Get the lead out, Garrett," he said to his partner. He was muttering to Julian as he dragged him away. "Come on, funny guy. I'll show you where they keep the cavity search kits."

Cameron had to work hard to keep up with the three taller and longer-legged men. "Is your partner always this way?" he asked Zane.

Zane glanced at him, and this time Cameron did see faint amusement. "No. Sometimes he's a little excitable."

Cameron stared at him, trying to decide if he was joking or serious. He couldn't tell with Zane's dry delivery. When he looked away from Zane, Cameron nearly ran into Ty, who had stopped and turned around to wait on them. Cameron winced. The man had to be made of solid rock. Ty looked from him to Zane. "If you're going to get friendly with the prisoners, take this one," he told Zane, unceremoniously shoving Julian at his partner. He took Cameron's upper arm in an iron grip and turned, pulling Cameron along with him toward the car rental desks.

Stumbling along, Cameron looked over his shoulder at Zane and Julian. "Is this your way of getting friendly?"

"'He has a bomb,' he says," Ty parroted in answer. He kept on, taking on a comically exaggerated Irish accent. "Oh look, Mr. Rubber Glove Man, he has a bomb. Och, we missed our plane."

Cameron laughed as he stumbled and bumped into Ty again. "Come on, man, you're like half a foot taller than me. Give me a break!"

"Stop talking."

"You need a Valium or something," Cameron said under his breath as he tried to hurry enough that Ty wouldn't drag him.

"Yes, I do. I should also be given a cigarette after what that TSA agent did to me," Ty snapped. He looked over his shoulder to find Zane and Julian lagging behind. "Garrett!"

Cameron watched as Zane held out a hand to his side, as if willing Ty to be patient. Neither he nor Julian looked to be in all that much of a hurry, which Cameron knew would just incense Ty more. Ty mumbled as he and Cameron came up to the rental desk. Cameron didn't even know if what Ty was saying consisted of real words, much less English ones.

By the time Zane and Julian joined them, the rental agent was almost finished telling Ty what models of car were available.

Ty turned to Zane and shook his head. "I refuse to drive to DC in a compact."

"There's no way we'd all get into a compact unless we lashed Cross to the roof," Zane said. Ty looked Julian up and down.

"They don't even have any SUVs," Cameron said to Julian and Zane.

"Maybe the trunk," Ty said.

Cameron gave him a disbelieving look before shaking his head, and he was seized with the urge to smack Zane as the man looked to be considering it.

Julian looked between them without comment, then rolled his eyes and looked away.

"Seriously, Zane, I'm not driving to DC in a fucking Chevy Aveo," Ty said after apparently dismissing the idea of stuffing Julian in the trunk.

"Train?" Zane suggested.

"We'd have to wait longer for that than the next plane," Ty muttered. Then a light entered his oddly colored eyes, as if an idea had struck him. "Let's head to the field office. Steal a truck."

"Borrow a truck."

"That's what I said."

"The office is nearby. We'll get a cab," Zane said, taking Julian's arm to turn him toward the door.

"Do you two do this kind of thing often? Because you really don't seem very good at it," Cameron said as he resettled his bag on his shoulder.

"Practice a little self-preservation, love," Julian murmured.

"Why? That's what I've got you for," Cameron said with a smile for his lover.

"Oh, gag me with a sock," Ty muttered as he pulled Cameron away and headed for the doors.

"You need a little love in your life," Cameron told him.

Ty narrowed his eyes but had nothing sarcastic to say to that.

"Really," Cameron said, just to get in a dig of his own for being dragged around. "It did wonders for Julian's attitude."

Ty shook his head and looked over his shoulder at Julian as they walked through the automatic doors. "Your boyfriend's coming on to me," he told Julian with the same sincere honesty that Julian had used to tell the TSA agents Ty was carrying a bomb.

Julian made an annoyed sound in the back of his throat.

"Zane's more my type," Cameron said, just to irritate Ty even more. Zane snorted before smiling again.

"Hear that?" Ty asked Julian over his shoulder. "He's kind of a whore."

Cameron huffed and elbowed Ty in the ribs as they exited the terminal. The man didn't even wince, which made Cameron want to find somewhere he didn't have a protective layer of muscle and kick him.

TY SAT in the driver's seat of a "borrowed" FBI sedan, drumming his fingers against the steering wheel. They hadn't been able to get away with an SUV, so the sedan would have to serve. It was roomier than anything the rental agency had been offering, and when the Chicago field office found the car missing, it would be a nice little "fuck you" to Dick for sending them into this mess without all the information.

Because it was painfully apparent that they didn't have all the information. They didn't even have the CliffsNotes version.

Ty smiled as he thought about the reaction the missing sedan would get from Burns, but he was still irritated just on principle. The first half of the day had been perfect, only to be marred by the addition of the two criminals in love in the backseat. Julian Cross got under Ty's skin simply because he felt dangerous. He was unflappable too, something Ty had rarely encountered. In fact, Ty couldn't think of a single person he'd ever met that he couldn't irritate to some degree. Cameron Jacobs, however, was annoying because he was so damn naïve it offended Ty's sensibilities. How the two had fallen in love and managed to stay that way Ty couldn't fathom.

Zane had insisted they stop to load up on supplies at the first drug store they came to. He was taking his sweet freaking time with it. Julian and Cameron were in the backseat of the car, handcuffed to the special rings welded to the floorboards, the child locks engaged so they couldn't get out. Ty sat with his gun resting on his knee, just in case Batman got creative.

"What could you possibly gain by making us miss our plane?" Ty asked when he got tired of hearing the two of them murmur to each other. "Now your ass has to ride seven hundred miles in the backseat."

Julian didn't answer him. Cameron leaned as close to him as his restraints would allow and looked to be ignoring Ty as well. Ty watched them in the rearview mirror for a moment before rolling his eyes and looking back at the doors to the store. His knee was bouncing, and he didn't try to curtail the movement. He was considering the radio when he saw Zane finally approach the car, several plastic bags hanging off each hand.

Ty reached down to pop the trunk for him as he neared the car, but he stayed put as Zane dealt with the bags. Then Zane got into the car, placing a couple of bags at his feet before shutting the door and pulling on his seat belt. "Vamos, compañero," he said.

Ty glared at him as he started the car. "Took you long enough."

Instead of answering, Zane leaned over, dug through a bag, then pulled out a can of Red Bull and held it out in front of Ty with an enticing waggle.

Ty raised one eyebrow and smiled crookedly. He took the can with a grateful "Thank you."

"Oh God, really?" Julian blurted from the back seat. "He's going to twitch himself through the moon roof."

"Shut up," Ty and Zane said simultaneously.

In the rearview mirror, Ty saw Julian reach sideways and touch Cameron's knee. It was all the contact they could manage.

"This should prove to be a long night," Julian said a moment later. "Perhaps the rest of us could be treated to coffee instead of Agent Grady's Red Bull-fueled spurts of nervous energy?"

"Coffee sounds good," Zane said.

"Me too," Cameron added.

"We'll find a McDonald's after we get out of the city," Ty said. He wanted to deny the request just for the hell of it, but he couldn't think of a good reason.

After an uneventful ride on the Chicago Skyway and over an hour later, Ty pulled off at the innocuous exit to Portage, Indiana. It took a few turns and a couple of miles to find the McDonald's, but soon the four of them had their rest stop and their coffee—Julian and Cameron having to make do with their hands still handcuffed. Ty had a cup of hot chocolate with molten properties, and they were on their way back to the highway.

It was two thirty in the morning, but Ty figured he could go another couple of hours on a can of Red Bull before they would need to stop at a hotel for a rest, since Zane had to be as tired as he was. Traveling at night would be quicker and less conspicuous, and the more the two in the back slept during this trip, the better.

The first thing Ty had done after borrowing the sedan was dismantle the active GPS locator; therefore, the GPS unit on the dash was silent and dark as well. They were using an off-brand portable GPS Zane had bought at the pharmacy for directions for their cross-country trek.

"Follow the yellow brick road," Zane murmured as the GPS unit chirped directions at them in a woman's voice, telling him how to get back to the toll road.

"I think I love her," Ty said as he petted the GPS attached to the dash with a suction cup.

"Until she talks back," Zane said as he settled back in his seat. They were coming up on the bridge they'd crossed less than ten minutes before. Close to the highway.

"That's what I like about her. She's bossy," Ty said with a smirk as he glanced sideways at Zane.

"Like that dominatrix you interrogated last month."

Ty whistled to keep himself from laughing.

"I feel like I need a psychology degree to be here," Julian muttered from the back seat.

"I don't know. They're kind of entertaining," Cameron said.

"Our definitions of entertaining vary wildly."

"You certainly do have authority issues," Zane drawled to Ty before taking a sip of coffee, ignoring Julian's and Cameron's asides.

Ty glanced at Zane and smiled. He was about to respond when he felt a hand come up from behind him, between the seat and door at his side. He shouted as he realized it was Julian reaching for the child-lock button on the door, but before he could grab for him to stop him, his seat belt jerked tight, pinning him to the seat and tightening over his throat. Scalding hot coffee poured over his shoulder onto his chest and lap, and the car swerved across the bridge as Ty slammed on the brakes.

"What the hell?" Zane held his sloshing coffee out in front of him and braced his free hand on the dash as the car fishtailed across the bridge before coming to a stop just feet from the guardrail.

Ty shouted as he fought to get his seat belt undone while pawing at his shirt front. He heard the back door open and struggled with simultaneously trying to get his own door open and trying to get the scalding material of his shirt off his skin.

"Get him!"

Zane was out of his door, and the next thing Ty heard was a gunshot, a spray of concrete, and a scream from Cameron, who had been about to climb out of the back seat to follow Julian.

"Son of a bitch!" Ty finally rolled out of the car. He stripped his shirt off and wiped at his chest with it as he rounded the car and took in the carnage. God, he sort of hoped Zane had shot the Irish bastard.

What he saw was Zane with his gun drawn and trained on Julian, who looked like he had stopped and frozen in midstride. Small chunks of asphalt lay scattered at his feet.

"Back in the car, Cross," Zane said in absolute monotone.

Ty cleared his throat and swiped at his cooling belt buckle with the coffee-soaked T-shirt. The frigid air hit his damp skin, and he began to shiver.

Julian held his hands up toward Zane and moved back to the car. "No need to get combative, now."

"Yeah, keep talking with the Irish accent. Makes it easier to shoot you."

Ty stepped over and grabbed Julian, slamming him against the side of the car. He secured the handcuffs Julian had picked, making them tight enough to leave bruises if they were left on long. They would need something more, because the man was obviously too slick for a single pair of restraints. He searched Julian thoroughly, finally finding the last sliver of metal he had missed on his initial search. Once he was satisfied Julian wouldn't be escaping again, Ty gripped him by the back of his neck, helping him into the car with a not so gentle shove after Cameron scooted back inside. He banged the man's head on the top of the door, muttering a careless apology as he shoved him inside and slammed the door behind him.

He looked over the top of the sedan at Zane. "You okay?"

Zane's jerky movements as he holstered his gun spoke volumes. He took a breath and twitched. "Yeah," he said after a long moment, though Ty knew it was partially a lie. "You?"

"Burned my nipples," Ty said, not able to say it without smiling.

Zane gave him a whisper of a smile, and the tension in his jaw and shoulders relaxed. "Open the trunk. I've got something that might help that."

Ty looked at him dubiously, wondering what Zane might have bought at a Walgreens that would help burned nipples—and why—but he decided not to ask. "Let's stop for the night, okay? Just stop and regroup, figure out a better way to keep Cross tied down. We'll tackle this shit in the morning."

"What about Burns?"

"Priority in this mission was low profile, not speed. He made that very clear. I think it's a good call to stop."

Zane nodded, and Ty leaned into the car to pop the trunk like he'd been asked. He looked over the seat at the two men in the back. "A for effort," he told them. Cameron looked a little pale, so maybe now he knew they meant business. To this point he'd been treating them like they might be just as cute and cuddly as the hired killer he called his lover.

Julian met Ty's eyes, but he didn't show a hint of emotion or an inkling of what he was thinking. The guy made the hairs on the back of Ty's neck stand up, and he found himself putting his hand on his gun without first being aware he was doing it.

Zane dug around in the plastic bags in the trunk for a minute, then walked around the car toward Ty. He had a small plastic package in one hand and a wad of brown cloth in the other.

"What's all this?" Ty asked as he straightened. He reached out to run a hand down Zane's arm, not caring that he shouldn't when they were working. Before this morning, he hadn't seen his lover in days, had barely touched him in a week, and he knew fishtailing in the car had to have set Zane's teeth on edge. Echoes of a nasty crash that had almost killed them both would do that.

Plus, Ty didn't care if the criminals knew he and Zane were an item. It was one thing to stay hands-off for a seven-hour flight. Entirely another for a two-day drive. He was tired of being so careful that it looked like he didn't care.

Zane offered him a more natural smile as he held up the plastic package. "Wet wipes." He then shook out the brown fabric. It was a T-shirt, and on the front it displayed a picture of a blue robot with yellow eyes and the words "Overkill is one of my many modes."

Ty laughed and took the shirt and the wipes. "Thanks, Zane."

"It sounded like you," Zane said before taking back the wet wipes to open the package so Ty could use them.

Ty watched him with a growing sense of calm. Just having Zane here with him was enough to keep him sane.

After pulling open the package, Zane glanced up at him. "All right, Grady. Strip down or you'll be sticky and miserable, and then we'll all be miserable."

Ty muttered at him but pulled his wet jeans off, right there on the side of the road. Several cars passing by honked at them, but this didn't even register on the scale as far as Ty's embarrassing life moments went. He put the T-shirt on, and they used his other shirt to pat down the front seat. Then they tossed his wet clothing into the trunk, where the smell of the spilled coffee wouldn't make him want to kill things. He changed into a pair of dirty jeans from the small bag he'd been carrying with him and slid back into the driver's seat.

He sat in the silence of the car and looked into the rearview mirror. "Next time he won't be aiming at you," he told Julian.

Cameron's eyes widened as he looked from Ty to Zane, but Zane was looking out the windshield rather than back at them and offered no comment.

"Understood, Agent Grady," Julian said. He didn't seem put out that his attempt had failed, nor did he seem upset with the overt threat to his lover. That bothered Ty more than he liked to admit, and the simple fact that Julian Cross made him nervous also made him angry.

And he wanted to know how the hell Julian had slipped those cuffs so quickly.

He started the car with a grunt. "Buckle up," he told them, even though neither man could comply because of their handcuffs. He pulled back out into traffic with a less than gentle yank of the wheel that sent both men toppling sideways.

~Chapter 6~

CAMERON looked out the window at the Comfort Inn, thinking it looked like it had landed right out of the seventies. Two floors, dark wooden plank construction, narrower and higher windows than in newer hotels, but it seemed nice enough for being out in the middle of nowhere, northern Indiana, off the toll road. It was almost three, and Cameron was exhausted. Surely Ty and Zane were too, and after Julian's attempted escape, they didn't seem to be willing to take any chances.

He dozed some while Zane was inside arranging their room, leaning his head against Julian, who had pulled as close as he could while handcuffed to the ring on the floor. The handcuffs were something new for Cameron. He'd watched in horror as Julian picked his lock in the car with a flick of his wrist and nothing more, wondering at how much practice something like that would take. His lover never ceased to amaze him with all his nefarious skills.

Cameron sometimes wondered about his own moral makeup, that something like that could sort of turn him on.

He smiled and turned his head to press his cheek against Julian's shoulder. Julian turned his chin to try to kiss the top of his head, an almost unconscious gesture, but he couldn't reach due to the way they were cuffed. He sighed, an exasperated sound that Julian rarely made, and he looked out the window, eyes narrowed.

Ty sat in the front seat, muttering to himself, his knee bouncing so quickly it was more a vibration. That Red Bull hadn't done the man much good, and it had only had an hour to wear off. Cameron was almost amused by the dichotomy of the two federal agents. Zane was so calm and steady and dark, taking things in stride, tolerantly handling any adversity that came their way until Julian's escape attempt. And then Ty seemed the complete opposite. He was wired to the sky, and he struck Cameron as a big floppy puppy, cracking jokes, attention bouncing from one thing to another, patience thin as a wafer. Ty was the Omega to Zane's Alpha.

They were both handsome, and while Zane was more Cameron's type than Ty was, there was something about Ty's rugged exterior that made him more approachable and attractive.

They certainly were the odd couple of partners, although Zane was the one who felt like a threat to Cameron now that he'd been exposed to them both. Julian obviously felt the same way. Cameron could still feel the tension invested in his tall frame. "Can't you relax just a little? You're so wound up," he whispered, looking up at Julian.

Julian turned and cocked his head to meet his eyes, then smiled. "No more than usual," he murmured, his voice low and gruff.

"I can tell," Cameron said, wishing he could get close enough to touch him with something besides his foot or his nose.

"It'll be okay. Just do as they tell you."

"Quit with the whispering," Ty said in a sharp voice.

Cameron could see the reflection of his eyes in the rearview mirror, looking back at them. "So you can scoff at us for having a quiet moment? I don't think so," he said with a sniff as he tried to cuddle closer against Julian.

"Kid, I don't think you really understand the situation, here, so let me make it perfectly clear," Ty said, voice going harder and hazel eyes flashing with anger. "You and your boyfriend are federal prisoners, and you do exactly what we tell you, when we tell you, without the attitude and without the cute little remarks. One coffee in my lap is all the free pass you get, and we don't have to fucking be nice about it. You whisper, I leave you on the side of the road and he rolls in the trunk. Got it?"

Cameron stared, wide-eyed. He nodded, suitably chastised and feeling stupid for his forays into the acerbic. He looked up at Julian. "Do you think Zane would really have shot you?"

"Yes," Julian said, sounding confident. Ty was nodding in the front seat as he looked out the window.

"I thought he was the nice one," Cameron said under his breath.

Julian put his lips to Cameron's ear and whispered, "Next time I'll dump the coffee on him instead."

Cameron sighed in exasperation. "You're deliberately causing trouble."

Julian shushed him as he glanced toward the front seat. Ty was rolling his eyes and rubbing at his temple. Cameron shifted closer to Julian and tilted his head until they could push their mouths together for a small kiss. Julian whispered against Cameron's lips, turning his head to hide the movement of his mouth from the mirror. "We have to get away from them before we reach Washington," he murmured. He kissed Cameron again to mask the words.

The kiss made Cameron's pulse race, just like Julian's touch always did. Cameron hummed to let Julian know he understood. He cursed the handcuffs; he wanted to shift himself further into Julian's arms and wished he could crawl into his lap, Ty watching be damned. He felt Julian smile against his lips. He'd obviously picked up on Cameron's desire to do so.

"Christ, please stop," Ty said from the front seat, voice plaintive.

Cameron pulled back and smiled at Julian.

Julian was looking at him in the same adoring way he always did, but he was also smirking. There was a hint of malicious enjoyment in his black eyes. "Do you object to all public displays of affection, Agent Grady? Or is it the fact that we're both men?" he asked without looking away from Cameron.

Ty answered with the loud slide action of his 9mm service weapon. "If you really must know, I'm of the opinion that it's rude to make out in a man's backseat."

"Well, technically, it's not your backseat."

"I've been on the road too long and I miss getting laid in my own bed. Don't push me."

Julian laughed and kissed Cameron again for good measure. Cameron shook his head afterward and settled down, turning a somewhat apologetic look toward Ty. "I'm sorry you've been away from home so long," he said, sincere. He wouldn't apologize for the kisses though.

"My own fault," Ty said, voice curt.

"Why?" Cameron could see Ty's eyes in the mirror, looking at him evilly.

"I'm too sober for you, Jiminy Cricket," Ty muttered. He looked out the window again and shook his head.

Julian hummed. "I don't suppose asking for a separate room would go over well?"

"Probably not," Ty said.

"I'm fine with two beds," Cameron said. "Can you see Ty and Zane getting any sleep in a double bed?"

"Ty and Zane will be just fine," Ty said in a falsely cheerful voice. "Cross will be sleeping in handcuffs on the floor."

"Kinky," Julian said, smirking.

"What do you mean?" Cameron asked, sitting up, peering at Ty through narrowed eyes.

Ty held up a third pair of handcuffs that clinked as he waved them.

"Funny," Cameron said with a frown. So much for a comfortable night.

The passenger door popped open and a cold blast of wind assaulted them. Zane leaned over to peer inside at his partner. "You can just park right here. We're going in the front and up to the second floor."

"What took so long?" Ty asked. If Zane was surprised to see Ty sitting there with his gun and his handcuffs in his lap, he didn't show it. It made Cameron wonder about the sanity of both men.

"It took her ten minutes to decide they didn't have any connecting rooms available. So, one room," Zane said as he gathered the bags out of the floorboard.

"Great," Ty muttered as he pushed open his door and got out of the car.

Julian ducked his head to peer out the window at them. "Luck is with us tonight," he whispered to Cameron.

"Why is that?"

"With one room it will be easier to disable them and get away."

"You're not going to kill them, are you?" Cameron asked, shifting uneasily in the seat. "I mean, they're just doing their jobs."

"Not unless they make me," Julian said as he looked back at Cameron. "The threat from Grady is negligible, but Garrett will kill both of us if he thinks he's justified. Remember that before you get too attached to them."

"You always tell me I trust too easily," Cameron said. "He just seemed like such a… nice guy." He shivered, though, remembering how Zane's face had been so cold and blank as he'd shot the asphalt at Julian's feet.

"He's not. Neither of them are."

His words were punctuated by Ty opening the back door and waving at Julian. "Come on, O'Doul."

That worried Cameron a lot, to think that men in law enforcement could be as bad as the criminals they chased. Not that he thought of himself and Julian as criminals, although technically, he supposed Julian really was. Or used to be. Or might have been.

As he climbed out of the car, he watched Zane, the wind riffling his hair, his gun gripped in a gloved hand. Cameron's eyes shifted to his lover. Julian and Zane looked similar enough that it was a little eerie in the harsh parking lot lights—tall, broad-shouldered, dark-haired….

When Ty stalked around the car to join his partner, all gruff attitude, hard muscle, and broad shoulders, Cameron barely quashed the urge to cringe away. He and Julian were in more trouble than he wanted to believe, and now he felt really stupid for ever joking around with the two men.

Ty pushed Julian against the car, a hand in the center of his shoulders, and he kept the hand there as he turned to face Zane. Zane stepped closer until they were right in front of each other. Each kept his eyes over the other's shoulder—Zane watching Julian, Ty watching

Cameron and the parking lot—as they spoke. Ty tilted his head so he was murmuring into Zane's ear. It had an oddly intimate feel as they stood there, and Julian was craning his head to watch them. Cameron wondered if he could make out anything they were saying.

Whatever they'd been discussing was decided, and Ty patted Zane's belly before stepping away from Julian and moving toward Cameron. "Come on, kid, let's go," he said as he held his hand out toward Cameron, waving him forward.

"What about Julian?" Cameron asked, dragging his feet.

"He and Zane are going to get to know each other down here. Come on," Ty said as he moved a step closer and took Cameron's elbow. He didn't tug on him, though, appearing willing to give him a chance to go of his own accord.

Cameron looked from Julian to Zane and back before nodding reluctantly. "All right," he murmured. Ty handed him his bag and shouldered his own as they started walking toward the front door.

When they got to the entrance, Cameron glanced back over his shoulder to where Julian and Zane still stood next to the car.

Julian had turned around, and he stood with his cuffed hands clasped in front of him. He nodded at Cameron.

"They're okay," Ty said in an oddly gentle voice as he pulled the door open and held it for Cameron.

Cameron didn't feel reassured, but he walked inside anyway. The interior of the hotel had the same feel as the exterior: too much brass, too much glass, and way too much disco fever.

They passed the front desk and headed on to the large set of stairs in the center of the entry hall. There was no elevator. Ty led him to the room just to the right of the steps and keyed the electronic lock, then pulled Cameron into the room as he flipped on the light.

Cameron couldn't think of a reason Ty would bring him up here alone unless Zane was going to do something to Julian. "Aren't they coming up too?" he asked as he stood just inside the door.

"After we're done," Ty said in an offhanded manner. The door closed behind them, and Ty pulled Cameron further into the room, turning on lights as he went.

"Done?" Cameron felt a pang of alarm. Maybe Ty was going to do something to him.

"Yeah, sit down," Ty said, distracted as he pointed at one of the two beds in the room and looked around. He walked to the window and peered out, then pulled the heavy curtains closed.

Cameron frowned but perched on the foot of the bed closest to the door as he tracked Ty's movement through the room.

Ty inspected the window and its frame before crouching to look at the air conditioning unit under it. He gripped the face of the unit and tugged at it. He picked up the chair and pushed at the small desk in the corner. He shoved at the miniature refrigerator with his toes and got down on the ground to look at the bottom of the safe attached to the wall. He turned the television on its swiveling stand, pulled out all the drawers in the room, plucked out the Bible, and flipped through the pages. He turned to look at Cameron as he held the book upside down and shook it.

"What are you doing?" Cameron asked. "I thought the Red Bull was wearing off."

"I'm looking for something solid. And I'm making sure there's nothing in here your boyfriend can use to kill or maim us," Ty said as he dropped the Bible back in the drawer. He knelt just behind Cameron and looked under each bed, then he slid his hands under the mattress.

"He doesn't need anything to kill or maim you," Cameron said as he realized he felt uncomfortable with Ty kneeling so close to him.

Rather than being impressed or intimidated, Ty just laughed. "I know," he said as he pushed himself to his feet.

"So why bother with the search?"

Ty sat down beside him on the double bed, too close to him. Yeah, he definitely made Cameron uncomfortable, like patrons at the restaurant that got too flirtatious. Only Ty hadn't done anything even remotely like that, so Cameron couldn't figure out what it was that made him uneasy. Maybe Ty was just one of those people who exuded that sort of feeling.

"You ever seen two big dogs fight over a bone?"

Cameron shrank back. "No. But I know what you're getting at."

Ty nodded. "In theory, the one with the spikes on his collar has the advantage. But really it's the one who ain't worried about protecting a puppy hiding behind him."

"Great. Now I'm a puppy." Then it hit him. "Wait. You're not talking about you, are you? You're talking about them, out there alone, fighting over… something?" Cameron's voice had risen as he started to panic.

Ty shook his head and began rubbing at the bridge of his nose. "It's a general metaphor. Don't take it literally," he said, but then he waved his hand. "Look, all I'm saying is you coming with him, it put him at a disadvantage. But you keep your dog on a leash, I'll keep mine on one too."

Cameron looked at him, uneasy. Then he nodded. "I'll try."

Ty nodded and stood.

The nerves faded once Ty wasn't beside him anymore. Yeah, it was definitely just a feeling Ty gave off.

Ty took his phone out of his pocket and dialed. Then he said, "We're good." He looked down at Cameron as he put the phone away. "You'll have that bed. Don't move," he said as he turned and headed toward the bathroom.

Cameron opened his mouth to object but swallowed it instead, shaking his head as Ty disappeared into the bathroom. The handcuffs comment made sense now. Well, he was in for a surprise, then, because if Julian ended up sitting on the floor handcuffed to a table leg or safe or mini refrigerator, then Cameron would be sitting right there next to him.

Cameron mulled over what Ty had said, and the unusual discomfort of the situation, until the door to the room opened and Julian walked in. He still appeared calm and stoic, but Cameron recognized the tension in his shoulders. As soon as he saw Cameron, though, he relaxed. Obviously he'd been having the same flashes of alarm Cameron had experienced when Ty took him up here alone, and that made Cameron feel both a little better and a little worse.

"Have a nice chat?" Cameron asked, putting on a smile he didn't feel.

"Oh, it was enlightening," Julian said, drawing the words out in amusement.

He took a step toward Cameron, but Ty appeared out of the bathroom before Julian could get past the door, and snapped the spare handcuffs onto one of Julian's wrists. Then he grabbed the back of Julian's coat, almost as if he were scruffing a cat, and dragged him into the bathroom. There was a brief and noisy struggle, complete with bangs and crashes, during which Cameron heard Julian say a few choice words he'd never heard his lover utter. A few moments later, Ty stepped out of the bathroom, primly adjusting his clothing as he gave Zane a dashing smile.

Zane's lips were pressed together hard. Cameron would have sworn that he was trying not to laugh.

"Secure?" Zane asked with difficulty.

"Unless he decides to rip the shower enclosure out of the wall... yes."

After hearing what had come out of Julian's mouth, Cameron wasn't too sure Ty should be so happy with himself.

Julian's dry voice drifted out of the bathroom. "You're an imbecile."

"But I ain't handcuffed to a shower."

"I want to sit with Julian," Cameron said.

"No," Zane said in a pleasant voice.

"Why not?" Cameron asked, standing and holding up his handcuffed hands.

"Because we fucking said so," Ty said. "Get in bed. Do it now."

Zane shrugged out of his coat and hung it in the closet before picking up his duffel. "You get in bed too," he told Ty with a jerk of his head toward the second bed. "I'm not sleeping."

Ty looked at Zane as if he wanted to object, but he kept his mouth shut. He stripped off the T-shirt he'd changed into earlier and toed off his boots. He fell into the bed in just his jeans and burrowed his head under one of the pillows. He reminded Cameron of a very large dog throwing itself to the ground to take a nap.

He wondered how Ty planned to just go to sleep on command after drinking an entire Red Bull, but as he watched, Ty didn't move, and soon his breathing evened out. Cameron stared at him in disbelief.

"He's asleep," he said without thinking.

"Yeah, he does that."

Zane didn't seem to be paying either of them much attention; he'd moved to the table in the corner and was pulling a stack of papers out of his messenger bag. He sat in the corner, running his hand through his hair to leave it unruly, fingers playing with his beard as he got to work. He looked a little more relaxed but still dark and dangerous. Rakish, even.

The gun went on the table right next to the papers. Only then did he glance back up at Cameron and raise an eyebrow.

Cameron wondered if it was too late to ask for a bathroom break.

AFTER an hour of writing down notes by hand, Zane caught himself staring across the room at Ty, who was sprawled on the bed nearest the bathroom, head under a pillow, body loose and relaxed. Zane doubted he was; Ty usually knew where he was even asleep. He could only remember one or two occasions when he'd done something while Ty was asleep and hadn't woken him.

Just being able to see him was reassuring in ways Zane would have avoided exploring in the past, but now he could admit why. He loved his exasperating partner beyond all reason. He saw him as a lifeline he had desperately needed, an inspiration in so many ways.

Several minutes passed before Zane tore his gaze away from Ty's half-naked body to glance around the room. Cameron was asleep as well, curled up under the blanket in the other bed. He looked young and innocent, though he couldn't really be, what with spending so much time with a man such as Julian Cross. Zane looked to the bathroom. It had been quiet in there as well. With a sigh, he pushed back from the table to stand and stretch. He had kinks all up and down his back after the flight and the car ride combined with the tension of the situation.

"Come lay down," Ty murmured in a low, hoarse voice, muffled by the thin pillow. He hadn't moved. Zane wondered how he did that sometimes, sensed things without seeing them. Zane had never mastered that art, even while being blinded from his injury several weeks ago.

Zane glanced at Cameron before walking over to stand at Ty's bedside and lifting the pillow off his head. "You should be asleep," he said as he set his gun on the nightstand.

"But I'm not," Ty whispered. "Come lay down with me."

Zane wasn't going to pass on a second request, not while all was quiet. He moved around to the foot of the bed and crawled up beside him, settling on his side and scooting up against Ty to lie in the crook of his arm. When he settled his cheek on Ty's shoulder, he felt a warm calm soak into him as he pressed close to Ty's exposed skin.

Ty growled and rolled, wrapping Zane up in his arms. "You need rest," he said. He lowered his voice and moved his lips against Zane's skin. "And I need you."

Zane slid his arm up and around Ty's neck as Ty pulled him close. It was about four a.m., and he'd been awake for almost twenty-four hours. But being this close to Ty after days apart wasn't conducive to sleep. "Baby," he whispered against Ty's throat before pressing his lips to the soft, warm skin.

Ty hummed and ran his hand up and down Zane's side, tugging at his shirt. He pushed his chin forward and kissed him. Zane sighed against his lips and inhaled Ty's scent, letting it flood through him. The sandalwood was still there, and Zane would have to remember to ask where it had come from. It was intoxicating, and he was barely hanging on to the thought that one of their prisoners was sleeping not even ten feet away. But one kiss—just one—he had to have it, and he tightened his arm around Ty's neck to deepen it.

Ty's hands gripped him hard, and he pushed Zane back just enough to be able to kiss him harder. "Is that kid asleep?" he asked in a quiet rush.

"Seems to be," Zane said under his breath as he tried to recapture Ty's lips. "We shouldn't do this." But he pawed at Ty anyway.

"Zane." His name was no more than Ty's breath against his lips. "I don't care if we should or not."

"God, I thought we got this out of our systems," Zane whispered, squeezing his eyes shut for a moment as his gut clenched with desire.

Ty kissed him again, pulling him until their bodies touched all over. "We can be quiet."

Zane had to smother his laugh in Ty's neck. "No we can't," he muttered with absolute certainty.

Ty pulled back and looked at him with one eyebrow raised. "Not even a little?" he asked with true disappointment.

"A little? You think I'm going to stop at just a little?" Zane shook his head and kissed Ty. He ached for Ty, inside and out, but this just wasn't the time. A professional hit man was locked up in the bathroom, and another prisoner was in the next bed. It would have been comedic if it didn't suck so much. "I want you more than anything," he murmured against Ty's lips. "And you can't possibly imagine all the things I'm going to do to you. But for that, we need to be at home."

"Goddammit." Ty pulled his head back and sighed.

Zane nodded regretfully. "But for now we have this," he whispered, burrowing in close.

Ty sighed again and pulled Zane closer, scooting up until he could rest his chin on top of Zane's head and Zane was snuggled up against his chest. "Go to sleep if I can't grope you. I'll stay awake."

Zane snorted but didn't twitch a muscle to move. "That'll be a pretty picture for Cameron to see if he wakes up."

Ty held his breath for a few moments and then let it out in an irritated rush. "Fine."

He pulled his hand out from under Zane's neck and rolled over, and then sat up and rolled his head from side to side. The immediate chill made Zane shiver, and he wrapped his arms around himself, watching Ty. He wished he hadn't said anything. He didn't want to sleep. He wanted to be awake, to soak Ty in. He reached out to trail his fingers down Ty's arm.

Ty turned his arm and let Zane's fingers glide over his palm. He pushed himself off the bed and stretched, then turned and leaned over

Zane, pulling the comforter up over him as he kissed him. "Go to sleep."

Zane sighed, warmed by Ty's quiet affection, and reached for his gun. Then he pulled one of the pillows partway under his chest and tucked the hand holding the gun underneath it, a security measure made second nature after his time undercover in the seedy Miami underbelly. Even the past several months sleeping unarmed with Ty hadn't made the position feel strange. "Don't kill Cross."

"No promises," Ty muttered. He moved away and clicked off the light Zane had been using.

It made the room mostly dark, just the light spilling under the room door to see by, and Zane watched Ty's silhouette for long minutes before closing his eyes. He'd just rest for a little bit.

He didn't know how long he slept, but there was gray light coming through the curtains when a noise awakened him.

There was a bang and a rattle like plastic rolling across tile, and then Ty shouted: "Where is it?"

Zane was out of the bed and at the bathroom door, gun in hand, in three seconds flat, pulse racing.

Ty stood in the middle of the bathroom, glaring down at Julian and holding a roll of toilet paper in his hand. Julian sat in the bathtub, handcuffed to the safety rail on the shower enclosure. He was looking at Ty like he thought he had lost his mind. Zane narrowed his eyes as he sized up the scene. He glanced at the wall where the toilet paper should have been, then back at Ty's hands, before turning a questioning look on Julian.

"Where is it?" Ty said again.

"I have no idea what you're blathering on about," Julian said, the epitome of calm. "Agent Garrett, I believe he needs more rest. Or perhaps it's time for his medication," he said, mimicking someone drinking.

"Shut up. Where's what?" Zane asked as he studied Julian and the cuffs. They looked intact.

Ty whirled around to look at him. His entire body was tense. His eyes were a sparkling green, and they flashed angrily. Zane's breath caught before he could help himself. His partner was stunning when he was like this. "The toilet paper holder," Ty said in quick bursts of words. He turned back on Julian. "Hand it over or I'll search for it myself."

Zane glanced around again, and he caught sight of the two plastic halves of the holder on the floor behind the toilet and next to the sink. He looked back at Julian and had to repress a smile. The man was clever, and an excellent liar. Zane didn't figure he would have thought of that himself. "You took the spring."

"I *tried* to take the spring, but it didn't have one," Julian told him. He didn't seem at all perturbed to have been caught.

Ty growled and reached into the tub to grab Julian's neck and yank him to his feet.

Zane put his hand on Ty's shoulder. "You can't just strip him down."

"Watch me," Ty said, and he pushed Julian face-first against the shower wall, then stepped into the tub with him.

Julian cleared his throat as he tried to reposition his hands in a way that his wrists weren't being torqued by the handcuffs, but he didn't protest the rough treatment.

Zane was torn between the urge to laugh and the more professional need to pull Ty off their prisoner. He also wasn't fond of watching Ty manhandle anyone like that unless it was him. He realized he was more tired than he'd thought if the sight of Ty searching a criminal had him jealous.

"Grady."

Ty was already patting Julian down. Quite thoroughly. He glanced back at Zane and jerked his head. He continued the pat down, and Julian moved his head so he could glance over his shoulder at them. He didn't show any emotion, merely looked at Ty.

"In most countries you'd have to pay for that."

Zane stifled a sigh and took a step back. It wasn't exactly kosher, what Ty was doing, but the assignment gave them unusual latitude to deal with such a dangerous asset. And maybe it would help Ty work off some of that extra energy. He turned in the doorway to glance out into the main room. Cameron was sitting up, turned toward the bathroom, peering Zane's way with a worried look on his face.

Zane heard Ty whuff from within the bathroom, and by the time he looked back, Ty had shoved Julian's face against the shower wall and was holding him there by the back of his head.

"Watch the elbows."

"Watch your fingers," Julian snapped.

"Welcome to TSA training, bitch."

"Want the other set of cuffs?" Zane asked, hoping to appease his cranky partner. "You could spread his arms out."

"Will someone please tell me the safe word?" Julian asked.

Zane snorted and leaned against the door, but he was watching Ty carefully. Something about Julian seemed to rub him wrong, and Ty's short patience was nonexistent with this man.

A moment later Ty reached around and slid his fingers under his belt.

"Agent Garrett, I really must protest," Julian said, though his voice was still calm.

Yeah, Zane wanted to protest too. Too much of Ty's bare skin was too close to another man for Zane's taste.

Julian started to speak again, but his words were choked off as Ty moved his hand further under his belt. Julian did react then, throwing his head to the side and beginning to fight as Ty pulled at the waistband of his pants.

"Ha!" Ty yanked something out of Julian's pants and held it up. It was a long, thin piece of metal. It had once been a spiral, but it had been straightened out. Julian cursed. Ty put a hand in the center of his back and shoved him against the wall, holding him there as he stepped out of the shower.

"Bravo," Zane said, shaking his head. He wasn't sure whom he was congratulating, though.

Ty waved the straightened spring at him and then tossed it into the sink on the other side of the bathroom door.

"Clever bastard," Julian muttered, sounding almost amused. "Do you have any idea how difficult that was?"

"Is this what the whole trip is going to be like?" Zane asked with a wave of his gun at the spring.

"I would wager so, yes," Julian said with a nod. "Perhaps if you allowed me—"

"No," Ty snapped. "Sit down, shut up, stop trying to escape." He turned to Zane. "Where's the kid?"

Zane nodded toward the open room.

"Go get him."

That got Julian's attention. He straightened, still standing in the bathtub, and he pulled at the handcuffs that looped around the safety bar. "No need to bring him into this."

"You brought him into this," Zane said. He took two steps out of the room and waved Cameron over.

"What's going on?" Cameron asked as he climbed off the bed and moved to join Zane at the door.

Ty stepped to the side so Cameron could see Julian. They hadn't let Cameron see him at all since locking him in the bathroom, and now Cameron's brow creased as he took in the scene. Zane knew it was a disturbing image, Julian disheveled, standing in the bathtub cuffed to the shower rail, and Ty bare-chested and fuming.

"Julian? Are you okay?"

Julian smiled at him. "I'm fine, love. Agent Grady just needed a cuddle. And possibly a piece of my spleen."

Ty held up the piece of metal and tapped it against the sink counter. Cameron looked from it to Julian and back. He didn't look like he was making the connection.

"When we left you said the only way you'd come along without a fuss was with your boyfriend," Ty said, but it wasn't clear which one he was talking to since he was looking at the floor near his feet. "But since you're making a fuss anyway, I don't see why we have to hold up our end of the bargain."

Julian raised his chin and his black eyes flashed, but he didn't react otherwise. When Zane had first seen Julian's reaction to Cameron in the apartment, he'd been sure Cameron would be the best way to control him. It was a combination of how the man softened when he looked at his lover but bristled, even the tiniest bit, when there was any threat toward him.

Cameron looked back and forth between them as if he was watching a tennis match. Zane had to admire how he seemed to be holding up under the stress. Many civilians would have fallen apart by now, especially in the face of Ty's impressive rage. "Julian?" His voice was low and cautious.

Ty shook his head. "Don't talk to him, talk to me," he said to Cameron in a low, barely controlled voice that would have scared just about anyone. It almost scared Zane. It did the trick, because Cameron shrank away from him even as he looked at him. Ty pushed away from the sink and stepped toward Cameron, holding up the spring. "He tries one more time to escape, and I promise you, you'll never see each other again."

Cameron stared at him, eyes wide and chest heaving as he breathed hard.

"Now, go whisper about that some," Ty said, voice downright cruel.

Cameron had gone white, and Zane caught a tremble in his hands before he gripped them into fists. But he nodded jerkily. "I'll talk to him."

"You do that," Ty said, and he stepped out of the bathroom. He pulled Zane with him and closed the door behind them.

Zane turned and went along as Ty walked toward the window. If that wasn't enough to calm Julian down, they'd have to tranquilize him.

They might have to tranquilize Ty too, if what Zane had just seen wasn't an act of some sort.

Ty paced toward the window and then turned back to Zane, looking troubled and no longer even remotely angry. Zane was impressed by his lover's ability to turn that on and off so quickly. He'd known Ty was a chameleon based on his performance as an Englishman on that cruise ship job they'd worked, but Zane had never seen Ty turn emotions on and off like that. "I feel like a monster, threatening that kid."

Zane raised one brow, surprised. "Why?"

Ty looked at him oddly. "Because he hasn't done anything wrong. Because he's got stars in his eyes, and he can't help it that he's in love with that jackhole."

"He chose to be here. He had to know what he was getting into. I can't imagine living with Cross is good for anyone's health."

Ty shook his head and looked down at the mangled spring. He spun it around between his fingers. "This guy, man. If he'd been able to retie his shoelaces, I'd have never noticed," he said in disgust as he tossed the wire into the trash.

Zane shook his head and set his gun on the dresser in front of the TV, in easy reach. "He used his toes to get to it?"

Ty nodded.

"Clever. Like someone else I know."

Ty glared at him before the expression softened. "Please don't compare me to the criminal."

Zane watched him affectionately. "Sorry."

"Hopefully, Cameron will keep him in line from now on."

Glancing back at the bathroom door, Zane set his hands on his hips as he considered. "Maybe if we leave them together in there another few hours, we could get some more sleep."

Ty nodded. "Sleep. We'll leave them to it." He grabbed up his shirt from the floor and pulled it over his head, then stepped over to Zane and kissed him. Zane took advantage of the chance, though, and slid his hands under the shirt before Ty even got it pulled all the way down.

"Did you enjoy patting down Cross?" Zane asked before nipping at Ty's earlobe.

Ty grunted distractedly, not picking up on Zane's teasing tone. "He got me a good one in the ribs. It's like he has extra hands."

Zane moved to slide his hands over Ty's ribs. "You bested him, though," he murmured, dragging his arm around Ty's waist and pulling their bodies flush.

Ty pushed away and looked at him oddly again. He shook his head. "This isn't a pissing contest, Zane. I just want to get rid of him as quick as we can. Guy makes me nervous."

"Yeah, I can tell," Zane said.

"You saying he doesn't bother you?"

"No. I'd put you up against him any day." He dropped his chin, rubbing his bearded cheek against Ty's.

"Are you trying to start something out here?" Ty asked in a warm voice.

"I wish," Zane muttered, splaying his hand flat along Ty's shoulder blades and rubbing the warm skin.

Ty kissed his cheek and moved away. "Then cut it out. And shave that damn thing off in the morning, huh?"

Zane huffed, but he allowed Ty to push him away. He wanted to be close, but they couldn't get distracted. Muttering under his breath, he walked over to the desk and his papers.

Ty went to the bathroom door and leaned against it, sliding to the floor with a soft groan. He was apparently intending to sit there the rest of the morning. After a roll of his eyes, Zane snatched up a pillow and flung it at him.

A moment later, he heard Ty's soft "Thanks, Zane."

JULIAN was surprised when the two FBI agents left Cameron with him in the bathroom. But he knew what they were thinking, and on the surface it made sense. He tugged at the handcuffs and raised one hand toward Cameron.

His lover climbed into the bathtub next to him and slid their hands together, lacing their fingers. "Have you been stuck like this all night?"

"Well, I *was* sitting," Julian answered, keeping his tone light. He slid the chain up the diagonal safety rail and spread his arms as wide as they would go, gesturing for Cameron to duck under. Cameron did, moving to stand in the circle of Julian's arms and reaching up to slide his hands around Julian's neck, tipping his head back to look up at him.

"Aside from threatening you, how have they been treating you?" Julian asked.

"Fine. Haven't said a word to me, really. I was sleeping until I heard Ty yell at you."

"He's just overly excitable." Julian kissed him. It was hard to pull him closer with the safety bar restraining his arms like it was. "Are you going to give me my lecture?"

"Do I need to?" Cameron asked, meeting his eyes.

Julian sighed and looked over at the door. "If we make it to DC, we'll never see each other again anyway." He looked into Cameron's eyes. "They're using threats to you to keep me under control. But if I'm reading them correctly, Grady won't hurt either of us unless we force him, and he won't let Garrett hurt you. Nothing is a bigger threat than what they're delivering us to."

"Will you tell me what's going on?"

Julian hesitated. He had spent most of their time together trying to shield Cameron from the worst of it. But now they were being dragged across the country, possibly to their deaths. Cameron deserved to know.

"It's the CIA, Cam."

"CIA? I thought Ty and Zane were FBI."

"I don't know what they are. But it's sure as hell not the FBI who wants to kill me."

Cameron's arms tightened around Julian's neck. "I won't let them take you away from me if I can do anything to stop it."

"Just look intimidated and docile whenever they threaten you. Let them think it's working."

"I don't have to act," Cameron murmured as he laid his cheek against Julian's chest. "They are intimidating."

Julian snorted before he could stop himself. He cleared his throat to cover it. He leaned back and looked down at Cameron. "You're not wearing anything sharp or pointy, by any chance, are you?"

Cameron frowned and let his arms slide down. "Sharp or pointy? I don't think so." He looked down at himself. He didn't wear jewelry—the only jewelry Julian had ever seen him wear was the Warrior's Cross pendant Julian had given him when they'd first met. But that necklace was long gone.

"Zippers? Shoelaces?" Julian asked as he looked down Cameron's body. He wasn't wearing shoes. And in reality, Julian couldn't imagine that he could manage to pick the lock with a zipper pull. "Damn, that spring was so perfect," he muttered in irritation.

"You about got yourself shot. Zane was up out of that bed with that gun so fast, it scared me."

"I'm surprised he's not accustomed to Grady shouting at random for no reason. They sleep with their weapons? That's good to know. If one of them is going to try to kill me, it will be Garrett. But no worries," he said as he pulled Cameron as close as he could. "We'll get out of this."

Cameron leaned against him again, tucking his head under Julian's chin. "It's a good thing you're such a good liar."

"I'm not certain whether that's a compliment or an insult."

"Me either," Cameron said before tipping his head back again and kissing Julian's chin.

Julian grinned. "I love you, you know."

Cameron gave him a tremulous smile. "I know. I love you too." He went up on tiptoe to kiss Julian fervently.

Julian had to bend to indulge in the kiss since he couldn't pull Cameron closer. He smiled against Cameron's lips. "We've never tried this with handcuffs," he said in a suggestive, teasing voice.

Cameron laughed. "Interesting idea. You can't pick me up, flip me over, or hold me down." He opened his eyes, and they sparkled mischievously.

"That's what you think."

The arched eyebrow Cameron gave him in reply was a clear dare, and Cameron's hands sliding down his chest to his belt buckle even more so.

Julian's smile was predatory as he stepped closer and pushed Cameron against the shower wall. He gasped and looked down between them. "My belt!" he hissed.

"What?" Cameron asked, plucking at it.

"They left it on me," Julian told him with a grin.

"So, that means I can put it in your mouth for you to bite on in a couple minutes?"

That got Julian's attention, and he looked back up with a grin. "Do you care if we make noise and they know what we're doing?"

A blush crept up Cameron's cheeks. "It's not going to make a difference in what they do with us, right?" His fingers manipulated Julian's belt buckle as he looked up into Julian's eyes.

"Probably not."

"Is this really stupid?" Cameron licked his lips as he unbuttoned Julian's pants.

"The only thing stupid in this room is sitting outside our door," Julian said, raising his voice just enough.

"Blow me, Cross," came Ty's disembodied voice from outside the door.

TY PRESSED his shoulders against the door to stretch his sore muscles, and he let his bare feet slide on the carpet until his legs were splayed in front of him. He sat there without any compunction about looking dejected in the dark.

Once he heard the unmistakable sounds coming from within the bathroom, he grunted in annoyance and rolled to his hands and knees to get off the floor.

"What the hell do they think this is, some stupidass romantic comedy?" he growled to Zane. He called through the door, "I have a gun and I like to use it!"

"That's only going to egg Cross on."

"I don't care," Ty mumbled as he walked toward the two beds. "He reminds me of you. Parts of him, anyway."

Zane looked up from the papers. The soft glow of the table lamp cast odd shadows, making his face appear gaunt. "Of me? How? Besides Cameron's 'tall, dark, and handsome' line."

"I mean he's outwardly stoic and fun to poke. Reminds me of when we first met."

Zane smiled and leaned back in his chair. "Much better than what you said about me back then."

Ty moved closer and sat on the edge of the bed near Zane, looking at him with nothing but affection. He was close enough to smell Zane's deodorant and the underlying scents of his shampoo and sweat, and combined with the trademark smells of a hotel room, it stirred all sorts of memories and emotions.

"You ever think about that first week?" he asked with a fond smile.

"Some parts of it, yeah," Zane said, edging up one shoulder as he spun the chair so he faced Ty, their knees bumping. "Usually when you're being particularly frustrating." He tipped his head to one side as his eyes raked Ty up and down. "Or particularly desirable."

Ty leaned forward. "Those couple of days in that hotel room with you," he said, voice low and intimate, "every time I looked at you I got butterflies. I couldn't decide if it was a good feeling or if I hated you for it."

Zane chuckled. "Oh, I was damn sure you hated me. And it was certainly reciprocated."

"Did you really hate me?" Ty asked, not necessarily offended, but curious.

"To immense proportions," Zane said with a nod, but then he rolled his eyes. "Didn't last, though. You were…." He drew in a deep breath and held it as he considered his words. He ended up shrugging. "Hurricane Ty. Blew me away."

Ty's smile grew warmer, and he reached out to take Zane's hand in his. "Sometimes I wish we could go back there and smack ourselves in the heads. But then I remind myself it wouldn't have been the same."

Zane squeezed his hand. "For me, there was no going back after you kissed me."

Ty looked up from their joined hands and met Zane's eyes. On his mini sabbatical he'd begun pondering what life might be like when neither of them worked at the FBI anymore; when they could walk down the street hand in hand and not care who saw; when they were no longer being shot at, blown up, or sent cross-country as errand boys. It was on the tip of his tongue to ask Zane if he thought they could be without their jobs and not go crazy.

But Ty knew he couldn't do it. Not yet. He had been born and bred to be a spearpoint. Zane was the only kink in the plan he'd always had, but Ty found that he didn't care. The moment Zane had kissed him, Ty had known he would throw that plan out the window.

Just remembering the terror and thrill of that moment made Ty's stomach flutter. He couldn't help himself—he reached out and slid his fingers along the back of Zane's neck and pulled him closer, leaning in to kiss him. Zane sighed and relaxed into Ty's arms as he rubbed his lips against Ty's, then placed a tiny kiss at the corner of his mouth.

"Why can't we just do one thing easy, huh?" Ty asked, frustrated by all the obstacles they seemed to deal with every day, the least of which was their own stunning inability to communicate with each other.

Zane raised his fingers to touch Ty's cheek. "I don't know," he said, though it was with equal resignation. "Except this," he whispered before kissing Ty again.

Ty hummed. "You have always been easy."

"You haven't," Zane said, but he softened the words with a smile.

A noise from the bathroom drew Ty's attention just long enough for him to miss the next intended kiss. He sighed and pressed his nose and mouth to Zane's cheek. "I know I'm not easy," he whispered. "I promise I'll make it up to you."

Zane shook his head. "I knew what I was getting when I realized I loved you. I don't expect—don't *want* you to change, no matter how crazy you make me sometimes."

"I like you crazy," Ty growled as he stood up. He leaned over Zane, propping his arms on the chair and forcing Zane to sit back as he straddled his lap and kissed him, long and hard. Zane hummed in approval and gripped his hips. He sighed when Ty straightened.

"Love you," Zane whispered.

Ty patted Zane's cheek. "That will never get old."

Another, louder sound from the bathroom caused him to growl in annoyance, and he stood and stepped away from Zane. "I better go take up my post again."

Zane nodded, letting his hands drag away from Ty's hips. He stifled a yawn and turned back to the desk. Ty stood there for a moment longer, watching his lover in the garish light.

If there was one thing in the world Ty was willing to give up everything for, it was sitting right there in front of him.

~Chapter 7~

JULIAN was secured in the back of the sedan as Ty fiddled with the GPS on the dash. Ty had spent a solid half an hour devising the most evil ways he could come up with to make sure Julian couldn't even get his hands together, much less pick any locks. They were waiting for Zane to finish checking them out, and Ty was keeping one eye on the two men in the back as he punched in the appropriate directions in the GPS.

With every button he pushed, the GPS unit offered suggestions. He shook his head at the list of Washingtons that it offered, eyes scanning for the right one. Movement in the rearview mirror caught his attention as he found the appropriate Washington, and he glanced up as he pushed the button, narrowing his eyes at his prisoners.

"Didn't you two get enough of that last night?" he asked in a low growl.

"I'm trying to restore blood flow to my fingers," Julian said.

"I'll restore your blood flow pretty damn quick if you try one more thing," Ty said, voice low and serious.

Julian rolled his eyes and sighed, shifting his shoulder and wiggling his fingers, which were hanging in the air. One hand was cuffed to the handle above the door, the other to the floorboard, wound around his leg first so he had to lean forward. Cameron was restrained in similar fashion. They had to be uncomfortable as hell, but Ty wasn't taking any chances.

He and Zane had discussed trying to head back to Chicago and find a flight, but a call in to Burns had informed them that a blizzard was heading their way and flights were being grounded left and right. They'd have better luck driving, and if they left right now they'd get ahead of the snowstorm and miss it entirely, even if they were having difficulties with their prisoners.

A few moments later, Zane joined them and Ty pulled out of the parking space.

"In point one miles, turn left on Willowcreek Road."

Zane was still shivering from the cold as the GPS began giving instructions, even though the car was finally beginning to warm. They weren't even out of the parking lot of the hotel yet and the GPS lady was bossing them around. The little arrow on the screen of the unit was pointing the wrong way, and they weren't facing anything resembling Willowcreek Road.

"You're going to have to do better than this, honey," Ty told the little unit stuck to the dash.

"I should get my phone out," Zane said as he settled in the passenger seat, newspaper on his lap, covered cup of coffee in hand. "Record you talking to it."

"Talking to what, your phone?" Ty asked as he turned the car toward the exit to the parking lot.

"In point one miles, turn left on Willowcreek Road."

"The GPS," Zane said, gesturing toward it with his coffee cup.

"She's more fun to listen to than you are. At least she knows what she's talking about."

"Ha ha."

"I kind of dig her," Ty said with a smirk.

"Yeah, well, the shine will wear off when all she does is bitch at you for seven hundred miles," Zane said.

"And that's different from you, how?"

When Zane turned to meet his eyes, Ty winked at him. Zane looked away, a smile forming.

"In point two miles, turn left on entrance ramp to Interstate 80/90, Indiana East-West Toll Road. In point one mile, stay left on Interstate 80/90 East, Indiana East-West Toll Road."

"Loosen up, honey," Ty said to it.

"Please stop talking to the inanimate object," Julian said from the back seat.

"You can give that up," Zane said as he opened the newspaper. He didn't look at Ty, but he was still smirking. "He talks to his guns too."

"That fits," Julian said under his breath.

Ty snorted at them both but remained silent as he followed the directions the GPS gave him. He took the toll ticket as they went through the entrance, handing it to Zane as they got on the toll road. As the miles began to roll by, Ty couldn't have been more relieved that he and Zane had managed to steal those few hours in Chicago. He wanted to reach out and touch his partner, rest his hand on Zane's knee, brush his fingers against his shoulder, anything. He refrained, though, the professional side of him winning out.

Zane seemed content as he read his paper and sipped at his coffee. Of course, Zane always seemed content. That was one of the things Ty loved about him. He was rock steady most of the time, dry and unflappable. A solid wall against which Ty's changing moods battered. Traits that made the moments Zane lost his composure even more entertaining.

They stopped at a travel plaza roughly an hour after leaving the hotel in order to get breakfast. As Zane took care of whatever the hell it was Zane did in travel plazas, Ty sat in the driver's seat, fidgeting. He wasn't going to be driving the next leg, but it was easier to see the two men sitting in the back in the rearview mirror from that side of the car, and to react with his dominant right hand if they put up a fight.

He couldn't get over the tension that had settled in his shoulders or the remnants of the Red Bull, and it was manifesting in a great deal of twitching, shifting, and drumming his fingers on the steering wheel.

"Intelligence operatives often pick food or travel areas as their cover, Cameron," Julian said from the backseat, where he sat examining his neatly manicured nails as his hand hung above his head. "Restaurants, gas stations. Lots of people in and out to mask suspicious behavior. A place like this, it must make Agent Grady very nervous."

"Try talking without making noise for a while," Ty said, his eyes still on Zane, who had not turned back toward the window at all.

"Are you okay?" Cameron asked him.

"I get fidgety if I sit too long," Ty answered almost against his will. He'd found that no matter what Cameron asked him, he seemed physically incapable of lying to the guy.

Cameron nodded, looking almost like he felt sorry for Ty. "Aren't you supposed to be able to, like, be still and hide? On… surveillance or something?"

"I don't do that kind of thing anymore." Ty looked at Cameron with one eyebrow raised and a slight smirk. "We have cameras for that."

"Really," Cameron said, heavy on the sarcasm. "So what does a federal agent do if he's not watching other people?"

"We cause all kinds of trouble. Terrorize innocent civilians, arrest the wrong people, take advantage of government healthcare."

Ty saw Julian put a finger to his own temple and pull the imaginary trigger.

Ty snorted and shook his head. Wouldn't that save them all a lot of trouble? He began to shake his knee side to side, starting the sedan rocking. He heard Julian sigh from the back seat.

"I understand why you can't sit still, Agent Grady." He sounded almost as if he were offering a consolation prize.

"I kind of doubt that." Mentally sparring with Julian Cross had long ago lost its luster.

"How long were you there?" Julian asked.

Ty's movements slowed, then stilled as his breaths came harder. The hair on his arms rose as a chill went through him.

"You scream 'prisoner of war', Agent Grady," Julian said, his voice low and almost sympathetic. "But you're too young to have been captured in the Gulf. That means Special Forces, black ops. Navy SEAL?"

Ty swallowed hard, ashamed to see that his fingers gripping the steering wheel were turning white. "I was Force Recon."

"The batshit insane ones. Of course, that makes sense."

"What is that?" Cameron asked.

"Agent Grady was a Marine. Force Recon is their answer to the SEALs or Army Rangers."

"That's impressive," Cameron said as his eyes cut toward Ty.

"It is indeed. Save for the fact that most Marines are slightly insane *before* they live through the hell of combat. Was it Afghanistan, then?"

Ty kept his eyes front and center, not looking in the mirror because he knew this man would be able to read him.

"Captured in Afghanistan, I'd wager. How long were you held?"

"I wasn't."

It was the same bullshit line Ty always gave when the subject came up. That operation was still classified. The answer, though, the answer only he, Nick O'Flaherty, and that weird little guy from Homeland Security knew, was twenty-three days, nine hours, and fifty-one minutes.

Ty glanced up to see Julian's reflection. His dark eyes seemed sympathetic. Ty looked to Cameron in the mirror—the young man had gone pale with the implication. Even though Ty had denied it, they both knew what Julian had said was true. Ty nodded, not intending to discuss the matter any further.

Maybe now Julian Cross would realize that Ty knew something about trying to escape.

"I'M DRIVING. I get to choose the music."

"No," Ty said as he continued to flip through the radio, searching for a station.

Cameron raised a brow as Zane smacked Ty's fingers and then hit the preset button, returning the radio to the classic rock station.

"Dude!" Ty said as he pushed the button next to it and turned the dial to find the station he'd just had it on. "Pay attention to the road."

Zane hit the first button again. "Sit back, copilot. You had sports talk all morning." He sounded calm, though Cameron couldn't see how he maintained it. Dealing with Ty on a regular basis had to be grounds for anger management classes. Or homicidal tendencies. Maybe that was what was wrong with Zane.

"So did you," Ty said as he hit another button at random. Cameron could see a smirk on his face as he looked at Zane. It was obvious now that he didn't care what they were listening to, he was just pushing buttons. Since Cameron was sitting behind Zane, he couldn't really see Zane's face to gauge his reaction, but his next poke at the first button didn't seem angry.

Cameron glanced at Julian. "You and Preston have such a different relationship than them."

"There are so many ways that statement is correct," Julian said in a bored voice. He wasn't paying the two agents much attention. Or didn't appear to be.

Ty pushed another button and turned up the volume. Zane hit the first button again but didn't mess with the volume. Cameron tipped his head to look into the rearview mirror at Zane's reflection. He couldn't be sure, but there might have been a smile on Zane's lips.

"How long have you two been partners?" Cameron asked. There was absolutely nothing about the landscape passing by to hold his interest after the first five minutes, and Julian was sulking or plotting, or both, so he might as well try to talk to them. Julian had told him to try and converse as much as possible; it would put their guard down, enable Julian to glean information, and make Ty and Zane less likely to hurt Cameron.

Ty jabbed at another button and put his hand over the radio controls so Zane couldn't touch them. "Too damn long," he said to Cameron.

"You love me," Zane said in a tone that was practically cheerful, and Cameron couldn't help but grin as Zane used the button on the steering wheel to turn the station.

Julian turned his head to look at Zane's reflection in the rearview mirror, and then at Ty.

Ty was watching Zane, eyes narrowed. He finally retaliated by turning off the radio and huffing at his partner.

"Come on, how long?" Cameron asked again. If he had anything going for him, it was that he was persistent. Julian could attest to that.

"About eight months," Ty said as he continued to eye Zane.

"Eleven months," Zane corrected.

"Uh huh," Cameron said, doubtful of the veracity of either statement.

"It's been eight months, official. By your logic it's almost two years."

"What?" Cameron asked.

"There was a short break in there," Zane said. "We didn't get along very well on our first assignment."

Cameron snorted. "And how is that different from now?"

"You heard him," Ty said with a sarcastic edge to his words. "I love him now."

"Yeah, I can tell," Cameron said, looking between them. Zane was actually smiling. It looked like he enjoyed needling his partner as much as his partner enjoyed needling him. "Why stay together if you didn't get along very well?"

"They were assigned, Cameron. They don't get to pick and choose," Julian said in a gentle voice.

"Well, but surely their boss wouldn't make them work together if they hated each other," Cameron said. "They do carry guns, after all."

"Do we look like we hate each other?" Zane asked.

Cameron held up his hand and waggled it from side to side in a so-so motion. "Sometimes, maybe."

"He can't tell what you look like with that beard," Ty said as he turned his head to look at Zane. Cameron could see him smirking again.

Zane's head turned toward Ty, and Cameron imagined it was so Zane could glare at him. "What's that have to do with it?"

"You look like a lumberjack."

Zane shrugged one shoulder. "'I'm a lumberjack and I'm okay,'" he answered in a low singsong voice.

"Stop," Ty said with real urgency.

"Please," Julian added.

Zane chuckled, and to Cameron's ear it sounded a little on the evil side. "You want to sing instead?" Zane asked as he glanced sideways at his partner.

"If I sing, I'll sing whatever I damn well want to. Might as well listen to my radio station."

"Nope," Zane said, and again Cameron wondered about his apparent saintly level of patience.

After leaning back, Cameron looked over at Julian. "They almost sound like you and Blake, sometimes. When Blake really gets on a roll."

"Must you continue to compare me with either of them in any scenario?" Julian asked as he looked at Cameron earnestly.

Cameron shrugged. "I have a small frame of reference for people who kill things."

"You sing for hundreds of people sitting in the stands at a ballgame, but you won't sing now," Zane was saying.

"No, I'm not going to sing," Ty said, incredulous as he glared at Zane.

"Why not?" Zane asked.

Cameron leaned toward the middle of the seat so he could peer through at Zane. He looked relaxed, left hand loose on the wheel, right hand free and resting on his thigh. A year ago, Cameron wouldn't have thought anything about that. Now, it occurred to him that Zane was probably keeping his hand free so he could draw his gun. Cameron frowned and sat back.

"Stop it, Garrett, I'm not singing," Ty said as he jabbed at the radio.

"How in the world did they get you to sing, anyway?" Zane asked.

"Sing where?" Cameron added, and then belatedly doubted the wisdom of making Ty any twitchier.

Ty looked at Zane pointedly. He glanced over his shoulder at Cameron. "He's talking about baseball games," he said to Cameron, and then he looked at Zane and spoke in a lower voice. "I just do."

"Season's suspended," Zane said. "City's refurbishing that field."

"And?"

Zane lifted one shoulder. "They called while you were gone about what to do with the Bronco."

Ty cleared his throat and hung his head. "Are they releasing her?"

"Yeah. I had them keep her in the impound lot so you could see her one last time," Zane said. "There's nothing to be done."

"We'll just see about that," Ty said with a determination that was almost frightening.

"You're talking like somebody died," Cameron said.

"She did," Ty said without moving.

Zane glanced up to make eye contact with Cameron in the rearview mirror, and he shook his head.

"My condolences," Cameron murmured, a little mystified. He looked over at Julian, brow raised.

Julian shrugged, a difficult action the way he was restrained, and he whirled his finger around his temple. Cameron sighed and glanced at Ty. He was starting to think Julian was right about Ty being crazy. Maybe Zane too, if he thought any of what they'd just talked about made any sense.

"Can I choose to ride in the boot, now?" Julian asked.

"Shut up," Ty and Zane both answered.

ZANE stepped out of the second travel plaza facility of the day with Cameron in tow, taking a deep breath of the freezing air. It had begun to snow, dropping fat flakes that were already beginning to pile up.

Zane shivered and glanced back inside. It was too cold to wait for Ty and Julian out here. With a steaming hot coffee in one hand and Cameron's arm in the other, he started for the car. He caught a glimpse of a hulking black SUV parked near the gas pumps, and something about it caught Zane's attention enough to warrant a second glance. He slowed, staring hard at it. Even as he did so, the car started, its lights blinking on, and it pulled away from the gas pump it had been using and headed for the exit.

"What's wrong?" Cameron asked as he watched the car drive away.

Zane pursed his lips. "Nothing. Come on, it's freezing."

The car didn't give him a bad feeling, and it was the first time he'd even thought about a suspicious vehicle on their tail. It was probably nothing to worry about. They headed back to the car, and Zane secured Cameron with a little bit less vehemence than Ty had that morning. He got in the passenger side and started the car, sighing in relief as the warm air touched his skin.

They had stopped for gas and something to keep Ty's hands busy, and Zane had been so close to buying a stress ball he'd found inside that he still regretted not making the purchase. Ty loved road trips, but he really needed to be the one driving. He wasn't cut out for the idle, easy passage of time that was required of passengers.

Soon enough, Ty and Julian returned. Ty shoved Julian into the backseat and clanked his handcuffs into place. They were arguing. Again. Zane turned in his seat to watch them.

"I refuse to search you every time you take a piss. Refuse!" Ty was saying through gritted teeth.

"Then don't do it, Agent Grady. It's very simple." Julian was watching as Ty went through the ever-increasingly complicated ritual of tying him down. If this kept up, Julian really would be riding in the trunk.

"Then stop trying to escape!"

"You wouldn't have one modicum of respect for me if I didn't try to escape."

"I don't have any for you now! The only thing I care about is getting your sorry ass to DC so I can go home."

Julian sighed as Ty slammed the door.

"What have you done now?" Zane asked him.

"That is a trade secret, Agent Garrett."

Zane rolled his eyes and turned back around in his seat as Ty threw himself into the car.

"You want to drive?" Zane asked as soon as Ty sat in the driver's seat.

"Yes, please," Ty said in a rush of relief.

Zane grinned. "Everything okay?"

"No. They didn't have any Cheetos."

"Tragic," Zane said as he took the lid off his coffee. "The coffee is fantastic, though."

"I don't like coffee, Zane!"

"It really is very good," Cameron said. "They don't over roast the beans like Starbucks."

Zane hummed in contentment as he took a sip.

"Shut up," Ty muttered as he jabbed at the GPS and hit the button that would continue their previous course.

The suction cup that attached the unit to the dash popped up, and the unit jumped off the dash into Ty's lap. He flailed briefly as he fought with the charging wire, trying to disentangle it and retrieve the unit as it slid down his leg and tangled in the steering column.

Julian chuckled drily from the back seat. "Looks like she likes you too."

JULIAN'S fingers had long ago lost all feeling, and the tingling sensation was marching its way down his arm toward his shoulder by the time the snow got heavy enough that the two FBI agents were discussing stopping.

"I think we can make it out of the storm," Zane was saying even as Ty shook his head.

"I'm telling you, Zane, if there's one thing West Virginia knows, it's snow. This is a car killer, and we're in a Crown Vic."

"You're saying we should stop for the night?"

"Yes."

"And let the snow pile up around us as Cross tries repeatedly to kill us and escape?"

"Well, not when you put it that way, Zane. Jesus."

"I really don't want to die in a snow storm in the middle of Indiana," Cameron said in a small voice.

"I said it would kill the car, not us," Ty grumbled.

"It's… sort of the same thing, though," Zane pointed out. "We don't even have winter coats."

Julian could clearly see the glare Ty shot at Zane

Julian glanced to Cameron and met his lover's eyes. Cameron still looked worried and overwhelmed, and Julian had been trying his best to remain outwardly calm for his benefit. It was getting harder to do, though, the longer this charade went on. Both attempts at escape had been foiled, and he had to admit, he was a little surprised. He smiled and gave Cameron a wry roll of his eyes despite his concern.

He was torn over what he wanted Ty and Zane to do. Every mile they drove brought them closer to DC and the danger that lay in wait there. But while stopping in the snow storm would afford him and Cameron the chance at escaping, how far could they realistically get in a whiteout blizzard like this?

Eventually, the snow was falling so fast and thick that it didn't matter what any of them wanted to do. Ty could barely see to drive the car, and as soon as they caught wind of an exit off the toll road that had a hotel, Ty headed for it. It took them half an hour to get from the exit to the hotel, inching along in the driving snow. Every minute that passed, the agents grew edgier and meaner.

"I could get out and walk and get us a room before the car could get there," Zane said.

"Zane, shut up," Ty said through gritted teeth. His knuckles were white on the steering wheel. Julian supposed it was partly instinct and mostly dumb luck that he was able to navigate at all. He was tense, though, and for someone wound as tight as Ty already was, making him more so wasn't going to help anyone.

Julian and Cameron wisely kept their mouths shut.

"You want me to drive for a while?"

"Zane, seriously, stop talking to me right now, okay?"

Zane cleared his throat and shrugged a shoulder, looking out the window.

Julian glanced over at Cameron again, trying to gauge how well he was holding up. "You okay?"

Cameron shook his head, eyes darting to the front to see if either agent was looking at him. Julian knew that Cameron was ashamed to admit to his fear in front of Ty and Zane.

The anger flared so unexpectedly that Julian gave a sharp gasp as it burned through him. Who were these two clowns to make Cameron feel like that? Who the hell did these assholes think they were dealing with?

He had to take several long, deep breaths to calm himself. "It's okay, love. There's no shame in being frightened."

Cameron looked at him, eyes pleading, expression miserable. Julian's chest twisted and the anger banked to a slower burn.

"It's okay."

Ty threw the car in park and rested both hands on the steering wheel. When Julian glanced at him, he had his eyes closed, visibly trying to relax after the stressful drive.

"I think we're in a parking lot," the agent muttered.

Zane cleared his throat again and looked back at them as he popped the car door open. "I'll go see about a room."

He left them with Ty in the car, and Ty reached to turn the car off, instantly throwing the car into an otherworldly silence. The chill began to seep into Julian's bones as soon as the heat turned off.

"Can't we at least have some heat while we wait?" Cameron asked, voice wavering.

Ty shook his head. "If we get stuck we'll need to conserve it."

"Stuck? Is that really a possibility?"

"No."

"Yes," Ty said in a louder voice.

"Agent Grady," Julian said through gritted teeth.

"He's not stupid, Cross, he deserves the truth."

"Not from you," Julian growled, barely able to rein in his temper. What it was about Ty that caused him to lose control so easily, he could not fathom.

"Well, he's sure as hell not getting it from you."

"I'm… I'm sitting right here," Cameron muttered.

"What do you think your boyfriend does, Jacobs?" Ty asked him, his hazel eyes seeming to pierce right through the mirror as he looked at Cameron.

Cameron swallowed hard. "He deals in antiques."

Ty snorted and shook his head, muttering to himself as he looked out into the wall of white around them. Occasionally they could see the motel's sign, the neon like a beacon of salvation amidst the world of white. But the chill and the silence were still oppressive.

Julian stared into the falling snowflakes, reflected blue in the moonlight, clamping down on the angry words running through his mind, trying to remain outwardly calm, for his own sake as much as Cameron's.

The passenger door popped open, and Zane stuck his head in. His hair was wet with melting snow, and his shoulders were covered with flakes. "We got the last room at the inn."

"Must be our lucky day," Ty muttered as he got out of the car and both doors slammed.

Julian met Cameron's eyes.

"I'll die before anything happens to you," he promised.

"That's what I'm afraid of," Cameron whispered.

"WE LOST them," Agent X reported to his superior without emotion.

"What do you mean, you lost them? How can you lose two FBI agents with a prisoner who don't know they're being tailed?"

"I believe we need to consider the possibility that they've caught wind of us," Agent X said. "They went through security at Midway like they were supposed to, but I believe they caused a commotion in order to flee. We never picked them up at O'Hare, and we later got reports of an FBI sedan being stolen. The GPS tracking on the sedan has been disabled. They're avoiding official channels, zigzagging and scrambling. It's classic maneuvering."

His superior sighed. "Yes, it would appear they know we're after them."

"We picked up their trail when they used a credit card at a hotel in Portage, Indiana. And again when they got on the toll road. They're trying to make the trip overland."

"That seems imprudent, to go to all that trouble and then use a credit card."

"I said they know we're after them, not that they're particularly smart. But we lost them again when they took an unexpected detour off the toll road into Michigan."

"Michigan."

"Yes, sir. Michigan."

"What's in Michigan?"

"Snow."

"What?

"A lot of snow."

"I see. Find them, understand? Our one true advantage was the element of surprise. I know Richard Burns, he's not an idiot. If he knows we're coming, make no mistake, he's put his best operatives on this. Whatever they're doing, it has a purpose. Julian Cross cannot make it to DC. Do what you have to."

"I understand, sir."

RICHARD BURNS sat in his darkened office, eyes on a computer monitor, brow furrowed. Years ago he had installed a special tracking device in Ty Grady's wristwatch for times like this. Ty could turn it on and off at will and only employed it when he was working a special assignment or in trouble, if he was able. Burns could also ping it remotely when he needed to. It was on now. Ty had turned it on moments after getting Burns' initial call.

His signal had popped up just west of Philadelphia, Pennsylvania, and made its way to Chicago just as Ty had been ordered. Now it was near the state line of Michigan and Indiana, holding steady.

Burns didn't understand why. Jonas exited the private washroom in Burns' office, having just showered, and he came to stand over Burns' shoulder, watching the computer screen in consternation.

"Why are they heading north? Are they evading someone?"

Burns shook his head and clicked a button that moved the grid onto one of two flat-screen televisions on the panel on the far wall. "They would have called in if they'd picked up anyone following them or run into trouble."

"Are you sure?"

"Yes."

Burns glanced at the other television on the wall, displaying a map from Weather Underground. Massive snowstorms were moving across the Great Lakes, the same weather system Burns had warned Ty and Zane about that morning. It was much more massive than he had thought, and Burns narrowed his eyes at the screen again. With the two maps side by side, it was apparent what was going on.

Ty was lost in the snow. Burns found himself smiling fondly, a laugh escaping as he rubbed at the bridge of his nose.

"What?"

"He's lost. Probably has no idea he's in Michigan."

"Lost? Does your man know how important this op is?"

"It doesn't matter whether I send him to Chicago to retrieve a wet works operative or to Kentucky to get me some goddamned fried chicken, he does his job and he does it well."

Jonas, of course, knew Ty Grady. He'd known Ty since he was born. But Jonas didn't know Ty was the one Burns had sent on this mission, and he didn't plan to tell Jonas that either, not unless he had to.

Burns had also debated over the benefits of telling Ty and Zane what they were getting into, and in the end he had decided it was best to leave them need-to-know. He didn't know who had followed Jonas' steps here or who had ears on him, and in the end, the less they knew, the less likely they were to be killed if they were captured.

Burns also knew that if they were aware of the whole story, they would fight and die for a cause that wasn't theirs simply because Ty would do anything for Jonas, just like he'd do anything for Burns or his father. Burns couldn't let that happen. Jonas was practically family—a man Ty knew and respected as a dear friend of his father—but Burns wouldn't risk Ty or Zane for him. Better they be innocent bystanders, blindly following orders, than complicit in what was happening.

Jonas looked at him for a long minute, then nodded and turned away. His hand moved to the pocket where he'd been keeping that burner phone, a nervous gesture Burns had noticed more than once.

"Do you want someone to get in touch with Trish?" Burns asked, recognizing the restless maneuvering of a husband who was beyond late for dinner.

Jonas shook his head. "The less she knows, the better."

Burns nodded. It was the mantra of every dark operative in history.

He looked back at the screen, a stab of guilt going through him as he stared at the blue dot that was Ty and Zane. Those boys had given up too much for this kind of work. Far too much.

They had stopped moving, and Burns guessed they had bedded down in the blizzard despite the early hour. A blizzard wouldn't stop the men coming after them once the CIA caught their scent, though. Nor would it stop Julian Cross.

~Chapter 8~

THEY had the honeymoon suite. Two rooms with the bedroom in the back, no windows, and one door in and out. To escape that bedroom, you had to go through the other half of the suite. It was so perfect that Zane was afraid to find out what the catch was.

As soon as they entered the room, Zane went to the heater and cranked it up. Cameron kept his head down, fleeing for the bathroom. He was upset, but Zane couldn't blame him.

Ty escorted Julian through the room to the bedroom, Zane trailing behind them to help secure Julian to whatever they could find. Ty had fished a handful of bungee cords out of the trunk with something close to unholy glee.

"Antiques dealer, huh?" Ty asked Julian, voice laced with amusement and contempt as he tossed his jacket onto the bed. He was still irritable and tense from the drive, and the target of his ire appeared to be Julian. Zane wondered what had been said in the car when he was gone to up the level of animosity between them.

"Yes."

"That's original."

"I don't strive to be original."

"And the kid?" Ty asked.

"What about him?" Julian asked, shoulders stiff.

Zane looked up at his partner as he flipped through channels on the muted television, trying to find the Weather Channel and wondering what it was about Julian Cross that annoyed Ty so. Ty had told him that parts of Julian reminded him of Zane. Well, parts of Ty and Julian reminded Zane of the way he and Ty had treated each other when they first met. The tension was palpable, but there was an added layer to it that Zane really didn't want to ponder.

"You know you're going to get him killed, dragging him all over the place like this."

"I wouldn't say *I'm* dragging him anywhere," Julian said, utterly calm.

"He has no idea what you do or who you are. You're doing nothing but putting him in danger," Ty said. "You really think he'd come willingly if he knew the truth about you?"

"Yes. And sometimes it's safer that way."

"Safer, my ass. Ignorance is not bliss, you know."

Cameron chose that moment to step out of the bathroom, unaware that he was the subject of their conversation.

Julian looked Ty up and down. "Are you telling me you've never lied to a loved one?"

Ty raised his eyebrows and shook his head, an entirely insolent look that would have made Zane want to smack him if it had been aimed at him.

"You've never kept something from your partner to keep him safe?" Julian asked, voice growing colder.

"No, I haven't," Ty answered without a moment's hesitation.

Julian's eyes narrowed, and he took a step closer. He and Ty were too close now. Close enough that they couldn't even look each other up and down without leaning away. Cameron shot Zane a nervous glance, and Zane stood, tensing.

Julian's voice was low and mocking when he spoke to Ty. "You've never lied to someone to keep them safe? Wife? Mother? Boyfriend?"

"No," Ty said, not reacting to Julian's last word.

"Fine, you've never done it. I'll believe that out of someone like you. But have you ever lied to someone you loved because you were following orders, Special Agent Grady?"

Ty didn't flinch, didn't react in any way other than a jump in the muscles of his jaw. "No." His voice had dropped dangerously.

The hair on the back of Zane's neck began to prickle because he knew damn well that was a lie, and Ty had managed it seamlessly.

Julian narrowed his eyes. They stood toe to toe, glaring evilly at each other, neither willing to cross that line and attack, whether verbally or physically. Zane stood back, watching them through wide eyes. He had no desire whatsoever to mix it up with Julian Cross, but if this continued he'd be happy to sit the man down.

"You're an excellent liar, Agent Grady," Julian whispered, his voice deceptively calm and borderline seductive. He leaned just a little closer, close enough he could have touched their noses together. He cocked his head. "You think I don't recognize you? My memory is not as selective as yours."

Zane straightened as Julian's words registered. He looked back and forth between the two men. They knew each other? What the hell?

"Julian, what are you talking about?" Cameron asked.

Looking at Ty, Zane could see that he had stopped breathing and gone still, like a snake about to strike.

Julian continued, his voice disturbingly intimate. "When last I saw you, you were speaking flawless French, plying a wealthy Parisian with drinks, and selling… antiques. Do you remember me now?"

Outwardly Ty didn't react. His face remained impassive and stony, revealing nothing. That alone was enough to tell Zane that what Julian said was the truth. But Zane hadn't picked up on the fact that Ty knew Julian. It must have been at least a few years ago, or Ty would have remembered. And Ty hadn't been to Paris since Zane had known him.

Unless Ty had been to Paris, and did remember, but hadn't let on that he did. A heavy ball of doubt settled in Zane's gut.

"I don't know what you're talking about," Ty finally said.

Julian continued to stare at him, and Ty still hadn't moved. Julian raised his chin, snorting. "What sort of man must it take to make even his eyes lie?" he asked, the words dripping with disdain and scorn. As far as he'd experienced, Zane knew Julian got a good read on people. But what had he seen in Ty to make him say something that cruel?

Ty continued to look at Julian, the anger and combativeness leaching out of his expression to leave him staring impassively. Not only had he gotten control of his temper, it had disappeared. Zane had never seen his partner like this.

"You call me a monster," Julian said, voice low. "At least I know what I am."

"I know what you are you too," Ty whispered back, not acknowledging the hit in any way.

The room fell into tense silence. Zane shifted his eyes toward Ty and waited. But Ty stood staring at Julian, face expressionless and body relaxed. He neither looked Zane's way nor even acknowledged that he and Cameron were there. It was like waiting for two dogs to fight, sensing that they were about to lunge and being helpless to stop it. Zane walked in a half circle to put himself in Ty's line of sight, perhaps six feet away. Until Ty came out of whatever headspace this was, it was better not to get too close.

Julian sensed him moving, and he gave Ty one last disdainful look and moved to sit beside Cameron on the end of the king-size bed.

All three of them watched Ty expectantly, and Ty stood glaring at them all. It was time for some kind of explanation. Zane could imagine Julian making something like that up; it would serve the purpose of driving a wedge of suspicion between Ty and Zane if they began fighting over it. It was a classic psychological technique. But Zane's gut told him that it felt like the truth.

Ty's eyes moved to meet his. His jaw tightened and he squared his shoulders, as if expecting Zane to launch his own attack. Instead, Zane slid one hand into a pocket and held out the other, palm up. He didn't want to fight about it. He just wanted to know; to know if Ty was in danger, to know if they were in danger because of this. As much as being kept in the dark pissed him off, Zane knew better than to demand answers from his lover and partner, especially in front of Julian and Cameron. That was a quick trip to an ass-kicking. Or worse, a stonewalling.

"Go ahead," Ty said, his voice grim.

Zane tried to keep his voice calm. "Do you want to fight? Because I don't. But there's a lot of numbers not adding up, and you know me and numbers."

"I don't want to fight," Ty answered. His eyes shifted to Julian again, a spark of anger in them.

"Then forget about him and focus on me," Zane said, letting his hand start to lower.

Ty looked back and raised his chin. "I swear to you, Zane, I'd never seen him before this case."

"You're a bloody liar," Julian muttered.

When Zane met those hazel eyes, he tried to see what Julian must have seen, but he just didn't. All he saw was the man he knew and loved telling him the truth. Everything in Zane confirmed it. "Then that means he's seen you. In Paris?"

"I've never been to Paris."

"Don't let him lie to you, Agent Garrett," Julian said.

"Shut up," Zane snapped.

Ty lowered his head, but his eyes remained on Zane's. It gave him a predatory look.

Zane knew that Ty was wound up too tight about this for it to be a simple matter. "This is one of those things you can't tell me about. That's crystal clear."

Ty exhaled sharply and turned away, running his hand through his hair as he headed for the door. Ty always aimed for open space when he was agitated, windows and doors and balconies. Like he was making certain he had an escape route. Only now it struck Zane as Ty wanting to get away from him.

Zane took a step to go after him.

Ty swept his hand out and grabbed the lamp off the dresser, then turned, ripping the cord from the base, and threw it against the nearest wall with a wordless shout of frustration that was lost in the shattering of the ceramic.

Zane flinched but didn't move. Julian stood but remained by the bed, where Cameron sat cringing away from the debris. Zane took a step toward them. It registered with him that he was afraid of what Ty was going to do, because Zane couldn't tell, and he'd gotten pretty adept at that. This was just one of so many unspoken truths between them. Maybe Ty feared them as much as Zane did.

"Goddammit, Zane!" Ty shouted as he continued to pace like a caged animal. As he ranted he waved one hand in the air, pointing accusingly at Zane and Julian and even Cameron as he did so. "What are the fucking odds of him knowing me? I worked that job for eighteen months without so much as a hint of trouble, and now of all people it's that fucking Irishman that's going to get that cover blown. Why couldn't you have just let me shoot him like I wanted to in the first place?"

Zane's brows rose higher the longer Ty ranted, and that rigid ball in his chest relaxed. If Ty could yell, it would be okay. It always was. What he was saying didn't help Zane feel any better, though. "Nothing's blown."

"Everything is blown! Forget whatever Burns wants with him, Zane! He knows me from Paris, and he just made me as a Fed!"

"Who is he going to tell? Who'll believe him?"

"Hey!" Julian said, affronted.

"Don't borrow trouble. We have enough as it is," Zane continued as he waved a hand at Julian.

Ty was silent; Zane couldn't even hear him breathing.

"Don't consider a year and a half of work thrown away before you know for sure," Zane said. "You're too fucking good at... whatever the hell it is you've been doing... to just chuck it because of one asshole with a bad accent."

"Hey!" Julian repeated.

Zane turned to face him as Julian took a step toward him. He realized their mistake too late. They had let themselves get pulled into an argument and dropped their guard before Julian was fully secured.

He attacked without further warning, launching himself at Zane and knocking them both to the ground. Zane heard Cameron cry out. Julian's body was solid and heavy on his as Zane hit the ground hard. Zane rolled as soon as his back hit the floor, flipping them over and kicking Julian over his head. He barely had time to gain his knees before Julian hit him from behind. They rolled across the floor.

Zane landed on his back again, Julian pinning him. He managed a jab to Zane's ribs, and he pulled his fist back again, aiming for a blow to Zane's temple that was sure to knock out the lights.

Zane flicked a wrist and a knife shot from its sheath. He palmed it, prepared to do real damage to Julian's midsection.

Ty stepped into his vision, catching Julian's fist in one palm before it could land against Zane's face. He twisted Julian's arm, and Julian arched his back and shouted in pain and anger. Ty turned gracefully until he was kneeling behind Julian with one arm wrapped around his neck, the other twisting Julian's hand back and up.

"Stop! Please!" Cameron cried as he stood up and stepped forward.

Zane pushed himself off the floor and grabbed Cameron, holding him back as they both watched Julian struggle against Ty's arms.

Ty clasped his hands together over Julian's shoulder, closing the choke hold as Julian tried to reach his face to find something tender to jab his thumb into. Ty closed his eyes and lowered his head, hiding his face against Julian's neck, making it almost seem intimate. They were too close for Julian to hurt Ty enough to loosen his grip. His elbows landed uselessly on hard muscle, his fists hit Ty's hips instead of his groin. Ty was too heavy and too low for Julian to flip over his shoulder.

Zane realized that Ty was whispering to Julian as he tightened the chokehold. "It's okay, you'll be okay," he was repeating to Julian even as he rendered him unconscious.

"He's killing him!"

"No," Zane said in a hoarse voice.

There was something fascinating and morbidly beautiful about watching it, though. Ty held tight to the larger man, wrapping him up, head bowed and expression calm when he opened his eyes again. It was perhaps the first time Zane had ever seen Ty's eyes go blank like that; he seemed almost meditative. Zen-like.

Julian tried to duck his head, attempting to open his airway, but Ty had closed the hold too quickly. After a few more seconds of struggling, Julian's body went limp. Ty continued to hold him for another few breaths, and then he released him and let him thump to the ground. When he stood he looked up at them, meeting Zane's eyes. Everything about Ty, from his body to the look in his eyes, felt calm and still.

It was like seeing a new person.

"Oh God," Cameron whispered. Zane let him go. He fell on Julian, taking his face between his hands and calling to him.

"He'll be fine," Ty muttered. He stood stock-still, staring at Zane. The stillness was unnerving; Ty was never still. He fidgeted and paced and vibrated and bounced and twitched and rocked when there was no other outlet for all the nervous energy he stored up. But now he was so still it was like looking at a statue.

Zane closed his eyes and counted heartbeats, just breathing, trying to hold onto composure that was cracking. Ty was scaring him, and Zane had no idea what to do about it.

"You're right," Ty said, the words stirring the tension in the air and cutting through it.

Zane blinked his eyes open and raised his head to look at Ty. He was still standing motionless, hands at his sides. He was looking down and his lips were parted, tongue pushing against the corner of his mouth as if he was deep in thought. Zane had seen the expression before, right before copiers started blowing up. He statistically had a very small percentage of heading that off, but Zane didn't know if he was up to it with so much uncertainty suddenly flowing between them.

"Well," Zane said with forced lightness, "the extent of my French is *voulez-vous coucher avec moi* and *ménage à trois*, so I hope you won't consider me a threat."

Ty looked up at him, his expression one of clear calculation. It passed and his shoulders slumped. "Don't be like that, Zane, come on. You had to know the kind of stuff I was up to on some level. And I haven't worked a job since we got assigned together."

Zane sighed. "Of course I did, Ty." He was sure Ty had no idea how much Zane knew about that kind of stuff. He shifted his weight back and forth, trying to shake off the discomfort this entire week had caused.

"Will someone please tell me what just happened?" Cameron shouted, his voice high and wavering.

Ty shook his head, looking down at Cameron and Julian's limp form. "He'll be awake in five minutes."

"What the hell did you do to him?"

"Blood choke. Cut off blood flow to his brain. He'll be fine."

"Ty," Zane said in a whisper.

Ty looked back at him, his expression softening. "I'm sorry."

"I know. Me too."

Ty frowned. "What for?"

Zane shrugged. "Either for letting the secrets go on so long or for pushing about it now, I'm not sure. Either way, it puts you in a bad spot."

"Excuse me, can one of you please help me here!" Cameron said as he lifted Julian's head off the ground.

Ty rolled his eyes and bent to shoo Cameron's hands away. "Zane."

Zane moved closer, bending to help Ty lift the unconscious prisoner onto the bed. The man was solid and a deadweight, way too heavy for his frame. "Jesus, he's made of granite," Zane said in a strained voice.

Ty grunted in agreement as they flopped him onto the bed. "Bungee cords," he said, breathless.

Zane went to get them, and he could hear Cameron's tremulous voice, asking Ty questions and demanding more satisfactory answers than Ty was giving.

"You know if it was you, you'd be trying to escape too!" he was shouting as Zane came back into the room.

Ty's eyes flashed dangerously as he squared his shoulders on Cameron, and Zane stepped between them.

"Cool it. Get comfortable. We'll tie you two up together tonight," he said, hoping the consolation prize would keep Cameron from squawking all night about his "dead" boyfriend. They made a cursory job of tying Julian and Cameron down, then Zane grabbed Ty's elbow and dragged him out of the room.

"Okay, talk," he demanded, unwilling to let it stew any longer.

Ty nodded, and his eyes shifted to the side to glance at the bedroom door before he looked back at Zane. "This is one of the things I wanted to tell you when we got home," he said in a low voice. "It wasn't my call to be able to tell you before. I wanted to, Zane, I don't like keeping secrets. But I couldn't."

"So what's so different about now?"

"Well, for one, I wasn't the one who spilled it."

"Granted. What about when we got home?"

Ty sighed. "While I was on the road I decided I didn't give a damn anymore. I'm not keeping anything from you from now on. I don't care if it's classified."

Something inside Zane started doing a Snoopy dance at Ty's words. He studied Ty for a long moment before saying, "I trust you."

"I know. That's what made it so hard." He stood there for another moment, leaning forward as if perched on a precipice. Then he shook himself and reached for his gun. He drew it out of its holster and checked the magazine as he strode toward the bedroom. Zane blinked after him for a moment before jumping in front of him. He took Ty by the arm and swung him around, getting between him and the door. "Whoa, Bulldog. That's not going to help." Zane paused. "Well, okay, it would help you feel better. But it wouldn't help the situation here and now, and it certainly wouldn't help any situation later."

"I disagree," Ty said in a calm voice.

"I am sure you do," Zane said, keeping one hand on Ty's forearm, not holding, not squeezing.

"I'm not going to kill him, Zane, just threaten them both until I feel better."

"That's a relief, but please listen. You would have to shoot his ass to kingdom come to scare him when he wakes up, and then we'd have a worse mess. Can't we just… settle this first, and then you can deal with him about the other? Hell, maybe that's why Burns wants him to begin with! Maybe that's why he sent you."

Ty stared at him mutinously for a long moment, long enough that Zane began to suspect his gentle persuasion might not work.

But then Ty rolled his eyes and sighed, sliding his gun back home. "Yeah, okay," he mumbled. Zane felt his heart start back up, and he sagged against the wall as Ty glanced around the room and spoke. "I need to put a call into Burns. This just went over our pay grade."

"Okay," Zane said, regretting the need for Ty to go anywhere right then. "Say hi to him for me."

Ty turned away from him with a nod, going to grab his coat off the bed. He was almost to the door when he stopped and turned. "Zane. Nothing else has been a lie."

Zane nodded. He wasn't sure he'd say Ty had lied to him at all—Zane didn't consider lies of omission lies—but he didn't want to get into a long, circular logic puzzle with Ty, of all people. His head would explode.

"Be careful."

Ty stood there for a heartbeat longer; then he advanced on Zane just like Julian had on him earlier. He took Zane's face between his hands and he kissed him, pushing him back against the wall and holding him there, his lips demanding against Zane's. Then it was over as suddenly as it had begun, Hurricane Ty passing by. When he stepped back again, he jerked his head in a nod. Then he turned and headed for the door.

"WHAT do you mean you know he knows me?" Ty asked Burns in outrage.

"Of course I know he knows you! Why do you think I sent you after him? He's listed as a possible contact on one of your old jobs."

Burns could hear Ty making a sputtering noise on the other end of the line that may or may not have been a minor hissy fit.

"You dealt with him in France!"

"No."

"Yes. I have the reports. His name was different, but this is the same guy. Julian Cross is a CIA codename. You worked together!"

"No! Dick! I have never seen this man in my life! I would remember that!"

Burns frowned, confused. Ty sounded genuinely upset and offended. "I don't understand," he muttered.

"Well join the fucking club!" Ty hollered on the other end of the line. "The guy from Paris that I worked with, the guy in that report, was a French guy, six one, white-blond hair. He was not a six-foot-five asshole Irishman!"

"That complicates things."

Burns could hear another series of sounds, culminating in a string of curses.

"Are you sure the man you have is Julian Cross?"

"I don't know, Dick, he doesn't have a fucking bar code I can scan!"

"This doesn't change your objective," Burns tried in a loud, authoritative voice, trying to pull Ty back on point. "You still need to get him to DC, understand?"

"Why?" Ty demanded in frustration. "What's this really about?"

Burns hesitated. "Need-to-know."

"Oh my God."

"Do whatever you have to do to get Cross here alive."

Ty was mutinously silent. Finally, Burns heard him exhale, a bid for calm. "Yes, sir," he said in a soft, composed voice.

ZANE sat watching Julian, waiting for him to wake and thinking about Ty and what had just happened. Zane had never seen his partner, his lover, react to violence in such a cold and calculating way. It was a new side to Ty. Was that how he'd been able to handle himself all these years, by simply turning off his emotion and essentially finding a happy place when he worked? Zane shook his head. He tried not to dwell on what it would take to do that.

When Ty came back from making his call, he found Zane in the bedroom and stood at his side, looking down at the two men on the bed. They had used the twisted bungee cords to tie Julian down and handcuffed Cameron to him to give them just enough contact to keep them from trying to escape when Julian awoke. Not that they'd go far in a blizzard.

Cameron had his nose buried against the back of Julian's shoulder and was looking up at them with one eye and hiding the other.

"Every time you two try something, it's one more bullet I put in his head in my dreams," Ty told Cameron. This time, Zane knew he wasn't acting.

Julian groaned. Cameron nodded, eyes wide. He scooted closer to Julian, looking genuinely upset.

"He'll be okay," Zane felt compelled to say. "He'll wake up in a few minutes."

Ty was already moving away from the bed and into the outer room. Zane stopped to turn the television to a different channel for Cameron before he followed, wondering what sort of damage control was needed here.

"I thought you were going to kill him back there."

Ty turned to face him. "Next time I will," he said, his voice cold and determined.

A shiver ran down Zane's spine, and he had to admit, a part of him liked it. "What is it about him that gets you so riled?"

"It's not him, Zane. It's you."

"Me? What'd I do?"

"He is a threat to both of us. You've seen what he's capable of, and I have to tell you, I don't think he's trying yet. I think he's just a fucking raptor testing the fences. When I look at him, I see him hurting you."

Zane's chest twisted in a way that wasn't unpleasant. He knew that feeling, being so protective and so desperate to keep his loved ones safe that it clouded his world. "I'm not worried."

"No?"

"I've got you here watching my back," Zane said with a serene smile. He didn't think he'd felt so calm inside in years. "And I've got yours."

Ty took a deep breath as he looked into Zane's eyes. Zane wondered what Ty saw when he looked into him like that. One day he would ask him.

"Okay," Ty finally said on a deep exhale.

"We've got a couple hours to wind down, get some real sleep." Zane waved his hand at the pullout couch.

Ty nodded, his movements not nearly as jerky or tense. He seemed to be coming to terms with what Zane had said, trying to assimilate it. "I'll be there in a minute. I just need a quick shower," he said as he pulled off his shirt and headed for the bathroom. The shower began running a moment later.

Zane turned and shut the bedroom door behind him. There was no telling when the storm would break. More privacy and space was better than less with the combined personalities in this little escapade.

He took the time to pull the couch out; then he went to the bedroom and stood beside the bed, looking down at the two men. Julian was awake, and he stared up at him evilly, his dark eyes glazed. Zane reached to take his pulse, checking it against his watch to make sure it was fast enough.

"You'll live," he muttered.

"He won't," Julian whispered.

Zane stared at him, investigating the feeling the threat gave him. He found himself smiling. "I look forward to your next attempt. He'll tear you apart."

Julian didn't respond, and Zane couldn't read him. He left the prisoners, closing the door and balancing one of the glasses from the small wet bar on the doorknob. Then he sought out his partner in the shower.

After watching Ty through the wavering plastic for a long moment, Zane reached out and pushed open the curtain. Ty jerked when the shower curtain squealed on its hooks. It was obvious that Zane had startled him, which was an unusual occurrence in itself. Zane stripped as Ty watched him, then stepped inside and closed the curtain behind him. Moving close, he raised a hand and slid it through Ty's hair, sluicing the water drops away.

Ty raised his head and lifted his face toward the ceiling. "Hey."

Zane didn't want to talk about what had happened. He didn't want anything but his lover to be relaxed and normal—as "normal" as Ty got, anyway. "Are you really okay?"

"Yeah, just… there are some things I need to tell you, Zane. And I want you to know from me, not by finding out from someone else like this. But I can't… I'm just wrestling with what's more important to me, my integrity or… you."

Zane blinked at him, taken aback by the subject. He'd thought Ty had been bothered by the fight. He'd had no idea this was what Ty had been thinking. But then, Zane supposed that was part of Ty's charm, the jumbled ball of yarn inside his brain that no one could unravel.

He took a deep breath to steady himself. "I think you need to go with what you can sleep with at night."

"It's you, Zane."

Zane smiled wanly as he reached for the soap. "I don't mean fuck at night, I mean sleep with. Whatever keeps your mind at rest."

"I know what you meant."

Zane's heart did a happy skip as he met Ty's eyes. He would never get tired of moments like this, when Ty proved beyond a shadow of a doubt that Zane was the most important thing in his world. "Tell me?"

Ty licked his lips, watching Zane even as the water beat down on them both. For once his expression wasn't guarded when Zane started asking questions. "Burns uses me on jobs he can't put the Bureau on but the CIA doesn't list as priority. We call them Misfits."

Zane nodded, licking his lips.

"And I know that he used to use you the same way."

Zane's eyes shot up to meet Ty's, wide and shocked. Ty was looking at him, holding his breath. He nodded. "How?"

"Jack Tanner."

"Jack Tanner told you?" Zane asked, aghast. Jack Tanner had been one of his instructors in the academy. He had single-handedly prevented Zane from dropping out and turned him into the agent he had become.

"No," Ty said. "You told me he used to eat dinner at your house."

"Yeah?" Zane said, confused.

"That's how he pulled me too. And then knowing what I do about Burns and the way he treats you… I put two and two together."

Zane's mouth was dry as he stared at Ty. "How… Jesus, Ty. Why didn't you say something?"

Ty shook his head. "You've had so much trouble with your past and getting over it," he murmured as he let his hands snake around Zane's back. "I'd rather you live in the present."

Zane swallowed hard. Ty was right, for the most part. Those were days he didn't want to relive.

"I'm not asking to talk about it. I just figure it's out there now. It's not something we need to hide or skirt around anymore."

Zane nodded, feeling dizzy. He couldn't believe Ty had put that together with so little to go on, but then he supposed Ty never did get enough credit for being as smart as he was. "Okay."

"Okay."

Zane leaned over enough to catch Ty's lips in a gentle kiss. It didn't last long. "I know you love me. And you know I love you. The rest will wait a little longer."

"Feels good to say that, doesn't it?"

Zane dragged one finger along Ty's lower lip. "Yeah. And I intend to keep saying it. Often."

Ty smiled wanly, but then he looked away as if he was struggling with what to say next. Or perhaps wrestling with a difficult decision.

"Tell me?" Zane murmured as he rubbed Ty's back, trying to soothe him. It was like working with a spooked horse, and it had been decades since Zane had tried to rein one in.

Ty hesitated before sighing. "Burns sent me—us—because he thought I knew Cross," he said in a low, tense voice. "It was in a report that he was a contact from a Paris job six years ago."

"Yeah?"

"He wasn't working under the name Julian Cross, but that's the name the CIA put in the file. I'm telling you right now, though, the man from Paris was not Cross. Not this Cross, anyway."

Zane frowned, mulling that over. "So either who we have isn't the original Cross, or the CIA guy you worked with said he was Cross but wasn't."

"We know our Cross is connected somehow, because he knew me," Ty said.

"Yeah. I don't know. Maybe he's like the Dread Pirate Roberts."

Ty looked at Zane warily.

Zane nodded and cocked his head at Ty. "What?"

"I'm just waiting for you to bust out the 'double cross' pun so we can get it over with."

One corner of Zane's lips curled up. "Want me to come up with one real quick?"

"No. Stop it."

Zane laughed and pressed his lips to Ty's cheek. Ty's body was still tense against his, and Zane could feel that there was still more his lover wanted to say. He reached up to put his hand against Ty's cheek, looking into his eyes, feeling that tangle of warmth spread in his chest like it always did when Ty looked at him like that. "What else, baby?"

Ty shook his head and wrapped his arms around Zane's neck instead, kissing him messily. They were still kissing when the water began to cool and Ty pulled away to meet Zane's eyes.

"We'll drop these two bozos off, then disappear for a night or two between DC and home, okay?" he whispered. "I'll tell you everything you want to know. And I'll make it up to you for bolting."

Zane nodded and smiled, fighting down his racing pulse as he looked into Ty's eyes. Now that was something to really look forward to.

~Chapter 9~

"WHAT mile marker are we near?" Zane asked as he peered at the map they'd bought that morning.

"129.3," Ty answered without cracking a smile or taking his eyes off the road.

Zane glanced at him and rolled his eyes. He set the map on the floorboard and took up his crossword puzzle book. A moment later they came upon a green mile marker. It read Mile 130.

Cameron watched it pass, and then leaned sideways to look at Ty in the rearview mirror. "How are you doing that?"

"Doing what?" Ty asked in a bored voice.

Cameron huffed and glanced at Julian, who was watching Ty with one eyebrow raised.

Ty tried to hide his smirk. He'd been doing it for a solid hour, and not one of them had managed to figure out how. Ty was once again behind the wheel, trying not to zone out as the road stretched out before them in a seemingly endless roll of pavement, snow, and Holiday Inns.

"He's either doing complex math equations in his head, or he's got GPS embedded in his ass," Zane muttered.

Cameron huffed and Ty allowed himself to grin. He glanced at Zane, his only real source of amusement, and he smirked as he turned his attention to the road.

"Okay, here's a quiz," he said. "It was the last set of questions they asked before I got accepted for Recon."

Zane looked up from his crossword puzzle to give Ty a sideways glance. "Are you this bored?" he asked in a knowing tone.

Ty shrugged. "Just trying to pass the time."

"I live to be your favorite source of entertainment," Zane drawled. "What are the questions?"

Ty glanced at him again, raising an eyebrow. Zane gave him an innocent look. Ty huffed at him, but he was still smiling when he asked the first question. "How do you put a giraffe in a refrigerator?"

Cameron groaned in the backseat. "If the answer involves knives I want out of the car."

Zane tipped his head to the side, his brows drawn together. He opened his mouth to reply, paused and narrowed his eyes at Ty, then hummed. "Open the door and stuff it in."

Ty glanced at him, trying to hide his smile. "Very good. How do you put an elephant in a refrigerator?"

Zane leaned his head back against the headrest as he drummed his fingers on his thigh. "I feel like this is a trick question. Same answer, though."

Ty was shaking his head. "You have to take the giraffe out first." He glanced in the rearview mirror at their prisoners. Julian was watching them, head cocked as he listened. Ty continued. "The Lion King is hosting an animal convention. All the animals attend except one. Which one is it?"

"Oh Lord," Zane said under his breath as he shook his head and looked out the window. A soft laugh from behind them drew his attention, and he looked over his shoulder to see Cameron biting his lip, trying not to smile.

Zane wrinkled his nose and looked back at Ty. "It's like those tests in grade school with a whole long list of questions to answer, and all you had to do was get to question three, sign your name, and turn it in."

"What's the answer?" Ty asked all of them.

"I refuse to participate on the grounds that I hate you both," Julian murmured.

"I feel like I should know this," Zane said under his breath.

"Is it the animal the Lion King is serving for dinner?" Cameron asked, a wry undertone to his voice.

Ty shook his head.

"The elephant isn't there," Julian finally said in an irritated voice. "Because you just stuffed it into the refrigerator."

"That's right," Ty said as he tried not to smile. "Last question. There's a river you have to cross that's patrolled by crocodiles, and you don't have a boat. How do you get across?"

"Ask the crocodile for a ride," Cameron said.

Ty shook his head.

"Swim," Zane said instead.

Ty turned his chin and looked at him for his reasoning.

"What about the crocodiles?" Cameron asked.

"The crocodiles aren't there. They're at the convention," Zane said with a shrug, and Cameron scowled at him.

Ty grinned before looking back at the road.

"You realize those are questions they ask schoolchildren to test their reasoning skills, yes?" Julian provided sardonically.

Ty nodded, still grinning.

"So did you get them all right when they asked you?" Zane asked.

"No," Ty answered. "For their purposes, you weren't supposed to get them right. They said they accepted me because my answers were wrong but precisely what they wanted to hear."

"I'm sure I cannot imagine what you came up with," Zane said, shaking his head. "You figured I'd pick it apart logically. Which is the total opposite of what you do."

"I wasn't sure what you'd do," Ty told him fondly.

"If you'd asked the last question first? I'd have said shoot the crocodiles," Zane admitted.

Ty shook his head, smiling.

"Grady's answer was build a bridge," Julian murmured from the back seat.

Ty looked up at the mirror, surprised. "That's right."

"How'd you know that, Julian?" Cameron asked.

Julian looked up, meeting Ty's eyes in the mirror. "Because it's what I would have said."

"How sweet," Zane muttered.

Ty's eyes lingered on the mirror before he was able to tear his attention away and focus on the road again. He shifted in his seat, unsettled and wishing he'd never said anything.

"What mile are we at now?" Cameron asked.

Ty's gaze darted to the side of the road, seeking out a structure. They came upon an overpass, and he found one of the tiny blue signs he'd noticed that told the mile to the exact decimal. "142.7."

A few seconds later, they came upon another mile marker.

"How the hell is he doing that?" Cameron asked as Zane chuckled.

Ty looked into the mirror, only to find Julian's dark eyes already watching him. He could tell that Julian knew exactly how he was doing it.

"How'd you two end up together, anyway?" Zane asked, oblivious to Ty's sudden discomfort and Julian's eyes boring a hole into his soul.

"I was his waiter," Cameron answered.

"How… romantic," Ty said as he honestly tried to find a more appropriate word.

"It was," Cameron murmured.

Ty and Zane shared a look. Ty supposed no one would call the way they met romantic either. Love was love, though. Ty wanted desperately to reach out to Zane and touch him. He refrained, tightening his fingers on the steering wheel instead.

"He's the most important thing in my life," Julian said, his low voice echoing what Ty was thinking.

"How did that happen?" Zane asked.

Julian raised one finger, all the movement Ty's method of restraint allowed him. "Love isn't a gentle thing. I've found it carries a club and a bullwhip and doesn't care when or who it strikes."

"My knight in shining plate armor," Cameron murmured.

Zane didn't try to hold back his soft laugh, though it trailed off. Ty glanced over to find Zane looking at him wistfully. "Kind of like getting pushed off a cliff," he said without taking his eyes off Ty.

Julian was silent for a moment, merely watching Ty and Zane. Observing them. "I don't consider it a problem. Loving Cameron is easy. He's the reason I try so very hard every day not to be killed," he said with a hint of what might have been humor.

"And the danger it puts him in?"

"I almost lost him to it when I tried to shield him from it," Julian answered unflinchingly, not even hesitating to say the words as Cameron watched him. "I kept things from him, things I knew would scare him. When he found out the true dangers of being with me, he was indeed scared and angry with me for keeping them secret, and he sent me away. We got a second chance. Now we deal in truth. He is his own man, he makes his own decisions. My conscience is clear on that note."

"Except when he's about to freeze to death in a blizzard," Ty murmured while trying to ignore the sword chopping at his own conscience.

"Ty," Zane whispered, shaking his head.

Ty huffed at him.

It was a few minutes before Zane finally asked, "How did you know that you loved him?"

"Difficult to say," Julian answered thoughtfully. "A number of things, really. The biggest, however, was the excruciating pain it caused me to think of life without him in it."

Cameron was smiling, watching Julian like he was the only thing in the world.

Julian laughed. "Something that torturous can only be love."

Zane snorted, carefully avoiding looking at Ty.

"I see you're familiar with it," Julian observed drily.

Ty glanced at Zane again, unable to keep his lips from curving into a smile.

"Yeah," Zane said as he turned around and eased back into his seat. "Yeah, I'm familiar with it."

Ty pulled the FBI sedan into the parking lot of the Commodore Perry Travel Plaza just as the sun was setting. It wasn't snowing, but even on the Ohio turnpike there was at least six inches of snow, and when the frigid wind kicked up, the top dusting flew in their faces and stung anything that wasn't covered.

They bowed their heads as they fought through the cold to the brand-new travel plaza building. It was mostly empty inside, with lots of open lobby space in a hexagonal shape around a center convenience shop.

Zane held tighter to Julian's arm.

"Ooh, Starbucks," Cameron said as he leaned toward the row of shops to their right.

"I thought they over roasted their beans," Ty grumbled.

Cameron snorted.

"I'd like to get some gum or something," Julian said to Zane as Ty led Cameron toward the restrooms.

Zane glanced at him and hummed as he studied the narrow aisles of the convenience store. "Try anything in there and I'll put you down."

Julian gave him a single nod.

Zane walked him over to the store, giving the restrooms a last glance. He and Julian meandered through the aisles of the convenience store, Zane watching Julian and Julian looking for something he didn't seem to be finding. When he reached for a pack of gum, his linked hands knocked over an entire row of condom and tampon boxes.

Julian cursed under his breath, glancing at the clerk as he lifted his hands to show Zane that they were empty. Zane sighed and glanced at the clerk as well. She was watching them with a wary frown. Zane waved at her and smiled, and when he looked back at Julian, the man was stooping to pick up the boxes. Zane watched his movements closely, making certain he wasn't doing anything nefarious. Then he plucked a pack of gum off the rack and led Julian to the desk.

Five minutes and a bathroom break later, they met Ty and Cameron in line for coffee.

"Everything okay?" Ty asked.

Zane spared himself a moment to just stare at his partner. He nodded before Ty could grow worried. They locked eyes, and Ty began to smile before he looked away.

They could not get home soon enough.

They filled the car with gas, Zane letting Julian stand in the cold wind to stretch his legs so he'd stop complaining, and then they hit the road again. An hour later they were closing in on Cleveland. Zane watched the Erie County water tower pass by, and he realized he was growing drowsy. He rubbed at his eyes and glanced at Ty.

"You doing okay?"

Ty jerked his head to the side and nodded. "Couple more hours we'll get something to eat, some caffeine. I think we can get to DC tonight if we both drive."

Zane nodded.

"Sleep," Ty whispered. "I'll wake you when it's your turn."

"Aw. That's sweet," Julian said in a wry voice.

Ty and Zane both ignored him.

Zane reached to lay his chair back, preferably on top of Julian's head, but as soon as his fingers found the button, the car made a sputtering sound.

Ty raised his hand off the wheel and looked at the gauges.

"What was that?" Cameron asked. The car jerked and began to slow.

Ty managed to get the car off the highway before it died completely. It chugged and grumbled and lurched to a stop. The engine went quiet, throwing the car into the otherworldly silence of a landscape covered with snow.

"What?" Ty said in irritation.

"Did our car just die?" Cameron asked, an edge of panic to his voice. "Are we going to freeze now?"

"Yes," Ty answered as he ran his hand over his chin.

Zane looked around them. The moon was out in full force, reflecting off the blanket of snow. They could see for miles, and it wasn't a comforting view. There was nothing around them. There wasn't even a glow of lights in the night sky that would signify a shopping center or small town within a few miles. "Fucking Ohio," Zane muttered.

Ty exhaled, and the slowly cooling air frosted with his breath. "Cross," he said, voice deceptively calm. "What did you do to it?"

"I haven't touched the vehicle, Agent Grady."

Ty looked at Zane, clenching his jaw. "What did he do in that travel place?"

"Got some gum. Knocked over some condoms. Took a piss, and stood in the cold."

Ty rubbed his eyes, lowering his head. "Did you put a condom in the gas tank?" he asked Julian.

Julian was silent.

"You put a condom in the gas tank."

Zane turned to look back at Julian. "How do you even do that?"

Julian looked away, meeting Cameron's eyes.

"If we start freezing, we're eating Cameron first," Ty grunted before unbuckling his seatbelt and climbing out of the car.

JULIAN had to restrain a smirk as the two FBI agents got out of the car. He could feel the cold seeping through the glass of the windows, and while it wasn't ideal to be stuck where they were, it would have to serve.

"Did you really kill the car?" Cameron asked in a low voice.

"You have to give me some credit for being subversive."

"Yeah, freezing to death in the middle of Ohio really turns me on."

Julian grinned, chuckling as he looked out the window at Ty and Zane. They stood at the front of the car, Zane calm as he spoke, Ty gesticulating wildly instead of using words. They were discussing something quite heatedly.

"What are they fighting about?"

Julian could take his guesses. "I would say Grady wants to shoot me. Garrett is telling him no, too much paperwork. Then Grady will move on to how to get help. Garrett will suggest calling for a rental, Grady will be more… illegal, and likely want to go steal one."

Cameron laughed.

"Listen, Cam. When I make my move, I want you to aim for the pressure points like I taught you and then run."

"Julian."

"I'm serious, love. These men are delivering us to our end. Either I'll be killed, or I'll be conscripted back into service, and either way, you won't be allowed to come with me. Do you understand?"

Cameron met his eyes, swallowing hard as he nodded.

Julian let his eyes linger on his lover for a few moments, and then looked back at Ty and Zane. To his surprise, Ty had turned and was walking off across the white field of snow toward a side road on the other side of a fence.

"I'll be damned," he whispered as he watched Ty put a hand on a fencepost and leap over the barbed wire.

"What?"

"He's leaving."

The front door popped open and Zane slid into the passenger seat. He brought a gust of cold air with him before he shut the door.

"You're just going to let him walk off into the snow?" Cameron asked.

"He'll be back," Zane assured them, as calm and steady as ever.

Julian looked from him to the retreating figure of his partner in the distance. This hadn't gone to plan at all. Julian had anticipated a rental being called, exchanging vehicles, the two agents being distracted and irritated enough that he could get the drop on them as he was transferred. He hadn't expected Ty to storm off into the darkness alone.

"Agent Garrett, while I don't pretend to particularly like your partner, I have to express some concern over this plan."

"Your concern is noted," Zane said, his voice stilted and curt.

"It's below freezing out there, Garrett."

"Julian," Cameron whispered.

Julian glanced at him and licked his lips, trying to force his shoulders to relax. He wanted to get away, but he didn't want to be responsible for the death of either of these men. They were only doing as they'd been ordered, just like Julian had done for so many years.

Zane turned his head to look back at them. "If either of you knew Ty like I do, you'd be more worried about us freezing than him."

An hour later, a pair of headlights flashed behind them, rousting all of them from a cold-induced doze. Julian craned his neck to watch the car approach. It slowed as it neared them, revealing itself to be a truck or SUV of some sort. Julian would have guessed it was an older vehicle from the shape of the headlights. The driver flashed the lights again before pulling up behind their sedan. The lights didn't shut off, and Julian could barely make out the figure that stepped out of the SUV and walked toward them.

Ty opened the driver's side door and ducked in to look at them. "Got us a ride," he said, voice hoarse and gruff.

Zane got out of the car and slammed the door. The trunk opened, and Julian could feel them removing things from the back to transfer. Julian flexed his fingers, trying to get the blood pumping. If they could catch Ty and Zane by surprise now, after the effects of the cold had made them slower and less aware, then they might be able to take whatever vehicle Ty had found and make a clean getaway.

His fingers were stiff and cold. His whole body was. He also realized, somewhat belatedly, that his mind wasn't working at full speed either. Ty and Zane weren't the only ones who'd gotten cold and sleepy.

"Shit."

"What?" Cameron asked, his voice sluggish.

"I'm afraid my plan has backfired. I didn't expect the exchange to take so long."

"Are you cold?" Cameron whispered.

The trunk slammed. Julian turned his head just in time to see Ty and Zane standing in the light of the headlights, Zane's hands on Ty's face. For a brief moment, Julian thought they were kissing. He closed his eyes and shook his head. When he opened his eyes again, Zane was merely feeling Ty's cheeks, apparently to check that he was warm.

"I believe... I might be hallucinating," Julian muttered as he tried to shift enough to get his blood flowing.

Cameron didn't respond, he merely looked at Julian, his eyes glazing over. The door popped open at Julian's elbow, and Ty reached in to unlock his handcuffs. Ty pulled him out of the car, and the blast of cold was enough to make Julian gasp.

"Cold, isn't it?" Ty asked through gritted teeth as he pushed Julian chest-first against the sedan.

Julian waited until Zane had freed Cameron. Then he rammed his elbow into Ty, catching him on the chin. Ty stumbled back and Julian turned, finally having gotten the drop on the man. He swung at him and Ty leaned away from his fist, dodging the blow. Instead of squaring against him to prepare for the brawl, Ty lunged at him. He jumped, turning sideways in the air, kicking out at Julian. He wrapped his arm around Julian's neck. One foot went between Julian's legs, the other on the outside of his knee. Then he wrenched his body sideways as he fell, wrapping Julian up and taking him to the ground.

By the time they hit the snow, Julian was completely immobilized, his legs tangled in Ty's, in a headlock as he struggled to free himself.

"Ty!"

"We're okay," Ty called back, his voice freakishly calm as Julian tried to find a pressure point or *something* to fight back with. "Get the kid in the car. I need your help."

Julian gritted his teeth. "Why is an ex-Recon Marine trained in Russian Sambo?"

Ty didn't answer, merely tightened his hold on Julian so he couldn't speak as they both shivered with the cold seeping into them.

ZANE hastily secured Cameron in the sedan before rushing over to the other side of the car, his gun drawn.

Both men were on the ground, Ty wrapped around Julian and restraining him with his body. It looked a little too much like they were spooning.

Zane grumbled under his breath and bent over them. "Quit messing around. I'm freezing," he told them, and then he put the muzzle of his gun to Julian's forehead and grabbed him by his collar.

They stood him up, Zane keeping his gun on him as Ty bullied him over to the other vehicle.

Zane didn't know where Ty had found the old Bronco II, but Zane was glad he had. Ty used every bit of bungee cord, rope, and handcuffs they had to strap Julian down in the back of the Bronco. Then they moved Cameron over and tied him down too.

When they were finally all in the car, the heat chugging, Zane felt like he could breathe easily again. He glanced at Ty.

"Where did you find this thing?" he asked, unable to keep from being amused.

"Old barn near that water tower we passed. It had a cracked cylinder head. I found one to replace it in a Ranger nearby and hotwired it. It won't go far, but it'll get us to a hotel."

Zane stared at him for a second before glancing behind them. Both of their prisoners were tied down, blocked by the rear seat. Zane reached out and set his hand on Ty's thigh, squeezing. "Nicely done," he whispered.

Ty set his hand on Zane's, letting their fingers lace together. He looked at Zane and gave him a tense smile. Zane didn't move his hand as they drove on into the night.

"WE FOUND the car, sir," Agent X told his boss as he stood on the side of the road in the freezing cold.

"They dumped it?"

"No, sir. It appears it broke down. I suspect the gas tank is the culprit."

"Why?"

"The engine is fine. The car won't start. I believe Cross sabotaged it. They left the keys in it, and there are signs of a struggle on the side of the road. Another car was here, possibly a truck or SUV. I believe they stole the car and switched over."

"Do you have a plan?"

"Yes, sir. They took their toll ticket. They have to have it to get off the highway. As soon as it comes up, we'll know what exit they've taken and we'll go from there."

"Very good. Keep me apprised. We have to get Cross before they deliver him."

"Yes, sir."

~Chapter 10~

Twenty minutes after Ty had dropped them off and told them he was going to stash the stolen car, Ty still wasn't back. How long did it take to dump a broken-down Bronco in rural Macedonia, Ohio? Zane sighed and looked at Cameron, who was sitting uneasily on the other bed, looking toward the bathroom where Ty had left Julian cuffed to the plumbing again.

"Go on," Zane said gruffly, waving a hand toward the bathroom.

Cameron blinked at him and then smiled gratefully. "Thanks," he said, and he hurried to join Julian.

"Leave the door open," Zane said as Cameron disappeared inside. "Just remember I can shoot him before he can get to the door."

Zane took off his jacket and slung it into the sink of the tiny kitchenette before thumping down on the end of the bed. He was tired. This trip was testing his patience. And what the hell was taking Ty so goddamn long?

It was another ten minutes, maybe more, before there was a scratch at the door and Zane heard the key card swipe. Ty pushed into the room, face flushed from the cold, flecks of snow melting on his shoulders. He was carrying a small paper bag.

He looked around the room as he stepped in. "Where are they?"

Zane gritted his teeth and swallowed the sharp remark that was his gut response. "In the bathroom," he said instead.

Ty nodded curtly. "That won't hold him all night," he said, not even bothering to try explaining why walking a mile or two in the snow had taken him nearly an hour to manage. Zane played the whole prospective explanation and resulting argument through in his head and decided to just not go there. Ty had done a lot of walking in the snow tonight.

"Our options are rather limited."

"What have you come up with?" Ty asked. He shrugged out of his coat, then tossed it onto the tiny table between the television and the kitchenette.

"I thought about cuffing him to the underpinning of the bed, but it's junk. He'd probably break it," Zane answered.

Ty stared at him, waiting for him to continue, and Zane resisted the urge to snap at him. Tempers were getting shorter, and it didn't help that they couldn't touch or even speak openly to each other in front of their prisoners. Zane reminded himself to stay calm. "We could attach him to the refrigerator. Even if he did get out, he wouldn't be going anywhere fast."

Ty was nodding slowly as Zane spoke. "How?" he asked in a flat voice.

Zane shrugged, mind churning. "Use his belt and the chill grate? Fasten it behind his back."

"And essentially give him a nice sharp metal weapon when he gets lose," Ty said, sounding disgusted. He picked up the bag he'd been carrying and opened it up to extract a gas station box of Benadryl. He held it up, looking at Zane grimly. "How many of these things would it take to put you down?"

Zane looked at the package, then up at Ty, and it was all too clear how far Ty had been pushed: too far. "Absolutely not. You're not drugging him."

"And he's not smothering one of us in our sleep," Ty said, voice sharp and serious. "I don't know about you, Zane, but I'm tired. I'm too fucking tired, and I'm afraid I'm going to fall asleep tonight, let down my guard, and not wake up."

"That's not going to happen. If you need to sleep, sleep. I can stay awake."

"No, you can't. You are just as exhausted as I am!" Ty tossed the box of Benadryl onto the table and pulled his gun out of its holster to check the clip.

Zane took in a deep breath through his nose, hanging on to his patience with everything he had. "You do need sleep, because you'd never try this in your right mind. Knock him out, tie him up, hell, strip him nude, but you're not drugging him." What if Cross had some crazy reaction to the drugs like Ty often did, and died? Burns would forgive them some surface damage to the asset, but dead wouldn't go over well at all.

Ty rammed the clip home, the noise unmistakable in the otherwise quiet hotel room. "You're right. Plan B then," he said in a deceptively calm voice. He pushed away from the table and headed for the bathroom, gun still in his hand.

Zane wasn't sure what was worse. He was certain—all right, almost certain—Ty wouldn't just shoot Julian. Well, kind of certain. Maybe. "Grady… what are you going to do?" he called, hearing the dread in his own voice.

Ty didn't answer him. Zane heard him push the door open and bark at Cameron to get out. Zane rubbed a hand over his eyes and waited, using the time to list possible worst-case scenarios, the fallout, how much paperwork would be involved, and if any said scenarios would afford him and Ty some peace and quiet sooner rather than later. Now that he thought about it, drugging Cross just a little might not be such a bad idea.

Zane rolled his eyes. He *was* sleep-deprived; just the fact that he had that thought was proof.

Ty grabbed Cameron by the arm and shoved him out into the suite. Zane watched the man stumble into the table, knocking over the box of Benadryl.

"What's going on?" Cameron asked, rubbing his hip.

Zane just shook his head. "Better stay out of the way," he said, jerking a thumb back toward the bed. Cameron nodded, keeping his eyes on the bathroom door.

A moment later Ty dragged Julian out of the bathroom, quite the noisy affair since Julian was threatening Ty with all matter of bodily harm if he touched Cameron again. Zane was pretty sure the only reason Julian didn't fight back was the gun in Ty's hand. Cameron had to hop out of the way as Ty propelled Julian forward and slammed him into the table, shoving at him from behind and pressing his face and chest to the tabletop.

Ty had done that to Zane a few times. Only he'd never pressed a gun barrel to the base of Zane's skull like he did to Julian's right now. It occurred to Zane that he should probably rein Ty in any time now. He was supposed to be the rules lawyer of the two of them, the one who kept his partner from blithely charging into serious trouble.

"You probably shouldn't cripple him," Zane said in place of further caution.

Julian turned his head just enough to meet Zane's eyes. For the first time since they'd picked him up in Chicago, the man looked worried. He didn't look scared like a normal person would be in that situation, but he did seem to be acknowledging that Ty had reached the end of his rope and just might shoot him.

"He'd already freed himself," Ty told Zane through gritted teeth. He was using his entire body to keep Julian pinned under him.

Zane glanced at Cameron, who gave him big, innocent doe eyes. "You're next," he warned the younger man. Cameron shrank back, guilt written all over him.

Ty gave the room one last scathing glance, obviously looking for something to secure Julian to that would keep him the entire night. But Zane knew there was nothing in the room that would alleviate Ty's concern, or his, enough to let them sleep.

Ty knew it too. He reached into his back pocket and pulled out his spare handcuffs, pushing into Julian from behind with the sharp part of his elbow. Julian winced but didn't make a sound as Ty put the handcuffs onto one of his wrists. Ty yanked the arm behind him, and Julian did gasp in complaint as his arm was jerked around.

"You're going to enjoy this about as much as I am," Ty snarled at him. Then he slapped the other half of the cuffs onto his own wrist with a loud clink.

Zane's eyes widened as he fought down a spate of hysterical laughter. What kind of fickle bitch was Karma that they kept getting these insane cases? He was about to comment when Cameron beat him to it.

"What are you going to do? Sleep with him?"

"No, Cam, we're gonna slow dance!" Ty shouted. He tossed his gun to Zane, where Julian couldn't reach it, and he took a step back and jerked Julian's arm to make him stand as well.

Zane caught the weapon out of pure reflex. Out of all the things Ty could have chosen to do, this hadn't made Zane's top ten. He was about to offer a crass comment when the deep shadows under Ty's eyes arrested him, and Zane just nodded his consent.

The way Ty and Julian fought reminded Zane of him and Ty when they'd first met. What had sparked them to go from hating each other like these two did, to loving each other like they did now? Some random tumble of Fate, a fly-by jumble of chance. Zane didn't know, but he thanked God for it every day.

Ty and Julian stood toe to toe, now locked together for the night. Ty held up the keys to the handcuffs so Julian could see them, then tossed them to Zane as well. Zane was tired of having things thrown at him. He pocketed the keys and shoved Ty's gun in the back of his waistband.

"Unless you smother me in my sleep and gnaw off my arm, I don't really see you getting out of this one," Ty said to Julian.

Julian was breathing heavily, obviously trying to calm himself. Then his shoulders sagged, and he nodded minutely. "A truce for the night," he said, voice soft. "I won't break your arm to get away, and you won't break my neck in the middle of a war flashback."

Ty's eyes narrowed. "Deal."

Zane looked back to Cameron, still standing off to the side like a spectator at a cockfight. "I guess you two are taking that bed," Zane said, hating the thought. He and Ty would barely fit on the double bed together, and they were friendly, to say the least. There'd be no way two big men like Ty and Julian could do it without contact.

When he looked back, Ty was staring at him. He looked like he hadn't slept in a week, worse than he'd looked before he'd bolted in Baltimore just weeks ago. He hadn't given details, but his trek through the snow to find a car had to have been harrowing.

Julian was messing with the sleeve of his shirt, and when he raised his arm, he pulled Ty's hand with it. Julian looked at Ty and flailed his hands in a rare display of frustration. "I finally get to sleep in a bed, and I can't even get out of my shirt now?"

"Shut up," Ty growled, and he pushed Julian toward the bed. He gave Zane one last glance, and Zane met his eyes long enough to nod, hoping it conveyed his tacit acceptance of the situation. He didn't have to like it; he just had to get to tomorrow.

CAMERON shot straight up, pulse going into overdrive, when a piercing alarm blared in the darkness now lit by red lights flashing from small boxes on the ceiling. It was so loud he had to cover his ears, and he panted for breath, trying to wake up and remember where he was and why Julian wasn't with him.

There was a shout and a cry of pain from the next bed over, followed by a thump loud enough to be heard over the blaring alarm.

He saw a tall shadow move in front of him, and he relaxed. "Julian?" he called out, trying to be heard over the wailing alarm.

But it wasn't Julian who Cameron saw when the shadow stopped at the foot of the sagging bed. Cameron's brain finally kicked in with the details: it was Zane standing in front of him; they were in a scary-ass motel somewhere in Ohio; and Julian was in the next bed, sleeping while cuffed to Ty.

Cameron started trying to push himself out of the hollow in the center of the drooping mattress, but Zane was already flipping on the light. It took some wiggling and a push to get off the creaky bed, and Cameron was finally able to see Ty and Julian. Or at least see where they were supposed to be.

Ty was sprawled sideways across the double bed, lying on his belly, arm stretched over the edge of the bed to the point that his muscles were straining and taut under his thin T-shirt. Cameron could see Julian's hand sticking up over the edge of the mattress, fingers limp and attached to the handcuffs on Ty's wrist.

Cameron winced and hurried over to crouch next to Julian, who was sprawled on the floor, arm turned back at an awkward angle. "Julian, are you okay?"

Julian groaned and turned his shoulders, trying to get off the floor while still in that position. "I'm okay," he muttered as he reached for Cameron.

Cameron leaned over to slide an arm around Julian's waist and give him some leverage to clamber to his feet. When Cameron looked up, Zane was standing right there, looking at the cuffs.

"Careful," Zane said, grabbing Julian's cuffed wrist and holding it still, stopping the yanking motion. "Ty? You okay?"

"Yeah," Ty said in a strained voice. He pushed to his hands and knees and shook his head. "Tried to go opposite ways."

Julian rubbed his shoulder and winced. The chain between them clanked accusingly. "Apparently I either weigh more than he does or I got out faster," he muttered with a hint of a smirk.

"And then you fell on your ass."

Before anyone could answer, the alarm shut off just as suddenly as it had started.

They all stood in the ensuing silence, Ty's harsh breathing really the only sound to be heard.

Julian moved his arm, rotating his shoulder, and Ty allowed his hand to go with the motion.

"I'm fine," Julian grumbled.

"Liar," Cameron said. "Should we check to see if there's a real fire?"

"Call the front desk," Ty suggested. He was still frowning, and he looked oddly haunted by the events of the evening. Julian's words about having flashbacks now seemed like more than mockery between the two men.

Zane moved to the phone and called the front desk. After a moment of listening, he hung up. "There's a short somewhere. They've got people coming to fix it."

"How long will that take?" Cameron asked, reluctantly pulling away from Julian to let him work out the kink in his shoulder. He'd no more than gotten the last word out when the alarm shrieked again for about five seconds and quit.

"Answers that question," Zane muttered.

Ty sat on the edge of the bed and rubbed at his eyes. Julian was forced to take a step closer, hovering over him and looking mutinous.

"Sit down and chill," Zane told Julian. "Or I can break out the bungee cords and fasten your wrists to your ankles. It's great for the circulation."

Julian turned his head to look at Zane, and Cameron recognized the look in his eyes. His lover was about to kill something. A glance at Zane revealed the same look, and it made Cameron very nervous. Zane and Julian seemed far too much alike for his comfort.

"Why don't you cuff him to me?" Cameron asked.

"Because you're not a resistant force."

"A what?"

"You're not exactly trying to keep him here," Zane said as he paced over to the window and looked out through the gauzy curtains.

"But he…." Cameron stopped, looked up at the intensity on Julian's face, and then nodded. "Yeah, okay."

Ty still had his head down, rubbing at his eyes. He sniffed but offered nothing to the conversation.

Zane looked over his shoulder at them, his eyes flickering from person to person. "It's 4 a.m. Get some more sleep," he said before walking past the bed to the light switch. "Come on, Cam."

"But Zane—" Cameron started.

Julian's hand reached out to catch at him in the dark. "Cam," he said in a low voice.

Cameron turned back to his lover.

Julian pulled him closer, pressing his lips to Cameron's ear. "It's okay," he whispered. His words were followed by another blast of the malfunctioning fire alarm. Ty gave a jerk.

Cameron winced as he felt Julian's arm jerked. "All right," he said.

Julian nodded and let go of him. "Good night, love."

"Oh God," Ty grunted.

In a fit of frustration, Cameron huffed at Ty. "Don't you have someone who misses you? Someone you miss?" The alarm cut off again.

Ty looked up at him, and there was an odd flash in his eyes as the light reflected in them. It instantly made Cameron nervous. Ty stood to tower over him. "You know what? I do," Ty said. "And the longer you two fuck around and draw this out, the longer I'm away, the longer I go without being with the person *I* love. So how about you take your goddamn simpering advice on romance and stick it up your ass!"

Cameron felt a pang of both shame and pain in the face of Ty's blunt honesty and obvious frustration. He'd never thought about the lives the two agents had been pulled away from to do this. He backed up until he bumped into something, only to turn around and find out he'd run into Zane, who was watching his partner, a slight smile pulling at his lips. Cameron shook his head and detoured around him, unable to say a thing in response.

Zane flicked the light off, and the room fell into silence. As soon as Cameron settled on the bed, the alarm cranked to life again. He curled up on his side, pulling a pillow over his head.

JULIAN waited until Zane had shut out the light again. Then he sat gingerly on the edge of the bed next to Ty. He was hesitant to speak at all; the agent's outburst had caught him just as off guard as it had Cameron. He absolutely loathed the moments where enemies became men with emotions and feelings.

"So," he said awkwardly, wincing in the dark.

Ty sighed loudly. The silence stretched on until Julian was fairly certain that both Cameron and Zane had dozed off once more.

Julian strained for something to say to the man that would border on polite, or even civil. But he was still fighting the almost overwhelming urge to throttle him. He cleared his throat and shifted, taking Ty's arm with him as he turned. "The last time I found myself handcuffed to someone and we had to sleep, we found it was actually more comfortable—"

"To sleep on your sides on the opposite arm, yeah," Ty said with a solemn nod.

Julian found himself staring in the low light, surprised. "You and your partner, you're not really the average field agents, are you?"

"Zane is not an average anything," Ty said, voice soft and hoarse.

Julian frowned, confused by the answer at first, but he realized what Ty was doing. The man was as good at avoiding an answer as Julian was. Only he did it with such good ole boy, backwater sincerity that it probably worked better than Julian's methods.

"I believe I've just discovered why you and I hate each other so much."

Ty snorted.

"I'm serious. You and I were the same person at one juncture. You took one path, I another."

"Are you saying you're my evil twin?" Ty asked. His voice was too tired to have any sarcasm in it.

Julian pursed his lips thoughtfully.

"Fuck it, just…. You take this side, I'll take that one, see if we can keep our arms from going to sleep."

Julian lay down obediently, disturbed and distracted by his new realizations. Outwardly he and Zane Garrett were very alike. But perhaps deeper down, Julian and Ty Grady were more alike than either man was comfortable with.

As if to accentuate his thoughts, the fire alarm blared to life again, and he and Ty both shot up in the bed before either could curtail the instinct. They sat in bed together, tense and looking at each other in the darkness, until the alarm cut off.

"I hate Ohio," Ty muttered before he flopped back to the bed.

"Amen," Zane and Cameron both said from the other bed.

ZANE examined himself in the bathroom mirror as he towel-dried his hair and then tossed the towel onto the counter. Placing both hands on the vanity, he leaned forward, taking in the beard and exhausted eyes. Ty was right: the beard didn't suit him.

He was also convinced that going on short sleep for days on end with his mileage was not conducive to his health or his looks.

"Looking good, Garrett," he mumbled. He picked up and shook out his new Henley before sliding an arm into it. He was putting the same clothes back on, but they weren't a mess. And after a shower he felt much better. He mentally patted himself on the back for picking up some deodorant, toothbrushes, and toothpaste when he was at that drug store in Chicago. It seemed like weeks ago.

They were coming up on four days that they'd been on the road. They had been long days, and even Ty's normally amusing antics were wearing on his nerves. Having to constantly keep his gun pretty much trained on Julian didn't help. Zane was thankful he'd gotten at least a little bit of time alone with Ty and some sleep, or he'd really be going nuts.

He smoothed down the shirt before opening the bathroom door. He was surprised to find not only Ty but also Julian standing right there at the door when it opened. Before he could react, Ty reached out and grabbed his arm, yanking him forward and snapping one half of a pair of handcuffs on his wrist.

He found himself handcuffed to their prisoner, who was looking at him with a sardonic smile.

"There!" Ty said happily.

Zane stared at him, incredulous, before reaching out and popping him upside the back of the head. "What the fuck?"

Ty danced away from him so he wouldn't risk another smack. "I couldn't find anything solid to attach him to, and you won't let me drug him," he said as he rubbed at his head. "And you're, you know… solid enough."

"You can cuff him to the damn toilet for all I care, but not to me!" He pulled his wrist up and shook it along with Julian's arm. "Give me the key."

"I must agree," Julian said.

The smile still on Ty's face made Zane want to wipe it away. Whether with a voracious kiss or a serious kick to the teeth, Zane hadn't yet decided.

Ty held up the keys to the cuffs and shook his head as he put them into his jeans pocket. "We'll get you something from Wendy's," he told them in what might have passed for a consoling tone.

Zane swiped out at Ty, but his partner took another step back and Zane was attached to the immovable object that was Julian, so he couldn't grab Ty before he edged around to the door. Cameron waited there already, looking uncertain and almost amused.

"What if they kill each other?" Cameron asked Ty. He sounded serious. Zane glanced at Julian, feeling the annoyance bubble just below a boil. He was probably right to be worried.

Ty idly scratched at his chin, looking at them. He glanced sideways at Cameron. "Should we place bets?"

Zane could hear Julian grinding his teeth.

"You—" Zane cut himself off before delivering a threat that wouldn't come from a partner. A working partner.

Cameron peered at Julian for a long moment before tipping his head to one side and considering Zane as well. "I bet there won't be blood when we come back. And if I win, Julian and I get a night uncuffed in a bed."

"Cameron!" Julian said, sounding shocked.

Ty considered for a moment, then reached out to shake Cameron's hand. "Bet."

Cameron shrugged and looked at Julian apologetically. "Now, don't throw the bet," he said, lips pressing down like he was hiding a laugh.

"You two are real comedians," Zane said, lifting his hand to point at Ty in accusation before remembering it was attached to Julian, and he shook it with a frustrated growl before looking at Ty through narrowed eyes. "You know that threat you make when I really piss you off with the puns? That's coming your way. Big time." Meaning Ty wouldn't be getting fucked for some time to come.

Ty smirked, as if he looked forward to the challenge. "How's the Benadryl option looking now, Nurse Ratched?" he asked. Then he jerked his head at the door, and he and Cameron exited before Zane or Julian could threaten them again.

Julian was silent for a long while, eyes narrowed, staring at the door. Zane figured they were having equally homicidal thoughts, not that it made him feel any better. If Ty didn't bring him back a damn Frosty, he was tearing a piece out of his ass, and not in a way Ty would enjoy.

Maybe. Zane wrinkled his nose. He knew damn well he'd be all over Ty as soon as they had at least half an hour uninterrupted time alone. He could fuck Ty twice in that amount of time if he was really motivated, and Zane was really motivated now. Just the fact that sex was his first thought instead of throttling his partner was evidence enough.

Julian finally cleared his throat and moved his hand, making the handcuffs jangle. He looked sideways at Zane, his expression speculative.

Zane raised an eyebrow and waited for what was sure to be a sarcastic remark veiled in icy politeness. It was Julian's style.

"I'm really starting to hate him," Julian said instead.

Zane snorted, thinking of last night and his thoughts about Ty and Julian mirroring himself and Ty when they first met. "Yeah, I know what you mean," he muttered. He raised their cuffed wrists and frowned at them.

"I could pick it if we had something suitable," Julian said as he turned his wrist over, taking Zane's arm with it.

"So could I, but Grady knows that too," Zane said as he looked around the room, casting about for options. "He's very thorough."

"Yes, I was forced to drag along behind him as he rid the room of every single shiny thing," Julian said. He looked around the room anyway, trying to find something Ty might have missed. "Shall we sit?" he finally asked dejectedly.

"I can guarantee he won't be getting takeout," Zane said under his breath as he turned in place and looked at seating options. There were the beds, one chair at the table, and the low dresser in a pinch. And as much as he wanted to be cranky, Zane knew being an asshole wouldn't make the time pass any faster. "Sure. Take your pick."

"Bed," Julian said under his breath as he took a step toward the closest one. Zane followed grudgingly, glad there wasn't anyone else here to see this. Eyes narrowing, Zane looked to the desk, where he'd left his gun. It was gone.

"He took my gun!" Zane said in outrage. That son of a bitch! He knew how Zane felt about being unarmed.

"You could pose that he took *my* gun," Julian countered with a hint of amusement.

"So he's already got more than his fair share," Zane said as he thumped down next to Julian on the edge of the bed.

Julian sat straight and proper, his back and shoulders rigid. He didn't feel tense, though. Merely sitting there to wait. Zane wondered if he'd looked like that, all stick up his ass, when he'd met Ty. With a sniff, he stretched out his legs toward the dresser and looked at the clock.

Julian's lack of movement was almost a novelty after so many months of being close to Ty. It was like sitting beside a stone statue. When he finally did move, it was to cock his head and look at the door.

"I believe they're back," he said, voice laced with surprise.

Zane frowned as he glanced up. It hadn't even been enough time to get there on foot, much less have food and be back. "He must have forgotten something." But that didn't sit right. Ty wouldn't have forgotten something when he'd planned like this. Zane pulled back his legs to stand, feeling uneasy.

As soon as he'd gained his feet, the flimsy door was kicked in and a burst of cold air flowed into the room as two men charged in. Zane didn't even think; he snatched Cameron's leather Dopp kit up from the dresser and backhanded it as hard as he could at the first man's face. He didn't know who they were or what they wanted, but their method of entry was enough reason to take them out first and ask questions later. Leatherface threw up his hands with a yelp, and the Dopp kit stopped his headlong charge as it busted open, scattering its contents all over.

Zane's actions pulled Julian off-balance, and they stumbled as he fell into Zane. Julian righted himself just in time to pull a hand up and block a punch from a second man; then he kicked out and sent the attacker sprawling to the floor. That put Julian between Zane and Leatherface, so Zane rammed the heel of his shoes into Rugburn's gut.

Julian turned with his movement, their backs against each other. He was jerked back when the handcuffs and Zane's arm kept him from moving further, but he managed a roundhouse punch at Leatherface before he was pulled the other way and stumbled at Zane's side. Zane grunted as their shoulders collided, and he purposely dropped his left arm so Julian could move it. But the few seconds of distraction gave Rugburn a window of opportunity, and he raised a leg to kick out, his shoe catching Zane's jaw. The recoil sent Zane stumbling back a step, jerking the chain taut between him and Julian, and the backs of Zane's knees hit the other bed.

Rugburn stood to attack again, but Julian pulled Zane's arm, and the chain between them, hard at his neck. They caught him just right, and there was a sickening crunch as Rugburn crumpled to the floor.

But Leatherface had gained his feet. He held a gun pointed at Zane's face, his eyes narrowing as he looked at them each in turn.

"Which one of you is Cross?"

Zane stopped, his free hand curled into a fist, and gave Leatherface a once-over. Suit and tie, leather shoes, standard holster under his suit jacket, plain brown trench coat. His appearance screamed government agent, though Zane doubted that. Why would another agent break in on their assignment? Which meant freelancers, especially since they were looking for Cross.

Julian pointed at Zane in answer to the question. Zane smacked his hand. "You're interfering in an FBI investigation. I suggest you stand down," he told Leatherface.

The man shook his head. "This is a national security matter." He turned the gun toward Julian. "You're coming with me."

Julian struck out at him so quickly it was easy to think it was imagined. He grabbed the gun and pulled the slide, his free hand moving in a flash, and the gun fell apart in Leatherface's hand. Julian swung at him with the slide, hitting him in the temple and dropping him in a heap.

"You're standing too close," he said to the unconscious man.

Zane couldn't help but admire Julian's speedy reaction. He'd have to remember that trick with the slide. "That was… impressive," he said as he touched his hurting chin. His fingers came away bloody from his lip.

Julian turned to look at him. He stared for a moment and then sighed. "Cam lost his bet. Let's see if one of these two has a set of handcuff keys, shall we?"

"National security," Zane muttered as he crouched down next to the man they'd hit across the throat and checked for a pulse.

Julian had to bend over and hang his arm so Zane could do it. "Dead?"

"No, but he may wish he was when he wakes up," Zane said, eyeing the vivid bruise already coming up across the man's throat. He started searching the pockets of the man's trench and came up with a wallet. What he saw when he flipped it open made his stomach turn.

Julian hummed. "Told you," he said evenly. "We should go find Cameron and Grady."

Zane studied the Langley entry ID, and from what he could tell, it was legit. He dropped it, pulled the man's gun and set it on the floor next to him, then dug out a set of keys. "You going to tell me what's really going on now?" he asked as he reached over to claim the ammunition cartridge from the other gun. They were both standard-issue Glocks, the same as his own.

"I'd rather wait to see if I can escape from you first," Julian answered candidly.

"You probably could," Zane said as he picked up the gun and stood, keys also in hand. "That doesn't help Cameron. Or the fact that the CIA wants your ass."

"You're right, of course. So unlock us and let's go."

Zane turned and calmly pressed the business end of the gun against Julian's midsection, the pommel brushing his own, they stood so close. "If they came at us here, we can be sure they went after Ty and Cameron too."

Julian didn't seem perturbed by the gun barrel in his belly. He glanced around the room and pursed his lips. "Cameron's bag is still mostly packed. Grab it and we'll go."

Zane nodded but pulled Julian over to the table instead, gathering their things as quickly as possible. "Get his stuff."

Julian did so, and he looked wryly at their joined hands. Zane wasn't about to unlock him now. "Darling, I didn't know you cared," he said to Zane in a voice that was smooth as velvet. The irony was not lost in the tone, though.

"You give new meaning to ball and chain. Come on," Zane said as he looked out the broken doorframe.

The corridor was clear, although Zane could hear the elevator moving with a whirr. He stepped out into the causeway, and Julian followed along, not offering another comment on their linked hands. After a mere moment's thought, Zane turned away from the elevator to walk swiftly to the stairs at the far end of the balcony. It could be Ty and Cameron in the elevator. Or not.

Again, Julian trailed along quietly, cooperating to the point that it was suspicious. At the stairwell door, Zane turned a serious, measuring look on him.

"What?" Julian whispered. "I'm being good."

"That's what bothers me," Zane muttered. With a shake of his head, he led the way through the door into the concrete stairwell.

They couldn't be quiet as they thundered down the stairs, but they were past the need for stealth now. Speed was their friend.

Zane stuck his head out of the stairwell when they got to the ground level, and seeing no one around, he pulled Julian with him and they hurried toward the main office.

They reached the entrance to the hotel, a wild cast to their eyes as they looked around for any more suspicious men in suits.

As they stood there, a sleek black sedan came tearing into the parking lot, taking the hairpin turn and sliding up to a stop right in front of Zane and Julian.

Zane took a step back, wishing he had unlocked the handcuffs in the room. They had a better chance of splitting up and dividing their assailants than they did of fighting them off. He felt Julian coiling beside him, readying himself for their final stand. Zane pulled his gun.

The heavily tinted driver's side window slid down, and it took Zane a moment to realize he was looking at his partner.

"Playtime's over, kids!" Ty called to them, voice urgent and gruff. "I put them down, but I didn't take them out. They'll be after their car."

Zane and Julian shared a look. They rushed for the back door, both of them diving into the car. Ty hit the gas before they could even get the door shut.

Cameron sat in the front seat, looking back at them with wide eyes. "Are you okay?"

Julian nodded. "What happened?"

"Two guys jumped us on the way to get food," Cameron answered. "Ty is like… a ninja on crack. He beat them up pretty spectacularly. Then we stole their car."

Julian let out a pent-up breath.

"This CIA issue stuff is really nice," Ty told them as he fiddled with the buttons. "Why the hell can't the Bureau spring for rides like this?"

Zane reached into his pocket and extracted the handcuff keys. "Ty," he said in a low voice.

"I know, I know, you can kick my ass later," Ty muttered. "Two suits get after you too?"

"All over us."

"Looks like we're not the only ones after MacGuffin back there."

"Are you seriously going to call me names after you almost got all of us killed?"

"You don't want to be called names, how about telling us a real one?"

"Blow me, Grady."

"That sounds Scottish."

Julian lunged with one hand, fully intending to throttle Ty even if he was driving. Zane reached out and caught his hand, restraining him.

"Let me do it, Garrett, it would make our lives so much easier!" Julian said through gritted teeth as he struggled to free his hand. There was no trace of the calm and controlled Julian Cross they'd met in Chicago.

Ty had that effect on just about everyone.

Zane pushed Julian back against the seat to calm him. He held up his hand and growled. "If anyone is strangling the life out of my partner today, it's going to be me."

Julian huffed but finally nodded. "As long as I get to watch."

~Chapter 11~

WHILE Ty was safely hidden away under the CIA vehicle, dismantling the GPS, Zane and Julian discussed their options. Cameron sat and listened, as he always did. They finally made the decision that they needed to get to DC as fast as possible, and to Cameron's surprise, Julian agreed that making it to DC was now what they wanted to do, rather than escaping.

"The enemy is too powerful. We need someone on our side. These two and their boss will have to do until we find someone bigger," he explained to Cameron.

It made sense, in a very Julian sort of way.

They headed for the nearest airport, which happened to be Pittsburgh. Ty and Zane didn't flash their badges this time, going for low-key as they went through the security checks. They had ditched their guns and wallets. Julian behaved himself, staying close to Cameron. It all went smoothly, which immediately put all of them on edge.

While standing in line with Zane to get a sandwich, Cameron watched as Julian moved around the sizeable shopping area in the airport, Ty trailing only a few steps behind him. Julian had assured the FBI agents that he wasn't going anywhere, but Ty didn't trust him.

Cameron couldn't help but watch his lover. When other people noticed Julian, they tended to do one of three things: stare at him, hustle away, or some odd, jerky combination of the two. Cameron shook his head as a couple of teenage girls stopped and watched him pass.

"I really feel for people sometimes," Cameron said once Julian was within hearing.

Julian raised an eyebrow and gave Cameron a fond smile. "And why is that?"

"Oh God, don't make him talk about his feelings," Ty muttered as he joined them.

Cameron shook his head. "You're like a shark. You walk around and all the little minnows go swimming away."

Julian hummed and glanced around the room. Ty began to snicker quietly, and Julian looked over his shoulder at him.

"Dude," Ty said as their eyes met. "Your boyfriend just called you a shark. That's a besotted burn."

Cameron saw Julian just barely roll his eyes as he looked away from Ty and back at him. Cameron edged up a shoulder. He heard Zane laugh behind him.

"While I appreciate the spirit of the observation, there is a flaw in your theory," Julian told him, voice lowering as he took a step closer.

Cameron tried not to grin. "Really? Because you do like to bite."

"Oh Lord, TMI," Zane muttered.

"This whole trip has been TMI, Zane," Ty grumbled.

Julian ignored both of their comments, returning them with a mere smile before he explained. "A shark, while frightening to us, is not a threat to the minnow at first sight. We know what a shark can do, the minnow doesn't."

Behind him, Ty rubbed his eyes. "Oh God, now I'm actually agreeing with him."

Cameron shifted his weight to peer around Julian at Ty. "Excuse me?"

Ty looked up and waved a hand at the airport around them. "Sharks eat fish, right? Or seals or… whatever. But if a seal is afraid of a shark on sight, then the shark will never get close enough to the seal to do anything."

Julian was nodding, looking moderately surprised that Ty knew what he'd been talking about. "What he's saying is if the prey recognized the predator as a danger, they would instantly flee. So the shark regulates its behavior. The majority of the time, a shark swims peacefully through schools of its prey, never causing trouble, never being pegged as a danger, barely noticed by the very things it hunts."

Cameron looked back and forth between them. "So... if you're not a shark, then what are you?"

Julian winced, and to Cameron's surprise, he flushed as he looked down at his shoes. "I've always associated myself more with a lion," he mumbled.

"I'll buy that," Ty said as he stepped away from the counter so Cameron could see him more fully.

"I'm not convinced," Cameron said, crossing his arms. He looked over his shoulder at Zane. "Does Julian look like a lion to you?"

"I refuse to answer that question on the grounds that it's stupid," Zane said, mimicking Julian's way of speech, before stepping up to order his food.

Cameron turned back to Julian. "Well?"

"Big cats are the only predators on earth who are known to kill for fun," Ty provided almost merrily.

"Meow Mix," Zane said over his shoulder in a flat tone.

"You said that before, at the apartment," Cameron remembered. "When Ty picked up Wesson."

"Wait, he picked up Wesson?"

Cameron nodded.

"How?"

"Grady has a codependent relationship with big cats."

"Why?"

"One tried to eat me," Ty said, the answer flippant.

"Actually, that explains so much," Zane muttered to himself, looking between Ty and Julian.

Cameron rolled his eyes. "Why a lion, Julian?"

"They're large and territorial. They're feared on sight no matter if they're hunting or sunning on a rock. They take advantage of environmental factors to hunt and kill their prey. And they occasionally go rogue."

"And start killing for fun," Ty finished with a flourish of his hand.

Cameron turned up his nose. "And what about you, Mr. Killing for Fun?"

"I don't kill for fun."

"I meant what are you? A bulldog?"

Zane let out a sharp bark of laughter. Ty grunted at them both, no longer enjoying the game now that he was the focus.

Julian turned to look at him. He nodded as if coming to a decision. "You see, Cameron, of us all, Agent Grady is the real shark."

Ty looked at Julian in outrage.

Cameron narrowed his eyes, studying Ty, trying to fit the description Julian gave earlier to what he'd seen of Ty. Julian and Zane both turned heads with their imposing dark looks and brooding auras. They were both somber and controlled. Like sharks patrolling their territory as they weaved through a crowd. Ty, though, sort of struck Cameron as a playful puppy in comparison, flopping along, cracking jokes, handsome face usually open and smiling.

Maybe Julian was right.

"Do you play poker?" Cameron asked Ty.

"Sometimes," Ty answered distractedly, still looking at Julian. "What the hell do you mean, *I'm* the shark? I'm not a shark!"

"You're a shark," Zane said as he turned away from the counter with a drink in hand, though his words sounded begrudged.

Ty gave him a wounded look, and Cameron almost felt sorry for him.

Julian nodded, satisfied. "Of all of us, he's the one someone in trouble would approach for help," he told Cameron. He waved a hand at Ty. "He doesn't seem outwardly dangerous, in fact, quite the opposite. So the wounded little fishies just swim right up to him."

"Okay, that's enough," Ty grunted, shoulders tightening.

"But he has probably killed more people than myself and Agent Garrett combined."

"Now you're just being mean," Ty muttered.

Zane shrugged. "You remember what Clancy said. You go around bitching and people still like you because you're charming. You can't help yourself."

"You're not helping, Zane!"

"Maybe Ty's a big cat too," Cameron said, not comfortable with the talk of kill counts and still feeling sorry for Ty and the wounded look in his eyes. Maybe Ty really was a shark, dangerous and dashing and still managing to make Cameron feel sorry for him.

"No," Julian murmured, still looking at Ty. "He's a shark."

Cameron glanced to Zane. "What about him?"

"I was born in the year of the horse," Zane said. He was leaning against the counter, waiting for their order.

"You're not a horse," Ty told him, sounding truly offended by the entire conversation now.

"I think maybe… a bear. A big grizzly bear," Cameron said as he studied Zane.

"A bear fits," Julian agreed.

"A bear?" Zane shrugged. "I've been called worse."

Ty was silent, looking at Zane with narrowed eyes. "Oh!" he said suddenly, pointing at his partner. "He's an elephant!"

Julian looked back at Ty and then at Zane, almost laughing, but then he nodded in surprise again. "That's… disturbingly fitting."

Cameron had to laugh when he saw the look on Zane's face. He was staring at his partner in clear disbelief. "An elephant?" Zane said.

"They're killers, man," Ty told him, voice trembling with laughter.

"As much as I hate to agree with him," Julian murmured, waving at Ty with a grimace.

"An *elephant*?" Zane repeated. "What the hell?"

"They lose their tempers and trample and gore and cause mayhem all the time," Ty said, his voice flippant but his eyes glittering.

Zane crossed his arms and narrowed his eyes, glowering.

Cameron cleared his throat and whistled as he turned to look at Julian. Julian was trying desperately not to smile.

"Elephants are unpredictable creatures," Ty told Zane, voice lower and mockingly earnest.

Zane cocked his head to one side. "Do tell."

Cameron edged away from Zane and reached down to pick up the second tray of food they'd been waiting for. "How do you two know so much about killer animals, anyway? I *know* you don't watch Discovery Channel, Julian."

Julian licked his lips, sharing a look with Ty that was oddly familiar, as if they shared a secret. "Studying the way animals stalk is an effective way to... sell antiques."

"Yeah," Cameron drew out, keeping his eyes on Julian and shaking his head.

Zane groaned and rubbed his eyes.

"C'mon, Simba, go buy me some lemonade while I find a table," Cameron said, hooking his arm through Julian's.

Ty and Zane remained behind them for only the briefest of moments, glaring at each other, before Ty broke away to trail behind them. Cameron got the very distinct feeling that they were communicating silently and that they would be discussing elephants the next time they were alone.

When Ty joined Cameron at the table, it was just the two of them. Zane had gone off to find a restroom, and Julian was waiting in line for a lemonade.

Cameron sat in the metal chair with his club sandwich as he watched Julian. It was always interesting to observe him interacting with strangers, whether he was a lion or a shark or a teddy bear. He was much the same as when Cameron had met him: mostly silent, otherwise soft-spoken and succinct. It had made for a challenge when Cameron served as his waiter at Tuesdays, the gourmet restaurant where they'd met. It still made him smile, thinking about how he'd been so sure Julian hadn't even known he existed.

Ty thumped down beside him and huffed, breaking his reverie. "You know how you can tell when someone's really in love?" Ty asked him out of the blue, his tone casual. He glanced sideways at Cameron, one eyebrow raised. "You're sitting here, watching him do something completely mundane, and you're grinning like an idiot."

"And what's wrong with that?" Cameron asked with a light laugh.

"Whatever, you make my teeth hurt," Ty grumbled, though Cameron could see the barest hint of something beneath the gruff exterior, perhaps amusement.

"I think you're just as sentimental as I am. You hide it better," Cameron claimed, remembering Ty's snappy response about being away from his loved ones. "I just don't have to hide it at all. It's really freeing."

"I bet," Ty murmured. Though his eyes still followed Julian's movements, they seemed to be staring off into the distance as well, as if he was seeing someone or something else. Cameron wondered, as he looked at Ty, what sort of person a man like him would love. Ty shook it off and glanced down, then looked away as if he sensed Cameron's eyes still on him.

Cameron took a bite of his sandwich. "Don't you get tired of it?" he asked. "This tough guy image?"

Ty didn't look at him, but Cameron could see his eyes gaining distance again. "It's all I've ever known," he answered, voice matter-of-fact and melancholy.

A glance showed Cameron that Julian was accepting the cups from the lady at the counter. Ty would totally clam up once Julian walked over. "It doesn't have to be that way. Julian was able to adapt," Cameron offered, hoping Ty might be able to see it could be done. "You just have to love the right person."

"What makes you think I don't?" Ty asked in an oddly distant voice.

Cameron was brought up short, staring at him with narrowed eyes. "I have a finely tuned macho bullshit detector, and it's shrieking," he said.

"You get a lot of macho bullshit from your boyfriend over there?" Ty asked in what seemed to be sincere curiosity. But with Ty, it was hard to tell what was said in seriousness and what wasn't.

Cameron shifted uncomfortably. "It doesn't bother you?" he asked, watching Ty.

"What? Bullshit? I work for the government, man." Ty laughed and shook his head.

Cameron repressed a smile. "No. That Julian and I are lovers."

Ty was already shaking his head, as if he'd known all along that was what Cameron had been referring to. "Now who's making generalizations? Just because I wear flannel doesn't mean I'm an asshole." His knee was no longer bouncing, and he seemed to have finally relaxed a little as he sat there. "Guy's willing to charge into a room full of guns to protect you and then drag you across the country in handcuffs to keep you with him. Seems like a keeper to me."

"Yes. He's a keeper," Cameron agreed, even though Ty's words were sarcastic. He cleared his throat. "And Julian is indeed a master of macho bullshit."

"Yeah, he seems the type."

"So do you."

"Oh, I know it," Ty said. He didn't seem to take it as an insult, or anything else, really. Just a fact. That alone intrigued Cameron. The more Cameron got to know Ty, the more he realized that the guy seemed to have absolutely no shame.

"So you met him at a restaurant," Ty said almost to himself.

Cameron nodded. "Tuesdays is a very nice restaurant."

"Tuesdays," Ty repeated. He mulled over the name for a while and then nodded. "I can see why that name would draw a man like that. Wait, wait, let me guess," he said in amusement as he held out his hand to Cameron. "Man that named it was a friend of his."

"What makes you say that?" Cameron asked in shock, his hand straying to rub at his throat, where the necklace Julian had given him used to hang before it was lost. He still missed its reassuring weight, if not the symbolism of it.

"European criminals. They love their mythology. Tuesday was Mars, the god of war. That restaurant is like a beacon to anyone wanting to deal."

Cameron almost laughed. He'd had to Google the information when neither Julian nor Blake would tell him. "You know more than I did."

"Well, that's what a federal agent does when he's not watching other people," Ty told him with a smirk.

"Read up on European mythology?"

"That too."

Cameron shook his head, amused that he was constantly being surprised by both Ty and Zane. They were anything but what they appeared on the surface.

Ty didn't speak again. He didn't even move, not a twitch of a muscle or bat of an eye. Cameron frowned and tipped his head, then tried to follow Ty's line of sight. But it didn't seem that he was looking at anything but the blank terminal walls over by the restrooms. Cameron sat back and took another bite of sandwich, turning his chin to offer Julian a smile as he joined them at the tiny table.

For once Ty didn't have anything snappy or clever to say to Julian. He was still sitting stock-still, now staring at the food counter where Julian had been standing.

Julian sat fluidly next to Cameron and handed him his lemonade. He glanced at the agent in mild surprise when he wasn't greeted with at least a derisive grunt, and Cameron saw him do a double take when he looked at Ty.

Cameron looked from Julian to Ty and back. "What?"

Ty inhaled deeply and turned to look at them. He shifted his shoulders so that he was facing Julian directly, and he met Julian's eyes with a look so grim that it almost scared Cameron. "To my five thirty," Ty said to Julian, almost under his breath. "What do you see?"

Julian's black eyes carefully drifted to gaze over Ty's right shoulder. Outwardly he didn't change, he still looked relaxed and somber, but Cameron could almost feel the alteration come over the table when Julian spotted whatever Ty had pointed out to him.

They met each other's gaze again and sat staring at each other across the table.

Cameron cleared his throat. "What is it?" he whispered.

When Julian looked at him, there was a hint of apprehension in his lover's eyes. That alone terrified Cameron, and he had to try to swallow twice to get the last bite of his sandwich down.

Ty cleared his throat and stood. "Come on," he prompted as he slid one arm into his jacket and used the motion to glance over his shoulder.

"What about Zane?" Cameron asked as he stood, abandoning his pretzel and drink on the table. They left the tray of barely touched food.

"Take your things," Julian said under his breath. He held his cup in his hand, looking down as he stirred it with his straw.

"Zane should be okay, we'll circle back for him if we can," Ty answered as he led them out of the café's sitting area and into the crowded concourse. After Cameron shouldered his bag, Julian took Cameron's hand and followed, not even hinting that he might try to escape while Ty was distracted.

Cameron tried to ignore the tension and dread curling in his gut. If he wasn't safe with Julian and Ty, he wouldn't be safe anywhere. But it wasn't himself he worried for. He caught himself before he could glance behind them to check for Zane. Soon he'd be coming out to find them gone.

When Cameron gave in and turned his chin, he saw a man in a dark suit step away from a magazine rack and begin making his way after them. Another man moved out of the alcove of a service door, and yet another got up from a table at a deli further down the causeway.

"Julian," Cameron whispered.

"I know, love," Julian murmured, voice tight.

Ahead of them, Ty stopped abruptly. Julian drew up and pulled Cameron closer to him. Three more men in various shades of dark suit had materialized ahead of them. Julian turned to face behind them, putting Cameron between himself and Ty.

"FBI?" Julian asked doubtfully, though there was a hint of hope as well.

"Wrong letters," Ty answered.

Cameron didn't like not being able to see, but taking a quick look made him more scared, not less. "What now?"

Ty actually reached back and put a hand on Cameron's arm, turning just enough to look behind them. Cameron heard his breath catch. "You're not meant to get to DC, are you?" he whispered to Julian.

Julian glanced behind him, and Cameron saw him lick his lips in a rare show of nerves. "I'm the last living witness to a high-level CIA man who was using CIA assets to carry out murder for hire. I'm the only person left who can identify him."

Ty cursed. "They're not here to take you into custody."

"Then what?" Cameron froze as one of the dark-suited men brushed up against a passing traveler. His jacket moved, revealing a gun stuck into the waistband of his pants. "Oh. We've got to get out of here."

"There's nowhere to go, love," Julian said, voice grim.

Ty was looking over the heads of the crowd milling around them, and Cameron could practically feel the man coiling against him, like a snake cornered and about to strike.

"They won't shoot us in the middle of the terminal and all these people," Cameron insisted. He cast around, desperate.

Ty turned around and grabbed Julian by the arm, yanking him closer until they were almost nose to nose. He didn't say a thing; they merely stared at each other for a moment before Ty let him go and turned to dart into the tiny gift shop several yards away.

Cameron gaped. Had Ty just cut and run on them? "What just happened?"

The six men were closing in, and the crowd seemed to teem with danger now that Cameron was aware of them. Julian squeezed his hand, squaring his shoulders like a lion might fluff its mane, trying to appear bigger as it was attacked.

A second later Ty came strolling out of the gift shop with a brown paper bag held to his lips. He was blowing it full of air. He calmly held it up, then shouted at the top of his voice, "He's got a gun!" and slammed the paper bag into his open palm.

Utter chaos ensued. Shrieks and yells filled the air, and the crowd stampeded every which way, creating a jumble of confusion and fear. Mothers snatched their children up and ran. Senior citizens ducked behind pillars and newsstands.

Cameron didn't think Ty could have caused more of a ruckus if he'd gotten up on a table and danced naked in front of the arrivals and departures sign. Apparently, disorder was Ty's specialty.

A moment later Ty was at Cameron's side, urging both him and Julian to move through the panicking crowd. He and Julian both ducked to hide their height, but it didn't take long until they were confronted with a charcoal suit amidst the zigzagging crowd.

Ty reached out for the man, who was drawing his gun, and he pulled him closer by his shoulder. He shoved the heel of his hand into the man's chin, snapping his head back, then rounded on him with his left and sent him to the ground. His actions were remarkably quick and powerful, all done in a split second and hard to follow. Cameron had only ever seen Julian move like that. Ty held up something he'd taken from the man, showing it to Julian over his shoulder. Julian still held Cameron's hand as they vaulted over the fallen man and broke into a run.

Cameron chanced a glance over his shoulder as Julian dragged him down the concourse, looking back at the mess and the agents coming out this side of the crowd. "They're still coming!"

The crowd was too thick, and there were just too many men after them for Cameron to see how they could get away. The exits were a logjam of people and confused airport security. There seemed to be nowhere to go.

Julian glanced back and turned, putting himself between Cameron and the pursuers. Ty was looking around the concourse, and Cameron caught a glimpse of the wild cast to his oddly colored eyes. He looked like a cornered animal, wily and dangerous.

"We're trapped," Julian said.

After a last look at their paltry options, Ty pointed a finger into Julian's chest, then waved them toward the exits. "Go," he snarled.

"What?"

"Go! Find Zane. I'll hold them off." Then he turned his back on them, facing the men coming after them with a roll of his shoulders and a tilt of his head.

Julian took a step back, momentarily stunned, but then he gripped Cameron's hand harder and pulled him, turning and running, leaving

Ty behind them to stem the tide of the oncoming suits. Cameron managed to glance back in time to see Ty launch himself into the first man; then they were obscured by the panicking crowd around them.

"But... Julian! They'll kill him!"

"They'll kill *us*, Cam!"

Stopping him was impossible against Julian's size and determination. They darted in and out of pockets of confused people, weaving their way through the masses and finally finding a side hallway that had an emergency exit at the end. Julian started toward it, but he hesitated, glancing over his shoulder. Cameron jumped on the vacillation.

"Julian, I know you two didn't get along, but please! He and Zane could have just given you to them, but instead they're trying to help us," Cameron said, pulling on Julian's hand, the upset getting stronger the longer they were away. Every second was a second Ty could be dying. "He doesn't deserve to die for trying to help us."

Julian met his eyes, and Cameron could see the indecision there. Then he shook his head and turned for the exit.

"Please! He'd come back for you, and you know it!"

Julian stopped and turned again, an anguished expression passing over his face. "Goddammit all to hell, Cam," he finally growled, the words rolling out beautifully in his Irish accent. "Stay here." And with that he launched himself back into the crowd.

Now both desperately afraid and insanely relieved, Cameron followed despite what Julian had said. The concourse had cleared some, but the space where they'd left Ty to make his last stand was a jumble of people and suitcases and café chairs. Tables were overturned, magazines littered the floor, and the contents of suitcases were strewn about where they'd been dropped.

Two men lay on the floor as well, one bleeding and motionless, the other writhing and screaming as he held his arm at an odd angle.

They reached the melee just in time to witness an impressive roundhouse kick to a charcoal suit's head that sent the man sprawling. But then a gun was pulled behind Ty, drawing his attention long enough for two more suits to swamp him. He disappeared under a hail of fists and expensive wool and silk. Cameron could see Ty lashing out, being held down and fighting like a wild horse trying not to be roped. He was kicked in the ribs, stomped on the side of the head as he tried and failed to roll away. Another gun was pulled and put to the back of his head.

"No!" Cameron yelled just as Julian went for the gun, knocking it and its owner to the ground. Zane appeared on the other side of the dog pile, wading in as if they weren't outnumbered and weaponless.

Julian's movements were quick and efficient, hands grabbing the suit's neck and chin and twisting with a vicious, sickening crunch. He shoved the man aside and reached to the bottom of the pile, pulling Ty out by his collar like he was scruffing a kitten.

"How did I know this commotion was your doing?" Zane yelled at them.

"Come on!" Cameron called. Before he could get more words out, he was shocked into crying out when someone grabbed him from behind. He immediately started to struggle against whoever held him. "Julian!" Cameron called out in real terror.

Julian looked up, dropped Ty's nearly limp body back into the fray, and raised the gun he'd confiscated. The shot was deafening, and the warm spray on Cameron's ear and cheek was evidence that Julian's aim was true. The hands released him, and the bulk that had been behind him fell away. Cameron reflexively lifted his hand to wipe at the splatter across his cheek.

Then Julian reached back down and grabbed Ty again, jerking him off the floor. "Come on!" he shouted at Zane. Zane knocked down the man with whom he'd been grappling with a vicious punch to the midsection, grabbed a gun off one of the unconscious men, and was only a couple of steps behind them as they ran toward Cameron, Julian dragging Ty with him.

The gunshot had caused more panic, and now TSA and other airport security were starting to appear, rushing into the wrecked causeway, trying to get people out of the way and assess the situation.

Julian wrapped his arm around Ty and supported some of his weight, ducking his head and hiding his face as they made their way past the overwhelmed security checkpoint. They followed the crowd, letting it sweep them toward the exits. Cameron ducked under Zane's arm to hide as they shuffled out. Zane flashed his badge at the man who tried to stop them to hasten their exit.

"There. Government-issue SUV at the curb," Julian said as he pointed through the glass doors. "I managed to get the keys off one of them."

Zane headed that way without even questioning it, and he went to the back door to try the handle. It popped open, and Julian shoved Ty inside and then climbed in after him, leaving the front for Cameron and Zane. Cameron scrambled in through the driver's side and over the console. Zane glanced around them before climbing in, calmly shutting the door and driving away into traffic.

Cameron turned in his seat to look at the two men in the back. "Ty? Are you okay?"

"Feels like somebody shoved a boot between my ribs," Ty answered, voice strained.

"That's actually exactly what happened," Cameron told him.

Ty hissed and then growled at Julian. "Quit touching me."

"I'm trying to make sure you're not dying," Julian shot back.

"Well, that hurts!"

"All the more reason to poke it!"

"Play nice," Zane said, but there was too much edge in his tone for it to be funny.

Cameron watched how he kept checking the rearview mirror. He wondered if Zane was checking for a tail or trying to get a look at his roughed-up partner.

"Will we get away?"

"For now," Zane said. "It'll take them some time to figure out who's where and what's missing, enough time for us to get somewhere and disable the GPS in this thing. But it won't last."

"That was fucking stupid," Ty muttered from the backseat. "I told you to go."

"Yes, well, unfortunately my conscience is a little more willful than most," Julian grumbled, and Cameron knew his lover was talking about him.

"They were CIA again, Zane," Ty said, voice soft and hoarse. He pulled a badge from his coat, waving it at them. He had lifted it from one of the men in the airport. "I identified myself and they didn't care."

"Rogue cell," Julian murmured. "They've got to be acting under his orders."

"Whose orders?"

Julian took a moment to explain what was going on to Zane, and it was mostly news to Cameron too.

"Burns must be protecting someone," Ty said, voice still strained. "Or investigating on the down low."

"Rogue or not, they've had the resources and the manpower to stay on us this long. I don't see that mess stopping them from keeping after us," Zane said as he shifted his attention back and forth from traffic and the rearview.

"We need to get somewhere safe. Unexpected," Ty said. Cameron couldn't see him, but he sounded worn and beaten.

"And soon. Your partner is bleeding," Julian informed Zane without a hint of sympathy.

Zane finally looked over his shoulder back at Ty. "How serious?"

"Shut up, that's not my blood," Ty murmured. His voice sounded weak.

"Ty," Zane said, his voice brooking no humorous pushover. Cameron heard leather squeak, and when he looked, he saw Zane's hands gripping the steering wheel so tightly his knuckles were white.

"What? It's not my blood!"

"Let me see it," Julian demanded, and a moment later there were sounds of a scuffle from the back seat.

"I am AB positive and this is distinctly type O blood!" Ty finally shouted at him. "Look at the little Os!"

"Jesus Christ, Grady, can you not take one fucking thing seriously?" Julian yelled back in utter frustration. Cameron wondered what it was about Ty that made Julian lose his composure so easily. If he weren't so secure in their relationship, he might actually be jealous of it.

Cameron gasped as the SUV jerked over to the shoulder of the road and came to a sudden stop. Zane threw it into park and turned in his seat. "Enough!" he shouted, grabbing Ty's wrist when it flailed within reach. Cameron shrank back, leaning against the passenger-side door as Zane growled. "Grady, give me a clear answer, dammit!"

"I'm not bleeding!" Ty insisted, sounding a mixture of exasperated and hurt that Zane didn't believe him. "Would you put the car back in drive before we're strafed by CIA fighter jets or something?"

"I swear to fucking God," Zane cursed under his breath as he let go, turned back around, and got the SUV moving again.

Cameron leaned his head back against the leather headrest and closed his eyes. This was like National Lampoon's *Vacation*, but with death, property destruction, and an Irish accent. He groaned and covered his face with one hand, only to touch sticky blood all down his cheek and jawline. He groaned again. The second time it sounded pitiful, even to his ears.

There was a tense silence for several seconds, and then Ty opened his mouth one last time. "I think the kid is bleeding."

"WHO *are* these people?" Agent X asked his superior in utter frustration.

"We've finally discerned their identities. They're FBI."

"Real FBI?"

"It would appear so. Richard Burns is pulling no punches when it comes to old friends."

"Do you wish us to continue? They killed two of my men."

"And stole two of your vehicles."

"I don't mourn the cars."

"Now that we're certain we know the names of the men involved, it will be easier to find them."

"If you say so, sir."

"Keep on them."

"Yes, sir."

He hung up and looked around the concourse of Pittsburgh International Airport. FBI agents. They had done this with two prisoners in tow and no weapons. He was beginning to wish he'd been sent to Alaska instead of this assignment.

"OKAY, if this is the CIA, what else are they doing?" Ty asked Julian as soon as they were satisfied that they'd lost any tails and disassembled the GPS in their stolen car.

"What do you mean?"

"We know they were pinging the GPS in the bureau car."

"Wait, I thought you dismantled that," Cameron said as he turned around.

"Bureau issue vehicles have two types of GPS. The backup is covert, meaning it's passive," Ty said.

"The Agency was pinging us with their remote systems," Julian explained.

"You knew," Zane said as he looked in the mirror at Julian.

"Well, at the time I was hoping to pit the sides against each other and escape."

"At least he's honest," Ty grumbled.

Zane glared at both of them for a moment.

Cameron waved a hand. "Okay, I get how they found us in the car you stole."

"Borrowed," Ty said.

"Whatever, psychopath. But how did they find us after?"

"Any number of ways," Julian said in a troubled voice. "Credit cards. The tolls when we passed through. Our cell phones. Depending on how high this goes, they could have even diverted a satellite."

"How high does it go?" Zane asked.

"I don't know his name, I just know his voice."

"You said cell phones," Ty murmured

"Yes. You turned the GPS off, but again, if it goes high enough, they can turn it back on remotely."

"Right. But do they have the firepower to listen in on calls?" Ty asked.

"Yes," Julian said with a simple nod.

Ty looked from Julian to Zane, and Zane had to take his eyes off the road long enough to meet Ty's eyes in the mirror. He could tell Ty was formulating a plan, and the fear behind those hazel eyes told Zane that Ty didn't like what he was thinking.

"What?" Zane asked with a growing sense of dread.

"If they're picking up on our calls, maybe we can call for help."

"What?"

"I'm sorry, I believe you lost me as well," Julian said.

"At least I'm not the only one," Cameron muttered.

"They're big, we're little. Their strength is the information they gather and how they do it. We have to turn that against them."

"A skewer," Julian said in a surprised voice.

"A what?" Ty asked.

"Chess. A skewer is a chess move. Use their strength against them. Their queen is opposite our rook. They're supported by their knight, and we only have a pawn. But if their queen takes our rook, our pawn takes their queen."

"I'm sorry, was that English?" Ty asked in exasperation.

Zane looked up at the mirror to see Julian again. He was a fascinating person once he opened up enough to allow them insight into his mind. Zane was glad he was on their side now.

"I'm agreeing with you, you wanker," Julian snapped.

"Well, stop, it's weird."

Julian grunted and sat back with his arms crossed over his chest.

"I have no idea how to play chess," Ty said in a flat voice. Zane glanced at his partner. Talk about fascinating, though, Zane didn't have to go further than Ty. Zane would never get tired of watching the way Ty's mind worked. "But yeah, I guess, that's exactly what I'm talking about. We need a pawn."

"A rook."

"Whatever!"

"You want to make a phone call to someone and make the Agency think we're heading there for help," Zane surmised, voice grim.

"Basically. Yeah."

"And where would we go instead? To DC?" Cameron asked.

Ty nodded, remaining silent as the sound of the tires on asphalt seeped into the quiet car.

"It's sound, in theory," Julian said with a frown.

"Who would you call? I mean…." Cameron trailed off, sounding troubled. "Whoever you call will be in just as much danger as we are."

Ty was still looking into Zane's eyes. Zane nodded, knowing exactly what his partner was thinking.

"I know a few guys who can handle themselves."

Zane waited a breath. He knew Ty was talking about his Recon team. And probably Nick fucking O'Flaherty.

"Call one of them."

JULIAN sat in the backseat of the stolen CIA Tahoe, watching Ty as he made the call. He was surprised when Ty spoke in French. He was quite fluent, even using a convincing accent. He sounded almost like a native speaker.

Julian blinked at him in shock, looking at the two men in the front seat to see if either of them was surprised. Cameron glanced back, but he didn't seem to comprehend anything other than it was a foreign language and it was far too dainty for a man like Ty to speak. Zane glanced up, eyes on Ty more than the road.

Julian had known Ty could speak French. He hadn't seen him in Paris like he'd led them to believe, but he knew from a reliable source that he had indeed been there. It was still a shock to hear him speak it. Julian knew enough of the language to decipher that Ty was basically telling the other man, "We're in trouble, we're coming to you to lay low."

Ty switched the phone from one ear to the other, clearing his throat. He spoke in English. "And Digger? Make sure you have coconuts when we get there, okay? Lots of them."

Julian could hear the tinny voice on the phone responding, and then Ty ended the call. He glanced at Julian and narrowed his eyes as he rolled down the window. The frigid wind whipped through the car, ruffling Julian's hair, tugging at his coat. Ty tossed the phone out the window and rolled it back up.

Julian stared at him, and Ty ignored him like only children and felines were typically capable of doing.

"Coconuts?"

"It's… *Monty Python*. Coconuts were the fake horse. It'll make sense to him."

"Right."

"I was telling him it was a ruse."

"Got it."

"Where to?" Zane asked in a solemn voice. The heavy sense of impending doom hung over them, making everything sedate and surreal.

Ty shook his head. "I feel like I just threw one of my best friends under a bus."

"You said the bayou would handle it, right?"

"Yeah," Ty whispered.

Julian looked between them. For the first time, the two FBI agents were beginning to take on an air of defeat. He had formed a grudging respect for both men, and he wasn't so blind that he couldn't see what they'd done. They could easily have handed him and Cameron over when they realized they were being followed and were outgunned. They had no vested interest in getting Julian to DC, other than they had orders. They were fighting and running and risking their lives simply because Julian and Cameron now needed their help. There was no other reason for it.

"I might know someone who can help us get to DC," he said after a few more moments of silence to ponder it.

He saw Zane's dark eyes looking at him in the mirror, and Ty was looking at him as well, messing around with his belt as if something was jabbing him.

"He retired several years ago, bought a… an antique store in Gettysburg."

"A real antique store, or the kind that can help us?" Ty asked.

"A real one, unfortunately. But I believe he could still help us. He flew biplanes, it was his hobby. He would loan us one for a price."

"Loan us one?" Zane asked as he kept his eyes on the road.

"A biplane? What are we supposed to do, duct tape ourselves to the wings all the way to DC?" Ty grunted. "I'm not a fucking Wright brother, okay?"

"Well, no, but this will all be over when I get to DC. Two of us could go, the other stay with Cameron."

"Can you fly a plane?" Ty asked with an incredulous glance at Julian.

"No. I was hoping you could."

"Do I *look* like I can fly a plane?" Ty snapped, getting more irritable the more he messed with his ribcage.

Julian pursed his lips as he looked at Ty. "I just assumed, since you enjoyed the TSA so much."

"Okay, let's stop right there," Zane said hastily.

"Julian, would your friend be able to find a bigger plane for us? One he could fly?" Cameron asked as he turned in his seat.

Julian shrugged. "We could ask him."

"Yes. Let's go ask him," Ty muttered. "That's fucking stupid."

"Fine," Julian said, his tone making it clear he was reaching the end of his patience. "We'll solve this like men."

"What do you want, MacGuffin, a duel?"

"No." Julian held out both hands, one palm flat, the other held over it in a fist. "Rock, paper, scissors. Two out of three."

Ty rolled his eyes and held out his fist, apparently willing to play. Julian hit his palm three times, and Ty kept time with his fist in the air.

But when Julian threw a paper, Ty reached into his jacket with his other hand and pulled his gun, aiming it at Julian.

"Ty!" Zane said in exasperation from the front seat.

"Glock, paper, scissors. I win."

"You are an ass," Julian muttered.

"Ty, put your gun away," Zane muttered, less sarcastic than his partner. "To Gettysburg, then?"

"Fine. And when we get there you can shave that fucking ferret's nest off your face," Ty said to Zane as he shoved the gun back into his coat.

"And on the way we'll get some Cheetos and Dr Pepper for Ty's blood sugar," Zane added, unperturbed.

In the front seat, Cameron clapped a hand over his mouth so no one would hear him snort.

~Chapter 12~

CAMERON looked up at Julian as they rode the elevator in the Gettysburg Hotel up to the third floor. "Do you think this man you used to know is still here?"

"I'd like to think so. If he's not, he's dead, and that would distress me a little," Julian answered, deadpan.

"Did you know him well? He was a friend?" Cameron asked.

"More an acquaintance. A coworker." Julian glanced sideways at Cameron and smiled. "He retired of his own volition. That doesn't happen often to people I know."

Cameron rolled his eyes and smiled as the elevator doors opened. "I imagine not, though I like to dream."

"You talk when you dream," Julian said in a low voice, fighting hard to keep the smile out of his voice. He took Cameron's elbow and let his fingers drift down his lover's arm as they stepped out of the elevator. Ty and Zane had let them go alone to scout the area. Julian knew they were testing him to see if they could trust him, and he also knew that Ty hadn't made it out of that brawl as easy as he was leading them to believe. He was hurt, and Zane had sequestered him in the hotel room as soon as they'd arrived.

"We have a room to ourselves tonight," Julian murmured to Cameron with a smirk. "I'm quite looking forward to it."

"Ty and Zane will still be next door," Cameron said, but his smile didn't fade. If anything, it grew wider.

"Like I care at this point." Julian allowed himself to grin as they came to the door of the first room. He gave Cameron a wink as he rapped his knuckles on the door three times.

"You never cared," Cameron murmured with a laugh. "About what they think, anyway."

"I maintain they're both idiots," Julian muttered, albeit more fondly than he would have a day ago.

The door opened. "I heard that," Zane said as he stepped back to let them in the room.

"I know." Julian waved for Cameron to go in first, then followed with a smirk at Zane as he passed.

Zane shut the door behind them a little harder than strictly necessary, and he stalked past them to thump down in the chair at the desk. His face was set in a deep frown as he glared at Ty, who sat sprawled in a wingback chair near the bed, bottle of water in hand. He'd been bitching about the lack of Dr Pepper for a few days now. He was apparently going through some sort of caffeine withdrawal, and he refused to drink Coke or Pepsi or even Red Bull. They were going to have to force something caffeinated down his throat soon, or he was going to kill them all.

Julian raised one eyebrow at Zane but didn't comment on his crankiness. The room was thick with tension that almost buzzed between the two FBI agents.

"What'd you find out?" Ty demanded of Julian.

"Well, dinner is quite pricey in the tavern downstairs, there's a ghost walk that begins at eight o'clock a few blocks away, and the young lady at the front desk is unnaturally friendly. I believe her to be a clone of some sort."

Ty pinched the bridge of his nose, as if desperately trying to keep himself from shooting Julian where he stood.

Cameron thumped Julian's arm. "You're not helping."

"That's all we found out," Julian said with a shrug. "There's a great deal of construction in town. And it's been a while since I've been here, so it will take me some time to orient myself. I'm afraid I was confounded when I arrived at Nestor's shop to find that it was no longer Nestor's shop. He's moved location, and while I did find the new building and leave him a message, it will be morning before we hear anything from him."

"Morning. Great," Ty said as he stood.

"We could all do with a night to sleep," Zane said.

"I'm antsy, Zane."

"You're high on exhaustion and Cheetos."

"One walk around the block isn't going to kill any of us."

"We don't know who's looking for us out there."

"Am I allowed to interject an opinion yet?" Julian asked with a frown.

"No. Shut up," Ty snapped.

"We need more information and more sleep before going back out. You can't just run around blind," Zane stated, his voice dropping into an angry growl.

"You're one to bitch at me about running blind," Ty muttered as he sat back down with a thump.

"Ty, put on your big girl panties and stop bitching, okay?" Zane growled, sitting up straighter. Julian noticed one of his hands clutching in and out of a fist. "There's no way in hell you're leaving this room tonight."

"Guys—" Cameron started. Julian reached out to touch Cameron's shoulder and stop him. He'd seen discussions like this in his line of work, and they sometimes ended bloody. With these two it seemed prudent to stay out of the argument.

"No way in hell?" Ty repeated incredulously. "What are you now, the stroll police?"

"We wait for Cross' contact and at least wait until dark to go wandering around," Zane said with finality. "And that's still a bad idea."

Julian cleared his throat. "Really, we won't hear from him until morning. Until then…." Julian shrugged and trailed off as he tried to gauge the tension between the two men. Zane's back was ramrod stiff as he sat unmoving, and he hadn't taken his eyes off Ty. Ty was the exact opposite, antsy and agitated, appearing to be moving even as he sat relatively still.

Cameron shifted closer to Julian, taking his elbow as he waited for the ensuing fight.

"I hate it when mother and father fight," Julian said under his breath.

"Shut up," Ty snapped at him, then turned on Zane, who stood to meet him. "Sit down, take a bubble bath or something. I need to take a walk."

"God*dammit*!" Zane lashed out without warning and hit the water bottle, sending it skidding across the carpet and splattering at Julian's feet. "I'm gonna end up in the fucking madhouse because of you!" He reached out and grabbed Ty's wrist, pulling him closer. "Loving you is going to make me fucking *insane*! I said no, and I *mean* it!"

Ty froze. Julian could only see half his face, but he appeared to be staring at Zane, mouth hanging open.

Julian realized he was doing the same thing. After several heartbeats, Zane closed his eyes and exhaled.

"I'm sorry. Did you say *loving* him?" Julian blurted incredulously. He pointed at Ty. "*Him*? You and *him*?"

"Julian...." Cameron tugged on his arm, trying to get him to leave the room, and Julian went along as he continued to gape at them.

Ty and Zane just stood there, frozen, Zane with his head bowed, Ty staring at him.

"I did not see that coming," Julian said to Cameron under his breath.

"Good to know you can still be surprised," Cameron whispered. "Now come on."

Julian nodded and turned with Cameron, glancing back at their companions. "We'll just be... somewhere else," he told them as he reached for the door.

There was no answer as Julian closed the door behind them.

"Wow," Cameron said quietly.

"Indeed," Julian murmured. He looked at Cameron speculatively, not sure how to parse the information they'd just been made privy to and not certain what to do now that they had an entire night to themselves.

Cameron looked back at the door. There wasn't any sound coming through it. "Come on. Let's go downstairs."

"And drink," Julian added, nodding. He smiled suddenly, giving Cameron a sly sideways glance. "Or. We could just turn in for the night. In our own room."

"Which is next door, and you'll be tempted to eavesdrop," Cameron said, waving at the room down the hall. "Compromise," he said, looking up to meet Julian's eyes with an answering smile. "Drink, then room. Just… give them a little time."

Julian gave an exaggerated roll of his eyes as he slipped his arm around Cameron's shoulders. "You're an insufferable romantic, you know that?"

"And you love me for it."

"I do." He glanced back at the door. "I wonder if they'll be done in time to realize joining that ghost tour is the best way to reconnoiter?"

"You're an insufferable predator," Cameron said, tongue-in-cheek.

"And you love me for it."

"I do."

ZANE squeezed his eyes shut as he waited for Ty to say something, but Ty smiled slowly and took a step toward him. "You totally just outed us to the criminals," he said as he pointed a finger at Zane.

"You make me insane, do you know that?" Zane blurted again with a wave of one hand. "Do you do it on purpose just to see me lose it?"

"Sometimes," Ty said with a smirk.

Zane sighed in utter frustration.

Ty bit his lip, watching his lover just because he could. He firmly believed that being able to rile Zane like he could was one of the aspects of their relationship that had saved Zane from tumbling back into his destructive past. Every now and then, Zane just needed to feel like he was alive. Everyone should be able to feel that. And if annoying him to the point of homicide was what it took, Ty was up to the challenge.

"What brought this on?" he asked after Zane was silent for a time.

Zane shook his head, his eyes drifting to the door of the room.

Ty gaped at him and pointed at the door. "From the criminals?"

Zane snorted, caught Ty's hand, and kissed his fingers. "Apparently some 'criminals' have better sense than I do."

"You're modeling your love life on that of a trained assassin," Ty laid out in disbelief. "I swear to God, if he pulled some Jedi mind trick on you and they're off escaping right now, I will put a bullet in his Irish ass!"

Zane laughed, the sound almost desperate as he swiped a hand over his face. "Well, now what do we do?" he asked, dejected. They had gone months without breaking their cover in front of anyone. It had almost been a source of pride for them. Just another undercover assignment.

Ty shook his head, looking at Zane again as unusual warmth began to spread through him. "I don't care if they know. I don't care if anyone knows anymore."

Zane looked at him sharply. "You don't mean that."

Ty shrugged. They both knew what their options would be if their relationship was discovered at work. It had nothing to do with them being gay and everything to do with the FBI's unofficial policy on fraternizing. "I think we take our chances when we get home."

"What?"

"They'd just reassign us partners within the work group. We'd still be working together. You'd end up with Freddy, they'd probably put me with Scott. It wouldn't be too bad. We could actually… you could get rid of your crappy apartment and we could live together."

Zane stared at him, his dark eyes taking on an almost molten appearance. Ty's breath caught in his throat as he tried and failed to continue speaking. Deuce had asked him once what it was about Zane that had first drawn him in. He'd been a broken man, an addict who was hopelessly lost in the past, drifting through life alone with little purpose and even less faith that it could get better.

Anyone with any sense would have steered clear. But from the first moment Ty had really looked into Zane's eyes, he'd seen behind them, into the man Zane was capable of being. He'd seen a phoenix waiting to rise from the ashes, and he still did. Every time he looked into Zane, he saw something extraordinary.

Zane shook his head, his breaths coming harder as they stared at each other. "What if you live with me and you change your mind?"

"Zane," Ty said in frustration. He held up one hand. "In the time you've been with me, have I *ever* changed my mind after deciding something? Even when we both knew I was wrong?"

Zane smiled weakly and shook his head.

"I love you," Ty said, the quiet words devoid of any self-consciousness or his usual bravado. "And I've never been able to say that before with such conviction. I can't remember a time that you weren't the first thing I thought of, and I want to spend the rest of my life with you. I don't care what stands in our way."

Zane's breath hitched, and he reached out for Ty. He caught Ty's face gently between his hands and kissed him, drawing it out until finally releasing his lips to run his nose along Ty's cheek. Ty closed his eyes, feeling the calm that Zane's touch always instilled in him sweep over him. He pushed his nose against Zane's as he slid his fingers into his hair. If he and Zane had any say in the workings of fate, Zane would be the last person he ever touched like this.

Zane let out a shaky breath and whispered. "Will you… will you make love to me?"

Ty chuckled and took Zane's face in his hands to kiss him. "Baby," he started, a thousand things going through his mind to say, every one of them a typical smartass Grady remark. He looked into Zane's sincere eyes and his smile softened. Zane's occasional purple prose was all part of his charm. Sometimes Ty even let him slide without poking fun at him. "I'd like that."

Zane grinned and gave him another gentle kiss, lapping at his lips to get Ty to part them. His hands settled atop Ty's shoulders before sliding down his chest, catching on the soft material of Ty's T-shirt, and around his torso to hug him close. Ty gave him a gentle tug, trying to get him to swing around and lie back with him on one of the antique double beds. Zane pulled back from their kiss and pulled off his Henley, tossing it to the floor, before reaching to slide his hands under Ty's T-shirt to strip it off him. There were two soft thuds on the carpet—Zane toeing off his shoes—then he shifted onto the mattress, pulling up his legs as he lay on his side alongside Ty.

"Baby," Ty whispered against Zane's lips. He had never felt this sort of heat and longing for another person. He didn't know how Zane did it, but Ty knew that there would never be anyone else for him. He wanted Zane to feel that too, to have that assurance both physically and emotionally. He would do whatever he had to do to make sure that Zane knew he was his.

He slid his hand into Zane's hair, gripping the curls at the base of his neck and using them to pull Zane's head back, just to be able to kiss him harder. Zane's lips were soft and gave under his as he drove the kiss. They lay wrapped around one another, and when he shifted more, Zane broke off the kiss with a gasp and rocked their groins together despite the layers of thin cloth between them. The look in Zane's eyes told Ty that he was on the right path. Zane's reply was lost between Ty's lips, but he dragged his legs apart so Ty could settle between them.

Ty groaned as Zane wrapped around him. He broke the kiss and pushed himself up, bracing himself with one hand as he used the other to tug at Zane's undershirt. "Get these off," he snarled.

Zane didn't hesitate. He pulled the shirt off as Ty pawed at it, and started unfastening his pants, hurrying to arch his back and start shoving them down over his hips along with his briefs. Ty had to crawl backward to let him get them off, and he pushed his own jeans and boxers down his thighs and got rid of them before he knelt between Zane's legs.

"Come here," Zane invited, holding out one arm to pull Ty back close against his warm skin.

Ty took his hand and kissed his fingers, then his palm, then his wrist. He tugged at Zane's hand, trying to get him to sit up instead. Zane did, sucking in a breath and sitting up without pulling his hand away, and it put him right in the circle of Ty's arms. Ty slid his fingers between Zane's as he kissed him. He had to lean over him to get closer, raising himself up on his knees. Zane spread his legs wider, propping up his knees and moving his feet out as Ty moved closer to him. A new wave of possessiveness and desire swept through Ty as he looked down at his lover. He ran his hand through Zane's hair, gripping the curls again to yank his head back and kiss him.

It only took a few seconds for him to tighten his grip and force Zane back down to the mattress. He used Zane's body to pull himself up and closer, settling between Zane's legs, pushing his hips against Zane's inner thighs, rubbing his hard cock against Zane's with a groan. Zane exhaled harshly as he shifted his legs further apart, making room for Ty as he slid both hands over Ty's shoulders and down his back and all over what skin he could reach. Not gripping or pinching or squeezing, just touching. He was murmuring too, desperate words that sounded like *I love you*.

Ty's hand went to the back of Zane's thigh, pulling at it to settle Zane's raised leg against his hip. He kissed him languidly, taking care to slide his lips and tongue against Zane's, wanting to give them both the chance to taste and feel each other before they lost all self-control. He rocked his hips almost unconsciously, rubbing their groins together as they kissed. Zane sighed against his lips as he followed Ty's lead and relaxed under him.

"I've wanted this," Zane said, breathless.

"You've had this, Zane," Ty said as he took a brief moment to push up and adjust his position.

"Not this," Zane argued. "We haven't had this."

Ty brushed his nose against Zane's, nodding in understanding. "We have it now."

He settled lower between Zane's legs, the head of his cock pushing against Zane's ass. He pulled at Zane's thigh again as he laid himself out over him and dove into another, more demanding kiss.

Zane curled his arms around Ty even as he shifted under the weight, trying to create friction between them.

Ty groaned appreciatively, his hand sliding up Zane's leg to grip and pull at his hip. "Lube in my bag or yours?" he asked breathlessly, cursing himself for not thinking of that a little earlier in the process of making them both almost painfully aroused.

"Both?" Zane answered with a soft laugh. As he spoke, his hand smoothed down his belly toward his erect cock.

Ty reached to stop him, knowing that if Zane started touching himself, they'd never make it to the lubricant. And he desperately wanted to be inside Zane tonight. He pulled Zane's hand up and held it down against the mattress.

"Two seconds," he said as he rose and looked down at Zane hungrily. "Don't start without me."

He caught the wicked smile before Zane hid it. Ty rolled backward and crawled to the end of the bed, leaning over to grab his bag and pull out the leather toiletry bag he carried with him.

"Want you in me, baby," Zane said from behind him.

Ty grunted and tossed the bag to the head of the bed as he crawled back up between Zane's legs. He let his hands slide over Zane's body, fingers digging into the hard ridges of muscle and soaking up the warmth of his skin, and Zane lifted up into his touch. Ty bowed his head to kiss at Zane's stomach, sliding his hand up to his chest and following its path until he was back where he'd started, between Zane's spread legs and kissing him. Zane moaned and hooked his calf over the back of Ty's thigh, his hand settling on Ty's waist for leverage as he tipped his hips up into Ty's.

Ty growled and pushed himself up, muttering as he reached for the bag and fumbled inside it. Zane gave another obscenely sexy moan as he continued to rub their bodies together, moving his hand to the other side of Ty's waist. Ty finally pushed the bag over and toppled all the contents out, finding what he needed from the pile and then using his forearm to sweep everything else off the double bed to the carpeted floor.

Zane laughed at his haste, but the heat and desire in his eyes were still shining.

Ty pushed up, looking at Zane and rolling his hips down as he watched their bodies moving together. "Fuck, Zane," he hissed as he bent down to nip at Zane's lips.

Zane nodded as he licked along Ty's full bottom lip. "Want me to turn over?"

"No," Ty growled. He leaned on his elbow, using his other hand to slide between them and down Zane's body. "I want you right here," he told Zane, stealing one last sloppy kiss before pushing back to his knees.

Zane's hands dragged down Ty's body as Ty moved. Ty ran one hand along the inside of Zane's thigh, unable to keep himself from touching. He enjoyed the play of muscle under soft skin, the occasional imperfection of a scar under his fingertips, the way Zane tensed and writhed beneath his hands. He became distracted by the drag of his fingertips against Zane's thigh. Zane quivered under him as he caressed. He was extra sensitive there, right at the juncture of his thigh and hip, not quite ticklish, and it was one of Ty's favorite places to touch and grip and dig his fingers into when they fucked. Ty ducked his head to kiss the spot he'd been stroking. Zane groaned and his eyes fell closed as he tipped his head back, and his hands closed into fists in the sheets.

Ty grabbed the back of his thigh hard and folded Zane's leg up as he leaned over him, bending just enough to kiss the inside of his knee. He reached for the little bottle of lubricant and pressed it into Zane's hand. Then he sat back and let his hand slide under Zane's other knee, his fingers gently stroking the very top of his calf, enjoying the sight of Zane's legs splayed around his hips.

Zane blinked his eyes open to look at Ty as he lifted the bottle and shook it a couple times before popping the top open. "What do you want?" he asked as he squeezed some of the lube onto his fingers.

"Make sure you're ready," Ty murmured. His hand moved up Zane's leg, not tugging or pulling, merely skimming over it until he reached his hip. "This is going to take a while."

Zane swallowed hard and reached for Ty, long fingers closing around his cock. Ty jutted his hips out, pushing into Zane's hand as he watched. Zane took his sweet time, spreading the slick lubricant all over, palming the head, dragging his fingers against Ty's balls. Ty reached to slide his fingers along Zane's, not guiding him, just enjoying the stroke of his hand.

"Ty," Zane whispered, desperate and needy.

Ty moved both their hands and pushed up to his knees, wrapping one arm around Zane's leg to lift it again as he pushed Zane flat to his back. Zane reached for Ty with one hand, palm brushing against his bicep, fingers glancing off his shoulder; his other hand curled around his own shin to pull it closer to his chest.

Ty didn't have to ask him if he was ready. That touch to his shoulder told him everything he needed to know. He kissed him, taking his time with it, enjoying the last moments of anticipation before he reached between them and guided himself into Zane. He rocked in place until the slick head of his cock slipped past the muscles that fought him; then he gave one languorous push.

Zane gasped out, his hand uselessly grasping for Ty's hip.

Ty lowered his head and let out a harsh sigh, resting his nose against Zane's chin as he flexed his hips and pushed deeper into him. The shift of Zane's body under him, the arch of Zane's back, the shortness of his breath, it all combined to keep him shuddering as Ty filled him up. His exhaled breath was warm against Ty's cheek as Zane started to moan.

Ty lifted his head and kissed him hungrily, sliding his fingers into Zane's hair and merely rocking his hips, wanting to make this last as long as possible. Zane calmed under him, joining in the rocking motion as their tongues slid together, and he wrapped his arms around Ty's neck to hold him close. It was slow and sensual, nothing but their gasping breaths and the wet slide of their kisses.

Zane lifted his knee higher, gasping when it pulled Ty deeper. Ty groaned, unable to continue merely rocking his hips any longer. His hand left Zane's hair to slide up the back of his leg instead, fingers digging in as he pulled back and thrust in.

Zane shivered under him and choked on a low cry of Ty's name. "Please, baby, you gotta... move. Harder."

Ty kissed him again, tightening his hold simply because he could. He continued the slow, even thrusts, enjoying the slide of their bodies rather than trying to reach the end too soon. Zane's fingers tightened on Ty's arms, but Ty stayed steady. The tension released, and Zane resorted to making needy noises in his throat and rolling his hips to meet each thrust.

Ty truly didn't think they'd ever done this. They'd intended to several times, but neither of them had the strength of will to go slowly when the other was begging for harder and faster.

He pulled Zane's leg up further as his thrusts got longer, but he managed to maintain the sensual speed, driving into Zane deep and pulling out slow so he could feel Zane's muscles squeezing and pulling at him. He relished the slide every time he pulled back, and every time he pushed back in, it sent hot waves of pleasure and desire through him.

"Fuck, Zane," Ty found himself whispering breathlessly as he pressed his face against Zane's neck.

Their bodies rocked with the languid rhythm. Zane's answer was a pleased hum.

Ty raised his head and searched out Zane's mouth. He picked up the rhythm, matching it with his tongue against Zane's. Zane's hum turned into a fully audible moan, and he started to move under Ty, rubbing against him all over as they kissed, rolling his hips and sliding his cock against Ty's belly.

Ty groaned against Zane's lips. He indulged in the kiss for a few more seconds before pushing himself up with both hands. Fucking Zane when he was really into it was a little like riding a mechanical bull. It was best to restrain him or Ty would end up on the floor.

He gripped Zane's hips, pulling back and tugging Zane with him. His hips rested on Ty's spread thighs, his legs splayed on either side of Ty. Ty let his hands roam over Zane's taut body as he rocked into him.

"Oh Christ, yes," Zane whispered. His back arched, and Ty dragged his fingers up Zane's belly.

He reached for the still-open lubricant with one hand and pulled himself almost entirely out, letting the head of his cock spread Zane's muscles wide. He held Zane's hip with the other hand and quickly poured a liberal amount on his own cock and on Zane, pushing slowly into him as he did it.

"Oh God, you're gonna fuck me totally insane, aren't you?" Zane asked, plaintive and breathless.

Ty tossed the bottle aside and nodded. "That's how I like you," he said, his voice tight and gruff. He took Zane's hips and pulled him closer, shoving into him hard as he settled him in his lap.

Zane's answer started as a huff, then rose into a higher yelp and gasp. "Please," he drew out, his voice heavy with arousal. It matched the pleasure written all over him.

Ty dug his fingers into the backs of Zane's thighs, dragging them down to his knees to wrap Zane's legs around him. Then he reached for Zane's slick cock, gripping it and spreading the lube with several slow pulls.

"Yes," Zane hissed as he lifted his hips to push himself into Ty's hand.

Ty closed his eyes and groaned loudly, letting Zane's movement do the work as he jacked him. He could hear Zane's labored, rough breathing and the rustle of the sheets as they moved. Zane's legs were tight around him, and then he felt the light brush of fingertips down his chest to his belly. He opened his eyes with difficulty, looking down at Zane's hand as it grazed him. He was distracted by the sight of his own cock pushing into Zane's ass, by his fingers wrapped around Zane, stroking him. His grip on Zane's hip tightened as he looked up to meet Zane's eyes.

They were glazed and nearly black as they focused on him.

Zane kept moving his hand, gently stroking Ty's flushed skin. He said Ty's name softly, even reverently.

Ty moved, bending over him again to kiss him roughly. He snapped his hips as he moved, and he continued the sharp thrusts as he made the kiss hard and messy. Zane bucked under him, trying to get more, his slippery cock sliding along the firm muscles of Ty's abs. He finally growled, gripped Ty's ass, and pulled him down hard. The movement sank Ty's cock deep into him, their bodies slapping together. Zane's cry of pleasure was muffled by Ty's mouth.

Ty broke the kiss with a gasp and thrust in hard again several times just to watch Zane's face display all sorts of emotion Zane was usually really good at hiding: pleasure, arousal, urgency, even a little desperation in his furrowed brow, tightly closed eyes, and abused lower lip, teeth still sunk into it.

Ty slowed the pace again, bending to kiss at Zane's lips. "I love you," he whispered, the words more a breath against Zane's lips than spoken.

Zane exhaled in a stutter and opened his eyes to look at Ty. He lifted his hand to trail his fingers over Ty's lips and cheekbone. Then he spoke, his words charged with emotion. "Love you too."

Ty kissed him gently again, then pushed himself back, rolling his hips to work his way in deeper. He pulled at Zane's hips and seated him once again in his lap.

He took Zane in hand again, stroking him faster this time as he picked up the speed of his own thrusts.

Zane's hands hit the mattress before settling on Ty's knees, gripping him. "Insane now…," he said, panting. His breathing sped up as he quivered under Ty, and his hips were moving constantly, moving Ty inside him.

"Come on, baby," Ty urged in a breathless whisper.

Zane gritted his teeth as he stared at his lover, and Ty watched his eyes go unfocused as his breathing stopped and he stiffened. His cock pulsed in Ty's hand. Zane convulsed in a series of inarticulate moans, evidence of his orgasm spurting over Ty's fingers. Ty watched hungrily as he continued to stroke him, fighting hard against the urge to pound into him through his orgasm.

He groaned, though, gasping Zane's name as Zane's body pulsed around him. With each stroke, his fingers and Zane's stomach were covered and Zane's moans grew louder.

Ty swore. "Next time I'll be sucking you off instead of watching it hit your belly," he growled, earning a desperate, plaintive groan from his lover in response.

Ty took mercy on him and brought his hand to a stop. He ran both hands all over Zane's body, smearing his come over him as he stared down at his face, dragging across his inner thighs and gripping his hips, then up his sides to squeeze his waist and pull him closer before running palms down to slide under his hips and lift him to pull him back fully into Ty's lap.

Zane opened his eyes as he tried to catch his breath, but with every touch, Ty could see Zane's overstimulated skin prickle with sensation, and the inhale broke off. "Baby," Zane whispered. "Don't stop."

Ty shook his head. He gripped Zane hard and rolled his hips, moving inside him with a slow groan. He ran his hands over the insides of Zane's thighs, looking down to watch himself pull almost completely out. He pushed at the backs of Zane's legs, forcing his knees up more toward his chest. Ty was still kneeling when he began to thrust his hips forward, head down and biting his lip as he watched the shaft slide in and out of Zane's tight ass. He loved to watch that.

"You are so fucking gorgeous like this," Zane rasped, one hand moving to cover Ty's.

Ty looked up at him before he was forced to let his head fall with a moan. He'd had every intention of finishing this as they'd started, torturously slow and gentle. But it was becoming increasingly difficult.

He let Zane's legs go and leaned over him, holding himself up with both hands as he looked down at his lover. His hips were still rocking, his cock sinking deeper into Zane with each thrust.

"Can you take more?" he asked Zane breathlessly.

"Yeah," Zane said before moaning and biting his lip again. "I'm really getting to like this whole slow burn thing."

Ty ducked his head and groaned in agreement. He picked up the strength of his thrusts again, gasping and moaning as he drove himself closer to climax. But he managed to keep the languid pace he'd set before. Both of them were damp with sweat even though the room was chilly, and everywhere Ty's skin touched Zane's seemed to be on fire. A drop of sweat rolled down Ty's nose and dropped to Zane's chest.

His movements became sharper, tinged with frustration as the slow build of pleasure continued. Each thrust rocked Zane, driving their bodies harder together.

Zane lifted his legs enough to wrap them around Ty again, changing the angle of Ty's thrusts, and he gave a long, forlorn cry as Ty hit his prostate. "Oh, God baby, so, so good."

Ty watched Zane as he ramped up his thrusts, keeping the same angle and pounding him hard for a few seconds before going back to the slower, deeper thrusts.

He loved watching Zane get fucked.

He wanted to keep at him, fuck him just like this until Zane came again, until he emptied himself deep inside Zane over and over and left them both totally spent, but he didn't think he could do it. It was too tempting to let go and take him hard and fast when he was so close to coming himself.

"Baby," he pleaded in a strained, harsh voice as he laid himself out over Zane again and pressed his forehead against Zane's chest.

"Don't stop," Zane begged again. He wrapped his arms around him tightly, tilting his hips back with each slow slide to try to take Ty deeper. "Please, give me more."

Ty's will to draw it out snapped. He raised his head and wrapped his arms around Zane, gathering him close. He briefly allowed himself the pleasure of fucking him, hard and fast, nearly pulling out of him each time before breaching him again and driving back into him. Zane cried out and dragged his fingernails down Ty's back as their bodies slapped together.

When Ty felt the orgasm almost on him, he stopped and held Zane close to him, breaths harsh and body screaming for release. When it ebbed, he rolled them until he was on his back and Zane sat astride him, Ty's cock still buried inside him.

It took a moment for Zane to get his balance, but he settled his weight on his knees and shifted on Ty's cock. He reached out to take each of Ty's hands, holding them captive as he began to rock forward and back, searching for the perfect angle.

Ty closed his eyes and pushed his hips up, groaning. Zane kept up the steady movement, occasionally grinding down but not speeding up. "My turn to make you insane," he said.

Ty opened his eyes to look up at his lover. He could see the shiny parts of Zane's skin that were covered in sweat, lubricant, and come. He licked his lips and panted out a pent-up breath. Zane riding him like this was possibly the sexiest thing he'd ever seen. His muscles were tense and his hips rolled sinuously, his thighs squeezing Ty, his cock half-hard again.

Zane continued to move his hips until he found the right position again. He put both hands on Ty's chest, fingernails dragging, and he rolled his hips in circles, using Ty's cock to massage his prostate and drive Ty insane as he watched.

Ty sat up the moment Zane stopped moving. He couldn't stand it any longer, no matter how much fun it was to watch Zane's hips roll like that. He wrapped his arms around Zane's waist and looked up at him, trying to thrust up into him from that position. He was so close to release his hands were shaking as he pressed his palms against Zane's back.

"If you can't ride me properly, I'm gonna have to flip you back over," he said before reaching up to jerk Zane's head down for a demanding, desperate, possessive kiss.

Zane hunched over to help with the kiss and without warning pushed up from his knees nearly off Ty's cock before slamming himself down, taking Ty's cock all the way with one smooth motion. "Properly?" he growled when he broke the kiss.

Ty's hands gripped Zane's waist, and he called out, encouraging his lover for more. He fell back again, hands sliding to Zane's hips. He loved to feel the supple movements of Zane's hips when they were fucking. Zane had never ridden him before, but they would definitely be doing this again.

"God, you're so hot," he groaned, pushing his hips up to shove his cock hard into Zane.

Zane started moving again, up and down, and then he'd sit flat and shift his hips forward, dragging himself along Ty's cock, before pushing back hard. Then he leaned over, braced himself on one hand, and started riding Ty in earnest, his balls and half-hard cock pinned between them.

Ty cried out and bucked his hips. He pulled his feet up to give him more leverage and tried to meet Zane's movements with his own. Their damp bodies slapped together, and he could feel himself pushing past that tight ring of muscle with almost every one of Zane's movements. It didn't take long for him to curl upward, the orgasm seeming to start in his toes and work itself through him.

His fingers grasped at Zane's shoulder and side urgently as he shoved his cock deep into him one last time, and Zane kept moving, riding him hard through the pulses of his orgasm. Ty finally cried out, a hoarse, desperate sound, fingernails digging into Zane's skin as he bucked his hips.

He shuddered as Zane finally slowed and leaned over to kiss him.

Ty's fingers shook as he reached for him. His entire body did. He kissed Zane with tangible relief, wrapping his arms around him and holding him. Zane sighed and settled over him, pressing his chest against Ty's sweaty skin and placing gentle kisses at his temple.

Ty didn't even try to calm his breathing, just let himself pant and gasp for air as he hugged Zane to him, then closed his eyes. "That was fun," he said, breathless.

Zane's soft rumble of laughter reverberated through both their chests, and he nodded.

"We're going to need a really big towel," Ty murmured as he turned his head to press his mouth against Zane's temple.

Zane chuckled again and sighed. "Shower."

Ty hummed a negative. "Then I won't smell like you when I wake up."

Zane pushed himself up on one elbow so he could look at Ty. "That's... ridiculously romantic."

Ty laughed. "Don't sound so surprised."

Zane nipped at Ty's bottom lip to stop the laugh. "I'm not."

Ty reached up to kiss him again, slow and careful. "Better let me up," he finally said with real regret.

Zane's fingers tightened on his arms for a moment before relaxing and releasing him. "For now," Zane allowed before climbing off him.

Ty lay there for a moment, still recovering. Then he sat up and swung his legs over the side of the bed, fighting down the light-headedness that he knew would come after mind-blowing sex. "Back in a minute," he said, and he headed for the door to the bathroom on unsteady legs.

He felt pretty confident in letting Julian and Cameron stay on their own for the night. After the noise he and Zane had made, the other two men could have no doubt what they'd been up to, and they were smart enough not to bother Ty and Zane tonight.

Ty smiled to himself. That, or they had used the golden opportunity to finally escape. At this point, he really didn't care.

~Chapter 13~

THE soft click of the door brought Cameron out of his doze, and he opened sleepy eyes as the bed dipped on the other side. It was Julian, back from a patrol of the hotel, most likely. Cameron smiled. Julian's protective instinct was one of his most endearing traits. He slid his hand out from under the pillow to reach for Julian's. Julian's cool fingers glided across his palm in the darkness. He felt Julian move, sliding himself into the bed with his usual careful movements.

"Go back to sleep," he whispered, almost at Cameron's ear.

Cameron hummed as he scooted toward Julian's warmth. "Everything okay?" he murmured before yawning.

Julian's arms wrapped around him, pulling him closer. He sighed as he settled Cameron against his chest and rested his chin on top of Cameron's head. It was the same contented sound he almost always made when he held Cameron to him. "I'm not sure. I've made several attempts to contact Preston, but he's… simply gone."

"Really?" Cameron woke up a little, though he nestled as close as he could get, inhaling Julian's warm, spicy scent. "What does that mean?"

"I hope it means he's smart and he's cut and run before he can be dragged into this too."

"You don't really believe that, though."

"No. Preston wouldn't run. I have an awful feeling."

Cameron wrapped around him with a frown, knowing there wasn't much he could do to alleviate the worry or stress.

They hadn't heard from the other room in a while, and Cameron found himself smiling as he thought about the two tough, acerbic FBI agents. "It's so cute. They're in love."

"It's like watching two kittens fight with machetes," Julian muttered.

"Julian."

"What? It's weird!"

"No, it's not. They're perfect for each other. Poor Zane, though," Cameron murmured. "In love with Ty Grady." He couldn't imagine how frustrating that would be. Then Julian inhaled, and Cameron chuckled slightly. Yeah, he could, actually. "Did I tell you that Ty cuddled Wesson when he was at the apartment?"

"He *cuddled* him?"

"He picked him up and cuddled him like a baby. I should have known right then that he was just as evil as you are."

"Interesting. You mentioned he picked him up. And Wesson let him?"

"He purred."

"Oh my God."

"And then begged for more."

"The little harlot."

Cameron laughed, hiding his face against Julian's shoulder.

"My opinion of them both has been slightly altered, I'm afraid," Julian admitted. "Grady's still a complete wanker, of course, but...."

Cameron blinked his eyes open and pulled back to see Julian's face. "Why is that?"

"It's twice as terrifying, working with someone you love. A mistake could cost you everything. It makes what they do that much more... impressive."

"That's what you do with me, sweetheart," Cameron said gently.

Julian laughed. "No, I can trust you to be smart and stay out of trouble. You're not... in the thick of things, usually."

Cameron swatted at his chest.

"You are everything to me," Julian whispered in his ear.

"You know you are impossible to resist," Cameron said with a sniff, cuddling back into his arms. He sighed and added, "I think I must have loved you before you spoke a word to me."

"All part of my charm."

Cameron smiled and tipped his head back so he could kiss Julian's jaw. "You're so humble."

"Which adds to my charm."

"Hustler," Cameron said as he reached up with one hand to tip Julian's chin down toward him.

Julian kissed him hard suddenly, holding him tight and delving into the passionate kiss. Cameron inhaled through his nose but snaked one arm up and around Julian's neck as he gave himself over. Julian could be disconcertingly tender, at odds with his demeanor and size, but he could also be demanding and rough, and Cameron loved it both ways.

Julian broke the kiss but didn't loosen his hold on Cameron as he took a deep breath. "Have I told you lately how lucky I am to have you?"

"No," Cameron answered as his chest began to ache. It did that around Julian an awful lot.

"I should tell you every day," Julian whispered to him. "Seeing those two struggling to love each other and forced to hide it from the world...." He shook his head sorrowfully. "You're everything to me, Cameron."

Cameron smiled as his pulse sped. "I'm a lucky man. I love you, Julian. If I didn't stop when you died on me, it'll never change."

Julian kissed him again, his long fingers spreading over Cameron's back as he tightened his arms around him. Cameron sank into his embrace, pushing away any thoughts of danger or separation. They were together right now, and that was what was important.

ZANE watched the sun go down and the room fill with darkness in the few minutes Ty was in the bathroom. He stretched on the bed, enjoying the slide of lube and come between his thighs. Muscle fatigue complemented by satiation lulled him into quiet thoughts as he waited for his lover to return. He tucked his arm behind his head and stared up at the ceiling as his mind wandered around reflections and memories of Ty—no big surprise there; that was where his mind almost always wandered.

The bathroom door creaked as Ty pushed it open, but that was all the noise he made as he crept through the darkness. Zane could barely see him, but the dim light picked up on his naked skin and the white towel he held in his hand.

It was always fun—and arousing—to watch Ty move, naked or not. He was like a wild cat, all lean, economic, smooth movement that was hypnotizing. He came closer to the bed, steps careful, eyes still adjusting to the darkness. He crawled up the bed and over Zane without a word, taking care not to rub against his sticky belly. He kissed him soundly before climbing off him and laying the towel on Zane's chest.

"You okay?" he asked in a low whisper.

Zane nodded and moved one hand to put the damp towel to use, but he kept his eyes on Ty. He just didn't want to look away.

Ty shook his head, grinning so that Zane could see the white of his teeth. He shifted, stretching out his shoulders before rolling onto his side and propping his head on his hand as he looked at Zane. It would be a trick for them to sleep in the double bed without one or both of them ending up on the floor at least once. But Zane figured he might just curl up around Ty close enough that it wouldn't matter.

Zane finished with the towel and tossed it to the floor. When he glanced back, that grin was still in place on Ty's lips. Zane snorted, enjoying the sparkle in Ty's eyes. He reached out and let his fingers coast down Ty's cheek to drift over the compass rose at his neck. "You know how to break me."

"That's the last thing on my mind," Ty murmured. He scooted forward and pressed his lips to Zane's. He didn't try to deepen the kiss or grope Zane like he usually did. It was a simple, sweet gesture, one that he ended all too soon as he rolled onto his back once more.

He put one arm under his head and stretched the other out under Zane's neck. "Come here," he said in a low voice.

Zane shifted to curl against Ty's warm body under the curve of his arm. He slid his hand over Ty's waist and settled his arm there so he could hold Ty as well.

Ty turned his head enough to nuzzle his nose and mouth against Zane's. He wrapped his arm around Zane's shoulders and held him close, bringing his other hand to his waist to rest on Zane's hand there. He was silent, his body loose and still. Zane had rarely ever felt Ty when he was truly relaxed. Even in sleep or after drinking, his muscles always seemed to be tight and tense, his body ready for action.

Zane hummed. "Wish I had this effect on you more often."

"What effect?"

"This one," Zane said as he slid his hand up Ty's torso until he could trace Ty's lax features with his fingers. "You're so relaxed. It's quite a sight."

"I'm always relaxed," Ty mumbled, though the smile in his voice told Zane he was merely poking fun at himself. He hugged Zane closer, kissing his forehead.

"Is this the result of your little sabbatical?"

"Partly. Mostly it's my dangerous lack of caffeine right now."

Zane smiled, and he couldn't help but ask, "Where'd the sandalwood come from?"

"Deuce. His crazy yoga girlfriend has gotten him on board the scent therapy stuff. It's supposed to relieve stress. I don't know if it works; I just think it smells good."

Zane laughed, and Ty chuckled along with him. The warmth soaking through Zane was heady and addictive. He couldn't remember being this content to just be still and next to Ty, although it was always pleasant. Now it meant even more, because Zane knew exactly how special this was.

He would never have imagined, even after their first night together, when Ty had held him all night, that they could ever have this.

"I was sure, when we met, that you were a straight-arrow ladies' man," Zane said. He pressed a soft kiss to the hollow of Ty's shoulder.

Ty laughed. "You were half-right."

Zane pushed himself up so he could look at Ty. "How's that work?" he asked, a smile pulling at his lips.

"What?"

"Half-straight? Half ladies?" Zane poked at Ty's belly, his finger hitting hard muscle. "You've never mentioned any other men."

Ty shifted again and reached up to run his hand down Zane's arm, letting his fingers play over Zane's muscles. "I think it's been pretty half and half, who I'm attracted to. Most of the other men I've been with have been one-time hookups," he admitted, words careful, as if he were trying to gauge Zane's reaction as he said it.

Zane wasn't quite sure what problem Ty thought he'd have with it; that pretty much described him too. "Are you expecting… shock?"

Ty snorted and shook his head. "You've just never asked me about this kind of stuff, I keep expecting your head to spin or something."

Zane laughed. He shrugged the shoulder he wasn't lying on. "I mean, I've obviously switch-hit and bounced around. It'd be pretty shitty of me to judge you for the same."

Ty nodded. "Well… you know I haven't been a saint. Most of the people I've been with have been… let's just say I remember the majority by the names of the bar or city I met them in," he said, unembarrassed by the fact. Ty had never tried to present himself to Zane as anything but what he was. That honesty was oddly assuring to Zane now that they were exclusive.

"Was there ever anyone serious?"

"A few," Ty answered. "A couple women I didn't love but I could see myself with long-term, one in particular, but…." He cleared his throat and shook his head. "The connection never felt right. It was always so much more natural with a guy. I was always scared to get too involved with the guys I met, though. There was only one I ever let myself fall hard for, before you."

It was fascinating, watching Ty from so close when his expressions were so open and honest. Zane tried to follow his eyes, but Ty clearly felt a little awkward with all the sharing, and he continued to stare at the ceiling. "I get the feeling it's been a while," Zane said, moving his hand over Ty's stomach.

"I was young," Ty said with a nod. "I don't know if we really loved each other or not. I'm not sure if you even know what love is at seventeen. Felt like it at the time. Enough to scare us. We decided we had to get away from each other before we fell too hard." He closed his eyes and took a deep breath. "That's why I joined the Marines, you know. I never told anyone that."

Zane blinked in surprise. "Really? I thought you were following the family tradition. Semper fi and all that."

"That just made it easy to explain. No one asked any questions; they all just assumed I was following in Dad's footsteps. I *had* thought about it before, it was something I knew I wanted to do, knew I'd be good at. But suddenly it was an escape route too."

Zane trailed his finger down Ty's chest as he listened, raptly watching Ty's face.

"See, my senior year in high school we were playing in a big rivalry game homecoming weekend. I was on defense. I don't remember why, I almost never played defense. But I was that night, and I sacked the other team's quarterback. He was a senior too, played all the same sports, so I knew him a little bit from all the games we'd played against each other. I broke his leg."

He winced with the memory, and Zane smiled. It was always fascinating to find out what Ty sympathized with.

"His last home game and he had to be carried off the field on a little cart. The next day I went to see him, tell him I was sorry. It was his left leg, full cast up to his thigh, so he couldn't drive a stick, couldn't get around. I felt guilty, so…." He laughed suddenly at the memory. "I wrote my phone number on his cast and told him to call me whenever he needed to go somewhere. We ended up… we spent a lot of time together. Hit it off."

"Was he your first?"

"Yeah." Ty reached up and idly twirled his finger through Zane's hair. "His name was David."

Zane tipped his head to the side to be closer to Ty's fingers. It was a remarkably intimate action, and he loved that Ty was doing it, seemingly without thinking about it. He smiled at the idea of a teenage Ty flirting with a guy he'd literally maimed the night before, writing his number on the guy's cast to get him to call him. It was sweet, in a very Grady sort of way. "Have you seen him since?"

"Couple times," Ty answered with a nod. "He's a lawyer down in Richmond."

Zane reached to touch Ty's cheek. "Does it bother you to tell me?"

Ty waited a moment before answering in a surprised voice. "Not really. I guess it's just been a secret for so long…."

"So how'd he turn out?" Zane asked, not wanting to press his lover on the topic of secrets. "Bachelor? Married?"

"Long-term relationship with a guy he met in college," Ty answered wryly. His smile fell and he shook his head, closing his eyes as he continued to play with Zane's hair. "He's the only thing I've ever run from."

"Being attracted to another man at that time in your life, I'm sure it was a shock to deal with," Zane said. "I probably would have run too."

The only thing Zane had known when he'd been that age was Becky. How would he have handled it if those feelings had been for another guy? He wasn't sure.

"Maybe," Ty murmured. "Am I the first guy you've been involved with? I mean, beyond the ones you left in the alley."

Zane pressed his index finger on the slight wrinkles between Ty's brows and rubbed, trying to get him to open his eyes. Ty batted at his hand, then caught it and kissed it, trapping it against his chest.

"Yes," Zane answered. "I didn't even consider being with a guy until after Becky was gone, but up to that point I hadn't considered being with *anyone*." It came out so easily, he surprised himself. Usually thinking about Becky at least echoed some sort of pain. But here with Ty, it didn't hurt. It was a chapter in his life that was finally over.

"Why'd you start?" Ty asked him as he held Zane's hand firmly to his chest to keep him from poking at his face again.

"Lust," Zane answered. "It was while I was undercover in Miami, working a smuggling operation from Colombia. We were treated to our choice of escorts, and there was this… well, he was the first one that caught my eye and I couldn't look away. I figured what the hell, new experiences. After a few times I figured out I enjoyed being with a guy more than any woman I'd been with. It was fun, a good way to blow off steam, really hot."

Ty nodded, remaining quiet as he rubbed his thumb back and forth over Zane's hand. He could feel Ty relaxing against him again, body loosening and growing more languid as he held him close. Zane smiled and shifted to lie down again, this time settling his cheek on Ty's breastbone. "So tell me about the one woman. One woman among so many," he quipped.

Ty immediately groaned and jerked under him. "I was hoping that would slip past you," he said, only partly joking.

"Not hardly," Zane drawled. He pressed his lips to Ty's skin for a moment. "Tell me anyway."

Ty cleared his throat. "Her name was Ava," he said in defeat. "I met her when I was in New Orleans. I almost proposed to her."

"Really?" Zane blurted, lifting his head to look at Ty.

Ty smiled and shrugged one shoulder. "I could never convince myself it was a good idea. I was right. It didn't stick."

"That's why I'm surprised," Zane admitted.

"Why?" Ty asked, shifting uncomfortably but meeting Zane's eyes anyway.

"Because you stuck with me."

Ty pressed his lips together, looking at Zane worriedly for a moment before reaching up and sliding his palm against Zane's cheek. "I didn't love her. And I wasn't the one who ended it," he admitted.

"I'm sorry," Zane whispered, even though deep down he really wasn't. Ty shook his head. Zane studied him for a long moment. "How long ago was this?"

"Right before Katrina hit," Ty murmured, frowning as he tried to remember how many years ago that had been.

"Five years this summer." Zane said. He paused, swallowing hard before asking, "Do you... does it still hurt?"

Ty laughed before he could stop himself. He clapped his hand over his mouth as if he was trying to hide the reaction, and he shook his head.

Zane pushed up to look down at him, not sure how to interpret that reaction.

"I'm sorry," Ty said hastily, reaching for Zane's arm to stop him from pulling away. "It's just your choice of words is…." He laughed again and took Zane's hand, pulling it to the side of his stomach, just under his ribs, to let Zane's fingers rest against his skin. "You feel that scar there?" he asked as he placed Zane's fingers along a faded scar Zane had noticed before.

Zane frowned and nodded, feeling the smooth raised line of scar tissue under his fingertips. It went from the front of Ty's hip to the back, like he'd been grazed. Then his eyes widened. "She did this?"

"Threw a butcher's knife at me," Ty told him, voice tinged with an odd mixture of amusement and irritation. "Her aim was usually better, so I'm pretty sure she missed on purpose."

"She was pretty set on *ending* it, then."

Ty shook his head and inhaled deeply as he relaxed back into bed. "It was my fault. She didn't know I was a Fed," he said with true regret. "By the time I realized I might have real feelings for her, I was stuck. Couldn't figure out how to tell her and not blow my cover. She didn't even know my last name. I don't know what I was thinking, I guess… I just hoped she'd still care for me after the case was over and I could come clean to her. But then, when Katrina was bearing down, they pulled everyone, UC or not, to help with evacuation and prepare for search and rescue. I went to her and told her to leave, that I'd found a transport for her and her family to get out safely. She refused until I promised I'd go with them. But I couldn't leave. I had to tell her why just to get her on the helicopter."

It was an easy question to ask why she'd been upset, but it wasn't one Zane needed an answer to. It was difficult when you lived a life undercover, and many people didn't take kindly to such thorough lies, even for the best of reasons. Ty had given up someone he thought he could love to save her.

"Why didn't you go back?"

"Well... I was sort of afraid she'd try again with a knife that was easier to throw," Ty answered, laughing. He bit his lip, looking up at Zane with eyes that shined even in the dim light. "No. The hurricane hit. The city just got... wiped off the map, pretty much. For days we did nothing but *survive*. Pull people out of the water, kids and animals and old people. Me and everyone else down there cried ourselves to sleep whenever we got the chance. All I could do was make sure they were all okay, everyone I'd known, you know, undercover. But every UC in New Orleans that got blown had to be transferred after the search and rescue became body recovery and they started getting people out. They didn't give us a chance to linger. That's how I ended up in Baltimore. I never saw her again after that night."

Zane didn't understand. If Ty had really cared for her, or even thought he might have loved her, how had he given her up so easily?

Ty shifted and looked at Zane with a sigh. "You look... disturbed. You're wondering why I didn't try harder to get her back, right?" Ty nodded, as if answering his own question. "I cared about her, I did. But after a week or two I realized that she wasn't the first thing I thought of when I woke up. And when something would happen during the day, she wasn't the first person I thought I needed to tell it to." He looked at Zane and smiled. "Not like you. I wasn't in love with her. She deserved someone who was."

Zane considered what to say. He wasn't going to give Ty platitudes; they'd be dismissed anyway. "I'm sorry you had to go through that. But I'm not sorry it happened. I wouldn't have you otherwise."

Ty pulled him closer. "Funny how life works, huh?"

"Yeah," Zane said as he eased into Ty's arms. They'd both lost a lot along the way. He needed to remember that.

The warmth of Ty's body next to Zane's and his easy breathing were both calming and familiar, and Zane found himself sinking into him.

"You okay with all that?" Ty finally asked.

"It's your past. Can't be changed any more than mine can. I'm fine with it. Unless we vacation there for Mardi Gras, then I might be on the lookout. I was there once with Becky. We loved it."

"If I ever go back I'll have to do it locked and loaded," Ty said. "I left too many pissed off loose ends down there, including one Cajun daddy who really liked voodoo."

Zane barked a laugh before he could stop himself. He knew how superstitious Ty was, and something about him being afraid of the voodoo-wielding father of a former flame was intensely amusing.

Ty rolled to his side to face Zane. He reached up to touch Zane's chin with his fingertips. "We still have a lot to learn about each other."

Zane figured that was a hell of an understatement. He smiled as Ty's lips brushed his. "That's not a bad thing."

"No." Ty grinned against Zane's lips. "I'm sort of looking forward to it."

Zane closed his eyes, the warmth of contentment stealing over him as they wrapped around each other and settled down to try to sleep. "Should we set an alarm?" Zane asked after a quiet minute. Ty's breathing had settled into a rhythm, low and even; Zane thought he might even have dropped off to sleep.

But Ty shook his head in immediate answer. He patted his chest before sliding his hand back over Zane's. "Alarm's built-in."

Zane smiled as he buried his face against Ty's chest. He drifted off to sleep, the warmth of Ty's body and the fading smell of sandalwood filling him with a sense of tranquility he had rarely experienced.

Zane estimated that it was several hours later, still well before dawn, when he awoke to the mattress dipping and Ty getting out of bed.

He had to move carefully in the dark as he rummaged for his clothing and got dressed. It was painfully obvious that he was trying to be silent, trying not to wake Zane. Zane lay listening, almost dozing. Ty sat at the table in the corner and pulled on his boots, and when he stood, he bent over the table for a moment, writing a note.

"Fuck, Ty, not again," Zane muttered.

Ty jumped and turned to look at him. "Jackass," he hissed. "You scared me."

"What are you doing?" Zane asked as he pushed up onto one elbow.

"Have you ever seen the battlefield in the moonlight?"

Zane shook his head.

"Come with me."

Zane blinked at him, a smile forming as he nodded. "Let me get dressed."

CAMERON didn't even get a chance to gasp for breath. He grabbed for the arms surrounding him and slapped a hand over the fingers that covered his mouth, trying to wake up as he felt himself being yanked up from the pillow.

"You're okay, love," Julian's soft voice assured him as he pulled him out of bed. There was an undercurrent of something else in his tone, though, something frightened and urgent. "Stay quiet."

Cameron nodded and drew a shaky breath when Julian moved his hand away from his mouth. He got his feet under him as Julian released him a moment later, but Cameron had no intention of moving an inch away. Something had spooked Julian, and that was never a good thing.

Julian was tense and silent, his dark eyes riveted on the door to the room and his ear cocked toward the wall that separated their room from Ty and Zane's. They could easily hear through the walls; they'd found that out earlier.

Julian had no weapon on him. If there was a threat now, they'd be facing it unarmed. "Get your shoes on," Julian whispered. "Don't make a sound."

Stepping away from the safety of his lover's hulking presence was more difficult than Cameron imagined it would be. He shoved his feet into his running shoes and crouched to tie them. Pulling the laces tight, he glanced up at Julian, trying to get a feel for the situation.

Julian stood stock-still, barely even breathing as he stared hard at the door. He wasn't looking directly at it, more to the side of it, as if trying to see it out of the corner of his eye. The soft sound of voices filtered through the thick walls, and Julian moved suddenly, whipping his head to the right to look around the room. Cameron stepped back as Julian practically pounced on the desk several feet away, picking up the desk lamp and yanking the power cord out of the base. He reached into the lampshade and unscrewed the lightbulb, then pulled the cord out of the wall. Looking from Julian to the door and back, Cameron scooted out of the way, putting Julian and the heavy wooden armoire of electronics between himself and the door.

"Cam," Julian hissed, barely audible in the darkness. "Fix the pillows on the bed, make it look like someone sleeping. Quickly."

Cameron rushed the three steps to the bed, grabbing some of the pillows they'd tossed onto the floor and making columns on the bed. He pulled the comforter up and was hurriedly shoving it down between the pillows when he heard a voice outside the door. He didn't even think; one of the first things Julian had taught him was to hide. Cameron turned, took one step to the side, and crouched down behind the solid armchair and ottoman to the left side of the bed, curling his frame up behind it so he was out of sight. He hoped.

"The other room was empty."

"They've got to be here somewhere."

There was more that Cameron couldn't make out. A moment later, the door to the bedroom splintered at the knob. There was another bang, and Cameron squeezed into a tighter ball as the door flew open. A shaft of light from the hallway fell upon the bed, and he saw the shadow of a man with a gun in his hand cast against the wall above the headboard not four feet away from him. The man didn't fire, though.

"Shit," he heard the attacker say, obviously realizing the ruse.

Another heartbeat later, Cameron heard the struggle start, and he knew that Julian had attacked the man. Cameron pried open his eyes and peered around the back of the chair.

Julian's back was to the wall beside the door. He had the cord of the lamp wrapped around the stranger's neck, twisting it from behind as the man struggled against him. Another man came through the doorway, gun drawn, and Julian reached out with one hand and slammed the lightbulb into the second man's face as he stepped through the doorway. He gave a bloodcurdling scream as he fell back out of the room, and Julian kicked the door shut as he tightened the cord around the first gunman's neck.

Cameron knew he was probably best off where he was, but he shifted to a crouch rather than staying on his knees so when Julian called he'd be ready to go.

The stranger sank to his knees, gasping for breath in the darkness as Julian held the ends of the cord tight. Cameron was grateful he couldn't see the dying man's face. The body fell to the ground with a thud, but Julian continued to kneel over him, pulling the cord tight. Shots punched through the thick door over his head, and Julian flinched and covered his head, rolling away from the door.

"Cam, stay down!" he called in a harsh whisper.

More noises came from outside, shouts and breaking glass, bangs and more shouting, and Cameron covered his head instinctively. Gunfire roared, two, three, maybe four shots. Then all was silent for a long moment.

"Two men down." The voice was sharp, clipped, and familiar, close to the door. Then, louder, "Cross? Are you in there?" Cameron let out his breath. That was Zane.

Julian didn't answer. Cameron could hear him breathing hard, somewhere in the darkness near the door. "Cross? Cameron?" Zane tried again, his voice still flat. Cameron bit his lip. Julian would have said something if he wanted to, so Cameron kept his mouth shut. Then he heard the busted door swing open and he glanced around the chair back.

As soon as the agent's shadow entered the doorway, Julian moved. He wrapped an arm around Zane's neck, holding the broken bit of lightbulb to his throat as he used Zane's body to shield him from whoever else was outside.

A second later, the light flipped on and Ty moved into the room with his gun drawn, eyes on Julian and Zane.

"I'm not fighting you, Cross," Zane said, keeping both hands down and out to his sides.

"Let him go, MacGuffin, we just saved your ass," Ty told him, the gun not wavering.

"No one could possibly know we were here. No one but *your* men. Check their badges," Julian ordered. He didn't let up on the pressure he was exerting on Zane's neck.

Ty held up his hand to calm Julian and bent down, rummaging through the dead man's pockets as he kept his eyes and gun on Julian. Cameron shifted behind the chair, staying down for now.

A moment later Ty pulled a badge and held it up, looking at it in shock as he flipped it open. It read FBI in big blue letters.

"See!" Julian shouted. "They're *your* people!"

"They're not our people," Zane said. "Let up, Cross. We both know I could have shot you twice before you had me."

"But you didn't, your fault," Julian said. "Grady, the gun."

"Go fuck yourself," Ty said as he continued to pat the dead man's pockets. He pulled out a clear spiral cord from behind the man's ear and whistled as he held it up. "These aren't Bureau issue."

Julian relaxed his grip on Zane as he looked at the earpiece. Cameron stood, wondering if he'd ever seen a man so close to Julian's size next to him. From the back, or maybe the side, he just might mistake Zane Garrett for Julian, and that was still disconcerting even after all this time with him.

"We knew there was something more to this," Zane reminded them, his back still against Julian's chest, though he didn't seem particularly fazed by the bloody broken glass at his throat. "I think it might be a little more important to be *leaving* right now."

"Agreed," Julian said instantly. He dropped the lightbulb and turned to look back for Cameron.

"How'd they find us? That's so fucking random," Ty asked as he stood. He sounded pissed.

As Zane and Ty kept talking, Cameron tuned them out. He'd be along for the ride regardless of his input. His eyes strayed from Julian, over to the mess of the bed, across the littered floor between them, to the crumpled body of a dead man with a lamp cord wrapped around his throat. Cameron let out a shaky breath. He knew that life with Julian was like this sometimes, but that didn't mean it was easy to handle or understand.

Julian moved toward him and hugged him fiercely, seeming to sense that was what he needed. And it was, to be held close and comforted. Cameron sighed and tipped his head back to find Julian's eyes. "Are you okay?"

Julian nodded. "You?"

"Yes." Cameron did not look down at the body nearby but instead toward the two men searching the other bodies, words flying rapid-fire between them. He hadn't been paying attention to know if Ty and Zane were working or insulting each other. For all he knew, it could be the same thing with them. "It's not safe here."

"No," Julian agreed as he looked back at the two agents. He squeezed Cameron's arm. "Get dressed, Cameron, okay? We're leaving as soon as these two idiots figure this out."

Cameron nodded. He wanted to ask questions, but the set of Julian's shoulders told him that now was not the time.

TY GROWLED as they stripped the dead bodies of all the weaponry they could find. He didn't like being in the dark, and he felt decidedly shadowed right now.

"Whoever they are, they've got top-notch gear," Zane said as he pulled a backup gun off one of the fallen agents.

Ty nodded unhappily. "Yeah, like their tricked-out fucking CIA spy cars. What could they possibly have tracked? We've tossed everything we have."

Julian stepped toward them, holding a gun he'd taken from one of the men before Ty or Zane could get to it. "We're leaving," he announced. He held up the gun. "With or without you."

Cameron stopped behind Julian, their smallest bag over his shoulder.

"Simmer down, Cross, all right?" Ty muttered as he picked up the dead man's fake badge again. He stared at it, the FBI logo emblazoning itself into his mind. "Ah, shit," he hissed as he stood up.

"What?" Zane asked as he stood as well. He checked the ammunition in the gun in his hand and snapped the cartridge back in place before looking at Ty.

"It's me."

"What?"

"It's me, they've been tracking me," Ty said as he pulled at the nylon strap of his wristwatch.

"What? How?" Julian demanded as he stepped forward.

Ty held up the watch. It was a Citizen Promaster Eco-drive dive watch with a black nylon band and a chrome and matte black face. He wore it everywhere he went, never even taking it off to sleep or shower. Richard Burns had given it to him when he'd graduated from the Academy.

Julian shrugged impatiently as he looked at it.

"It has a tracking device in it."

"It what?" Zane blurted.

Ty glanced at him, apologetic. "Burns had a tracker put in it so he could follow me on assignments. I only activate it when I'm dark or think I'm going to die, but it can be pinged remotely in case I go off grid and he needs to find me."

Zane was staring at him, wide-eyed.

Ty shrugged and dropped the watch, raising his booted foot to stomp it. Julian grabbed his arm before he could bring his foot down.

"Leave it. They may think it's you lying dead on the floor and give us some extra time."

Ty nodded, and he spared one last glance for the watch on the expensive rug before he followed the others out.

"Was it a special watch, Ty?" Cameron asked as they made their way down the back stairwell of the hotel.

Ty shook his head, too troubled to answer. Burns was the only one who knew that tracking device was there. How had the CIA known to ping it?

"My man just went offline," Burns said, voice grim as he leaned against the desk and stared at the large screen on the wall.

"What could do that?" Jonas asked as he stood to join Burns.

"Well, he could have turned it off. But he wouldn't, not when he's in the wind like this. Something's wrong."

"Can you turn it back on remotely?"

Burns nodded and went to his computer. A few clicks later and the tracking device in Ty's watch came back to life, the blue dot flickering before it gained strength. It was still in Gettysburg, Pennsylvania. It had been there for over twenty-four hours.

"They haven't moved," Jonas observed, brow furrowed.

"No," Burns whispered. "He took the watch off."

Jonas turned, looking at him in alarm. "Why would he do that?"

"He figured out that we weren't the only ones using it." Burns slammed his hand down on his desk.

"How do you know that?"

"Because I know how he thinks. Someone must have found them."

"We have no way of tracking them now."

"No."

"What's the plan?" Jonas asked.

"Their orders were to get Cross here to me. We have to trust them to do it."

"Richard, I don't trust anyone that much."

Burns met his friend's eyes and smiled. "Luckily, I do."

~Chapter 14~

TY KNEW the names of the valet and the concierge, so it didn't take anything for them to make it inside the swank Regatta building in downtown Philadelphia. They rode the elevator all the way to the eighteenth floor, to the penthouse suites. Instead of knocking on 1802, though, Ty pulled out a small lock picking set and bent toward the doorknob.

"You could just knock," Zane said as Ty fiddled with the lock.

"Shh." There was a click and Ty opened the door. "Let's hope he hasn't changed his code," he said as he slipped in and disappeared.

Zane sighed and turned to glance at Julian and Cameron. Both men had been quiet since leaving Gettysburg. They all had. Ty especially had been concerned about the watch he'd left behind, but Zane couldn't decide if he felt guilty for having been the reason they'd been found or if there was something more troubling him. Knowing Ty, he felt guilty about *something*.

It was clear now that someone very powerful did not want Julian Cross to get to Washington. Zane had to wonder why Burns hadn't told them what they faced, but that was just how Burns worked.

There was a small sound within the condo, a sweeping sound and a barely audible click. Zane had enough time to turn his head and peer through the doorway before he saw a shadowed figure moving inside. He moved to stand with his back against the hallway wall, next to the open door, chin turned to the side to watch for movement. It wasn't that he was scared of who was inside—quite the opposite. He just knew the Gradys well. He didn't want to get shot, smacked, or stabbed, accidentally or otherwise.

There was silence for a few moments, and then a sudden shout, and the sound of a scuffle ensued.

"Ow!" Ty cried out finally. "Deacon, it's me!"

When Zane peered around the doorframe, he could barely make out the scene in the dim light from the moon through the windows. Ty lay on the floor with his hands held out in front of his face, his younger brother standing over him wielding a wooden baseball bat, raised and ready to swing it down again. A sharp bark of laughter escaped before Zane could stifle it, and he leaned against the doorframe, chuckling.

"Ty?" Deuce Grady said as he lowered his bat and looked down at his brother, who was still cowering on the floor. He looked over at the doorway and then back down at Ty. "What the hell, man? You have a key!"

"Oh, Jesus." Zane beckoned for Julian and Cameron to come closer. "I didn't know he had a key," he said, giving up on hiding the somewhat strained laughter bubbling in his voice.

"Man's an idiot," Julian muttered.

"Sometimes I'm inclined to agree," Zane said under his breath.

Inside, Deuce was helping Ty to his feet. "I don't have it with me and I was trying not to wake you," Ty hissed, keeping his voice down. "We didn't want to draw attention in case anyone was watching. Garrett, quit laughing and get them in here."

Zane stepped into the penthouse and looked around. It opened into a grand foyer with high ceilings and large windows that displayed a huge terrace with views of the Ben Franklin Bridge and the Delaware River. There was marble flooring, and directly to the right of the entrance was a designer kitchen all in sleek, cool colors. There was a den and a solarium, where it looked like Deuce had set up his office. It was a million-dollar home, Zane had no doubt.

"Jesus, Deuce. This is… nice," Zane said as he looked around the penthouse.

"Thanks," Deuce said, sounding confused by their sudden arrival but too polite to ask them what the hell they were doing there in the middle of the night. "It serves as my office too, so I can justify a little luxury."

"Nobody cares, Slugger," Ty muttered.

Deuce looked down at the baseball bat still in his hand and shrugged, unapologetic.

Beside Zane, Julian cleared his throat and reached his hand out to Cameron, wrapping an arm around his shoulders and pulling him close.

"What is this, your version of a camping trip?" Deuce asked Ty as he set the bat aside and moved to help with the bags they'd carried in.

"We've run into some… trouble," Ty said with a wince.

"Run *away* from some trouble," Zane corrected as he shut the door behind him.

"I see," Deuce said. He flipped on the kitchen light and turned to look them over. "I don't see blood."

Zane smiled and stepped up to hug Ty's brother. "It's good to see you again, Deuce."

"I wish I could say the same," Deuce said, though his voice was still warm and amused as he returned the hug. He glanced at his brother, who was unconsciously rubbing at his forearm where he'd apparently blocked one of Deuce's swings with the bat.

"Uh," Ty said as soon as Deuce looked at him. He cleared his throat and dropped his hands. "This is Julian Cross and Cameron Jacobs. They're in protective custody," he told Deuce as he waved his hand at the two men.

"Oh, now it's protective custody?" Julian muttered. "No more get on your knees, let me bungee you to the roof of the car?"

Ty glared at Julian and Cameron. "Gentlemen, this is my brother, Deacon."

"Call me Deuce. Protective custody," Deuce repeated. He glanced at the two men, then at Ty and Zane again speculatively. "And your gimp brother got the drop on you with a baseball bat? Really, Ty?"

Julian made a sound in the back of his throat that may have been a stifled laugh.

Cameron looked among them and rolled his eyes. "Could you direct me to the bathroom, please?" he asked Deuce.

Deuce turned and pointed toward the dark hallway. "First door on the left."

Ty was grumbling and rubbing his forearm as he moved to the nearest chair and threw himself into it. "Where's uh… what was her name? Yoga girl?"

"Livi," Deuce said with a smile. "She went home last night, had to feed her dog."

Ty nodded. "Best to keep her away while we're here."

"Sure, let me just call her up and tell her I'm harboring my brother, his partner, and their two federal fugitive buddies for a few days, take herself a spa weekend. That won't get me accused of anything nefarious."

Ty waved a hand through the air, obviously not caring.

Deuce glanced at him before turning his attention back to Zane and Julian. "Dare I ask what you've done to deserve protective custody?" he asked Julian.

"I deal antiques," Julian answered in a soft voice.

Deuce nodded, looking Julian up and down. He turned his head to look at Ty speculatively. "That's a euphemism for 'I kill things', isn't it?"

Ty closed his eyes and nodded.

"It's classified," Zane murmured as he pulled off his jacket and tossed it over one of the bags. Julian was silent and still behind him.

"All righty, then," Deuce said cheerfully. "Do you need food, showers, or beds?"

"Beds," Ty answered, voice thin and exhausted. He had been taking the bulk of the driving, simply because he was the best suited to being able to keep himself awake and he'd known where he was going as they'd set out for Philadelphia. But he had reached the end of his stamina on the outskirts of the city.

After they'd fled Gettysburg, they'd basically had three options: head for DC as fast as they could and risk hitting a CIA roadblock, go home to Baltimore and hope the CIA wasn't sitting on their homes, or abscond to Philadelphia in the hopes that their pursuers wouldn't expect it. In the end they'd decided that trying to get to DC would be suicide; every road in and out could be watched, and they couldn't risk driving into the hornet's nest. Baltimore had been viable, but they'd feared it would be watched too. Since the CIA had known to find Ty's tracking device, they obviously knew who Ty and Zane were now and where their home was. They would spend a few nights in Philadelphia, as long as they dared, and then try to sneak their way back to DC somehow. They just needed a night's sleep before they could figure out how to do it.

Ty was rubbing his eyes. "Those two can take the guest bed. Zane and I will fight over the couch."

Deuce just nodded. "Come help me unearth the air mattress, we'll toss it in the floor here," he said as he jerked his head at Ty and turned to head down the hall.

Ty pushed himself out of his chair and followed.

Julian waited until both men were out of sight before taking a step further into the room to look at Zane. "Which one of them is adopted?"

Zane snorted. He knew on the surface, the two Grady brothers seemed very different. While Deuce did look a lot like Ty—he was an inch or so taller, much less broad, his hair was lighter, and his eyes were greener—their personalities could not have been more different. Ty was often abrasive and blunt, wielding sarcasm like a weapon, while Deuce was more diplomatic and kind, finding the gentlest ways of saying even the harshest of things. They had completely different tastes in everything from clothing to decorating to the cars they liked to drive. Their similar looks and quick wit were really the only things they seemed to share. Zane knew better, though. Deep down in their psyches, both brothers were really just waiting to get old enough to sit on a porch and bang things with a shovel.

"You ought to meet the rest of the family." He arched his back, listening to the audible pops of his spine as he stretched within the confines of his gun holster. "But they're good people," he added, looking at Julian. "Deuce is one of the best."

Julian merely looked back at him. Finally, he nodded almost imperceptibly. "I decided I liked him the moment he hit Grady with a baseball bat."

"Deuce doesn't take shit from anybody, Ty included. Or maybe Ty especially." He shrugged and leaned over to pick up one of the bags, and his mind moved on to more serious concerns as he looked back at

Julian. "We'll stay here for a day, get some rest and food. Let me know if you and Cameron need anything."

Julian nodded again, swallowing hard as his eye strayed to the hallway where Cameron had disappeared. It was easy to see that Julian was worried now. Before, he'd either thought he could keep the situation under control or he'd been masking his apprehension well.

"Anywhere we touch down now will be a hot zone," he said, his voice still soft and barely audible. "Agent Grady's brother will be in danger as well if we stay too long."

"Ty is well aware," Zane said, though he shared Julian's concern, at least for Deuce.

The low light mostly masked Julian's reaction, but he seemed tense and reserved, as if he wanted to say something he was keeping himself from saying.

Ty's voice filtered down the hallway. "How are you going to hit me with a bat I freaking gave you for your birthday? That shit's commemorative."

Deuce's response was muffled by his laughter.

"Do you believe in God, Agent Garrett?" Julian asked suddenly, his eyes on the hallway.

The question caught Zane off guard, but he wasn't sure that was Julian's goal. Religion didn't have much place in Zane's life anymore, like a lot of other things. But did he believe?

"Yeah," he said quietly. Zane figured he'd have long ago been in the ground if it wasn't for some higher power watching out for him.

Julian was nodding. "You should. It's a bloody miracle your partner has lived this long," he murmured. He began moving toward the kitchen. "Man's an idiot," he muttered under his breath as he passed Zane.

Zane didn't laugh this time. In years past he had sat uncounted times in the dark of night, smoking, shooting up, drinking, wondering if the coming morning would be the one when he didn't wake up. Sometimes he'd even prayed for it.

But not since Ty. Yeah, he believed in miracles.

"It's not like I knew it was you," he heard Deuce insisting as he came back down the hall.

"That's what Grandpa said when he broke my nose."

"Again, you deserved it." Deuce emerged from the hallway carrying a plastic storage box that probably contained the air mattress he'd mentioned. Ty dropped an armload of bedding on the floor. Deuce set the box on the couch and looked at Zane, then glanced around to see where Julian had gone. He gestured between Ty and Zane, and his voice was pitched low when he asked, "Y'all need separate places to sleep?"

Zane blinked away his preoccupation. He could muse over divine intervention another time. "No, they know everything. And one of us needs to keep watch anyway."

Deuce inclined his head, looking at Zane carefully before nodding. He turned to look at Ty, but Zane couldn't see Deuce's expression when he looked back at his brother.

Ty was ignoring Deuce's pointed queries, or at least pretending to, taking the lid off the storage box and poking around inside.

"This thing got a pump?" he asked as he pulled the heavy air mattress out.

"No, Ty, you have to blow it up," Deuce answered in a flat voice. "We'll take turns, should have it done by August."

"I love you too," Ty muttered as Deuce moved past him to head back down the hall, presumably for the pump.

Zane watched as Ty messed with the mattress. "This is where you came, isn't it?"

Ty looked up as he laid the mattress out and knelt to spread it flat. He nodded before Zane could say more. "He always knows how to talk me off the ledge."

"I'm glad." Zane turned in a half circle and then sat on the couch nearby. A part of Zane, a very small, dark part, had been worried that Ty had fled to Boston and Nick O'Flaherty when he ran from Baltimore.

Ty merely nodded as he stretched to flip over the last corner of the air mattress. He stood carefully, obviously sore and stiff, and he rolled his shoulders and neck as he straightened. He turned and jumped when he found Julian standing in the doorway to the kitchen, watching them.

"Jesus Christ!" Ty hissed at him. "Stop doing that!"

Julian's lips twitched in what might have been a smirk. Zane couldn't help but feel slightly vindicated. Ty did that to him all the time.

"Tell your brother not to touch the handle of the front door," Julian said as he stepped over the flattened mattress and moved to sit in a leather club chair close by.

"Great," Ty muttered.

"How's Cameron holding up?" Zane asked.

Julian shrugged, looking down the dark hallway. "About as expected. I think he's still in the washroom."

"How do you rig a doorknob with kitchen utensils?" Ty asked, still exasperated but also sounding a little too keen to learn a new trick.

"A large percentage of accidental deaths occur in the kitchen. It's a dangerous place," Julian drawled, almost seeming to enjoy himself.

Zane turned his attention to Julian. "Will you still be with us in the morning?"

Julian's eyes cut over to Zane, but nothing else moved. "If I still intended to run, I would have done so already. The time for escaping cleanly has long passed. As far as I'm concerned, the more weapons and people who know how to use them, the better."

"Including baseball bats."

"I'm sure we've all been in situations where we longed for something as appropriate as a baseball bat."

Zane nodded as Deuce came back down the hall. He stopped and tilted his head at Julian. "I believe your friend needs you," he murmured, his voice gentle and soft. He sounded almost like the psychiatrist he really was.

Julian stood immediately and moved toward the hallway. "Good night, gentlemen," he said as he left the room.

Zane watched him go, feeling confident that he could trust the man to keep his word. He seemed to have reached a decision to stick with them after the Pittsburgh airport, after Ty sacrificed himself to let them escape. Besides, Zane knew Cameron needed downtime, and Julian would probably move heaven and earth to give it to him. Zane turned his gaze to Ty and figured he understood. His partner was exhausted. They all needed time to rest.

Deuce had moved to help Ty plug in the electric pump. His limp was less pronounced than it had been the last time Zane had seen him, but he still let Ty do all the kneeling as they hooked the pump up and turned it on. Deuce was still wearing the boxers in which he'd been sleeping, and for the first time Zane could see the railroad track scars on his leg and knee.

He stood with his hands on his hips as Ty knelt beside him, both of them watching the air mattress inflate with their heads tilted to the side, like a pair of puppies trying to figure out a strange noise. Zane had to smile. He could really see the resemblance. How their mother had raised them both without having a nervous breakdown was anyone's guess.

"Hey, Ty, can we talk for a minute?" Deuce asked after a moment.

Ty glanced up at him and then over at Zane with a nod. "You got this?" he asked.

Zane nodded and gestured for them to go on. He watched them curiously as Ty followed Deuce down the hall to his bedroom, then turned his attention back to the air mattress and flipped the pump back on. The noise would make it impossible to overhear what they were saying, and Zane knew better than to allow himself the temptation of eavesdropping anymore.

"WHAT'S up?" Ty asked as he watched Deuce close the door to his bedroom. Deuce wasn't exactly a private person, and he knew Zane better than he did most people, so Ty couldn't fathom what he had to say that couldn't have been said in the living room.

Deuce turned to look at him, crossing his arms over his chest and covering his mouth with his hand. Ty recognized the signs all too well.

"Something's wrong."

Deuce shook his head. "No, I just… I need your advice."

"Okay." Ty said the word carefully as he studied his brother. He glanced around Deuce's bedroom. It was immaculate, as usual, all flat and modern and… weird. He pointed at a tray on top of the dresser. "Seriously, is that a blunt?"

"Well, I wasn't anticipating the FBI breaking down my door tonight."

Ty closed his eyes and shook his head. "That's fair. What's the problem?"

Deuce took a deep breath. "It's about Livi."

"Yoga girl."

"She really has a real name."

"Okay," Ty said with a smirk.

Deuce rolled his eyes and paced toward the window. "What did you think of her when you met her?"

"She's cute," Ty answered, confused by the question but willing to go along with Deuce's unique way of getting around to a point. He'd spent a day with Deuce after leaving Baltimore, and he'd met his girlfriend when she'd dropped by. "She was genuine and smart and probably very bendy. Good job."

"Ty."

"What? I'm not really sure what you're getting at. I met her for like five minutes."

Deuce stared at him, looking almost ill, and Ty stood waiting for him to continue. They stood in silence for a few moments, Deuce fidgeting and Ty forcing himself to be patient.

"Deacon," he finally said.

"She's pregnant," Deuce blurted in a rush of relief. Ty couldn't mask the surprise, and Deuce read him well. "Before you say anything, yes, I love her. Yes, I'm excited as hell. And yes, she's very bendy." For the first time, Deuce cracked a smile. He seemed to be trying to contain his excitement, but Ty recognized it anyway.

Ty nearly laughed in relief. He waved a hand through the air and stepped closer to hug his brother. "Congratulations, Deacon," he said as Deuce clapped him on the back.

"Thank you," Deuce said as he pushed away and took Ty by his shoulders to meet his eyes. "The problem."

"Why does there have to be a problem?"

"Because there's always a problem."

"Okay, what's the problem?" Ty asked with a growing sense of dread.

"Livi wants to be married before our families find out."

"What?"

"She doesn't want to tell her parents she's pregnant before we're married."

"Well, that's kind of a time-sensitive condition."

"That's the problem."

"That leaves you, what, like a month? Maybe less?"

Deuce nodded.

Ty blinked at his brother as the problem hit him. He gasped and pointed at Deuce's face. "You want to elope!"

"Yes," Deuce said in relief.

"Deacon!"

"I know!"

"You can't do that to Ma, she'll kill you. She'll kill me! Not to mention seriously bad relations with your future in-laws."

"Now you see my problem," Deuce said as he waved a hand through the air and sat on the end of his bed.

"I'm assuming this wasn't planned. How does that happen, anyway?"

"I think you've been doing dudes for too long if I need to answer that."

"Touché," Ty murmured with a frown. He grimaced and shook his head, bypassing half a dozen smartass remarks as he sat down beside Deuce. He really gave the question some thought, as much thought as he was capable of when being hunted down like a dog by the CIA.

"I mean… Deacon, if this is what you really want to do, then I'll cover your play. I'll do whatever you need to take the heat off after. Unless you do it without me there, and in that case I'll disown you."

Deuce smiled and nodded, and he put his arm around Ty's shoulders. "I knew I could count on you," he said quietly.

"But… if you're asking for my advice?"

Deuce nodded.

"Wait. Tell everyone, let them be excited about a baby, let them know you're committed to her whether you're married or not, and go from there. Don't go… sneaking around and trying to hide things from your families. You'll… you'll regret it."

Deuce looked at him in silence, his eyes sympathetic and warm. If anyone understood how well Ty knew what he was talking about, it was his brother. "Thanks, Ty."

Ty nodded, and they sat in silence for a long time, long enough that the pump to the air mattress stopped its loud whine and the light coming under the bedroom door turned off.

Deuce took a deep breath. "I'm going to be a daddy."

Ty smiled as he watched his brother's profile in the dim light. He could hear the mixture of excitement and fear in Deuce's voice. Then the smile faded as cold realization began to seep through him. "You're going to be a daddy," he echoed, almost to himself. He stood suddenly, looking around the room and patting his jeans as if he'd lost something.

"What's wrong?"

"We have to go," Ty said as he looked at Deuce with wide eyes.

"What? Why?"

"If someone tracks us here, I mean they shouldn't, but if they do—"

"Ty, it's okay. I knew someone was after you when you broke into my house. I know it's a risk for you to be here."

"No, but it's not just about you now, and this isn't just *someone* after us." Ty was already heading for the bedroom door.

Deuce hopped up to follow him, barely able to keep up on his bad leg. "Ty!"

"This isn't up for discussion, Deuce, it really isn't," Ty said. He banged on the bedroom door as he passed by, and Zane had turned the lights on again by the time they got to the living room.

"What's wrong?" Zane asked as soon as he saw Ty's face.

"We can't stay here, we need to move."

Zane looked between the two of them, seeking some clue in Deuce's face before he met Ty's eyes again.

"He's being ridiculous," Deuce told him.

"What's this all about?" Julian asked from behind them.

Ty turned to look at him. He was still wearing his jeans and T-shirt, but it was obvious that he'd been asleep.

"We can't stay. We need to move."

"No. No! One of you, talk some sense into him," Deuce said to them.

"What's wrong?" Zane asked again, more insistent. Ty met his eyes and tilted his head toward Deuce. It wasn't his secret to tell, and he hoped Zane would just trust him.

Deuce sighed in exasperation. "My girlfriend is pregnant. We found out yesterday."

Julian snorted. "That is the most remarkable non sequitur I think I've ever heard. You're right, he is Grady's brother."

Cameron jabbed Julian in the ribs, causing him to double over and groan pitifully.

Ty glared at him for a minute, but he could see that Zane knew exactly why Ty wanted to leave. "It's not just you we're jeopardizing by being here now," Zane said, looking from Deuce to Ty. "You're going to have a family. He's right, we have to leave."

"Come on," Deuce said as he stepped closer to Zane. "I know damn well that if Ty thought there was any danger to me with you coming here, he wouldn't have come to start with."

Zane looked between them again. Ty held his breath as they waited for Zane to respond. He silently pleaded with his partner to back him up.

"I'm sorry, Deuce. He's right," Zane finally said with a shake of his head. Ty sighed in relief.

"Just stay for the night, okay? You're all exhausted; you're barely functioning. And hell, if someone's going to be coming to kill me, I'd really appreciate it if you'd stick around with your guns and pointy things 'til morning, you know?" Deuce said in exasperation.

Ty cleared his throat and met Zane's eyes.

"That's a fair point," Julian murmured.

Ty nodded. "You're right," he said to Deuce.

"I know," Deuce said with a bright smile. He reached out and hugged his brother, holding onto him tightly. "Go to bed, okay? Be here in the morning?"

"I promise," Ty muttered.

ZANE had to look away as Deuce hugged Ty tighter. He could sympathize with the feeling, knowing Ty was in danger and wanting desperately to hold on to him and keep him safe.

When he finally let Ty go, he turned and hugged Zane as well. Zane smiled as he looked over Deuce's shoulder at Ty.

"We're keeping you up, Deuce," Zane murmured as he pondered the two brothers and patted Deuce's back. "Why don't you go back to bed? I'm sure Ty knows where things are if we need anything else."

Deuce let him go and looked him over, then looked at Ty, who was nodding in agreement.

"Just stick to your regular schedule in the morning, but don't touch the front door," Ty muttered.

"Why?"

Ty gestured helplessly to Julian.

"Just trust him; don't touch it," Julian said with a curt nod. They all stared at him. "Trade secret."

Ty rolled his eyes. He reached to the small of his back and took out the backup gun he'd taken off one of the bodies, checking it before handing it to Deuce. "Put that under your pillow."

Deuce looked down at it with a heavy sigh but didn't take it. "Yeah, okay. But you can keep that. My regular schedule doesn't involve shooting myself in the ass in the morning."

Cameron laughed and then clapped a hand over his mouth. Ty snorted and shook his head. Deuce looked up to meet Zane's eyes again, a worried frown creasing his brow.

Zane offered him a weak smile.

Deuce nodded and looked back at Ty as he turned toward the hallway. "Good night," he said as he left them.

Ty turned his head to watch his brother limp toward his bedroom.

Julian and Cameron stood there awkwardly for a moment. "Well. Good night, then."

Cameron gave them both a weak smile as he turned and followed Julian back into the guest bedroom.

Ty poked at the mattress with his foot.

Zane glanced toward the dark hallway, then leaned forward to reach out and touch Ty's lightly bruised jaw. "He got you," he murmured, his fingers feather light as they ghosted over the slight stubble. "You okay otherwise?" He'd not even gotten a chance to ask since the fight at the hotel some hours ago.

"Honestly?" Ty asked with another weak attempt at a smile. "I'm terrified, Zane. Everyone in the world I care about is mixed up in this now. I sent CIA cleaner teams to one of my friends and then led them right to my brother."

Gut clenching painfully, Zane slid his hand along Ty's neck. He wasn't sure he'd ever heard Ty so freely admit to fear. "We'll deal with it."

"And I'm suddenly going to be an uncle."

"That's good, Ty. It's good news."

Ty nodded and looked back down at the mattress, poking at the corner of the sheets with his toes, unwilling to look at him.

"Ty."

Ty met Zane's eyes and swallowed hard. He reached out without a word and slid his arms around Zane's neck. Zane pulled him close, surprised. He held him and Ty hugged him tight, still not speaking. Then he kissed Zane's neck and stepped back.

"Let's fix these sheets and go to bed, okay?"

"What's wrong with the sheets?" Zane asked.

Ty barked a laugh and shook his head.

They remade the bed quickly, Ty's corners still somehow perfect even on an air mattress on the floor. He stood to grab the heavy quilt and laid it out over the bed, then tossed the two pillows back onto the head of it.

He toed off his shoes and unbuckled his belt, then slid his jeans off and folded them neatly to set them on the couch. "You want couch side or floor side?" he asked Zane before pulling his shirt over his head.

"Floor side." If he wasn't going to be sitting up, he wanted to at least be able to move immediately. All he really wanted was to hold Ty to him.

Ty moved closer to him, sliding his hand against Zane's face before he bent and crawled onto the bed. Zane's eyes followed Ty's every movement; he didn't notice any hitches or winces that would indicate hidden injuries. It was rare enough for Ty to admit to being scared; Zane didn't know if he'd be hiding injuries now. He simply looked exhausted, just like the rest of them.

He stretched out under the covers and rolled onto one side, curling up again and facing the couch next to the mattress.

Zane had already stripped down to his boxers before the commotion. He turned off the light and stood in place to let his eyes adjust, watching the lump in the dark that was Ty as he waited.

Even in the darkness, Zane could tell Ty was still tense as he lay there. He had every right to be; he'd just learned that his brother was going to be a father, the same brother he could possibly have put in danger simply by coming here.

Zane finally moved and knelt next to the mattress before climbing onto it carefully, trying not to rock Ty too much.

Ty immediately reached back for him, resting his hand on whatever was closest as Zane moved behind him. The gesture settled Zane, and he scooted close enough to spoon up against him, sliding one arm under Ty's neck and draping the other over his waist. Ty scooted back into him, fitting against him perfectly. Calm began to seep through Zane's mind and body.

"I love you," he whispered, intending to say it as much as possible, at every opportunity, for the rest of his life.

Ty patted his hip a few times in response; then he was still and quiet. He wasn't rocking or jiggling a leg or tossing and turning like he often did when he was lying in bed before sleep overtook him. He was just still and calm as his breathing evened out. It was a little disconcerting.

Zane kissed his shoulder again before letting his head settle on the pillow. He sank into the darkness as he listened to Ty's breathing and the quiet sounds of the condo at night. He hoped the next day could be even half this peaceful.

THE distant ringing of a phone rousted Ty, but he was still lying in the warm cocoon of blankets and Zane's arms, staring at the ceiling, when Deuce skidded into the living room.

"Get up," Deuce said in a panicked voice.

Ty shot up, rolling over Zane and clambering to his feet gracelessly, spurred on by the tone of Deuce's words. Zane flailed and wound up rolling off the bed with him. Ty left him on the floor as he stood. "What's wrong?"

"Livi's on her way, you have to fix that doorknob."

"How close is she?"

"In the lobby, Ty!"

Ty sprinted for the kitchen, almost dreading what sort of contraption he would see attached to the doorknob. "Why didn't you tell her not to come up?"

"It was the doorman, she didn't call ahead."

"Well, call her and tell her to wait in the hall!" Ty said as he knelt in front of the doorknob. "What the shit is this?" It was so innocuous that he almost reached up to touch it. A row of connected straws wrapped around the base of the knob and led to the nearby coffee maker like a string. The knob itself was covered in tin foil, and Ty could see foil sticking out from inside several of the straws. "I...."

"Ty, come on, take it off."

"I'm not even sure where to begin."

"Ty!"

"Did you call her?"

"Her phone's not picking up, she must be in the elevator."

"What's going on?" Zane asked from the doorway to the kitchen. His hair was mussed, and he still looked half-asleep. A moment later Julian joined them.

"Cross! How do we dismantle this thing?"

"Carefully," Julian answered, voice calm and quiet. "The current's in the foil."

"What if we cut it?" Ty asked.

Julian hummed, not sounding optimistic.

"Ground yourself," Zane said as he brought his boots over and clunked them down beside Ty's knee.

In the moment of calm while Ty was sliding his feet into the boots, they heard the elevator ding in the hallway outside.

"Oh God," Deuce said as he held the phone to his ear. "Come on, baby, answer the phone."

"Give me some oven mitts."

"You're going to shock the shit out of yourself," Julian murmured. "I want to take this moment to thank you profusely for letting me watch."

"Shut up!" Ty and Zane both shouted at him.

Zane handed Ty the kitchen shears, and Ty tapped the end of one of the straws with the blade. Sparks flew, and he could feel the current running through the straws.

"Holy shit!" Zane cried, as if he hadn't really thought it would work.

"You're not helping!" Ty told him, his voice wavering.

"That was incredible!"

"Zane!"

"I'm sorry, that was just really… I'm sorry."

"Can we bask in its glory after we dismantle it?" Deuce growled as he dialed Livi's number again. "It's going straight to voice mail."

"I…." Ty winced as he pulled the oven mitts on.

"Ty! You're about to electrocute my girlfriend!"

They heard keys jingle outside the door.

"Livi, don't touch the door!" Deuce called.

"Deacon?" a dainty voice said on the other side of the door.

"Answer your goddamn phone! Ty, cut it."

The hair on Ty's arms rose as he held the scissors up to the straws. "Oh, God, this is gonna hurt."

"What is going on in there?" Livi asked, and the keys jangled again.

Out of the corner of his eye, Ty saw Cameron dart through the kitchen to the coffee maker on the counter. He reached behind it and yanked the plug out of the wall. The buzzing sensation on Ty's arms ceased, and then he heard Livi's key slide into the lock on the other side.

Nothing happened.

"Oh, well, that would have been easier. Well done, Cam," Julian said in a pleased voice.

The door opened before Ty could scramble away, smacking him square in the cheek and sending him sprawling backward.

He lay on the tile floor, holding his face as Livi walked into the condo. "Oh my goodness, Ty! I'm so sorry!" the woman said as she put both hands to her mouth and bent over him. Livi was a beautiful girl, possibly less so just then since Ty could see two of her. She had intelligent robin's-egg-blue eyes and hair so blonde it seemed white when the sun hit it. She was lithe and athletic, everything Ty thought a yoga instructor would probably be. She also led with her shoulder when she opened a door.

Zane took his arm and hefted him to his feet. Ty shook his head to clear the gauze. "So nice to see you again," he muttered to her. She still had her fingers over her lips, staring at him with big blue eyes.

She turned and looked at Deuce, giving him a helpless gesture. "What the hell is going on?"

"Livi, you remember my brother, Ty. This is his partner, Zane Garrett."

"Hi," Zane offered in a low voice that sent a shiver up Ty's spine.

"And these are their… friends, Julian and Cameron," Deuce said as he waved at the other two men.

"Nice to meet you," Cameron mumbled.

She greeted them each, overwhelmed by the surprise, then looked at the doorknob and the string of straws, shaking her head. "What is all this?"

"It was a security measure. We're running from the CIA," Ty told her, not even attempting to spare her. "They're trying to kill us."

"Well, kill him, specifically," Zane added as he pointed at Julian.

"I sell antiques," Julian said, monotone.

She narrowed her eyes, looking amongst them and then at Deuce. "Is this some sort of boys' weekend that I'm not supposed to intrude on? Because I can totally leave before they hurt themselves trying to lie convincingly."

Deuce gave her a warm smile and shook his head. "I think the only one lying is him," he said, pointing at Julian.

"So, I'm... I'm sorry, tell me again?" Livi stuttered as they all sat in the living room of Deuce's condo.

"We're serious," Ty told her. "The CIA is trying to kill us."

"Him," Zane muttered.

"Would you stop that? Come on!"

"It's more accurate to say they're trying to kill him."

"Zane!"

Julian rolled his eyes. "I believe what Agent Garrett is trying to point out is that you are likely in no danger because of our presence here."

Livi nodded, looking at him dubiously.

"They're lying," Cameron said, his voice remarkably offhand. "You are in danger because we're here, they're trying to protect you so you won't worry. They do that."

"Cam!" Julian said, stunned into gaping at his lover.

Ty smacked his forehead and covered his face with his hand.

"Wow, you guys are... I could make a mint off your therapy," Deuce muttered.

"I'm sorry—I really am—I'm just tired of this macho bullshit!" Cameron said as he waved a hand at them. He turned to Julian. "Can you honestly look at me and tell me you're not scared?"

Julian tried to respond, but his mouth was still hanging open.

Cameron looked at Ty and Zane where they sat together on a square ottoman. "And you two, you're just ridiculous! You're so busy bitching at each other and trying to look like you don't care that you don't realize you're throwing your lives away waiting for it to be the right time to admit you're in love."

"Cameron!" Julian finally managed to say, waving at Deacon and Livi as if Cameron might not remember they were there.

Cameron cleared his throat. "I'm sorry."

Livi glanced over at Ty and Zane, then looked at Deuce. "So when you said partner, you meant like *working* partner? Because that didn't really come across so much as they were a couple."

Zane pinched the bridge of his nose, but he appeared to be smiling.

"Really?" Ty asked, sounding concerned.

"You scream 'we're screwing'."

"Huh."

"Well, now that we've got *that* cleared up," Deuce said as he stood. "What are you going to do?"

Ty and Zane looked at each other, and then both men glanced at Julian. Zane was shaking his head, but Ty's eyes moved from Julian to Cameron.

"What do we do, Cam?" Ty asked in a soft voice.

"Excuse me?"

"Look, you're right. People like us, sometimes we can't see the forest for the trees. We were all trying to figure out how to dismantle that freaking doorknob when none of us thought to just pull the plug."

Cameron nodded.

"We haven't asked you, not once, what you thought we should do," Ty continued.

Julian tore his eyes away from the FBI agents and looked at his lover. Ty was right. They'd been pulling Cameron along without so much as a thought to what he might want or think.

Cameron met his eyes, uncertain.

"Go ahead, Cam."

"Well… we can't fly or ride a train. You've been saying that driving into DC is suicide. So why not get there another way?"

"Another way," Julian repeated.

"Oh God," Ty muttered.

"Water," Zane said, sounding surprised and irritated that none of them had thought of it before.

Julian slid his arm around Cameron's waist, squeezing him.

"Getting our hands on a boat won't be easy," Ty said, sounding grim. "We'd have to take a smuggler's line down the coast."

"Avoid the Coast Guard, and slip into port without a course plotted or papers," Zane added. "That's if we can find a boat."

Livi perked up and smiled. "Daddy has a boat."

Deuce cleared his throat. "I think they're thinking more inconspicuous than your dad's yacht, honey."

"Oh wait, I think they took it to St. Vincent."

"Yacht?" Ty said with a smirk at his brother.

"She's smart, beautiful, and loaded. What's not to love?" Deuce drawled, matching the smirk with one of his own.

"I'm a trust fund baby—both of you shut up," Livi said.

Zane was smiling at her and Ty was shaking his head, eyes focused on the pure-white carpet. "I know someone who has a boat."

Zane looked at his partner, one eyebrow raised. Ty glanced sideways at him and winced.

"Who?" Zane asked.

"You're not going to like it."

~Chapter 15~

THEY used Livi and her incomparable charm to gain access to the private port on the Delaware River where her father kept his yacht. She sweet-talked one of the skippers into letting them take a small boat out for a "joy ride," and in less than an hour they had set sail down the Delaware toward open water.

By the time night fell, they had reached the coordinates they'd been given. They anchored there, bobbing in the choppy water, to wait.

Zane and the others thanked Deuce and Livi for their help and then went out on the cockpit to let Ty say goodbye. Zane watched through the window as he hugged Livi. She put her hand to her belly in a gesture Zane knew meant Ty was telling her he was happy for them. Zane's lips twitched in a smile. He liked Livi, and he couldn't wait to hear about her meeting Ty and Deuce's family. It also made him sad, though; he wouldn't be introduced to Ty's family in the same way she would be any time soon.

Ty gave Deuce a tight hug, holding onto him for longer than he usually did as he spoke to him. Then he handed Deuce the last of their cash, and Zane knew he was telling his brother to get out of town for a few days and not to use his credit cards.

Zane had to fight back a jangle of nerves. He had to believe that the CIA agents after them wouldn't hurt anyone unless they were in the path of Julian Cross. Deuce would be fine. He hoped.

A beacon of light on the water caught his eye, and he squinted into the moonless night.

"Ty!" he called as a completely different type of nervousness settled over him. "He's here."

When Ty had mentioned Nick O'Flaherty's name, saying his old Recon buddy had a boat they could use, Zane had sort of expected a dinghy. He had imagined Nick inhabiting some seedy apartment over an Irish pub in South Boston. That was the impression he'd gotten from Ty's oldest friend when he was blind and could only hear him speak. So he was surprised when a sleek sixty-foot Outer Reef 580 Motoryacht glided into the view of the little boat's running lights.

Julian whistled from the railing where he was watching the yacht. "Not cheap. I thought you said your friend was a cop."

"He is," Ty said as he checked the magazine in his gun.

"Is he on the take?"

Ty looked up to glare at him. He didn't answer, instead heading for the stern of the boat to call out to Nick and help him secure the gangplank they would use to switch boats.

Zane was scowling as he watched Ty and the shadowed figure on the other boat. Julian was right; that was not a bargain basement way to live. Zane found himself wondering how Nick afforded it.

He drew a steadying breath and then rolled his eyes. He shouldn't be nervous. Nick knew who he was, even if Zane had never laid eyes on Nick. He watched as Ty spoke with the man, able to overhear them in the still night.

"Let me guess," Nick's Boston accent said in amusement. "Strippergram?"

"Yeah, let us in so we can steal your watch in the morning," Ty muttered. The sense of humor explained why this man and Ty had become such close friends, but it also made Zane want to hate him a little more.

"We'd better get going if we intend to go unnoticed," Nick called out as soon as they had the gangplank secured.

They boarded the yacht one at a time, Zane's stomach in knots. Zane realized that he was desperately hoping that Mr. Nick O'Flaherty was an unfortunate-looking individual.

It was a few seconds later, when they all gathered in the salon, that Zane truly got a look at Nick for the first time as he hurried past them toward the pilothouse. He looked about Ty's age, ruggedly handsome and clean-shaven with short strawberry-blond hair and ivy-green eyes. He was a few inches shorter than Zane, but then, most men were. He was built solidly, not as broad as Ty or Zane at the shoulders, but obviously fit. Damn him.

He wore faded jeans, a thick cable-knit sweater, and boots. The gun in his jeans told Zane he'd been expecting trouble.

They followed him through the boat, Ty moving into the pilothouse with Nick as the others stood in the galley in the middle of the yacht.

"Garrett, good to see you in one piece," Nick said with a nod as he slid into the pilot's seat.

"Well, it's good to see anything," Zane said, unable to look at Nick without thinking about how he had kissed the man Zane loved. He pushed that aside for now.

"I think we got here clean," Ty said as he turned and waved for Julian and Cameron to join them.

"Same. What the fuck have you guys gotten into?" Nick asked.

Ty shrugged and looked around the pilothouse uneasily. Nick watched him and then turned in his seat to look at Zane.

Zane didn't know how much Nick had been told, because Ty had spoken to him in Farsi on the phone. He stood in the galley of Nick's yacht, trying to think of anything to fill the awkward silence that didn't end with punching Nick in the face.

He couldn't come up with anything, and so they stood in silence as Cameron gave Nick a weak smile and stepped forward to shake his hand. "I know you don't know us. But thank you."

"Ty says you need help. You got it." He offered his hand to Cameron, then to Julian when the Irishman moved closer, introducing himself to each of them.

Zane pursed his lips as he looked around the yacht. It was sumptuous, all black leather and lacquered teak wood, shining stainless steel and top-of-the-line everything. The furniture in the salon was all built-in, heavy and luxurious, with a large television in place on the wall that separated the salon from the galley. Stairs led from the galley to an upper deck. When Zane looked around, it didn't feel like it fit Nick at all. But then, he didn't know Nick very well.

"So," Nick said with false cheer. "Tell me about the people trying to kill you this time."

"The less you know...."

"Bite me, Grady."

"Bathroom?" Zane asked before the conversation could devolve further.

Nick pointed toward the steps that led down, right beside where he sat. "Take a right, that's the VIP head. Left is the master. Whichever."

Zane headed for the stairs, feeling like he was descending into the pit as he ducked and hunched his shoulders to make it down the curving stairwell. He discreetly looked around the lower cabins to try and get a feel for the man who'd made a move on his lover just a few weeks ago.

The most prominent pictures on the walls were of Nick in uniform, surrounded by smiling Marines. Very similar to Ty's photos at home. Zane stopped and stared at one when he caught sight of a younger Ty. There were six men, all in various stages of dress, some standing, some kneeling, looking as if they had been roughhousing or playing during downtime while deployed on a carrier. Ty and Nick were front and center, wearing only pants and combat boots, both tanned from hours in the sun and salt air, their dog tags prominent on bare chests. All six men were grinning, arms around each other. Ty was holding a football, balancing it on the tip of his fingers as he displayed it for the camera.

Zane could hear Ty filling Nick in on the basics of what had happened, giving him the condensed version in typical Ty fashion. He turned toward the head before he could let himself get sucked into that vortex of uncertainty again. Ty may have looked happy in old pictures, but Zane knew Ty was happy now too.

When he returned, Nick and Ty were still discussing what needed to be done. Cameron was sitting in a corner booth that was tucked into the other side of the pilothouse, and Julian was looking askance at the low ceilings as if he might hit his head when he took a step.

"How long will it take us to get to DC?" Ty was asking Nick.

"A day, two if we can only travel at night."

"No, we need to keep a regular schedule. Travel by day, anchor at night."

"You sure?"

Ty nodded as he rubbed his hand over his face.

"Have you dumped your cells?" Nick asked.

"Cell phones, a few cars, credit cards, badges, guns, my watch. Everything we could think of that might have been bugged or can be tracked electronically."

"At least you're not wearing tinfoil hats yet."

"Only when we sleep," Ty muttered.

"You told me on the phone that you called Digger. Was that true, or were you trying to give me a message?"

"It was true. I told him that we were coming to him so whoever was listening could overhear, and then let him know that it was a decoy."

"Coconuts?"

"Yeah."

"So, somewhere in the bayou, Digger is preparing for the arrival of an unfriendly?"

"In theory."

Nick glanced at Julian and Zane and then rubbed his hand over his mouth. "God help the poor bastard that shows up on his doorstep," he muttered.

Ty huffed a laugh. "We tried to lay low a couple places, but they kept finding us. I finally realized they were pinging the receiver in my watch. We headed to Philly, but... I can't risk Deacon."

"Understood."

Zane wondered if Nick had any qualms about Ty risking *him*. He didn't let on if he did.

"I pulled out the limit from every ATM I passed while I was on duty, so I've got a couple thousand for you. That's the best I can do, but I can give you my card when we make port."

"Thank you," Ty whispered.

Nick nodded and then glanced at the rest of them. "You all look like half-eaten sushi."

Zane found himself fighting back a smile, and he nodded instead.

"You're a police officer?" Cameron asked Nick, who nodded. "Isn't there something you can do? Someone you can call to help us?"

Nick looked at him for a moment with a sympathetic frown, and then he glanced at Ty.

"The CIA is slightly out of his reach, love," Julian murmured. He put his hand on Cameron's shoulder and squeezed, trying to comfort him.

"I'm sorry," Nick said, sounding sincere.

Ty met Zane's eyes, and Zane knew exactly what he was thinking. They were going to get Cameron out of this alive even if it killed them.

"These two need a bed together," Ty murmured to Nick as he waved a hand at Julian and Cameron.

Nick raised an eyebrow but nodded without commenting. "You can take my cabin," he told Julian. He stood, making sure Ty had the wheel first, and then he gestured for them to follow as he ducked down the stairs. Julian and Cameron followed with murmured good-nights to Ty and Zane.

Zane moved to sit in the booth near Ty. He wasn't sure what Ty wanted to do, though he expected visiting with Nick to be high on the list tonight. Zane didn't really want to visit with Nick, though, and he sure as hell didn't want Ty doing it. It bothered him enough that Ty knew his way around Nick's boat. But he had to trust Ty, and it had to start somewhere, so why not here?

"You okay?" Ty asked as he fiddled with the controls of the yacht.

Zane pursed his lips. "Every time I look at him I want to knock his lights out."

Ty shrugged as he kept his hand on the wheel and then glanced down the stairwell. "So do it."

"What?"

"Do it, Zane. If it'll make you feel better, slug him."

Zane took in a deep breath, truly contemplating it. But he knew it wouldn't make anything better in the end, and he was suspicious of Ty's easy agreement.

Nick returned a few moments later.

"VIP cabin's all set up," he told them as he stepped into the galley and opened the refrigerator. He still had his gun stuffed in the small of his back. "Clean sheets and everything."

"Improvement over last time," Ty muttered.

"You had a sheet last time. And it was sort of clean."

"Yeah, on top of a pool float that was anchored to the flybridge," Ty said as he pointed up.

"You were on a pool float because it squeaked when you moved; we had to make sure you were still breathing!"

Ty gave a dismissive grunt and wave as he put the boat through its paces, apparently preparing to set it at anchor.

"Few years in a suit and Princess is suddenly too good for a pool float," Nick whispered to Zane with a smirk as he handed them each a water bottle. "I've got food, beer, sodas, and water in the fridge. Garrett, help yourself."

"Thanks," Zane said, half laughing, wondering how often Nick got away with calling Ty a princess. He resented that Nick was a likable guy. He really wanted to hate him and be rude to him.

"Go on and sleep," Nick told them. "I'll get us settled for the night and keep watch."

Ty left the wheel and stood. He looked from Nick to Zane, as if waiting to see if Zane was going to deck Nick. When Zane didn't move, Ty took a few steps toward Nick and took his forearm instead of his hand, gripping it hard. "Thanks, Irish."

"You know it," Nick said, and then he nodded at Zane and turned to slip into the pilot's seat.

Zane followed Ty down the stairs to the smaller of the two cabins. There was what appeared to be a queen-size bed tucked into the room, with wooden steps on either side to climb into it. Ty stuffed their bags onto a shelf that circled the bow-shaped room, then looked at Zane and smiled, albeit uncomfortably. He rubbed his hands up and down the material of his jeans just below the pockets, a nervous habit he only displayed when he couldn't find anything else to do with his hands.

"He's a decent guy, isn't he?" Zane asked, dejected.

"Zane."

"I really want to hate him."

"So hate him. You have every right. Being drunk is never an excuse to do stupid shit. You'll have to hate me too, though, 'cause I was there and I kissed him back."

The words hit Zane in the chest like a sledgehammer. He stared at Ty until he realized that he wasn't breathing and he cleared his throat. His voice was flat when he spoke. "Really."

Ty let out a pent-up breath, his shoulders slumping as he looked away from Zane, unable to meet his eyes.

"Did you like it?" Zane asked, his voice going lower, full of barely repressed anger that he was surprised to hear.

"Zane, come on, what's the point in that?" Ty asked, sounding frustrated and angry and possibly a little scared by the question.

Zane narrowed his eyes to scrutinize his lover. Ty had his lips pressed into a thin line and was staring at him with his hands on his hips, his eyes unreadable.

"Yeah," he answered, spitting out the word. "A little."

Zane couldn't help the twisting sensation in his chest. He didn't want to think about that, and he certainly didn't want his very active imagination providing him with any visuals. He pressed his lips together hard and looked up at the low ceiling to let out a long breath. "I kind of wish I hadn't asked."

"I kind of wish I had lied," Ty said in a soft voice.

Zane shook his head. Ty stepped up to him, hesitant, as if he thought Zane might rebuff him. He reached out and touched Zane's cheek, stepping closer to brush his lips against Zane's chin.

Zane closed his eyes. Ty was being just as brutally honest as he always was, even if it hurt him and even if it hurt Zane. There was something comforting in that. It didn't wipe away the knowledge that Nick O'Flaherty was in love with Ty and had been for years or that Ty had shared and enjoyed a kiss with him.

Zane set his forehead against Ty's cheekbone, letting his hands slide around Ty and pull him closer.

"Zane," Ty whispered, uncertainty clouding his voice.

"I know. It's okay. I just hate that you're so close to him."

Ty jerked his head and pulled back. Zane let him go. "I haven't spoken to him since he left Baltimore, Zane. I used to talk to him at least once every day, even if it was just a random text, but that's stopped. He's leaving me alone out of respect for you, for us, and I have to tell you, baby, I miss him."

Zane snorted in annoyance.

"But if that's what you need, I'll do it. Do you understand? I'll do anything you need me to do. Because I have never felt like this about anything, and I'm terrified of screwing up and losing it."

Zane held his breath, meeting Ty's eyes. "He's your best friend, Ty."

"If it's you or him, there's no question who I'll choose."

Zane was ashamed of the effect those words had on him. He felt like doing the Snoopy dance around the room. Instead, he said: "I don't want that."

Ty nodded. "Let it sit for a while. Okay? Let's just live through this first."

"Yeah," Zane murmured, though his eyes were drawn up, to where Nick still was.

Ty was silent. Finally, he swallowed hard and shook his head. "I know you're worried. Nick knows me pretty well. I think you'd probably have to go to Deuce to find someone who knows me better." He looked up, as if measuring his words. "He knows what love means to me, when he's not drunk off his ass like we were that night. It never should have happened, and he knows it."

Zane had to deal with both a little spot of relief—that Nick knew better than to push—and a small spark of pain at the same time. It was true: he didn't know Ty as well as Deuce or Nick. Zane allowed himself a melancholy moment. Sometimes it seemed that Ty could read his mind, but Zane was still fighting through gauze when it came to Ty.

"They've known you a lot longer than I have," he said. "A lot of history there I'm not connected to."

"Stop it," Ty said gently. His voice was warm and affectionate, and his fingers slid up and down Zane's arm as he stepped closer and wrapped Zane up in a hug.

Zane huffed but smiled against Ty's shoulder. He liked that Ty knew him so well. It was like a splash of cold water to the face every time he started to sink into thinking he was a mystery. "So tell me something."

"Anything," Ty said in a low whisper. Just like the first time he'd answered with that, months ago in a tent, Zane's stomach did a happy flip. He steeled himself to ask the only thing he could think of just then.

"How the hell does Nick afford this boat?"

Ty's fingers came to a stop, and he seemed to be holding his breath as the muscles against Zane's body tightened. Then he sighed and relaxed again, his fingers dragging against Zane's neck as he stepped away.

"Come on, Ty, this isn't city cop salary stuff. This isn't even saving every dime he made in the Marines and eating Ramen noodles every meal."

"It's his home, it's where he lives. You ever asked yourself how I afford a historic row house in the middle of Fell's Point?"

"Not really," Zane said with a frown. "I always figured you were just really adept at not spending money."

"Jesus, Zane," Ty said with a laugh.

"You never buy anything, you never have anything extravagant," Zane continued, mumbling as he began to feel sort of stupid for never wondering about it. "How *can* you afford it?"

Ty shook his head, looking up as if he could see the deck above them. He met Zane's eyes again before turning away. "I'm going to bed."

"Ty, come on."

Ty picked up the nearest pillow and chucked it at him. Zane caught it and threw it back. "You brought it up."

"It was a payoff, all right? When they kicked us out of the Marines, they had to make sure we wouldn't go crying to the press, so they paid us a lump sum and sent us on our way."

Zane stared at him, not exactly shocked but close enough to it to gape. Ty closed his eyes and turned his head away.

"How much?" Zane whispered.

"Enough."

"Why'd they do it? What'd you guys get into?"

Ty turned to meet his eyes, then gave a curt shake of his head. "That's enough story time for one night. I'm going to bed."

"THEY'VE completely dropped off the grid again," Agent X said as he spoke to his superior.

"How is it possible that they keep evading you with two prisoners to keep under control?"

"I'm beginning to believe that Cross isn't a prisoner, sir."

"Excuse me?"

"I hesitate to conjecture, sir, but… I believe he thinks they're trying to help him."

"Why in God's name would he think they're trying to help him when all they want to do is deliver him to the man who wants him dead?"

"That I can't say. But why, sir, would they attempt to deliver him at all if they merely want him dead? Why not kill him in Chicago?"

"I don't know."

"Is it possible they don't know what they're doing?"

"Anything is possible, I suppose. We'll try to take them alive."

"Yes, sir."

"Hunting them down is becoming futile. I haven't heard anything from the team we sent to Louisiana. But we knew that was a ruse."

"Yes, sir."

"Come back to DC, we'll sit on the Federal building. We know that's where they're going. I'll send a team to Blake Nichols in Chicago. Perhaps we can find some clarity in all this."

"Yes, sir."

Agent X hung up the phone, looking at it in frustration. If Randall Jonas got his hands on Julian Cross, the last shred of evidence against him would be gone. Jonas was responsible for too many deaths. They couldn't let these FBI assholes deliver Cross to his death too.

HOURS after crawling into bed with Ty, Zane still lay awake, staring at the stars through the windows, listening to the soothing sound of Ty's breathing. Ty's body was warm against his, something familiar in the midst of this absolute clusterfuck.

There was something incredibly romantic about where they were. The moon and stars were astounding out on the water, twinkling above them, unfettered by the lights of any city. He could hear the waves slapping against the hull, the creak of the boat as it bobbed at anchor. The gentle rocking under them would have been the perfect backdrop to curling up with his lover and making love all night long.

He shifted in bed, turning his head so he could look at Ty. He was trying not to think too hard about anything, but Ty was always at the forefront of his thoughts. Where the hell had the money come from? Why was Ty so uncomfortable with the subject? Was he telling the truth about the military paying them, or was that another classified cover? And then there was Nick.

When he'd first found Ty in the airport in Chicago, Ty had said he wanted to talk about a lot of things when they got home, to get everything in the open. Ever since, Zane had pondered what Ty could possibly have in mind. Obviously, Nick had been one of those things. He was angry and hurt, even though Ty hadn't really done anything wrong but react to a kiss and then admit to liking it. He hated the bond Ty had with Nick, but he also hated to ask Ty to give it up.

A glass clinked from above, and Zane raised his head to listen. He heard another small sound, and he slid out from under the covers, trying not to disturb his partner as he clambered out of the oddly shaped bed. Ty usually woke at the drop of a hat unless he was truly exhausted. All the driving and running and fighting had used up everything Ty had in him. He didn't even toss his head when Zane got out of bed.

Zane stood at the end of the bed and looked down at him, wondering about the panic that Ty had been feeling that night weeks ago when he'd left Zane asleep and bolted. Was there a force in nature that would make Zane walk away right now?

He shook his head, determined to let that stay in the past, and he grabbed his gun and headed up the stairs for the galley.

When he peered over the edge of the stair railing, he could see Nick standing in a weak pool of light coming from the sink. He cleared his throat to let Nick know he was there. Nick turned to look at him, glass in hand.

"Did I wake you?" he asked in a whisper.

Zane shook his head and climbed the rest of the steps, moving toward the little corner booth that was situated in the pilothouse. He set his gun on the tiny table and slid into a seat, turning to rest his elbow on the back so he could look into the galley. Nick had been really quiet, actually. Impressively so. Zane was just too attuned to noises in the night.

"Mind if I get a drink?" Zane asked, his voice hoarse and dry.

"What's your pleasure?" Nick asked as he turned to the refrigerator behind him.

"Water, tea, coffee, doesn't matter."

Nick messed around in the refrigerator and finally pulled out a plastic bottle of water. He set the bottle and a glass of ice on the counter between them with a flourish and smirked. "Caffeine'll keep you awake."

"I'll be awake anyway," Zane answered, but he pulled the bottle and glass toward him. "Thank you."

"No problem," Nick said with a nod. He picked up his own glass again and leaned his elbows on the countertop. "What's keeping you up? Aside from the people trying to kill you."

"I don't sleep much. Even when people *aren't* trying to kill me," Zane said, smiling.

Nick was nodding, watching Zane, though he probably couldn't make out much since the only light in the room didn't reach the corner where he sat. Zane wondered what Nick might talk about, if asked, or if he might share something about Ty that Zane didn't know. Ty was their common ground. It was just talk between new friends, right? Only this friend knew Ty was *with* Zane, and he'd had his tongue down Ty's throat a few weeks ago.

Zane shrugged that imagery off. He'd have to deal with it soon, but he wanted to see what he could get out of Nick first.

"I guess none of us sleep much. Ty's down there muttering in Farsi," he said as a way to break the ice.

"He does that still?" Nick asked in amusement.

"Only when he's asleep or really, really pissed off," Zane admitted, sliding the glass back and forth on the table near his gun. He kind of enjoyed the dig, letting Nick know that Zane was the one who held Ty at night. It might have been beneath him, but he didn't care. "When he sleeps, he doesn't sleep quietly."

Nick gave that a melancholy smile. "We were all like that, to a degree. You can be disqualified from making Recon if you snore, but what they don't realize is that after half a year, every one of us talked in our sleep. Or screamed."

Zane emptied his glass and reached for the bottle to refill it. "I don't think that's something I've ever done. Talk in my sleep, I mean. Keep it bottled up, I guess." Not to mention that a large part of the time he'd been undercover, he was sleeping with someone—or someones—he didn't want knowing who he really was.

"Not healthy," Nick chastised, smiling and lifting his own glass to his lips.

"Are you a friend of Deuce's too?" Zane asked wryly.

"Ty's brother? I've met him a few times. I don't know, something about combining the Grady traits with psychological training didn't sit right with me. Made me nervous."

Zane laughed. "Grady traits? Like blustering out of tight spots and courage under fire?"

"And being crazy enough to pull off the impossible."

"Gummi bears."

"Cheetos. And that look, like he knows exactly what you're thinking and he finds it funny."

"I hate that," Zane muttered, setting down his half-full glass.

"Me too," Nick said, laughing and looking down at the ice in his glass again. "God, I miss him sometimes."

Zane looked up at him, an uncomfortable feeling in the pit of his stomach. He didn't want to imagine what it was like to miss Ty.

Nick was silent too, watching Zane in the dim light again and drinking his water without further comment. Finally, Nick smiled and looked away with a shake of his head. "Ty told you, didn't he?"

It threw Zane for a moment, and he stared at Nick, wondering if he was headed for a showdown of some sort. "Yes."

Nick nodded, still looking down at the glass he'd set on the counter. "I was hoping he'd forget."

"He told me that night. As soon as he got home."

Nick nodded. "His brand of morality is pretty unique," he said as he looked up to meet Zane's eyes. He straightened and put both hands on the counter. "I owe you an apology."

Zane frowned, not sure how to handle the straightforward approach. "Am I actually going to hear it?"

"Depends," Nick answered with an easy shrug. "Do you deserve it?"

"Yes," Zane said, meeting Nick's eyes.

Nick raised one eyebrow and cocked his head to the side. "Ty told me he was involved with you, that he loved you, and I should have respected that. I didn't, and for that I'm sorry," he offered, sounding sincere.

Zane nodded, noting how precisely Nick worded that apology. "Now tell me how you really feel," he said, keeping his tone dry. He didn't want to start an argument, but he did want to know where Nick stood. And he did still want to slug him.

Nick snorted and gave him a grim smile. "I think you're one lucky son of a bitch, and I kind of want to hate you. The hell of it is, I know Ty. He won't come looking for me unless you give him a good goddamn reason to."

"I know I'm lucky," Zane said as he realized that the little bundle of nerves he'd always had to deal with when he thought about love and Ty just wasn't there. Was that confidence? Trust in his lover? Zane wasn't sure, but he liked it.

Nick lowered his head, shaking it minutely. "In that case, for what it's worth, I'm sorry for making a move on your boyfriend."

It sounded so absurd that Zane huffed a laugh. "Thanks."

"Yeah." Nick stood for an awkward moment, obviously not sure what to say or do.

"If you weren't so damn much like him, I'd probably have been able to hit you," Zane told him, wondering where the urge to share was coming from and kind of wishing it would stop.

Nick looked up at him, expression guarded. "If we can be friends, it'd make our lives easier. And Ty's."

Zane nodded.

"You can tell he's tense. I've been wondering if that's because of me, or just life. But then, he never did like it when people tried to kill him."

"No one likes it when people try to kill them."

Nick smirked at that. He picked up his glass and turned to get more ice from the freezer. He moved deliberately, trying not to make any noise. He glanced toward the stairs again. When he turned back to the counter, he reached for his own bottle of water to refill his glass.

"He said you've been on the run pretty much nonstop," he said to Zane. "You've got to be as exhausted as he is, why are you really up?"

"Honestly? You."

"Ah."

Zane glanced toward the stairwell, then back to Nick. "How close *are* you?" he finally blurted out. "I have no frame of reference, other than the oorah and your tongue down his throat."

"Whoa, okay."

"Well?"

"Right. Uh… we met on the bus ride to Parris Island. Stuck together for the next… ten years, I guess."

"That doesn't answer my question."

"Then you're going to have to be more specific."

Zane shrugged. "I don't know. I've never been able to really talk to one of Ty's friends before, besides his brother. I guess I figured you might have some insight."

Nick was already shaking his head before Zane finished. "Just treat him like you would when you unravel a slinky. That's the best I can give you."

"That's disturbingly apt," Zane murmured.

Nick's lips twitched as he looked down at the glass in his hand. Zane looked at him, truly studying him. He was beginning to understand why this man was Ty's best friend, coming out and kissing him aside.

"Anything else?"

Nick's smile fell, and he nodded. "I've lost count of how many times over I owe him my life." He looked at Zane hard, narrowing his eyes in the darkness. "There's something you're dancing around," he said, confident in his assertion.

Zane sighed. He figured he must be really worn out if he wasn't hiding his emotions as well as usual. Nick was reading him, and Zane wasn't sure he cared. "I'm worried. This mess could go so bad so quickly, and you know him. He'll be right in the middle of it."

"Ty was made for messes. He and the cockroaches will be the only things to survive the final meltdown."

Zane looked down at the almost empty glass he held and then set it carefully on the counter. "I wouldn't bet on the cockroaches."

Nick was quiet, but Zane could feel his eyes on him.

"You and Ty… you were prisoners of war, weren't you?" he said, looking up to meet Nick's eyes carefully.

Nick inhaled sharply and rubbed his hand over his mouth as he looked away.

"I was wondering… I don't want to ask him details. He doesn't know I know."

Nick looked down at the counter and shook his head, then pushed away from the counter and paced away, running his hand through his hair.

Zane winced. "I'm sorry, I…."

"I just, uh… it's still classified. Not something I really like to chat about," Nick stuttered. He was truly flustered, and Zane realized that it didn't suit him.

"I thought maybe it would help me understand you two better. Understand him better. I'm sorry, I…." Zane shrugged. He had worried about asking Ty the details, but he hadn't even considered the effect the mention of it would have on Nick. He realized that it had been cruel to bring it up. Despite wanting to hate this man, Zane found that he didn't.

Zane's words hung in the air between them. Zane wasn't sure if Nick would give him details. Zane wasn't sure that he wanted details, but he felt like it was something that had forged Ty into who he was now.

Nick returned to the counter, watching Zane, looking like a man with something heavy on his conscience. It was another look that didn't suit him, and Zane frowned as a shadow crossed Nick's face in the weak light.

"We were in captivity for over three weeks," he told Zane without being prompted again. "Twenty-three days, nine hours, and fifty-one minutes."

"Jesus," Zane whispered.

"We were captured when our Chinook was taken down by an improvised rocket-assisted mortar. We're not really sure how it happened; one minute we were in the transport, the next we were both waking up in a cell. The investigators said that the five us who were in the middle of the helo were thrown. He and I were the only two taken.

They think it was because we were further from the wreckage. I don't know. We were detained, questioned, and tortured for information."

Zane shook his head. It was worse than he had imagined. He had guessed months ago that something had happened while Ty was in Afghanistan. Little clues had dropped over time, and Zane had collected them: Ty's incessant nightmares and nocturnal muttering. Fear of small, dark, enclosed spaces. Hating being restrained or even forced to sit still for long. Recognition of interrogation tools and techniques. The POW sticker on the Bronco. The words Zane had overheard when Ty had spoken to Nick. And then Nick had confirmed it.

But when Nick laid out the details, it was so much worse than Zane had feared. Almost three weeks in captivity, being drilled for answers and tortured.

Nick gave him a moment to let the reality sink in and possibly to give him a chance to stop the narrative. Then he continued. "Ty kept pissing them off by speaking in different accents every time they questioned him." He laughed. It was a bitter, thin sound. "He spent a whole day pretending he was Russian and telling them they were doing it wrong."

Zane couldn't help but smile. That sounded so much like the man Zane knew. Even in the midst of an ordeal like that, he was still *Ty*.

"They kept us together in a cell that wasn't big enough for either of us to stretch out in. But we had each other, kept each other sane. When they'd come and drag Ty out, leave me there alone, that was the lowest I'd get. They could torture me all they wanted, do whatever they wanted to me. But sitting in that cell alone, wondering if he was coming back... those times are where my nightmares go." Nick swallowed hard and looked away, his green eyes glistening as he tried to force the emotions back so he could continue. It affected Zane as well, and his chest already hurt in sympathy.

"Finally they started getting desperate. They realized that we were drawing strength from each other. Instead of separating us, though, they tried to drive a wedge between us. They'd take us out together, make us do the work. If we didn't hit hard enough, we had to hit again. If we didn't cut deep enough, we had to cut again. I don't know how long it really was, but we estimated it was about a week that we spent torturing each other, beating the shit out of each other at gunpoint."

Zane let his eyes fall closed. He had taken enough of Ty's punches in the past to know how bad that must have gotten. He and Nick both must have been beaten to a pulp.

"But it didn't work," Nick murmured triumphantly. "They wanted us to resent each other, turn on each other. It just made us stronger, more determined to live through it together and escape. I don't think they really knew what to do with us. We wouldn't crack, we wouldn't die, they weren't willing to execute us. Ty wouldn't shut up."

His eyes began to peer off into a distance only he could see. Zane watched him, apprehension and nerves swamping him. He could sense that Nick hadn't reached the worst part yet.

"Then they came up with something that would work." He looked up at Zane, his hard eyes coming back into focus, bright with anger and memory. "One day they strapped Ty down to this table. I could hear the noise from my cell, and I knew from the way he was fighting, he thought he was going to die."

The thought hit Zane hard, and he closed his eyes, wondering if he should ask Nick to stop. But morbid curiosity got the better of him, and he forced himself to open his eyes again.

"When they got him tied down, they brought me in there with him. They had him bent over the table, a rope over his back to hold him down. His hands were handcuffed behind him. They put cuffs on me, and I thought for sure they were going to make me cut him open." Nick shook his head, raising his chin and glancing at the ceiling. "Then they told me I could either tell them what I knew or I could fuck him on that table with a gun to both our heads. And if I didn't do it, they'd do it for me."

Zane stopped breathing as he stared at Nick, suddenly frightened out of his mind. He'd expected to hear about torture, but not that. Was that what had happened to Ty to make him hate being held down?

Nick sat silent, eyes on the window, fingers trembling on his glass as he recounted what had to be one of the most terrifying, difficult experiences in his life. In anyone's life. Zane dimly remembered that

Ty told him once that they shouldn't compare wounds. Now it made terrible, crystal clear sense. He felt sick.

Nick's voice wavered when he continued. "I was ready to tell them everything. I would have. Anything they asked, I would have given it to them. Everything Ty and I had stood for and fought for, I was ready to hand it over just like that." His eyes welled and he closed them, possibly ashamed at the memory, but that just forced the tears out, and a pair tracked down his handsome face without him seeming to notice. "But Ty…."

Zane knew without a doubt what Ty would have said, and he closed his eyes against the pain of it.

"He told me to do it." Nick nodded as he said it, as if affirming what Zane had already guessed. "He ordered me. Fucking pulled rank, like I cared at that point. He was still a *Marine*, and that's all he cared about. I couldn't process what they were going to make me do, what Ty was *ordering* me to do. I was standing next to this table, my best friend strapped down on it, a gun at my head, trying to decide whether I was a Marine with brass balls like Ty or a coward. And Ty told me to kiss him." He laughed suddenly, the sound oddly incongruous with the story he told. "He had to tell me twice. And when I did he slipped a key into my mouth."

Zane's heart seemed to lurch back into beating.

Nick hummed deep in his throat, the sound both content and somehow ominous. "We didn't leave anyone in our path alive."

Zane could barely get in a breath to speak. "So you didn't have to—" His voice broke off, and he didn't try to continue. He didn't want to know, and yet he *had* to.

Nick's green eyes focused in on Zane again, as if he was just remembering that he'd been telling Zane the story instead of reliving it by himself. His eyes flickered away, and he shook his head. "No. I don't think either of us would have come back from that."

The relief almost knocked Zane over. He gripped the edge of the table with one hand to stay balanced. After what seemed like a silent forever, he spoke in a hoarse voice. "That explains a lot about you two."

Nick nodded and swallowed hard. "I was in love with him. I'd already made up my mind to tell him after our tour was over. Consequences be damned, I just needed him to know. But after that…." He shook his head and cleared his throat. "There are some friends you don't risk for your own peace of mind. Some things… at the time it wasn't worth the risk of losing him."

"Last month when you…."

"I knew I'd already lost him."

Zane nodded. "And now?"

"Now what?" Nick asked. He leaned against the counter, body relaxed again as if he'd taken a weight off his shoulders and handed it to Zane to carry. It struck Zane as singularly unfair. "Am I still in love with him?"

"I know you still love him," Zane said. "I know he loves you. Maybe not the kind of love you want, but…. What I want to know is what you plan to do about it."

Nick sighed sharply, as if the question annoyed him. "I've known Ty for twenty years, Garrett. I was enthralled with him after the first week." He shrugged. "But time blunts these things. If you want us to stop caring about each other, you're shit out of luck. We did three tours in Hell, and that kind of thing bonds you to a person for life. But if you're asking if I intend to make another move on him, the answer's no. I've regretted what I did every day since." He was still meeting Zane's eyes, unwavering, and somewhere deep down, Zane could feel the warrior in him, feel the dangerous, capable, upstanding person he could be if he wanted. He was like Ty in so many ways.

He didn't know Nick, but he knew Ty. He trusted Ty, and he knew Ty wouldn't do anything to hurt him. But hearing the words from Nick, receiving the promise that he wouldn't make another advance, that he regretted doing it in the first place, it did ease some of the worry in Zane's mind.

"Garrett. He's never looked at me like he looks at you," Nick said in a soft voice. "He's never looked at *anything* the way he looks at you. Besides. He hates the Sox. We'd never work."

Zane huffed and shook his head. "You're kind of a dick, you know that?"

Nick shrugged.

"Thank you."

"Least I could do," Nick whispered.

Zane stared at him for another minute, trying to wrap his mind around all the things Nick had told him, and telling himself that this man was and would always be a huge part of Ty's life.

"I think I'm going to try to sleep."

"Probably a good idea," Nick said. "I've got your back tonight."

Zane stood and carefully didn't examine the feeling those words gave him as he pushed his glass toward Nick. "Thanks," he murmured as he turned away. He made his way back down the steps to the cabin where Ty lay asleep, but Zane knew he wouldn't be sleeping easily tonight, not after learning what he had.

He crawled into bed, seeing his lover with new eyes as he pulled the covers up around their shoulders.

Ty muttered something in the foreign language Zane was becoming used to, and rolled away from him, pushing back at him so Zane would hold him. Zane scooted up behind him, wrapping him up and pressing against his warm body.

"Are you awake?" Zane asked, barely letting the words come out.

Ty hummed and pushed closer to Zane. "No."

Zane smiled, letting his fingers drag against Ty's skin. As conducive to romance as the setting may have been, all Zane wanted to do was hold Ty close and sleep with him in his arms.

Ty turned his head. "Did you hear what you needed to hear?"

Zane pulled him closer. "I think so. Yeah."

THE next morning, Nick was guiding the yacht toward Washington, DC, and the rest of them were huddled in the booth where Zane had sat last night, trying to come up with a plan.

"Look, I don't care if you're the big bad assassin, and I'm not intimidated when you glower at me. You're not coming with me," Ty was saying to Julian as the two men went in verbal circles.

"I refuse to be dragged along any longer. We will have a say in our next move, or I will leave you bound and gagged during the night for the Coast Guard to find," Julian growled.

Ty slammed his hand against the table and pointed a finger in Julian's face. "Why can't you talk like a normal person?" he shouted in frustration.

Julian snorted in disdain and crossed his arms.

"Fine! When we make port, you come with me to headquarters, Cam stays somewhere safe with Garrett, and you start using contractions when you talk to me or I swear to God—"

"Agreed," Julian said in annoyance.

Ty grumbled as he grabbed up his coat and stalked toward the steps that led to the flybridge, where there were more places to sit in the open air. "I need air," he snarled to the rest of them.

"What exactly is wrong with the way I talk?" Julian asked as he got up and followed him up the steps.

"I hate you and shut up. Why are you following me?"

"Because air is free," Julian shot back before they slammed the hatch door closed and muffled the rest of their argument.

Quiet reigned for a full minute before Zane started to chuckle, a wry smile on his face. He tipped his head sideways to look at Cameron. "I really do think they enjoy it."

Cameron shrugged. "I know Julian does."

"Reminds me of Thanksgiving with my parents," Nick muttered as he sat at the wheel, still examining the nautical chart he'd been reading when Ty and Julian had started in on each other.

"As long as they both come back intact," Cameron said, pushing away his coffee cup and standing. "I'm going to take a shower." He disappeared down the steps

It left Zane acutely aware that he was sitting alone with Nick.

There was silence for a long moment. Even the rustle of the paper had stopped. Finally, Nick turned and looked at Zane over his shoulder. "Ty does love a good nemesis."

"Ty could start an argument with Gandhi if he put his mind to it."

"You should have heard him and Sanchez go at it. Four different languages, neither of them ever understood the other. A Latino guy screaming in German and a mountain hick shooting off French back at him."

Zane snorted.

"Hey, listen…. You said last night that you wanted to understand him better."

Zane looked up at Nick and nodded.

Nick reached into his jacket and pulled out a CD case. "I dug this up. It's uh… it's a bunch of videos we took while we were in service." He handed it to Zane. "Thought maybe you and Ty could watch it together."

Zane blinked at him, momentarily stunned by the simple gesture. He recognized it as the peace offering it was. He reached out to take the CD case and looked from it to Nick. "Thank you."

Nick nodded and then turned his attention back to the charts and navigating the waters toward DC.

"Sidewinder, right? Where'd the name come from?"

"That's just what they called us. I think it was because no matter what they sent us into, we always managed to slither out of it."

Zane laughed. Yeah, that sounded like a team Ty would have led. "Did Ty have a call sign?"

"Nah, that's just pilots," Nick said after a minute or two. "We had nicknames. They changed every couple months depending on who moved in and out. But Ty was team leader, meant we just called him Six."

"He didn't have a nickname?" Zane asked.

"None he'd want me to repeat," Nick muttered, a smile in his voice. "Just Six."

"YOU better damn well call me when you're safe," Nick told Ty as they stood around Julian, shielding him as he jimmied the lock on a car parked in the parking lot of the public marina where Nick had rented a slip.

"Someone will. Check on Deacon for me, okay?"

"Done."

"And go home. Don't stick around and get caught in any blowback."

"Ty."

"Promise me, O. You'll go home."

Nick huffed but he nodded.

Ty met his eyes for a few seconds. He didn't look scared. But he didn't look confident, either, and that made Nick nervous. Ty's biggest asset was his ability to make those around him think he was bulletproof.

"Are you sure you don't need another gun?"

Ty shook his head. "This isn't your fight, O. And if things go bad, we need someone who can tell what went down."

Nick felt a ball of cold steel settle in his chest. He hated being left on the sidelines, but Ty was right. He nodded, and Ty turned away from him to slide into the car Julian had unlocked. He sat in the driver's seat and reached between his legs to mess with the wires underneath the steering column, and in a matter of about thirty seconds, Ty had hotwired the car.

Nick waved as they drove off, the old blue Chevy Suburban lumbering through the parking lot and turning out of sight. Nick took a deep breath and tried to settle the nerves that prickled through his chest. Ty could handle himself, and Nick had seen enough of Zane Garrett to have formed a confident opinion of his skills as well. The man was formidable, a good match for Ty. And Julian Cross was a piece of toast that would always drop butter-side up, but Nick wasn't sure if being lucky would do them much good. Even the luckiest dog in the litter had its bad day.

He was turning to head back to the dock and his boat when he caught sight of a black SUV turning the corner on the other end of the parking lot. The windows were tinted, and there was nothing remarkable about it except for the thick antenna on the roof.

It stopped in the middle of the lane, and Nick stood there and looked at it for a few seconds. The SUV revved its engine, and Nick broke into a sprint for the gate to the dock as the SUV roared down the lane toward him. It hopped the curb and barreled down the sidewalk as Nick reached the gate and shouldered through it. He could hear the doors slamming behind him as he sprinted down the dock, and when he heard the gate give way, he leapt onto his boat and rolled to the deck so he could crawl inside without being open to gunfire.

There was nowhere to run; he would never get the 580 moving in time to escape. All he could do was buy enough time for Ty and the others to make it away cleanly. He scrabbled through storage compartments, tossing life preservers over his shoulder and finally hitting gold. He grabbed it and kissed it, murmuring to it as he scrambled to the galley, where he'd have the most cover.

When two men in dark suits kicked down the heavy oak door in the salon, Nick stood behind the galley partition, aiming a double-barreled shotgun at them.

"Oh, son. You broke down the wrong door today," he said with sadistic glee before he opened fire.

~Chapter 16~

BLAKE NICHOLS walked onto the floor of his four-star restaurant and took a deep breath as he headed for the bar, where two men in expensive suits waited.

"Mr. Nichols?" one of them said as he approached them. He reached into his suit and extracted a badge, flipping it open to show Blake his CIA credentials.

"Can I help you?" Blake asked, not reacting to the badge.

"We know you've been in touch with a Mr. Randall Jonas. We need you to tell us what you know."

"Oh really?" Blake laughed, shaking his head at the audacity of the man. "And why should I do that?"

"Because you're Julian Cross' friend. And we're trying to save his life."

"Excuse me?"

"Mr. Cross is the last man alive who can identify Randall Jonas as the architect of over fifty known murders. We have no other proof. Jonas destroyed it all before he escaped."

"Escaped?"

"If those FBI agents deliver him to Jonas before we can intercede, Mr. Cross will be dead and Jonas will be free to access his account in the Cayman Islands and disappear. We don't want that to happen. And we assume you don't either."

Blake held his breath, his mind racing as he tried to decide how much to give away. "Jonas said he was being set up."

The CIA agent nodded. "We've been tracking his movements for two years, trying to gather enough evidence to bring him down. He caught wind of the investigation, destroyed everything, and ran."

Blake narrowed his eyes, suspicious.

"We know he sent a man named Arlo Lancaster here to Chicago a year and a half ago to kill Cross and you. Ever since he learned Cross was still alive, he's been trying to find him. And with your help, he finally did."

Blake found it hard to breathe as the truth sank in.

"The FBI?"

"Two rogue agents, sent by an old friend of Jonas to bring him in. We assume he's either being duped or he's working with Jonas. Either way, this ends in Julian Cross dying when he's delivered."

"Oh God."

An hour later, after seeing the threadbare evidence the CIA had compiled on Randall Jonas, Blake called Preston as his stomach tumbled. There wasn't enough to convict the man, but it was enough to convince Blake.

"I delivered him right to the bastards," he spat out as soon as Preston answered his call.

"An honest mistake, sir, I'm sure," Preston murmured.

"You make damn sure those FBI agents don't make it to their boss, you understand me?"

"Yes, sir."

"Do whatever you have to. Jonas cannot get his hands on Julian, or Jules is a dead man."

Preston was silent for a moment. When he spoke, his voice was low and dangerous. "Understood, sir."

BURNS stood as soon as he heard the commotion outside. For his assistant to be railing at someone like that, it had to be Ty. Relief flooded him. They hadn't heard from him in days. Burns had begun to face the very real fear that Ty and Zane might be dead. He heard the telltale response to his assistant in a gruff voice, and then the door to his office was shoved open.

"You can't just barge in like this whenever you want. Director Burns has a standing order not to be disturbed!"

"Go eat your granola, Nancy, don't worry about it!" Ty shouted.

"It's okay, Nancy!" Burns said in a stern voice as Ty shoved a man into the office and then slammed the door in her face.

Both men were disheveled and breathing hard, as if they'd just run up the steps of eleven stories and not taken the elevator. At first glance, Burns thought he was looking at Zane, but when he looked at the man directly, he realized his mistake.

"Director," Ty said to him in a sarcastic, hoarse voice. "Door-to-door delivery. Sorry we're late."

"Jesus, Dick, you didn't tell me you sent Earl's boy out there!" Jonas blurted in outrage.

The man Burns now recognized as Julian Cross tensed and took a step back, face grim. His eyes darted to Jonas and back to Burns. "What is this?" he asked. He turned on Ty, grabbing him by his shirt collar and slamming him against the door to Burns' office. "You lied to me!"

Ty seemed shocked, staring at him in confusion. "What are you talking about?"

"Let him go," Jonas said, and Burns saw him draw a gun from the small of his back. It had a silencer on the end of it. Certainly not standard-issue.

Julian eased his grip on Ty's shirt and shoved him one last time against the door before turning to face Jonas.

"What the hell is going on?" Ty asked as he looked at Burns.

Burns met his eyes with a growing sense of apprehension. He wasn't sure he knew what was going on anymore. "Randall. Put the gun away," he said.

Jonas shook his head. "You didn't tell me you sent Earl's boy after him," he said again through gritted teeth.

Burns glanced back at Ty, who was standing with his hands out like he was balancing on a thin piece of rope.

"You want your mastermind?" Julian asked in a disgusted voice. "There he is."

"What?" Burns blurted out as he looked between them.

Jonas glanced at him, his eyes hard. "I'm sorry, Richard. You were my last chance to get to him."

"You used me?" Burns growled, taking one step forward in his anger. Jonas turned the gun on him, then back to Julian and Ty as he stepped further toward the corner of the room.

"Disarm yourself, Richard, or I shoot him right here."

Burns clamped his teeth together and carefully removed his weapon to set it on the floor.

"Now you two," Jonas said to Julian and Ty. "All your weapons."

Ty still looked stunned. He had known Jonas since he was a little boy. He'd spent family vacations with the man.

He took his standard-issue sidearm out of its holster and tossed it to the ground, eyes never leaving Jonas. Julian slid a gun from the belt of his trousers and tossed it away as well.

"No backups?" Jonas asked with narrowed eyes.

Ty shook his head. "No, sir," he said, sounding as if he hated himself for using the same term of respect he probably always had with Randall Jonas. Ty's habits were hard to break, though.

Jonas glanced at Burns again. Burns knew he was trying to decide whether to kill them all or try to convince Ty and Burns to go along with him in his scheming.

Ty took one step forward and slid over, putting himself between Julian and Jonas' gun.

"Stop moving, Tyler," Jonas said as he took a step back to match.

Ty shook his head. "I can't let you shoot him, sir."

"Boy, I told you to move."

"Ty," Burns whispered. He knew now how deep Jonas' betrayal went. He didn't know if Jonas had it in him to shoot the son of one of his oldest friends, a man he'd literally rocked as a baby, but Burns didn't want to find out.

Ty lowered his head like a bull preparing to charge. "I can't let you shoot him."

Julian moved behind Ty, shifting from one foot to another.

"Stop moving!" Jonas shouted.

"You're going to have to go through me," Ty said. His words wavered, like he knew how high the possibility was that Jonas would do just that.

Jonas' eyes narrowed, and the muzzle of his gun trembled. Burns held his breath, afraid to move for fear of setting Jonas off. He could not stand here and watch Ty be shot in front of him. He would not.

"He's the only one who can take me down."

"Not anymore," Burns said. "We all can. Are you going to kill us all, right here in my office?"

"If I have to," Jonas said. His eyes hadn't left Ty and Julian.

"I've known you since we were eighteen!" Burns shouted.

The crack of the bullet hitting the glass window behind them made them all jump. Burns dove to the ground as he tried to decide where the sniper's round had come from. The bulletproof glass had spiderwebbed in concentric patterns around the high-velocity round that was still lodged in it, just feet behind Jonas' head.

Jonas ducked and then brought his gun up to take his shot at Julian. Burns called out. Ty covered his head with both hands and spun out of the way, and Burns realized that Julian had grabbed him and shoved him, drawing a hidden gun from the small of Ty's back. He dove to the side as he fired. The boom of the Glock overpowered the dull thuds of the silencer.

Burns could do nothing but cover his head. Everyone scrambled for cover.

"Jesus fucking Christ!" Ty cried as soon as the shooting hit a lull. "You prick! You shot me!"

"I couldn't possibly have shot you from this angle," Julian murmured from where he hunched behind an arm of the same sofa Jonas was using as cover.

"Ty?" Burns called out.

Another sniper round hit the window, close enough to the first bullet to crack the glass more. Eventually the sniper would get through.

Jonas lunged to his feet and sprayed a volley of bullets at the corner where Julian had taken cover. Burns scrambled for the weapon he had discarded, diving to the floor and rolling as he brought the gun up. Jonas had the gun trained on Julian, who had run out of bullets and was on his knees, hands held high. Burns raised his gun to fire, but his finger had barely brushed the trigger when Ty rammed Jonas from behind.

Jonas' gun went off, spraying ceiling plaster everywhere. They landed hard, Ty's bulk knocking the air from Jonas as he skidded face-first across the plush carpeting. Ty rammed an elbow into Jonas' back to keep him down.

Burns pushed to his feet and aimed his gun at Jonas. "Ty! Get him out of here!"

Ty hesitated, looking from Burns to Jonas.

"He's not safe until he's at Langley!" Burns growled, jerking his head toward Cross. "Go!"

Ty rolled and struggled to his feet, holding a bloody hand to his side. Julian took his elbow, both of them staggering toward the door.

"Richard," Jonas groaned as he pushed off the floor. "You don't know what you're doing, Richard. Don't let them get away!"

"Shut up," Burns gritted out as Ty and Julian fled from the office.

Jonas met his eyes, his body tensing. Burns looked into the depths, reliving every moment he'd known Randall Jonas, from boot camp to the morning he'd pulled Burns out of a fire in the jungle to the day he'd been a groomsman at his wedding.

"I trusted you."

Jonas twisted to look up at him. Burns tightened his hold on his gun, hand trembling as the betrayal sank in.

Jonas gave a derogatory snort and met Burns' eyes. "That just made you easy to use."

JULIAN heard the last gunshot, the sound deafening as they ran for the stairwell. Ty skidded to a halt, turning back. "Dick!"

"He had the upper hand," Julian said, grabbing Ty's elbow to pull him along. Ty hesitated, but when they saw agents flooding the hallways, he turned and ran with Julian to the emergency stairwell.

They stormed down the steps, every bang and clang of the stairwell putting Julian's teeth on edge.

"It's brilliant, really," he gasped out. "Send unsuspecting errand boys to do the dirty work. It's his signature."

"I don't fucking believe this," Ty muttered. "Does this mean me and Zane were the bad guys?"

"I believe so, yes."

"Son of a bitch!"

They hit the ground floor level, and Ty pushed through the door into the lobby. Sirens were going off; the entire federal building was mobilizing. Ty flashed his badge at a security guard who tried to stop them. When the guard stepped in front of them, unwilling to let them leave, Ty grabbed him by the hand, twisted it, and turned into his body, dropping the beefy guard with a move as graceful as a ballerina.

They darted past as other guards came after them.

"Zane is gonna kill me," Ty said as they burst through the doors and sprinted down the street into the sparse crowds of tourists.

"He's not the only one!" Julian shouted as they darted between people and across the street. "We have a sniper to worry about now as well."

ZANE sat with Cameron at the café they'd designated as the rendezvous. He despised being left behind, but Ty had given a convincing argument that he and Julian would be able to slip through better just the two of them. They were also hoping, on some level, that Zane would serve as a decoy for anyone watching the building waiting for Cross to show up. He had walked up and down the sidewalk several times, hoping to draw attention, as Ty and Julian had slipped inside in a flower delivery van.

It was a lot easier to sneak into FBI headquarters if you were an actual FBI agent.

When he caught sight of two men running down the street, Zane sat forward and tensed, barely keeping himself from reaching for his gun.

When they got closer, he saw that it was Ty and Julian. "Uh-oh."

"What?" Cameron asked as he peered into the crowd.

"Looks like something went wrong."

"We have to move," Ty gasped as soon as they reached Zane and Cameron. From the looks of them, they had both sprinted there.

"What happened?"

"It was Jonas."

"Who?"

"Jonas, he was the guy."

"I don't know who that is."

"He's CIA, he had Burns pull us in, but he only wanted Cross to kill him," Ty stuttered.

"Ty, breathe."

Ty shook his head, gulping air and holding to his side. Blood seeped through the material of his T-shirt.

"There's a sniper on a roof somewhere. We don't know whose side he's on, and we need to get out of sight," Julian said, rapid-fire and barely discernible with his thick accent.

Zane and Cameron moved, grabbing their last remaining bag of gear, Zane leading the way. There was nowhere to go that they would be able to hide. But they could duck into a restaurant or museum and be out of the sniper's sights. They headed for the massive complex of the Verizon Center, and Zane darted into The Greene Turtle as the others followed. Cameron was gasping for breath after the sprint, and Ty was leaning against the railing of the curving staircase that led down to the restaurant's basement, panting and holding his side.

"Can I… help you?" the hostess asked them.

"Table for four, please," Cameron said, breathless, holding up four fingers. "Away from the windows, if that's possible."

"Of course," she said, looking at them askance as she grabbed menus.

Zane took Ty's arm and began to lead him down the stairs. Julian followed, dragging Cameron with him as he explained to the waitress that they'd be right back. They didn't want her growing suspicious enough to call the police on them, but Zane doubted Cameron's attempts had helped their cause.

The basement of the restaurant had two oddly situated bathrooms and a wide open space used for parties and probably hiding Jimmy Hoffa. They tumbled into that dark, cavernous space and collapsed against whatever was nearest them.

"You've been hit," Zane said to Ty as he knelt next to where Ty had sunk against a wall.

"It grazed me. It's not bad." He met Zane's eyes. "It's not bad."

Zane looked at him worriedly, then glanced at Julian.

"It wasn't me," Julian snapped, the heat in his voice aimed at Ty.

"You shot from under my arm!"

"There is no possible way I hit you from that angle! It was a ricochet!"

"You want to go over the laws of physics?"

"If I was going to shoot you, I would have shot you somewhere more memorable!"

"Okay!" Zane shouted, putting both hands out to calm them.

Ty grunted at him and pressed his hand to his side, glaring at Julian.

Cameron hugged close to him, and Julian pulled him in and rested his chin on Cameron's head, closing his eyes as they embraced.

"I'm afraid I'm out of ideas," Julian whispered.

Zane looked back at Ty. He shook his head, unable to meet Zane's eyes. "Burns said to get him to Langley."

"That won't be happening," a new voice said from the doorway.

All Zane could see was the outline of a man, a long-barreled rifle slung over his shoulder. As he watched, the man pulled the rifle down and aimed it at him and Ty.

"PRESTON!" Cameron called out in obvious relief.

When Ty scrambled to his feet, he found himself facing the matte black muzzle of a sniper's rifle. His heart stuttered and his body flooded with ice.

The muzzle lowered to reveal its owner as the man stepped into the pool of an emergency light, and Ty stared at the blond man in shock.

"Thank Christ. Preston, what took you so long?" Julian grumbled as he rushed forward.

"Terribly sorry, sir," Preston drawled, smirking as he glanced around and met Ty's eyes. "Hello, Tyler."

Ty couldn't find his voice through the surprise.

Cameron glanced between them. "You two know each other?"

"We're acquainted," Preston answered as he hiked the rifle onto his shoulder.

"Do tell," Zane said as he stood next to Ty. "Who the hell are you?"

Preston raised one eyebrow at Zane but didn't answer him, instead meeting Ty's eyes and giving him an enigmatic smile.

"He's Preston, Julian's driver," Cameron said.

"Driver," Zane said, voice wry. "Do you sell antiques too?"

"No, I kill people."

"Preston!" Cameron said, appalled. "I thought you were staying in Chicago."

"I had other business to attend to."

Ty finally found his voice, though he was still staring back at the man as if he'd risen from the dead. "He was… French. You were French," he said accusingly.

Preston shrugged. "So were you. We both got what we were after."

"This is the guy from Paris that Burns thinks is Cross?" Zane said, pointing at Preston. "So this is the guy all this has been about?"

"No, dear, please keep up," Preston said with a curl of his lip.

Ty stood there, shaking his head, mind churning to connect the pieces.

Preston turned to Julian. "Smith and Wesson are in your car, sir. Ready when you are."

"What about my dogs?"

"With your lady friend from the restaurant."

Cameron looked crestfallen, but Ty was too distracted by Preston's sudden appearance to feel sorry for him.

"Grady and Preston were both after the same mark in Paris a few years ago," Julian said to Zane. "They met during what I hear was a drunken, debauched night of… selling antiques. That's how I knew Ty had been there. I never saw him."

"Such unnecessary details," Preston murmured.

"Ty, seriously," Zane grunted.

"How is this my fault?" Ty asked in exasperation.

"Do you have a history with every guy with a gun in the Northern hemisphere?"

"Oh, like you don't have some winners back there you hope we never run into. Let's head to Miami and see what comes out of the woodwork."

"Ty."

"I like guys with guns!"

"Oh my God," Julian muttered as he rubbed at his eyes.

Zane crossed his arms over his chest and gave Ty a look that said they'd be discussing this later. Ty rolled his eyes and pointed at Preston. "Why are you here?"

"We learned that you were delivering Mr. Cross to the very man who wants him dead. I'm here to kill you and rescue him."

"You're a bit late for that," Julian muttered.

"Bulletproof glass, or I would have been right on time."

"Fair enough."

Zane put a hand out and looked from Julian to Ty. "So wait a minute… we're the bad guys?"

"Sucks, right?" Ty muttered.

Zane huffed. "If we're the bad guys, that means the CIA isn't trying to kill Cross. They've been trying to save him from us!"

Julian and Ty stared at him, then glanced at each other uncomfortably.

"This is stupid," Cameron muttered as he rubbed his hands over his face. "I can't believe this is real life."

Ty shook his head.

"If the CIA and Preston and whoever else are trying to save him and not kill him, why don't we just drive him up to Langley and this is all over?" Zane said, sounding almost excited.

Julian shook his head. "Please. If you deliver me to them, my life is over. Whether I'm alive or dead, they will own me again."

Ty met the Irishman's eyes, a pang of familiarity running through him. He knew what that claustrophobic fear felt like. No one deserved to be pressed into service.

"Can't we just… disappear?" Cameron asked.

They all looked at him with the same mixture of sadness and contempt. There was no disappearing if you had something the CIA wanted.

"If someone doesn't go in to clear all this up, they will never stop following you, Cam," Zane said. He looked at Julian. "You know that."

"That's why I'm here," Preston said, stoic as ever.

"No," Julian said immediately.

"There's really nothing to argue over, sir."

"What?" Cameron asked.

"Preston intends to turn himself into the CIA in my stead."

"What? Why does it have to be one of us?" Cameron asked, a little plaintive.

"The only solution is to give them Julian Cross," Ty murmured. "Or run for the rest of your lives. And Preston is in their books as Julian Cross. Am I right? The two of you shared duties under one codename?"

Preston nodded.

"No wonder they thought you were Batman. You were two people."

"Antiques dealers don't play fair," Julian muttered, voice low and wry.

"This is not a difficult decision, gentlemen," Preston told them, voice devoid of emotion. He handed his rifle to Julian, who took it without question. Then he turned to Ty.

"Wait," Julian pleaded, a rare show of emotion playing across his face as he stepped between them. "Preston, please."

"Sir, I really must insist that you not make this difficult," Preston whispered.

"Oh, Preston," Cameron murmured, pain in his voice.

Julian was silent, the two old companions sharing a moment of understanding before Julian wrapped the blond man in a tight hug. Then he hung his head and stalked away like a wounded lion pacing in a cage, unable to meet Preston's eyes. Preston held his hands up to Ty to be handcuffed.

"Put your hands down," Ty said in a hoarse voice, inexplicably touched by the show of loyalty between the two. They had obviously been partners for many years, and Preston was essentially giving up his freedom for Julian. Sure, he wasn't going to be imprisoned, but he would be under the thumb of his former employer all the same, unable to live the life he could otherwise. Most importantly, he was giving up ever seeing Julian again, because as soon as they did this, Cameron Jacobs and the man known as Julian Cross would disappear.

It was enough to earn Ty's respect.

Ty glanced at Zane. "The CIA knows what Cross looks like," he said in a measured voice as his eyes traveled down Zane's body. "Walking Preston in there won't work. We need to give them what they're looking for or we won't even make it through the door."

Zane tipped his head to one side, met Ty's gaze when it returned to his face, and then, with a twitch of his lips, nodded. "Yeah. Sure, that'll be fun, actually."

"What? What will be fun?" Cameron asked.

"Special Agent Preston and I are going to turn 'Cross' in to the CIA," Ty drawled with a growing smirk as he nodded to Zane.

Cameron's jaw dropped as he looked between Julian and Zane, obviously remembering that he was the one who originally said they looked so much alike. "Isn't that going to be dangerous?"

Julian nodded grimly. "That's why they're all grinning like idiots. Lucky bastards."

Zane smiled and flipped the gun around in his hand to hold the barrel and offer it to Preston. "Special Agent Preston, your company-issue firearm."

"It does have a certain ring to it," Preston murmured as he took the weapon. "All right, lads, say your good-byes," he urged as he headed for the door, obviously not intending to say his own.

"Zane," Cameron said, stepping over to touch his elbow. "Thank you."

Zane patted his hand and glanced at Julian. "Keep him on a leash, would you?"

"Yeah," Cameron whispered.

Julian looked between them and nodded, his jaw tightening. He stepped forward and held out his hand to Zane. "Agent Garrett. It's not easy to earn my respect. Well done."

With a nod, Zane shook his hand. "It's not often people like us get a second chance. Enjoy it."

Julian nodded tightly, and his eyes shifted to Ty. He held out his hand, and Ty didn't hesitate to reach out and take it. "Take it easy, Killer."

"Agent Grady," Julian said solemnly. "If the world didn't have sharks, we couldn't have kittens either."

"What?" Cameron asked.

"That doesn't even make any sense," Zane muttered.

"Yeah, it does," Ty said, meeting Julian's eyes and nodding.

"They don't even exist in remotely similar ecosystems," Cameron said.

Julian smirked and let go of Ty's hand. "You are far too literal," he told Cameron as he wrapped an arm around his shoulders.

"Take care of yourself, Ty," Cameron said, voice wavering as Julian led him further into the darkness of the large basement room.

Zane turned back to Ty, then stepped close enough to cup his cheek and kiss him thoroughly. Ty closed his eyes as Zane curled his other arm around him and pulled him close, and let himself get lost in it. He didn't care if Zane was staking out his territory like a stray dog. After today they might be spending quite a lot of time in jail; it might be his last chance to be staked out.

When Zane finally pulled away, leaving Ty wavering, Preston offered a low whistle.

Zane ignored him as he reached up to touch the compass rose, his fingertips lightly brushing Ty's skin as well. "In case we're wrong and I get shot on sight."

Ty shook his head. "Won't happen."

They looked to where Julian and Cameron had been, only to find them both gone.

Ty and Zane shared a glance and shrugged. Their prisoners had finally escaped. Zane held the cuffs out to Ty with a smile. "Ready to go fuck with the Agency?"

A cold ball of determination settled in the pit of Ty's stomach. He took the handcuffs and grinned wolfishly. "They messed with the wrong Feebs this time."

~Chapter 17~

THEY didn't even make it past the gate guard at Langley.

"You're not expected," the man said as he examined Ty's FBI credentials.

Ty pointed to the camera over the man's shoulder. "Give the face recognition software some time. We'll wait." He pointed at his face and smiled as he looked into the camera; then he reached over and took Zane's head, yanking him sideways so the camera could see him as well.

Two minutes later, the guardhouse was surrounded.

They were escorted through the lobby, past the wall with no names, to an innocuous conference room where three men sat waiting for them.

They stood when Ty, Zane, and Preston were shoved into the room.

"Gentlemen."

"You're the big kahuna?" Ty asked as he kept a tight grip on Zane's elbow. They had handcuffed Zane behind his back and frogmarched him into Langley like a criminal. Ty had enjoyed it a little too much.

"What is the purpose of this?" the man asked. His face was thin and sallow, and he had snow-white hair that seemed to stand on end. His suit probably cost more than Ty's whole wardrobe, and Ty didn't buy cheap. He was flanked by two younger men, Agent X and Agent Y, the former looking tired and amused, wearing a canvas jacket and jeans, the latter wearing thick-rimmed hipster glasses and a tie that was way too thin to be company issue.

"We heard you were looking for Julian Cross," Preston said, voice devoid of an accent.

"This is not Julian Cross," Agent X said in a low voice.

"We figured the beard was enough of a threat to national security to bring him in," Ty said as he waved a hand at Zane's face.

Zane turned his head and glared at him.

"Release this man, please," the Big Kahuna said, and Agent Y stood to walk over to them. He unlocked Zane's hands and stepped back, looking at all three of them with narrowed eyes.

"This is Zane Garrett," the agent said as he turned to look at his superior.

"What?" Ty said as he turned to look at Zane. Zane was trying not to grin as Ty dragged his gaze up and down him. "Wow, he does kind of look like him." He poked Zane's stomach. "Say something Irish."

"Irish I was at home," Zane said, managing not to smile.

The Big Kahuna stood and smoothed his hand down his tie. "Mr. Cross, we're pleased you came in. Randall Jonas has been a thorn in our side for a long while." He was looking at Preston.

"I can't say I'm pleased to be here," Preston murmured.

Agent Y looked from Ty to Zane to Preston. "Sir, this is not Julian Cross."

"Yes, he is," Agent X said with a smile.

"What of Randall Jonas?" Preston asked.

"He was shot while trying to escape."

"Shot?" Ty said in surprise.

"The investigation has already concluded."

Ty blinked at him, not able to really process that information.

The Big Kahuna smiled and waved a hand at Agent X. "Take these men into custody. Let them see what it is to be on the wrong side of the Company."

TY SAT in a white-and-chrome padded room, his legs shackled to a table, his hands chained together to a ring on the tabletop. The jumpsuit he wore had no markings, buttons, or zippers. Not even a tag. He was wearing shoes with no socks, and nothing under the jumpsuit. They'd taken everything from him, even the compass rose pendant Zane had given him.

He stared at his reflection in the mirror, knowing there was someone on the other side. He drummed his fingers on the table, trying to make the rhythm slow and measured to dispel the nerves that zinged through him. He'd been held all night in this observation room, given only water in a Styrofoam cup. When he'd told his guard that the CIA was killing the planet with Styrofoam, the man had left with his cup and never come back.

The door to his room opened with the loud clank of heavy metal, and Ty watched as two men in suits sauntered in and sat opposite him at the table.

"Special Agent Beaumont Tyler Grady, correct? Also known as Tyler Beaumont and… Sam Hill?"

Ty stared at the man, raising one eyebrow. "We meet again," he said, allowing himself a small smirk.

The agent looked up at him, and his partner glanced at him before looking back at Ty.

"We apologize for the necessity of the strip search. But it seems you have a reputation for… producing keys."

Ty shrugged. "Don't worry about it, that's not even the first one I've had this week," he said, voice wry. He looked at Agent X and grinned widely. "It was the most fun, though, huh?"

Agent Y blinked rapidly, as if trying to hide his reaction.

Ty grinned and pointed two fingers at Agent X. "This guy, man. He likes it rough," he said with a chuckle. He topped it with a suggestive wink at Agent X, pointing his thumb and pinky at himself and mouthing "call me."

"That's enough," Agent Y murmured. Ty enjoyed that the man was uncomfortable, probably more than he should have. "Your task was to retrieve and deliver a CIA asset by the name of Julian Cross, correct?"

"No, no, you've got this all wrong. I was sent to get milk. I got 2 percent instead of skim and everything went ballistic. I mean you'd think I brought home soy milk or something!"

"Special Agent Grady, you can drop the act now or you can do it next week."

"Next week's no good for me. Do you have a calendar?"

The two CIA agents sat stolid, staring at him.

"Wow. Tough crowd." Ty hummed and looked down at his hands, beginning the tune to the "Battle Hymn of the Republic."

"Special Agent Grady, the sooner you answer our questions, the sooner you go home."

Ty stopped humming only to let it turn into a whistle.

The two agents waited for a few more moments, then stood and exited, closing the door behind them with an echo of finality.

Ty couldn't help the shiver that ran up his spine, but he looked up at the mirror with a grin, the hum turned into muttered words, and soon he was singing. He mangled the lyrics to the chorus, though, replacing the word "hallelujah" with "paranoia" and making up his own words to the rest of the song.

He hadn't finished the song before the door opened again. He glanced at the newcomer, relief washing over him. "Am I glad to see you," he told Richard Burns.

"Yes, well, I wish I could say the same," Burns growled as he tossed a pair of handcuff keys on the table. They slid past Ty's fingers, just out of reach. Ty tried to reach them with the tip of one finger as Burns sat opposite him.

"That's so unnecessary," Ty mumbled as he continued to try and reach the keys.

Burns sat snickering at him for a few moments before he finally took pity on him and reached out to cut through the zip tie and unlock the handcuffs. He handed Ty the keys so he could release his feet.

"Everything's settled down?" Ty asked as he ducked under the table.

"That depends. The CIA currently has in its custody two FBI agents and one Boston police detective who is demanding they pay for the damage to his boat."

"He's okay?"

Burns nodded. "Emptied a double-barreled shotgun at a couple of Company lackeys, and then they arrested him. He spent all night claiming he thought they were the Men in Black coming to scan his brain."

Ty bit his lip so he wouldn't laugh.

"They returned him to his boat this morning, and he's on his way home. Safe."

Ty breathed a sigh of relief at that.

"Julian Cross is responsible for the deaths of half a dozen CIA agents."

Ty nodded, pressing his lips tightly together. It was true that every man who'd lost his life had fallen to the hands of Julian Cross. "That's unfortunate. It was self-defense, though, he thought they were trying to kill us."

"We're aware of that, Ty, but here's the problem the Company has right now. It seems the man you brought in was not, in fact, Julian Cross."

"No?" Ty asked, feigning surprise as he sat back up and doing it badly just to annoy his superior. "Huh. That's weird."

Burns hummed, meeting Ty's eyes and trying not to smile. "You want the CIA to believe that you mistook your *partner* for your prisoner, handcuffed him, and delivered him to Langley?"

Ty shrugged. "I mean... he grew a beard. It was an honest mistake."

Burns nodded. "Fair enough."

Ty stared at him, waiting for the other shoe to drop. A man appeared at the doorway, all clean-cut and dashing and looking official with his badge and gun. Ty looked Preston up and down in surprise.

"They've changed my code name to avoid further confusion," Preston said with a smile. "Thank you for escorting me safely from Chicago, Special Agent Grady."

Ty blinked at him, not sure what to say to that. So he just kept his mouth shut. Preston nodded and turned to go. Ty looked back at Burns.

"I'm filing this under my Rubik's Cube," Burns murmured. "Come on, let's get out of here."

Ty hopped up to follow. "Can I get my things back?"

"Working on it."

Ty grumbled but didn't ask again. The first person he saw when he exited the room was Zane, already dressed, freshly shaven, and ready to go. Ty pointed at him as he glared at Burns.

"You rescued him first?"

"We've been watching you through the mirror for ten minutes," Zane told him, trying not to smile.

"They've been training rookies off you, Ty," Burns said as he walked away.

Ty glared after him, then glanced at Zane with a grin and threw himself at his partner to hug him before Zane could dodge him. Zane laughed and closed his arms around Ty, returning the enthusiastic embrace.

"Gentlemen," Agent X said as he approached them. Ty let go of Zane's neck and turned to look at the man. He held a bundle of Ty's clothing and possessions. "You did an impressive job this week."

Ty and Zane shared a glance. "Thank you, I guess," Zane said warily.

"The Agency would like to extend an invitation to both of you."

Ty leaned his head forward as if he'd heard wrong.

"An invitation?" Zane repeated.

"You're offering us a job?" Ty asked, incredulous.

Agent X nodded. "We here at the Agency believe that if you can't kill it, you hire it."

Ty barked a laugh. Zane just shook his head and turned away, trailing after Burns.

Ty wagged a finger at Agent X, who was smiling ever so faintly. He took his things from the man. "You're kind of all right, man," Ty told him, still laughing. "Later, gator."

He turned to amble off after the other two, content that the ordeal was over and he could finally go home. With Zane.

ZANE was already wrapped around Ty, kissing him senseless as he pressed him against the front door of his row house. Ty fumbled behind him for the doorknob, turning the lock and causing the door to open, tumbling both of them into the house.

Zane kicked the door closed and grabbed at Ty again, but Ty pushed at his hands and tensed, looking around the living room of his home.

"Wait, wait," he whispered urgently, eyes scanning the darkness behind Zane. "Someone's been here."

"What?" Zane asked as he turned and reached for his gun. "How do you know?"

Ty drew his weapon and edged into the narrow room. "Couple years ago a suspect broke in during a case. I set up backup systems."

"Seriously? Like what?"

"Zane!" Ty hissed, waving at Zane to be quiet as he edged further into the room, heading for the kitchen. Zane followed, backing him up as he felt the tension of the last few weeks begin to invest itself in his shoulders once more. What else could they possibly run into before this month was over? Was it possible that he had set Ty's alarms off when he'd come here at night? He prayed for a simple answer.

Ty moved past the bar, turning and pointing his weapon at the kitchen. He stopped short and straightened, lowering his gun as he stared at the kitchen floor.

"What?" Zane asked, breathless.

Ty shook his head.

"What is it?"

"It's... alive," Ty mumbled as he stuck his gun in its holster. "It's Smith and Wesson."

"Cross' cats?" Zane moved into the kitchen and flipped the overhead light on.

The two large long-haired orange cats sat in the middle of the kitchen, eating cat food out of a bowl. They glanced over at Ty and Zane. One of them growled deep in its chest and then went back to eating. As it ate, it continued growling.

"Oh my God," Zane whispered.

Ty was reading a note left on the counter, paying the two monsters no mind. "He says he'll retrieve them after he and Cam have settled somewhere. 'Don't get too attached,' he says."

Ty put the note down and looked at the two cats. One of them was still growling as it ate, making obscene smacking and hissing sounds.

"I knew that bastard hated me," Ty grumbled as he turned to head up the steps.

"But... Ty," Zane said as he looked at the cats. They had left the food bowl behind and were stalking toward him, looking at him with luminous green eyes. "Uh."

One of the massive orange cats hissed at him. Zane stepped back, out of their way, as they sauntered past him toward the stairs, their tails swishing like the two evil Siamese cats in that Disney movie. Zane gaped at them as they trailed after Ty up the stairs.

THE day after returning to Baltimore, Ty and Zane finally found themselves back at their desks and back to work, with absolutely no downtime as a reward for what they'd been through. The rest of the work group greeted them enthusiastically, Scott Alston even giving Ty a hug in greeting before he handed him a stack of paperwork.

"Welcome back," Michelle Clancy said as she came up and put her arm around Ty's waist as he sat on the edge of Zane's desk.

He laid his arm over her shoulders, then glanced over her and frowned. "What's wrong, Red? You look like someone kicked your puppy."

Clancy shrugged and gave him a weak smile. "They transferred Tim yesterday."

Ty raised an eyebrow and glanced at Zane. "Who's Tim?"

"Financial Crimes guy," Zane murmured from his seat. He looked at Clancy. "Why'd he transfer?"

Clancy shrugged one shoulder and laid her head against Ty. She looked like she was holding back tears. "I think they found out we were dating. Sent him to North Carolina."

"Jesus," Zane whispered.

Ty stared at the top of her head, feeling as if his heart had dropped into his stomach. "Why didn't they just reassign him?" he asked, surprised when he found his voice hoarse.

Clancy shrugged. "They wanted to make an example of it, I guess." A tear slid down her cheek, and Ty pushed away from the desk to offer her a hug. She accepted it gratefully, something the hard-as-nails little redhead rarely did. He looked over her head to meet Zane's eyes, seeing the same fear in them as he was suddenly feeling.

They had planned to be open and out when they got home, planned to move in together and stop feeling like they needed to hide.

Now, though….

"Grady, Garrett!" Dan McCoy called from his office.

Clancy thanked Ty as she wiped her eyes and hurried away, leaving Ty and Zane staring at each other. Ty could feel the fear growing in both of them.

"Hey, fruitcakes! Now!"

Zane stood, and Ty followed him to McCoy's office, feeling like he was moving through water. Of all the things that had happened in the last month, he thought maybe Michelle Clancy's news was the hardest for him to take.

Ty AND Zane filed into McCoy's office to find Richard Burns sitting there waiting for them. McCoy closed the door for them, and Ty thumped down into one of the chairs. Zane followed a little more gracefully.

"We've still got all kinds of paperwork pending, but now that the CIA is deigning to tell us what the hell was going on over there, I expect this all to clear out pretty quickly," Burns said from his seat behind Dan McCoy's desk as he shuffled papers. He'd come all the way from DC to speak to them, rather than make them drive any more than they had to at that point.

Zane nodded absently, listening with half an ear, tapping his pen idly on the pad of paper in front of him. Another crisis past, another case closed, but so much had changed in the handful of weeks they'd been away. He felt off-balance being back at home in Baltimore. He felt like the world had changed, with all the revelations between him and Ty. Zane felt like he'd changed. The nervous swirling inside him was gone, replaced by an almost eerie calm. The uncertainty he always fought was taking a backseat to confidence he'd forgotten he possessed. And the most glaring change of all, he knew beyond a shadow of a doubt that the love he was feeling for Ty was the real thing and that Ty reciprocated that conviction.

As Burns kept talking, moving on to a précis of what they'd missed, Zane glanced to his side. Ty was slouched, palm pressed to his cheek as he leaned his head on his hand. One foot rested on a knee, bouncing to a rhythm only he could hear. He was watching Burns attentively, but whether he was listening attentively was anyone's guess. Zane gave him a fond smile and tuned back into what Burns was saying.

"... if anyone from over there contacts you directly again, you tell them to talk to me, got it?" Burns asked, thumping his fist on the desk.

"Yes, sir," Ty murmured. He shifted in his seat, putting his foot on the floor and leaning forward expectantly. "If contact is made in person, are we allowed to hit or throw anything at them?" he asked, deadpan.

Zane chuckled and leaned back as he watched Burns roll his eyes.

"As entertaining as it might be to watch, I doubt that will happen," Burns said.

"Yeah, we also sort of doubted that agents of another federal organization would try to hunt us down and kill us," Zane muttered.

Ty glanced at him dubiously as if he disagreed, but he was smirking as he looked back at Burns.

"Is there anything else?" Ty asked almost cheerfully.

"No." Burns waved a hand at them. "Go home. Relax. Come back to work Monday."

Zane blinked. "But it's Wednesday."

"Shut up, Garrett," Ty muttered as he stood and patted Zane on the shoulder. "Let's go before he changes his mind."

Zane immediately got to his feet. "Thank you, Director."

"Get out of here," Burns said with a melancholy smile.

Ty hesitated as he looked down at Burns. "Dick. I… I'm sorry about Jonas. I know how close you were."

Burns nodded, pursing his lips. "He was a spook. And no matter how good your intentions, spooks always end up transparent in the end." Zane glanced at Ty, uneasy. "When you get home, dump your second phone."

"Sir?" Ty said, obviously too surprised to voice anything else.

"Get rid of it, Ty. I won't be calling it again."

Ty nodded, still looking shocked and just a little hurt by the words. Zane almost reached out to put a hand on his shoulder but stopped himself.

"You've given enough. There's nothing more precious than trust, boys," Burns said, voice somber. "You've got it. Don't do something stupid and lose it, huh?"

"Yes, sir," they both murmured before heading for the door.

They were almost to the elevator before Ty turned to look at Zane appraisingly. "Trust."

Zane cut his eyes to look at him. "I don't think that's going to be a problem."

Ty hummed, a sound similar to the one he made in bed. Zane's body noticed. "Long weekend," he said instead of commenting on trust again. "It's dangerously close to the 'vacation' word."

"And yet, you still said it." Zane slid his hands into his pockets as they walked.

"I like to live on the edge." Ty reached out and punched the button, then turned to lean his shoulder against the wall next to the elevator doors. He watched Zane.

Zane stifled the urge to shuffle his feet and simply returned Ty's look with a raised eyebrow. Ty didn't speak as he met Zane's eyes. The elevator doors opened up, and he nodded for Zane to step in. Zane let out a slow breath as he did, turning to lean back against the side wall as Ty joined him.

As the elevator doors slid shut, Ty leaned against the mirrored back wall and sighed. "I've interrogated people who looked more relaxed than you."

Zane offered Ty a wry smile. "I don't want to have to hide. But… I don't want to be sent to North Carolina either." He felt a little more comfortable when he could look at Ty openly rather than constantly reminding himself not to watch his lover's every move. That was tiring. Zane didn't remember doing that to himself before.

Ty nodded, swallowing hard. "We can still be together." His manner was calm and soothing, but beneath the surface Zane could hear a hint of nervousness, so rare in his partner that he wasn't sure he hadn't imagined it.

Now that Zane had the opportunity to say something, everything in his head sounded so… silly. He gave in to the nerves and rubbed the back of his neck. "You still want me to move in?" he asked, chancing a look at Ty.

Ty pressed his lips together and nodded, glancing down at his feet. "We could have all your things moved by the weekend. We can pull it off. Don't you think?" he asked as he looked back at Zane. "Say you're renting a room from me or something."

Zane tilted his head to one side as their eyes met again. "I think I could pull anything off if it meant waking up with you every morning," he said, his voice barely audible.

Ty nodded, not looking away from Zane. "Well," he started, a smile forming as his hazel eyes warmed. "Why don't we start with tonight, and we'll go from there."

The relief made Zane laugh, and he nodded. How the hell did Ty make everything seem so simple? "I'd like that."

Ty chuckled, the sound low and warm and familiar. "Life is hard and confusing, Zane. Love doesn't have to be."

Zane raised both brows in mild surprise as the elevator dinged and the doors slid open. His instinctive response would have to wait until they were out of the building. He walked alongside Ty down the hall as they headed into the parking deck. "No more fortune cookies for you," he said as he caught Ty's eye. "You're way too Zen."

"I'll quit my fortune cookie moments of Zen when you stop making awful puns."

"But I'm such a punny guy," Zane mock complained, one hand over his heart.

"Quit it, Cheeseball." Ty swatted at Zane's head for emphasis.

Zane grinned and ducked, turning to walk backward in front of Ty. Ty looked him up and down with a rakish smile. It warmed Zane almost to the point of distraction. "So Chinese is out for dinner. Anything else sound good?"

"Let's go out."

"You just don't want to be left alone in the house with those cats."

"They're not so bad. Once you get used to their heads spinning. But seriously, let's go sit down somewhere where you get real silverware and I can grope you under a classy tablecloth."

Zane laughed. He didn't care where they went, as long as they were together. "It's a little early yet, just now four."

Ty sneered and looked across the parking deck in the direction of his rental. "Let's go drive that thing into the harbor and see how long it takes the insurance adjustor to get there," he said, his eyes shining just enough to make Zane fear he might actually do it.

"Let's not and just fantasize about it at an early dinner." Zane would rather Ty not go postal over another vehicle just yet. He reached out and snagged Ty's arm as he turned to walk beside him. "How about a trip to the batting cages, then we can clean up and get a decent dinner?"

Ty looked sideways at him, grinning widely. He nudged him with his shoulder as they walked, the smile turning warmer and somehow more intimate without really changing. "Are you asking me out on a date?"

Zane smirked. "I guess I am. If by 'date' you mean we end up naked and sweating."

Ty laughed. "You do know how to charm me," he said, looking away and shaking his head.

"Hey, I can be charming," Zane said, bumping Ty's shoulder as they came to a stop at Ty's rental.

Ty turned to him, leaning against the sedan and crossing his arms loosely against his chest. He was still smiling. Not his usual smirk or crooked grin that always warned Zane when he was up to something, but an honest, serene smile. "Yes, you can be," he said after a few moments of comfortable silence.

The concession made Zane's pulse speed, and he knew he was smiling like a fool. He inhaled deeply and willed away an impulse that could only bring trouble. They had to be more careful than they had been. They could do it.

"Pick you up in an hour?"

"I'll be waiting," Ty promised in a low voice that was smooth as honey. Somehow he seemed to know the effect his words had on Zane, and he was antagonizing him with the gentle flirtation.

Zane narrowed his eyes and glared at Ty for a moment before turning toward his own truck, trying to ignore how flushed he was. He'd get back at Ty tonight, in the privacy of their home. The home they would be sharing from now on.

Ty would be there; that was all that mattered.

The Cut & Run series

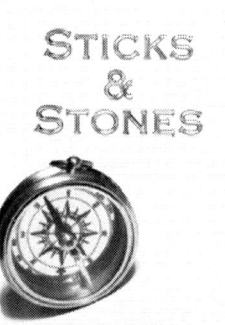

Cut & Run
Madeleine Urban
Abigail Roux

Sticks & Stones
Madeleine Urban
Abigail Roux

Fish & Chips
Madeleine Urban
Abigail Roux

Divide & Conquer
Madeleine Urban
Abigail Roux

Toccata e Fuga
Madeleine Urban
Abigail Roux

http://www.dreamspinnerpress.com

ABIGAIL ROUX was born and raised in North Carolina. A past volleyball star who specializes in pratfalls and sarcasm, she currently spends her time coaching middle school volleyball and softball and dreading the day when her little girl hits that age. Abigail has a baby girl she calls Boomer, four rescued cats, one dog, a crazyass extended family, and a cast of thousands in her head.

Visit Abigail's blog at http://abigail-roux.livejournal.com/. You can also send her mail at:

Abigail Roux
P.O. Box 552
Wallburg, NC 27373-0552

Also from ABIGAIL ROUX

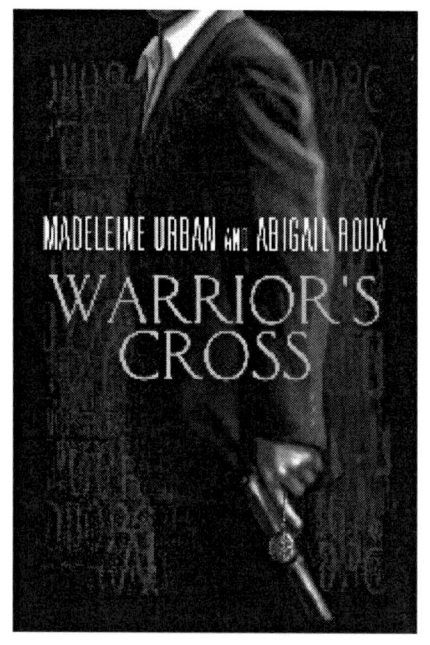

ACCORDING TO HOYLE

WARRIOR'S CROSS

Caught Running

THE ARCHER

http://www.dreamspinnerpress.com

Also from ABIGAIL ROUX

http://www.dreamspinnerpress.com

For more of the best M/M romance, visit

Dreamspinner Press

www.dreamspinnerpress.com

Lightning Source UK Ltd.
Milton Keynes UK
UKOW041815090712

195714UK00012B/161/P

9 781613 725122